Best wishes for a scenic and adventurous read!

Gratefully,
Robert L. Williams
(Bob)

PUCK

BOOK ONE: PAPU BANTA

ROBERT A. WILLIAMS

Strategic Book Publishing
New York, New York

This is a work of fiction placed in an historical setting. Some places and figures are actual, while most are wholly contrived, as is the story itself.

Copyright 2008
All rights reserved – Robert A. Williams

No part of this book may be reproduced or transmitted in any form or by any means, graphic, electronic, or mechanical, including photocopying, recording, taping, or by any information storage retrieval system, without the permission, in writing, from the publisher.

Strategic Book Publishing
An imprint of AEG Publishing Group
845 Third Avenue, 6th Floor - 6016
New York, NY 10022
www.StrategicBookPublishing.com

ISBN 978-1-60693-162-2   1-60693-162-8

Printed in the United States of America

Book Design: Linda W. Rigsbee

CREDITS

For the summary account of the Battle of the Rosebud relived in chapter one and biographical segments on the life of Chief Washakie, grateful acknowledgment is offered to Benjamin Capps, *The Old West: The Great Chiefs* (New York: Time Inc., 1975), pp. 130, 137-159; and to Virginia Cole Trenholm and Maurine Carley, *The Shoshonis: Sentinels of the Rockies* (Norman, Oklahoma: the University of Oklahoma Press, 1964), pp. 244-253. Other historical data and insights were gleaned, with grateful acknowledgment, from Foster Rhea Dulles, *The United States Since 1865* (Ann Arbor: The University of Michigan Press, 1959). All Scripture references are from the Authorized King James Version of the Bible.

DEDICATED TO:

Jackie

Jan

&

Jenn

who would not let this idea rest
unpublished.

And to
the memory of

Blanche A. Penny Robinson

A beloved sister-in-law

In whose home
the first pages of this book
were drafted.

ABOUT THE AUTHOR

Robert A. Williams is a native of New Mexico. He grew up four miles west of the Pecos along the Goodnight-Loving Trail in what at one time was Indian Territory. As a youth, he worked alongside family members on his grandfather's farm in the alfalfa and cotton fields. He rode and cared for horses and mules, and often rode his grandfather's wagon into town. He had a penchant for the Old West cowboy movies featuring such stars as Roy Rogers, Gene Autry, Wild Bill Elliot, Lash LaRue, and others.

In addition to his fondness for the Old West, the author holds three undergraduate and graduate degrees and is an ordained minister, having been pastor of several country churches. He is also the Founder and Director of *The Encouragers,* a Christian ministry of "helps," and a longtime volunteer Bible teacher for the Adult Rehabilitation Center of the Salvation Army in Dallas, Texas. He is the author of three non-fiction books and several magazine articles. "*Puck*" is his first attempt at fiction. He and his wife, Eve, presently live in Dallas.

CONTENTS

Dedication v
About The Author vii
To the Reader xi
  1. Homeward 1
  2. The Village 33
  3. Catching Up 45
  4. The Decision 61
  5. Preparation 77
  6. Accommodations 89
  7. Departure 99
  8. Fort Washakie 111
  9. The Search 129
10. The Switch 155
11. The Surveillance 185
12. The Showdown 201
13. The Vigil 219
14. The Hiding Place 237
15. The Camaraderie 249
16. The Interrogation 269
17. Pay Dirt 281
18. The Revelry 291

TO THE READER

The idea for this book began in the apartment of my sister-in-law, Blanche A. Penny Robinson, on an occasion when my wife Eve and I were visiting her on vacation. At one point, I picked up a *National Geographic* magazine and read a documentary on Jackson Hole, Wyoming. Until that day, I had always been a nonfiction writer, but was toying with the idea of writing a western novel. I felt this should be done mainly during vacation time as a diversion from other more pressing projects. That day, I wrote two pages that eventually became part of the first chapter.

Approximately a year later, while I was on a hunting trip in Colorado, staying in the mountain cabin of High Country Holdings, of which my friends James and Pat Gibson and Ralph McCalmont were partners, I happened to pick up a Western novel written by an acclaimed Western writer. As I read, I recall commenting to Pat that I thought I could write similar material. At intervals on my return trip home, I outlined and wrote pages of ideas that would eventually become part of "*PUCK*."

On other vacations I continued the note taking, but when I got down to the serious business of the actual writing, I penned various segments that would eventually go into the book. The current book is actually the result of a diversion that took place almost automatically, a totally different episode from the one first intended and for which most of the notes had been taken. I had anticipated completing the episode on "Papu Banta," and then return to the original episode as Part Two. However, by the time the first episode was nearing completion, the length seemed too formidable to add another sequence. Hence, the original notes will go into Book Two if readers welcome Book One with any telling interest.

Once I had written chapters one and two, my wife and I, along with my younger sister, Jan, went on vacation to Jackson Hole, Wyoming and the surrounding areas of Montana and Idaho. Strangely, what I discovered of the terrain and the flora and fauna of the regions coincided fairly well with what I had already written regarding the setting. Upon returning, I made some changes and additions in chapter one, based on findings of the trip.

Accordingly, "*PUCK*" is couched in a historical setting, making use of many places and historical figures of the region. Of course, many places and character names are entirely fictional, as is the story itself. The actual governor of Wyoming Territory at the time, Francis E. Warren, is used in the story, but he actually did none of the things ascribed to him in the scenario. Fort Washakie is also of historical note, though the names of those involved in the fort are fictional. Story linkage with the Battle of the Rosebud in the first chapter is historical, and the names carrying it out, along with Chief Washakie, who participated, are also real. The main character of the novel is completely fictional, though the reader, by the end of the book, may desire for him a place in reality. Except for the few historical figures mentioned by name in the book, all other characters are fictional, any name corresponding to anyone in real life being wholly coincidental.

The name I selected for the little Indian girl in the novel, Papu Banta, was chosen in honor of a birthday pal of mine—Dorothy O. Banta Reddell—our birthdays falling on the same day of the year. Banta was Dot's maiden name, her biological background also being of Indian heritage. She is also a Daughter of the American Revolution.

I have dedicated the book to my two sisters, Jacqueline (Jackie) Weitner and Janice (Jan) Williams, and to my niece, Jennifer (Jenn) Johnson, who would not allow the idea of "Puck" to rest unpublished. I have also dedicated the novel to the memory of Blanche A. Penny Robinson, in whose home the first pages of this book were drafted. (Sadly, before this book went into print, my sister, Jackie, to whom the book is dedicated in part, died. Gratefully, she had read the manuscript and viewed the artist's concept for the cover.) I credit my wife Eve with assessing every chapter of the novel as it was being written, and eagerly looking forward to successive chapters until the book was finished.

I would also like to express my gratitude for those persons, other than my family, who read the manuscript and offered helpful comments and encouragement. These include Jim Almond, James and Pat Gibson, Jim and Allene Hemmingway, Ralph McCalmont, Willy Morris, Glen Reddell, Charles and Nelwyn Spruell, and Nelton Warren. I would be remiss not to express my appreciation to the personnel of the WL Writers' Literary Agency and all those of Strategic Book Publishing, who had a hand in the production of the book.

The writing of this novel has been a diversion of sheer delight.

Robert A. Williams
Dallas, Texas

CHAPTER 1

HOMEWARD

The steep climb into Teton Pass was not difficult for the big Chestnut, even though his rider was a tall and hearty man, muscular and firmly set in the saddle. Gentry was almost as sure-footed as Sandy, the little dun and black mule tethered to the pommel, trailing instantly behind. The black stripe that draped the mule's withers, like a shoeshine rag pointed at either end, could hardly be seen for all the gear he carried. One would think the weight of the portage would slow the pace. There was no mistaking the intensity with which the threesome moved, as the downward side of the Pass toward the rising sun would soon expose the panorama of home.

For the past three years, Puck (short for Puckett), the name by which everyone in his home village knew him, had been a highrider on the Parr Belmont Cattle Ranch along the Wood River in Idaho Territory. He had gone there about the same time in June of 1887, just after the great 1886-87 blizzards, and had loved every minute of his work, that is until the last few months due to some rapidly changing times and changing people in the cattle operations. He never thought he would see the day when laziness, drunkenness, and greed would dictate the future of the cattle business that at this point was a struggle in itself, due to the decline of the cattle boom during the great blizzards of four years past.

In recent months, Puck had especially grown tired of coddling cowboys on the ranch who, after their monthly weekend binges in the villages, returned to their duties too sick to work. He never minded helping out with an excessive workload when helping an associate would actually get work accomplished for some important and immediate deadline. What he detested was the shirking of duty, especially when the reason behind it was a night of drunkenness and ribaldry in town. He detested even more the leniency of his boss who seemed repeatedly to brush off their irresponsible actions by such remarks as "Oh, let 'em be. They deserve a little play now and then." Though Belmont's ranch had not been hit as hard as others, did he realize such action on their part was cutting into his much-needed profits? And even more, the work still had to be done, most of which fell to Puck in a stretch of overtime and working alone, which was not even in the realm of his hired duty. He was a highrider, one who policed the operation, guarding against would-be bandits, and who was largely responsible for seeing that the operation ran smoothly and efficiently. Now, he was indulging drunken cowhands, mollycoddling his boss's lack of ethics, and sweeping out more bunks than his own. These were the personal reasons that were filling his craw to consternation.

Something of his philosophy of stewardship was also being challenged. Due to the booming cattle market, prior to the two big winter blasts, cattlemen had become rich and with their wealth had gained prominence and the assumption of political power. Their success had raised the stakes for the burgeoning homesteaders who had brought more cattle into the region, namely Mexican Longhorns from Texas by way of Wyoming to the east and Herefords from Kansas to the southeast. With the glut, the buffalo and antelope had been greatly pushed out by an overabundance of cattle vying for the better grasslands. Those not pushed out were killed in great numbers by U.S. Cavalry units and fur traders for meat, hides, and heads—meat to keep the soldiers content, and buffalo capes and mounted heads to whet the vanity of Easterners.

In those accelerated times, success had gone to the ranchers' heads. Belmont, for one, early in his cattle operation, had seen to the welfare of near-by Shoshonis who were going hungry for lack of game. Often as not, treaties with the U.S. government for assistance, as promised in exchange for the use of Indian lands, had been broken. Puck had seen the plight of the disadvantaged and starving Shoshonis during the past two winters, and had noted the attitude of Belmont and his kind change in deference to his own fat bank accounts in lieu of finding humane ways of aiding the suffering Indian population. He could no longer take the arrogance and greed associated with his work—at least among the cattle establishments north and west of the Snake River.

He could see potential uprisings on the horizon, and if that were not the case, with a drop in the beef market sure to grow stiffer, his job would be in jeopardy either by economic downfall or by virtue of his own moral principles. He would not wait for either to dictate the direction and purpose of his life. Already, he could see whisperings of tragedy on the swell. Every sign since the great blizzards seemed to predict the continued death of the cattle business. Sheep ranchers, for one, were driving their sheep through rangelands that were devastating the grasslands. The sheep cropped the grass so short that it became impossible for cattle to graze. So far, there had been enough for all, except in a few instances in which Puck had necessarily been drawn into a few minor battles among the differing ranchers. More and more, he detested any participation in scraps precipitated by greed. Added to this, the winters, if not longer, seemed longer due to the exceptionally bitter cold over two of the past three winter seasons. During the worst months, with the grasses being used up, it was getting more difficult to retain feed for the cattle. Anger was growing in every camp. Cattlemen could care less for the grazing needs of sheepherders, and vice versa. Farmers, likewise, had long since been fencing off their homesteads, which prevented further use of those range lands for ranchers and herdsmen. Range wars had erupted over grazing and watering rights and looked to be mounting, as farmers were now falling on hard times. Puck did not intend to be caught in the crossfire for the wrong reasons.

The horizon looked good in other directions, and Puck could dream. The horse business was stable and perhaps even on the rise. Then too, farming, despite its encroachment on potential ranch land, had followed the cattle boom as the next great economic development, even though its decline was also in the air, leaving the future looking uncertain. Expensive wood fences were no longer required to divide the grasslands. Fences could now be built of barbed wire that had been invented just a few years earlier in 1873. Windmills solved much of the watering problems, as farmers and ranchers were no longer totally dependent on streams and rivers for water. Water could now be drawn from under ground. Agricultural insights were growing as to how the drier, more arid lands could be utilized. Financing the farming operations was now the big question. Trouble was in the air, even here. Farmers were becoming indebted to the great Eastern banks for loans to finance operations, and many were losing their farms to the holding companies when the notes could not be paid. There was no guessing on Puck's part that times were changing, and fast.

Puck weighed every aspect of his profession. To press on as a highrider would not be a problem for some time to come, he hoped, but remaining in the atmosphere of greed, arrogance, and the lack of moral stamina would not be his undoing. He was just independent enough to see to that. His decision to leave Idaho, to give up a good salary, and to free himself of unnecessary stress at the hands of unreliable cowboys and greedy cattlemen, had not come too soon.

The one thing that disheartened Puck about leaving the Wood River region was his having to leave a good Indian friend, Chulo, a Shoshoni brave about twenty-seven years of age, who had served as his interpreter in cattle business dealings with his people. Puck knew the Uto-Aztecan language of the Shoshonis enough to get by in conversation, but he did not trust his knowledge on matters that required precision.

Chulo was not an Indian name, but rather an archaic Spanish word meaning *pretty*, which his mother had adopted when he was born, largely because a Spanish trapper, happening into the camp, used the word to describe the newborn. The baby's mother was so pleased by the trapper's remark that she latched onto it for the baby's name. Of course, no one really knew the real intonation of the trapper's use of the word. The usual Spanish word for *pretty* is *lindo* or *bonito*. The word *chulo*, on the other hand, is often used playfully to address someone who is just the opposite, such as calling a fat person *slim* or a tall person *shorty*. In calling the baby *Chulo*, did the trapper see "Little Ugly" in the Indian basket, or was the baby actually pretty? Chulo, as a man, was not ugly, but then he was not, well, you know....

Puck's interest in Chulo was not in his name, but in his character and friendship. When other cowboys on the ranch left for the villages after their monthly pay, Puck rode to the Shoshoni lodges and mingled among the people to learn of their ways. On these occasions, Chulo would take Puck on antelope or elk hunts and show him the Indian way of stalking. The Indian had been a delightful companion for over two years, and Puck was a bit grieved that his leaving Wood River meant also his leaving his friend Chulo behind.

All of that was behind him now as he leaned forward on the saddle horn surveying the trails leading into Teton Pass. This morning seemed restful enough, but the past three and a half days of travel had been grueling, a journey equally taxing on rider, mount, and pack animal alike. Crossing the border into Wyoming Territory seemed a long way from where they had started.

That first day they had left the Belmont Ranch on the Wood River just north of Chulo's Shoshoni Indian bailiwick. They had traversed the reservation, passing through Kimama and Minidoka by evenfall. That night they had camped in a grassy spot among the cottonwoods and western red cedars along a freshwater hill-country stream. After a fitful sleep and rising early in the shadows to a scant breakfast, harnessing and re-packing the animals took its morning toll in duress before the three had gotten underway again.

At first light, Puck recalled, the shadowy troop had headed due east toward the Snake River. Reaching the river, they had crossed it and had cut a path northeast along its front. At one point, they had proceeded around the east side of the river's minor lakes where, in Puck's mind, all the irregular patchwork of quarries and potholes meshed together, a reservoir was badly needed. The rovers had difficulty skirting the water reserves, but the big Chestnut, who had all but sonar for high ground, by midday had led them into the rolling hills away from the river. The band, then, had settled in long enough for Puck to have lunch, for the animals to water and graze, and for an hour's much-needed *siesta*. Of the three, Sandy had been the most restrained, as the pack on his back allowed for no rolling or dust-bathing the sweat away. Luckily for Gentry, his saddle had been removed only because it was needed for the highrider's pillow.

That evening after a fatiguing ride, the troupe had arrived at a Bannock and Shoshoni Indian haven, a work camp sponsored by the United States Army, where acquaintance had been made and quarters had been secured to end the second day on the trails. Hospitality could not have been better. Indian boys even fought over feeding and caring for his animals for the night. The older women had brought food. The men had invited him into their nightly conversations, and Indian and white man had shared important histories, as young Indian maidens had kept refreshments in supply.

The young maidens had been flattered to be serving the handsome white man. For all it was worth to those innocent vestals, Puck was, in reality, a handsome fellow, though not much taken by the fact himself. He sported a head of dark brown hair, just short of turning black, waving gently around the ears and down to his collar in the back, revealing more than a slight need of a haircut. He exhibited a mustache that was full but neatly trimmed that also blended with the density of his sideburns raised slightly above his ear lobes. His eyes were the center of attraction, usually demanding a double take of those seeing them for the first time. They were a deepening brown with a golden tint, punctuated by black pupils, eyes that on that night glistened in the firelight and seemed a pleasant precursor to his vivid smile. He displayed a pleasing, sanguine personality and carried himself in a robust fashion that spoke of confidence, but showed the least hint of arrogance. His manner gave him an air of approachable goodness, and he looked to the world as if he wouldn't hurt a fly—until he stood up. His six-foot frame, with shoulders like beams and arms like pistons of a dynamo, seemed a demanding presence that took command of the moment. Yet, he conveyed himself with dignity and quiet strength. Most persons in his presence felt relaxed by his winsome spirit. His voice was of delightful resonance, authoritatively deep, yet mellow. He appeared discerning of everything going on around him, and receptive and curious of almost everything he saw.

The youthful, innocent maidens, with their buoyant smiles and occasional equivocating snickers, could hardly keep from looking Puck's way as they served the tiny circle of men. Puck played to their eyes, which may have been a mistake. One of the girls, a bit taller and more developed than the others, carried herself in a saucy manner and kept glancing flirtatiously in his direction. Her black eyes, sparkling like the black beads on her leather vest, could entice and mesmerize a rattler, and Puck was easier prey than that. Had he instigated something he might have difficulty quitting? Such actions were not his normal style, but now it was either spread salt or thistledown; he was no intriguing eunuch, and Indian maidens usually got what they wanted. As cold sweat bathed his brow, he reluctantly took advantage of the conversation going on around the circle to break his quixotic spell. There are times when enough is enough, and this was certainly one of those times.

The Shoshonis were recalling the most heralded figure among their tribe, one who was still alive on the Wind River Indian Reservation that had been declared Shoshoni territory on July 4, 1868. They spoke of Chief Washakie, acknowledged by all their people as a man of iron will and by his enemies as "the greatest of all Indian warriors." Was it to indulge their white visitor that night that they talked of Washakie's policy of total cooperation of his people with the white man? Was Puck aware that above all other Indian tribes, the Shoshonis had facilitated the white man's settlement of the West? Their posterity as a people could not be described better than through the leadership of their beloved chief. Stories of his accomplishments, both in war and peace, were endless points of discussion on evenings like that one of which Puck had been a special guest.

Though the conversing Shoshonis were not aware of Puck's own avowal of their undisputed aid in the winning of the West for the white man, he was indeed a student of Indian history. He was, in fact, part of that history as a young boy. He was well aware that without the help of the Shoshonis, thousands more of the settlers would have been killed and the time period for victory might have been extended by decades. Puck was also conscious of the many episodes of the white man's inhumanity and cruelty toward the Indians in the taking of their land and, in many instances, pushing them aside with nowhere to go. After the fact, there was one thing of which Puck was certain—the white man must never forget that the newly acquired land is a *stewardship*, not a *possession*. And yet, Puck was afraid that the white man had already forgotten the real value of his conquest and had let it dwindle into nothing more than the dying glory of ill-gotten gain.

Puckett knew that he was in for a long night when the circle began to chatter away at the great and many episodes that characterized the life of their austere leader. One incident recalled another, and into the night the memories flowed freely.

They recalled one incident in which an Army officer learned of a particular Indian brave among Washakie's people, Six Feathers by name, who incessantly beat his wife. The officer confronted Washakie about the matter, and finally convinced the chief that such was not an appropriate means of settling differences. Not only was the chief wrong in permitting it, but it also demonstrated that he did not have control of his people. Embarrassed at having his authority questioned, the chief went to Six Feathers and ordered him to stop his uncivilized behavior. He made it clear that he would no longer tolerate any Indian man beating his wife. Not long after, Washakie caught Six Feathers again beating his wife, whereupon he pulled out his pistol and shot the man dead on the spot.[1]

Washakie, the circle made it clear, did not tolerate any challenge to his authority and especially with respect to his policy of cooperation with the white man. When one of his sons roused the camp to retaliate against the white man for his broken treaties, Chief Washakie confronted him, saying, "My son, rather than see you take up arms against the white man, I will strike you dead at my feet."[2] Other young bucks tested his verve at a point when they thought the aging Washakie was growing weak—becoming too compatible with the whites and too lenient with their Indian enemies, the Sioux and Cheyenne. The war blood had ceased to flow in his veins. He was growing soft and indecisive. Arguments erupted among the braves regarding who would take his place as Shoshoni leader. This so angered the Chief that in silence he left the camp and proceeded to prove his prowess. A few days later he returned to the camp, displaying seven scalps of the enemy whom he had encountered and taken in battle single-handedly. "Let him who can do a greater feat than this claim chieftainship," he charged. "Let him who would take my place count as many scalps."[3] The question of his courage was settled and no one ever again challenged his authority.

The greatest war excursions of Washakie had been those of aiding the white man against the Sioux, 20,000 strong, the fiercest Indians on the northern plains. They had already confiscated the hunting grounds of the Omaha and Iowas in Dakota Territory. They had then virtually swept the Black Hills clean of the Kiowas and Cheyennes. On their way to overcoming the Shoshonis, they swamped the Crow in eastern Wyoming. And then, on a day in 1865, a war party of two hundred Sioux attacked Washakie's summer lodging camp on the Sweetwater River, stealing four hundred of his best mustangs. Washakie led a counter raid, beat back the enemy, and recovered his horses, but at great personal expense—his son was killed by the Sioux and scalped before his very eyes. Vowing to avenge his son's death and the losses among his people, he complained to the U.S. authorities at Fort Bridger that the outnumbering Sioux were invading his reservation at every turn.

By 1876, the Sioux had become allies again with the Cheyenne, making it almost impossible for the Shoshonis to live in peace. That year, Brigadier General George Crook of the Platte Authority was directed to rally forces against the hostile Sioux and Cheyenne on the northern plains. Crook, on the authority of William Tecumseh Sherman, who took Grant's place as commanding General of the Army in 1869, was touted "the greatest Indian-fighter the Army ever had." Be that as it may, Crook was wiser than to think that he and his army of white men could out-maneuver the sharp thinking of the Indian warriors of the enemy without help from other Indians docile to the white man. He would need Indian scouts. Accordingly, when his orders came to march from his garrison at Fort Fetterman in southeast Wyoming north toward the enemy front of hostile Sioux, he sent couriers to the Shoshoni camps of Washakie seeking aid, which Washakie was overjoyed to offer.

At the same time Crook was enlisting the aid of Washakie, Colonel John Gibbon had rallied his forces from Fort Ellis in the south of Montana Territory. In April of that year, he met with the chiefs of the Crows on their reservation along the Yellowstone River, hoping to marshal scouts for his cause. In a speech before the clan, he prudently aroused their bitterness toward the Sioux. He said "I have come down here to make war on the Sioux. The Sioux are your enemy and ours. For a long while they have been killing white men and killing Crows. I am going down to punish them. If the Crows want to make war upon the Sioux, now is their time. If they want to prevent them from sending war parties into their country to murder their men, now is the time. If they want to get revenge for Crows that have fallen, now is their time."[4] Thirty Crow braves immediately responded to Gibbon's quest for scouts, and others promised to link up with General Crook within two months.

In early June, Crook had established his garrison with fully supplied quarters on Goose Creek, a clandestine offshoot of the more major Tongue River on the Wyoming-Montana border. If he thought his presence was unknown, he was mistaken; a message was sent to him by a Sioux party from none other than Crazy Horse himself. The burden of the message was that any soldier who entered territory north of the Tongue River would die.

Crook knew what he was up against and approximately where the enemy might be found, but he had to await the three Crow chiefs, Medicine Crow, Old Crow, and Good Heart, and their warriors before he could move out. On June 14, the Crow warriors arrived, 176 strong, and were later joined that same day by eighty-six Shoshonis led by Washakie himself, along with two of his sons. Crook's force was now composed of 839 cavalrymen, 201 infantrymen, and 262 Crow and Shoshoni Indian warriors, including their leaders. Even with the recruiting of Indian warriors and scouts, 1,302 men seemed ridiculously small to rout Crazy Horse's mass of Sioux, boasting 4,000 in number.

At this point in the conversation, Puck noticed the circle of men growing more excited with the energetic recall. Only fourteen years had passed since the Battle of the Rosebud, and the foray was still intimately alive in their minds. One in the circle who had fought ferociously in the campaign was Little Bob, who now took up the telling of the story. He talked with pride of the veteran warriors who had been drilled to precision by the great Washakie. He told of his bravery and dispatch right alongside the Army officers in the heat of battle. He could not be more pleased to be speaking.

Little Bob proceeded to tell what took place two nights before the great battle. During the day, the Shoshoni and Crow recruits had traveled sixty miles before arriving at Goose Creek where the Army command was camped. To the surprise of Crook and his men who consulted with them that night, the two Indian divisions had opted not to sleep but to prepare for battle. In their minds, that meant a night given to the war dance. The chanting, howling, and tremolo, mixed with the tambours and drumbeats, lasted the night, raising Indian ardor to fever pitch. The tribes were ventilated, unified, and brought to a dauntless peak of courage. Now they were ready for the assault.

Two days later on June 16, Crook's total brigade crossed the Tongue River into enemy Sioux territory. His scouts had preceded him, risking deeper surveillance into danger, and soon returned to report the sighting of Sioux activity. The detachment camped early that evening on Rosebud Creek, but rose before first light and proceeded down the Creek. A few hours after dawn, Crook halted the column in a hill-girt basin through which a lesser tributary passed. There he ordered the soldiers to unload the horses and let them graze while the rear units caught up with the command. Washakie and the other chiefs did not like the move. They saw soldiers scattered on both sides of the creek, resting, and unprepared for battle. Crook reasoned that the Sioux garrison would be a great village stronghold, and until scouts could locate its whereabouts, there was no reason to tire the soldiers. The chiefs knew, to the contrary, that if Crazy Horse were to be a target, he would be a moving one. Accordingly, they readied their men for any event, stationing their braves along the north ridges skirting the basin below.

Washakie sent scouts into the intervening hills to look for signs of the enemy. In less than an hour, the scouts returned flailing their horses in a frantic gallop. One of the scouts had fallen into enemy contact and was returning wounded. "Sioux! Sioux!" the shout went up. Trailing the scouts' dust with instant speed, a horde of advancing Sioux, draped low, inconspicuously, along the sides of their mustangs, swept against the few Army sentries patrolling the amphitheater. The hills to the west and the ridges to the north emptied of hostile Indians at break-neck speed, advancing against the only Army unit prepared to battle—the vanguard of Shoshoni and Crow warriors. The Indian regiment countermanded the oncoming Sioux and, despite being greatly outnumbered, held the enemy at bay until the soldiers could prepare to rally.

Little Bob told of the fierce onslaught that kept them busy until General Crook could arrange his troops in the valley and send troops to their relief. He laughed as he told of their beloved Chief Washakie as he rode alongside the officers in the heat of battle, half-naked, trailing his war bonnet on the ground behind his mustang mount, and conferring with Crook by interpreter. Like a phantom moving everywhere at once, the chief encouraged his braves. Little Bob told of his own part alongside his chief, when Captain Guy Henry was shot through the cheek and left flouncing on the ground covered in blood. Washakie, Little Bob, and several other scouts had stationed themselves around the fallen man until troopers could get him to safety.

In the initial attack, the Sioux were driven back by the Shoshoni and Crow alliance, but they returned in greater force and continued the melee. The report of rifles, along with their smoke and the dust of the cavorting horses filled the air. Horses fell dead or were disabled; men were crushed while others lay dying. Blood mingled in the crush of grass and wild roses that carpeted the basin floor beneath their feet.

When the dust had settled, the battleground had been secured, but that was all. General Crook then dispatched Captain Anson Mills and his company northward up Rosebud Canyon in search of the enemy camp that he anticipated was only miles ahead. Crook would follow close by in the event that a Sioux attack ensued. Here again, Crook had made another mistake. The Sioux had maintained their positions, and soon attacked the frail Army flanks left weak by the absence of Mills and his company. Crook dispatched runners to retrieve Captain Mills and his men. Mills, rather than back tracking the canyon trails, ascended the canyon walls and cut a half-moon path through prairie sage back to the battlefield with his men. This proved to be a profitable move, as his company found itself flanking an auxiliary of Sioux warriors bearing down on Crook's men. Taken by surprise, the Sioux found themselves caught between the two divisions. They broke into a break-neck run around the flanks of Crook who, again, had been unprepared and served as little support to the rush of Mill's pursuit that soon petered out behind the enemies' faster horses.

Checking the casualties, Crook surmised that the Sioux forces were too many in number to make further pursuit, so he ordered the company back to the camp at Goose Creek. Crazy Horse and his bandits were left free to ride again, which they did eight days later in the massacre of Lieutenant Colonel George Custer's battalion at the Little Bighorn, only thirty miles to the north.

Little Bob brought the Shoshoni memories and legacies to a gentle close and thanked the men for allowing him his commemoration of their great chief. A hallowed yell of victory arose in the Indian chamber as the circle of braves and older men ended their revelry. Elsewhere, the camp lay silent. Women and children had long since retired. Even dogs lay motionless at their sentry posts. The fires had dwindled to coals. Night air, thick with rising moisture and coolness, intimated the lateness of the hour. A limpid moon was already waning to meet the morning in just a few brief hours.

As Puck thanked his hosts and excused himself for a much-needed rest before dawn, he was astonished to see one lone Indian maiden, the black-eyed beauty, enter the meeting room. With a guise of cleaning and straightening, she busied herself, intentionally making herself conspicuous at the doorway out of which Puck must pass to his quarters. As he passed, her dark eyes met his and an engaging smile crossed her lips. Curiously, Puck returned the smile, bowed a quick sign of adieu, and brushed by her out into the night.

The next morning, as Puck now recalled, their getting away from the Indian settlement, with its morning *pow wows*, native pleasantries, and a breakfast of blood-pudding, berries, and *pemmican*, was a task out of the ordinary, given no sleep. Amenities finally satisfied, a late start had found them facing an already climbing sun, as Puck mounted and pulled up the reins, swinging the freshly fed animals toward the edge of the Indian camp. They picked their way slowly through the workings of teepees and deer meat draped on drying poles, eased around the sacred dancing ground, and passed in review of the chief's lodge, waving an obliging good-bye to the leader. Chief Broken Bow, known to the Spanish trappers as *Arco que Brao*, nodded in response as the troop faded into the trails at the edge of camp.

The day would be a good day, still, if the file could step it up briskly and move out with incentive. Puckett was about to encourage the team onward, when suddenly a lone figure sidestepped into the trail from behind a tree and clasped the bridle of Gentry, almost startling the animal into an all-out panic. Puckett pulled him back forcibly as Sandy broke in fear to one side and then the other behind the big horse, kicking up rock and dust in the foray. There at the edge of the meadow, now stepping back out of the path of the animals stood the black-eyed Indian beauty of the night before, her raven hair glistening in the sunlight, her sashes blowing in the breeze. Around her shoulders was draped a bulging *parfletche* of unknown content, and on her feet high top moccasins strapped tightly for running. She stood shivering, not of cold, but of fright.

Puckett dismounted and dropped the reins around a protruding stump and walked slowly toward the Indian, arms raised in disbelief and surprise. When he had reached her, she had slipped to her knees in deferment, eyes bent to the earth. He reached down and, grasping her hands, gently raised her to her feet.

"Wha—, What's the trouble my dear young woman?" he asked, somewhat shakily himself. "Why are you out here on the trail away from the camp?" The maiden lifted her eyes in abeyance and spoke almost embarrassingly.

"Hanacumseh want go with big man!"

"What do you mean you want go—I mean want to go—with me?"

"Hanacumseh like what see!"

"*Hanacumseh*, is that your name? Whose are you? I mean, to whom do you belong in the camp? And what's this strange urge to leave the territory with a white man?" Puck was straining for words. He had a case of envelopment on his hands, a star-struck beauty tugging at his arm. The maiden would not turn his hand loose. Puck led the Indian out of the trail and sat her down on a mass of rock protruding from the ground. "Now, tell me your story," he continued to plea. "What is this all about?" The young lady hesitated, her eyes welling with tears.

Puck dared to compose her. "Now, straighten yourself and look up at me. Something serious must really be troubling you. Shoshonis don't cry that easily. And I'm sure nothing to spout over, so let's see, look here and tell me."

This time the girl spoke more freely, as she wiped her eyes.

"My father is Big Eagle, and I am number three of my brothers and sisters. Number one is my sister, Little Fox, but she no longer stay here. She go away with new brave for husband in *Wihakakta Ce Papi.*"

"In *Wihak*—what?" Puck interrupted.

"She go away with new marriage in Moon of Greening Grass," Hanacumseh interjected.

"*Moon of Greening Grass* is white man's April," Puck broke in again. "You are telling me that your older sister got married only two moons ago."

"Yes, that what I say," the girl continued. "My father gave good horses for her brave's hand, and made big dance for many peoples. My mother and other mothers in lodges made new dress and blankets for Little Fox."

"You should be happy for her," Puck enjoined, as he dropped to his knees before her.

"Hanacumseh is happy for her, but not happy for Hanacumseh," the young beauty hastened to add. "Hanacumseh is sad for reason of my father's word. He make promise to me that very soon he find me handsome brave and make gifts for beginning new life like Little Fox. But two moons pass and no brave. No party! No dress! No new life! When you come to camp, I like what I see. You pretty white man with happy face. You big, with good arms and strong voice. You, too, look for new life. That is reason why Hanacumseh ask to go with you." The vestal slinked back against the stone with a sigh of relief and anticipation.

"I—I'm afraid I do not know what to say," Puckett shrugged, showing perplexity. "Look, Hana—" he had already forgotten the full name, "I'm flattered, that is, I'm complimented by your interest, but you must understand many things about yourself and about me before you can pack up and leave your family." He eyed the *parfletche* that draped her shoulder. "And, look, this little satchel here—that is, this little wrapping of your goods—how far would this take you? I mean..." Puck searched for more words, and the more he sought, the more he saw he was not making any headway, even if he were communicating the point. He sighed and hunkered back on the heels of his boots, wondering what the next move should be. In a whisper to himself he wished Chulo were there, but there was no possible help on that point. Then an idea came to him. He raised his eyes to heaven as if thankful to some kind of spirit that had linked up with him. Once again, he took the damsel by her hands and lifted her to her feet. Wistfully he entreated, "Hanacumseh, that is a beautiful name, and you are a beautiful Indian maiden, and I do not know any man who would not find you charming—that is, pleasing and lovely. But aren't you a little impatient?" The girl looked questioningly at him. "Impatient, impatient," Puck repeated to himself. "She doesn't understand impatient." He gave up on the point and continued.

"I mean, look, maybe I have an idea. Listen to me. What if you and I return to camp and I will go and talk with your father. Maybe I can help him understand your dreams and maybe he will give more attention to your future. You really should give him more of a chance."

"You and I will go to my father and ask him to find brave for me?" the girl repeated in her own words. "If my father has no brave and does not find my new life fast, then you will take me with you?"

"I did not say that, Hanacumseh," Puck broke in. "I only think that you are asking much of your father after only two moons—even less than two moons. We are now living in the first days of the *Strawberry Moon*—I think you call it *Wipazuka Waste*. We call it June. Your sister married late two moons ago. Your father must have time to find the very best brave for his lovely daughter. It would not be good for him to bring home an ugly or mean brave to such a pretty girl, and do you not want to look among your peoples for a man of good character who would honor you in your new life, then suggest such a one to your father? Together you and I could help Big Eagle with his promise."

"We try," the maiden resigned.

With that move, Puckett led the Indian girl to where Gentry and Sandy stood waiting and lifted her into the saddle. He then pulled himself up behind the cantle of the saddle behind her, and reined the animals toward the camp. His riding behind her and braced against her for the ride, told him one thing for certain—she was no girl. How old she was he had no idea, but she displayed the contours and firmness of a well-developed woman, a beauty that would turn the head of any man who could see straight. The day was being lost for time, but it wouldn't be spoiled, Puck thought, if he could satisfy this young woman with one final effort at the camp.

As they rode into camp, young braves rallied to take lead of the animals. They were a little puzzled seeing one of their own riding in the saddle with a white man. In the rush and noise of entering camp, women began to dislodge their living quarters to see what was happening. Flaps flew open everywhere. Puckett pulled up the train and dismounted. He helped the Indian to the ground and turned the animals over to the braves. Motioning toward the tent dwellings, he graciously intoned, "Take me to Big Eagle."

The pair found Big Eagle flaying at some animal skins, getting them ready for tanning, a job usually set aside for the women folk.

A surprised blush swept across his face when he saw the big white man leading his daughter to where he was working.

"What has my daughter done that you come returning to camp with her at your side?" the burly Indian questioned. Not waiting an answer he continued, "Hanacumseh, what is the meaning?" he protested.

Puck raised his palm in greeting and began to relate the story, enhancing it only enough to help Big Eagle understand. Turning to the maiden, he urged, "Hanacumseh, why don't you go find your mother and I will talk with your father." Though that was a question, it wasn't a question, and she turned away agreeably. While she was away, the two men discussed the great issue of the day. Puck learned that the daughter was twenty-two years of age, her older sister was twenty-four. He went on to explain as best he knew how, just how strong longings, or perhaps even jealousies, really are when it comes to sibling rivalry. Then, too, *rivalry* was not the right word because Hanacumseh was happy for Little Fox. She just wasn't "happy for Hanacumseh." Big Eagle not only understood, but thanked Puck for showing so much care for his daughter. He agreed to bear more intensity with his promise. His daughter would find happiness. Gifts, horses and ware were not his concern. The well being of his daughter really did concern him.

"Chief," Puck spoke up, though Big Eagle was not actually chief, "it really is none of my business, but if you run out of hunting room for just the right brave, I know someone two day's ride from here who would make your daughter the finest of husbands." With that remark, he gave Big Eagle the directions to the summer camp of Chulo, his friend.

Hanacumseh returned momentarily with her mother and was surprised that the two men had left off talking and were both now scraping away at the animal hides. Apparently, the two women had been discussing the womanly dreams of Hanacumseh and had brought a little wisdom to bear on the matter. Her mother looked at Puck and smiled knowingly of what he had ridden up against earlier that morning. She had once dreamed herself.

Turning to Hanacumseh, Puck began to speak. "I know you want new life at the pace of mushrooms popping up on the hillside overnight, but please remember, you are not a mushroom, and you are not looking for mushrooms. You are a beautiful young lady looking for fulfillment in your life, and you will find it if you give your father a chance. He respects your desires and he is a man of integrity—that is, of good promise. You must listen to him."

With those words, Puck crossed his heart with his arms and bowed gently before all three in a sign of love and respect and bade them the best of life among their people. He excused himself under the necessity of getting on down the trail toward Wyoming Territory and his little home beneath the great Tetons. Big Eagle had already called for his horse and mule and had them standing outside the lodge.

They rode through the haze of steaming wash-pots, passed around hanging clothing and blankets, and neared the edge of the camp for the second time that day. As Puckett neared the spot where he had been constrained earlier that morning, he thought almost jokingly to himself, *"You know, there were three other maidens serving last night...."* With that thought striking steel, losing no time to let it settle, he spurred Gentry into a gallop and beat a path pell-mell for the outlying meadows without looking one way or the other. After a half-mile run he straightened up in the saddle out of his crouched position, relieved that the camp, with its cultural morés, was now behind him.

The troop proceeded northeast and shortly after noon had crossed the Blackfoot River. From there they had then traveled the twenty miles or so to Grays Lake River Outlet and had made a beeline for the Snake River that, true to its name, had meandered snake-like from the north dropping down in a southeasterly direction from Ririe Station into Swan Valley.

After the night in Swan Valley, Puck had driven his animals headlong for the Wyoming Territory and Teton Pass, where they would find entrance into the magnificent and the wild, an inviting door into what Puck regarded as God's country.

At great length, the wayfarers peeled downward now into the backside of the Pass anticipating the moment of truth when what Puck had been waiting and hoping for would play into view. Suddenly, as if a door had been opened from the foyer of paradise and the trellised curtains of the grand show had been fanned aside by the winds of time, the breathtaking view opened into the great expanse that Puck called home. Pulling the animals into the shade as a respite from the late morning sun, he now stood overlooking a vast panorama, a mountain-girt valley, fifty miles long and eight miles wide at the foot of the Tetons, known as Jackson Hole. "Hole" was the jargon of French-Canadian trappers for a flat valley encircled by mountains. To Puck, it was more like an elongated crater, whose origin stymied the imagination.

Indians had dominated the territory until 1807 when John Colter, hunter and trapper, ventured into the valley from Staunton, Virginia, and settled temporarily beneath what later came to be called the Teton Mountains, or as the French-Canadians had dubbed them, *Les Trois Tetons*, The Three Teats. Teewinot Mountain stood at the southern-most end of Jenny Lake. The lake had been formed by tributaries of natural springs and snow melts, and was connected to the larger Jackson Lake to the north where

Colter was said to have built his first log cabin couched in its bay.

As beautiful as the place was earlier in the century, which Puck had the advantage of absorbing now, seventy-five years had passed before anyone thought seriously about homesteading its magnificent presence. The likes of Jim Bridger, Kit Carson, Jedediah Smith, and William Sublette, like Colter himself, were trappers and hunters, not the least bit interested in setting roots. It was left to J. Pierce Cunningham to homestead the area late in the 1880's.

The sight of the valley reminded Puck instantly of his boyhood days, playing in and out of the mountains and among the lakes and tributaries, and making his home just east of there at Togwatee Pass. Even his name had its roots in this lonely mountain hideaway. Puck's real name was Buster George Puckett, but those who had known him for any length of time knew better than to call him "Buster" or "George." So, following his surname, they called him "Puck" for short. He liked "Puck" as a reference, but hated "Buster" because that name appeared to him to be an anonymous address with a lot of disrespect associated with it. "Buster" seemed to be the name of anyone in the wrong place at the wrong time. For instance, he had once overheard Brandon Wise, the Togwatee banker—if you could call it a bank—scolding his cleaning boy, Billy Yeager, with the threat, "Okay, *Buster*, you're to stay out of my files. Just clean and git!" On another occasion, he had heard Jeremy Ames censure his son when he found him in the hayloft catching a few extra winks of sleep before getting to work for the day. "When you git through lounging around, *Buster*, you can git to doing the things you're fed for!" Hence, to Puck, "Buster" seemed to be everybody's name and he was just independent enough not to like even a hint of it in reference to him.

As for "George," that name was even worse. When his younger cousin was born, the parents had wanted a boy they could call

"George," but when the baby turned out to be a girl, they named her "George" anyway. Early on, Puck thought—erstwhile mistakenly—that "George" was a girl's name, and detested even the thought that the elder Pucketts, William and Clare, would name their son George. The fact that there were no other men or boys around named George, so far as he knew, only compounded the derision. He had long since broken his peers from the use of "Buster" or "Buster George." Even the men of the village knew enough to abide by the correct appellation. They soon learned that "Puck" was the name. "Puck Puckett" was good enough.

Now that he was grown, there were not many men around those parts like Puckett. Even as a youth, he had blazed every unprotected trail of Indian Territory alone. Weaned early from his home, he had traveled the Wyoming trails of Bannock, Crow, and Arapaho. He had hailed as far as Minnesota and the North Dakota Territories and had faced down the most war-like Indians of the plains—the Cheyenne. He had contended many times with the renegade bucks of the Cheyenne camps. Though there was no disrespect for the Cheyenne people, he had never been overly concerned with them as a whole. He had befriended many of them, they being rather congenial people when left to themselves, but some of their pigheaded braves, often feeling their youthful mettle, were a different story altogether. There is no counting the number of skirmishes that the young Puckett had braved and won, but not without a price. Now that he was a man, he did not think himself rid of the possibility of new tussles always threatening around the next bend.

In 1850, when the early white settlers began arriving in what was later to be called the Wyoming Territory, established by Congress in

1868, the Plains Indians had already established it as their own natural homestead for hundreds of years. Before white settlers arrived and displaced them, they found Arapaho, Bannock, Blackfoot, Cheyenne, Crow, Flathead, Nez Percé, Shoshoni, Sioux, and Ute Indians already there. The displacement spread them far and wide, leaving many tribes homeless and wandering in hunger and sickness. If there were any shame on the part of the white man, no one read it on his face.

Puckett himself, did not help create the displacement; he was born into it in 1858. Thirty-two years had passed since he was born in a covered wagon, just outside Missionary Minnie Blaylock's temporary hostel, which was in the vicinity of Jackson Hole before it had even become a village. The meager place had been built to help Indian women in the birthing of their babies and to care for them in the few days just following. The missionary had actually gotten caught there during a winter storm on her way to Colorado Territory and had to put down temporary roots until the spring thaw in May. William and Clare Puckett had been on their way from the Dakotas to visit sick relatives in Idaho when they were caught by the blizzard, and were directed to the hostel by friendly Indians. Clare was in labor and was so far along that there was no time to even transfer her from the wagon to the warmth of the hostel. Two Indian midwives, helping the missionary, took fist-sized stones heated in the hostel fireplace and wrapped them in blankets to lay alongside the laboring Mrs. Puckett for warmth. A lantern had provided light and helped knock the bitter chill from the air into which the new baby was first introduced. For the first few weeks following his birth, the hostel had become Puck's first home, until Indians had helped the Pucketts build a one-room log cabin near the hostel site.

In the spring of that year, the Pucketts moved on to Idaho and

Missionary Blaylock on to Colorado, but early in Puck's boyhood, upon the family's trek back to the Dakotas, they had so liked the Teton area that they decided to take up new homestead there, rather than return to the Dakotas. Because there was still no settlement in the basin, they went twenty-five or so miles east to a small settlement at Togwatee Pass. Here Puck had grown up as a boy and had visited the valley of the Tetons quite often with family members and adventurous peers. Togwatee Pass had been Anglicized after *Togwotee*, a Shoshoni sub-chief under Washakie, a medicine man of the Sheep Eaters tribal segment, and a valued scout of the white man during the Indian wars.

The railroad had entered Wyoming Territory when Puck was only seven, and this feature of the expanding of the West was bringing more settlers into the areas surrounding the Jackson basin. J. Pierce Cunningham had been the first to enter the Teton crater in the late 1880's to take up homesteading. Under Cunningham, the area had begun to grow up almost overnight, largely due to the burgeoning cattle business on the heels of the railroad and the discovery of oil in the Dallas Field near Lander, Wyoming. By then, Puck had become a young man and his parents had died within months of each other, his father of smallpox and his mother of pneumonia. Puck stayed on with his aunt in Togwatee Pass until the little settlement began to dry up, mostly due to homesteaders shifting a few miles West to the Teton basin. He and his aunt moved to the valley and established roots where she was able to establish a dress shop that made her more than a meager living. Puck signed on at all kinds of jobs from highriding, to riding shotgun on the Sabreline Stage, to standing sentry at Brandon Wise's newly established village bank, moved from the Pass to the Valley. Once fully established in the new setting, Puck had gone off on his adventurous escapades into Minnesota and the Dakotas and had returned to Jackson Hole only a year before taking the Belmont job in Idaho in 1887.

"Jackson Hole" soon became a name on everyone's lips. It is purported that William Sublette, fur trader and merchant, had named the valley *Jackson's Hole* after one of his partners, David E. Jackson. In any case, the name stuck. It was here in this meadow-laden paradise between the Tetons and the sagebrush flatlands that Puckett had come to call home.

Now, in early June of 1890, as he stood overlooking the valley, visions of his past and future danced deliriously in his head. With the rousing spell of memories broken and dreaming dispelled for the moment, Puckett eased the big horse farther along the trail below a steep rim in the rocky cliffs. He had to come down north of Teton Pass, over the series of rippled peaks, winding in and out of a trough of crevasses and canyons on the Idaho side, with their abundance of flowers and trees. He eventually emerged at Granite Canyon. Amid the dazzling masses of trees and ferns and herbage of every guise and color, he reined the animals in a downward slant toward the valley, meandering in one direction and then another. He rode brusquely into a maze of smaller canyons and bluffs, edging his way closer to the bottom and to the little Teton village glistening faintly in the distance.

Two miles into the basin, he rode amid the towering pine, buck brush, and assorted grasses. Another mile and he could see vestiges of Phelps Lake banked against the mouth of Death Canyon. The South, Middle, and Grand Tetons began to faintly come into view as he descended further into the valley below. Had he stayed the course, rather than winding toward home, he would pass Taggert and Bradley Lakes. Further on, he would reach Jenny Lake, and ultimately Jackson Lake. Instead, he struck pell-mell toward the village. Above him two bald eagles wafted on the wind. A massive pair of moose foraged on the verdant brush at the beginning of the Willow Flats. In the distance, he was sure he saw a small herd of majestic antelope embellishing the silvery sage. Beyond that beauty, appeared the Gros Ventre Butte and the undulating plains that reached for miles until fading out on the far eastern horizon.

The late spring and early summer flowers carried their own idiomatic colors whimsically decorating the pebbled grassland beneath the horses' hooves. In shadows where a few patches of lingering snow still graced the woodland floor, little purple Hepaticas had peeped out from among the fallen leaves of winter. In the sunlight, Indian Paint Brush, with its scarlet petals and yellow pistils, looked pinkish-orange at a distance. A smattering of Lupines, with their wand-like clusters of decorative blue, yellow, and white flowers, made tiny stands on the grassy overhangs. Bunchberries, brandishing their tiny little purple blossoms surrounded by white petal-like bracts, looked almost like spatters of paint thrown indiscriminately against the terra cotta coating of the earth. Ghostly white Indian Pipe, hanging like crystal bells, shot up in the manner of toadstools from the rotting tundra below. Fireweed, known better in Yukon Territory and often called Willow Herb, stretched their three-foot wand-like tendrils in air and waved their rose-purple pods in the wind. The perfume of a blossoming myriad of other plants floated on the humid mountain air—Alpine Forget-me-nots, White Mules Ear, Lewis Monkey Flower, Glacier Lilly, Globemallow, Balsam Root, and Marsh Merrigold. Their splendid aroma now mixed with the smells of horse lather, rawhide, and sun-dried grasses at the edge of the beaten trail. Puckett was not at a loss as to which smells were the most familiar, but the sweetness of the summer air was a delightful change for the otherwise stiff ride along the hillside.

If the flowers were a godsend, the trees enamored Puck even more. All along the route and especially in the canopy of the forest, Puckett had noticed the beauty and variation of the timber. Some of the trees still held leftover fragments of their winter apparel deviating from amber and brandied copper tones to cinnamon and rich burgundy. Tree trunks of both hardwood and pulp, along with trailing vines and brambles, showed their magnificent browns, from burnt umber to saddle tan, from silhouettes of black and brown to lichen gray and moss green, with intermittent sheens of buff and beige where they shimmered in the sunlight. Every now and then, spring-like growth held forth color like changing autumn leaves. At times, the foliage doffed combinations of yellow, gold, and russet, fading into raw sienna, or perking up to scrappy orange. At one point, one tree brandished brilliant salmon rouge. One could hardly discern whether it was gold turning to rose, or rose turning to gold. One almost mistook it for various other flowering trees still blossoming along the trails.

For the most part, with spring fading away and temperatures rising to summer attention, the forest canopy was full of yellow-green and forest jade, with shadings of gray-green and olive drab. The red needles of the pine-like larch tree had given way to a yellow-green crown. The Ponderosa Pines, Idaho White Pines, and Sugar Pines had maintained their deep thalo greens throughout winter, but were mixed now with the new growth of brilliant forest green. The Douglas and White Firs, and the Lodgepole Pines (so named for their use by Indians as teepee lodgepoles), maintained their usual evergreen appearance. In the periodic intervening meadows, the Engelman Spruce boasted a bit of blue cast to taunt their evergreen cousins. On the lower slopes and general flatlands, the Incense Cedar and Western Red Cedar showed a mixture of evergreen and copperas-changing needles due to an abundance of newly rising sap.

If ever a soul longed for the symbolism of renewed spirit, he found it here in the yellows and greens of new life burgeoning on these timbered hills.

Puck chuckled faintly and smiled approvingly of God's great rustic commonwealth, which reminded him of his own country-born status. For a moment, horse and rider stood motionless. Sandy pulled up in compliance. Then, in an instance that challenged eternal gaiety, Puckett reverberated from the inner recesses of his soul drowning out the previous chuckle and washing away his placid smile. "What a God! What a land!" he shouted.

More than ever, Puck was determined that in these beautiful hills he would find truth and slake the thirst of his soul. He was no saint by a long shot, but the trying indifference of mankind to the revelation of God would not be his undoing as he had seen happen in many weary sojourners in the West. For him at least, God would not be a relic of some Palestinian past. He would be the invigorating enabler of the enriched present and the sure bulwark of the gallant future. One day at a time would be enough for Puck in being convinced of his rich destiny.

How could he not be convinced? How could anyone not be convinced? You can't ride across God's green earth for three days without being reminded of the mind behind such wonder. To consider the personal consciousness that observes it, makes creative use of its resources, and industrializes its products, staggers man's imagination second only to the glory of his own dignity and worth. Still again, to endorse its peopled expanse and to see the difference and sameness among the races is sheer glory of its Author. Let those who would attribute such splendor's rise to anything short of the personal back of the universe, if they so choose, but as for B. G. Puckett there was no denying its reality and nothing to quash his search for reason and truth, those rational and spiritual balancing forces that free men's souls.

The beauty of the panorama matched the beauty of the moment. Dreaming innocence and grandeur already on his mind, Puckett felt a soliloquy coming on. You know, those moments when one's serene spirit dredges up the inner depths, calling forth reasons to exult silently to oneself! Trapped by his reason to be, the meaning of his life peeled forth. He whispered to himself, more inwardly and hushed than anything else, while the content of his life broke the noonday air. Only the birds would ever tell if he were to speak aloud, but his thoughts were his own. He looked out into the beauty of what surrounded him and realized that life was meant to be big and full. Nature closed around him. He was charmed and awed at its disclosure. Racing non-bewildered through his mind, the hope of destiny beckoned, as willows and streams and birdsongs enlivened his soul's gaze. No splendor like God's splendor! The "made" by the "Maker" loomed up before him, enticing his pathetic vision and wafting him higher on its pinioned flight. The verdure of grand terraces, little wind-spattered ponds of silvery blue water dancing like pewtered sunshine on a rain-pattered sea, lofty firs and billowy pines and spindly quaking aspens rising gently against the azure sky pointing like the fingers of God toward the eternal—it took his breath away! He fell stricken in humility before it all. He settled back and dreamed, but dreamed big, knowing that God is bigger than the dream. He was flattered that God even knew him, and he ventured upon the possibility that this was the only fact of which he was really certain.

With this ennobling spirit established and purpose set, Puck spurred Gentry farther down the hill toward the waiting village below. Horse, rider and pack mule, weary but sound, turned the bend toward home.

CHAPTER 2

THE VILLAGE

On Saturday afternoon the village was bustling with people, horses, carriages, mules, and wagons, everyone dressed in finery and moving with dispatch along the settlement's main street. Teeming patches of playful children frolicked in and out of the store fronts and down the boardwalks, fitfully startling horses tied to the railings, and being blessed out soundly by prim and proper old ladies trying to get around them. A few town drunks already inebriated, to the veiled delight of saloonkeepers, stumbled along arm-and-shoulder mumbling to themselves in the afternoon heat, or trying to sing some little ditty they faintly remembered from youth. Over to one side, two dogs fought it out royally, without the slightest rationale occurring to them that nothing would be different when they got through fighting. A few stray chickens fluttered noisily, feathers flying, before the rush of the incoming stage, its driver sawing frantically at the reins to stop the jaded horses—nostrils flared, frothing at the mouth, harnesses white with lather—and dust billowing up from beneath the tumbrel's wheels.

The town's steam whistle blew its two o'clock warning that the day was aging rapidly. Soon the encroachment of sunset and nightfall would overcome the day and bring on gala encounters in the lighted halls. Life would rev-up to fever pitch, or perhaps settle down to get ready for Sunday-go-to-Meeting, at least for those who were able to endure the night with any kind of sanity and still be fit to wobble out of bed at first light.

Puck and the animals had entered the village, having come down from Teton Pass, along the flat valley west of the Snake River. Then they had crossed the river, had wound through a few rolling foothills and into the flat basin of the village nestled below Snow King Mountain to the south and Cache Creek Canyon to the Southeast. In spite of the unmistakable weariness of the three, the animals' ears perked up at the clamor and din of what they could not understand, and Puck rallied in the saddle momentarily, somewhat elated at being on home turf again.

As they edged their way down the street purveying the scene, Puck was surprised at how much the village seemed to have grown. A hive of people swarming in every direction was to be expected, but there was new wood everywhere. Structures that he had not seen before had grown up along the boardwalk on either side of the street. Logs, planks, and plaster of every shape and form rose theater-like against a radiant summer sky. Signs scripted on pine and parchment indicated the burgeoning success of new blood and business in the village. Puckett was visibly stunned, but too tired and thirsty to register the change before him.

The dust from the stage was just now settling as the troop passed the stage terminal next to the Quincy Hotel. The stage drivers, Clarence Miles and Cliff Bandy, were disembarking, and the manager of the stage terminal, Josh Fuller, was loosening reins at the head of the four-horse team. As Miles opened the stage door for his riders to unload, he shouted back over his shoulder. "Josh, check out the front off-wheeler, if you will. He's either losing a shoe or may have a stone bruise. If he's unstable, would you have Seldon Howard at the livery stable exchange him for the trip out?"

As Josh uncoupled the doubletree to free the horses from the coach, a young lad disembarking the stage, and having overheard the stage driver, questioned his dad. "Hey, Pa, what's an off-wheeler?" The father, picking up a duffel bag and a valise, answered the boy matter-of-factly. "An off-wheeler is usually the right horse, son, and in any case, the horse farthest from the wheels." The man was not sure he was completely correct, but it seemed to satisfy the curiosity of his son, so they ambled off toward the hotel, the question forgotten.

Puck reined Gentry toward the Primo Saloon, pulled up to the watering trough, and allowed the animals to slake their thirst before he tied them off at the rail and entered the saloon to satisfy his own thirst. The owner of the saloon, Cousin Billy Stiles, did not appear to be around at the moment. It was just as well, because Puck was not there to talk, but to quench his thirst and settle back a few moments from the long ride into the village. Everyone in town, whether related to Stiles or not, called him Cousin Bill, and the Saloon got its name from that reference. *Primo* was Spanish for *Cousin*.

Puck plopped down at the bar on a barstool and placed his hat on the counter, revealing a disheveled array of matted hair. A few other men were spotted around the room, but none that seemed familiar to Puck, so he turned toward the bar, wiped his brow, and cradled his head in hands.

Tige Rooter, the bartender, hardly recognizing the figure, ambled over to the slump of a man hard pressed against the counter. Though tuckered out, Puck looked up in his congenial manner to be respectful of another's presence. The light dawned for both men as they recognized each other at the same time.

"*Wal*, Puck," Tige almost shouted, "I had no *idee* that was you sittin' there! If you're not a sight for...*wal*, I won't say it! But you are anyway! Where'd you come from anyhow?"

"Oh, I rolled in over the hills a little while ago. Been over in Idaho and just got homesick for the old home folk. You know, you're to be honored. Or maybe I should be. You're the first person I've talked to since I rode into town?"

"*Wal*, okay! You deserve a drink on me, don't *ya* see! So, what'll *ya* have?"

"Well, I know you don't have iced tea or ice cream sodas, so I'll have to settle for a beer. I'm too thirsty to be particular."

"Puck, you never were much on the alcohol, but anyway, this one's on the house, so drink up."

Puck and Tige conversed a spell, talking of pleasantries that were more than just killing time. The exchange was downright enjoyable. Puck learned a little more about the changes going on in the village, and found out that Rooter had bought part ownership in the saloon, but only with the stipulation that the *Primo* name remain. Rooter then excused himself to serve some customers at the end of the bar.

Puckett eased down with the drink and leaned against the bar for support of his fatigued body. Just then, he was interrupted by a boisterous voice to one side of him. "Say, mister, don't you clean up on Saturday?" Although the remark came by way of a sneer rather than a smile, Puck passed it off with a shrug and continued sipping his drink.

"I mean, Ivey's Store down the street has a good assortment of soaps!" The cowboy wouldn't let it lie. He just stood there dressed in his finery with a smirk on his face that would defy good sense. He looked as if he might have shaved twice in his lifetime. His skin was suave and dull, but had just enough sheen to reveal that he had primped to meet the day. He was as tall as Puck, but much more slight of build. He carried a crooked elbow that wouldn't totally straighten out as he reached for the stool next to Puck. He stood rather tall, even when seated, due to the irregular feature that his torso from waist up was almost longer than his legs. The bolero jacket he wore, though it was supposed to look short, looked rather scant on a man of his Lincolnesque stature. He would have worn a frock coat much better. His unsoiled gray-blue hat matched his coat and slacks. The gun he wore was so polished that it appeared never to have been fired. He sported a wide leather belt with a large silver buckle and a luxurious pair of boots whose tops glistened openly due to his pant legs being stuffed gingerly inside. Though Puck had never seen the man before, everyone in the village knew him as Buel Tankersley. Puck never moved.

"I said, Ivey's Store down the—"

Puck didn't let him finish, but turned on the barstool to face the stranger in the duds. "My friend," Puck asked casually, "Is Doc Judd still in town?"

"Why? You need'n a doctor?"

"No, but you will be if you don't mind your own business!" Tankersley eased away slowly, half mumbling and half chuckling to himself. He betrayed his insecurity as he found a table of men seated and joined them laughing in derision at the show he had just put on. He kept pointing at the bar in Puck's direction and flapping his jaws to the patrons at the table, always ending his nimble-witted gestures with smoldering laughter.

Puck had finished his drink and was about to leave when a saloon dance girl sidled up to him. "Say, Cowboy," she intoned, "don't pay any attention to Buel. He's just a Monkey Ward Cowboy and a bother to everybody. Hang around with me awhile and I'll shake the dust off your boots!"

"Make yourself easy, Miss. I'm afraid I'll have to pass. Anyway, it would take more time than you've got to shake the dust off these boots. I've got several days of trail dust clinging to these leathers, and as you can see, they look about as tired as I do. But thanks just the same." With that, Puck put down his glass and headed for the door.

"Well, Cowboy, I can at least see you to the door." The lady took him by the arm and sauntered slowly toward the exit, hoping to see his brown eyes again on some other occasion.

A faint chuckle filtered from the tables in Puck's direction as Tankersley moved slyly toward the door as well. With a devil-may-care nonchalance, he neared the couple making their way to the front and coyly stuck out his foot. Puck, diverted by the feminine charm, did not see the protruding foot and tripped over the gangly clodhopper. He fell forthright onto the floor, almost taking the bar princess with him. The sting of the pine floor against his already tired knees aroused anger, especially when he looked up and saw Tankersley standing over him.

Puck unfolded his doubled frame upward in one motion, grasped the drugstore cowboy's lapel with one hand and popped a forearm between his eyes. The rogue bristled and staggered backward, blinked his eyes for focus and came lumbering toward Puck with vengeance. The pair wrestled rabidly, intolerant of surroundings, knocking over hat racks and sending chairs flying. They rolled lewdly on the floor, then climbed to their knees. Finally, the two were on their feet again, clinched in a death hold, rocking one way and then the other, flailing with backhands, each trying to better his territory, not merely maintain his ground. In a moment, the force of two lumbering giants crashed through the saloon doors, swinging them wildly on their pins, and popping them against the jambs. The gray-blue hat scooted through the doorway with them. High Pockets was winded and stumbling blindly, his tousled hair blocking his view. Puck saw his chance. Grabbing him from behind by his collar and his fancy leather belt, Puck, two-handedly and with convincing force, marched the miscreant across the boardwalk, over the rail, and headlong into the brackish horse trough below. With a ceremonious splash, the lanky figure sank fully beneath the murky surface, Saturday duds and all. Puck, under the heat of wounded pride, unthinkingly picked up the stranger's hat and tossed it in after him.

Leaning over the trough, Puck reached down to retrieve the villain. Grasping him by the collar, he hailed, "Okay, fella, climb on out of there if you've had enough!"

The man dragged himself to the edge, bobbing up and down, spewing the brackish sun brew, and splashing his way out of the box. Dripping, he stood there with sagging duds, looking like your average waif. He composed himself as unstately as a soaked rat sitting on the edge of a rain barrel.

Then brushing himself off, shaking his hat in hand, and with a sour smirk on his face, he growled, "Look what you've done! Look at these duds! And you've ruined my sombrero! Who do you think you are?"

"Look mister, I didn't ask for any of this. This is what happens when you mess with tired, dirty cowboys who have nothing to lose." Puck actually felt sorry for the man, especially registering a little guilt for having tossed the man's hat into the water without call. "I'll tell you what I'm going to do," Puck continued. "I think you are better than you look and better than you act." Reaching forth his hand, Puck opened his palm revealing two gold coins. "Here, take these. They ought to cover the cost of getting your hat cleaned and blocked and maybe even restore your suit. You can clean your boots and gun yourself!"

"Well, what about this horse grime and moss in my hair and on my face? Huh? What about this crud?" How will I ever *git* shed of this scum?" He draped his hands and wiggled his fingers as if to shake the filth free.

Puck snickered soberly and retorted, "Ivey's Store down the street has a good assortment of soaps!"

The barroom buckaroo scowled and grumbled again, "Can't you

learn to fight on dry ground? At least it would save a fella's clothes. I have a notion to..." The sentence hung in midair as an older citizen standing by interrupted him.

"Son, you better be glad the man has offered you reparations as he has. He really doesn't owe you anything. So, you better pick up and git along or I'll throw you into the trough again myself."

With that embarrassment, the drugstore waif resigned, poured the water out of his pretentious boots, gathered his reins, and led his horse down the street—led his horse, that is, because his saddle was cleaner than his clothes. He wasn't about to add to his losses by soiling it too. At least his gray mare and tackle retained their beauty, even if he stood out unappealingly beside them. The wrinkled sop of a man, still mumbling to himself, meandered on down the street, turned the nearest corner to avert public embarrassment, and was gone.

Puck remained standing on the boardwalk being dusted off by Tige Rooter and the saloon princess. "You needn't make such a fuss," Puck said, somewhat ashamed. "I'm sorry for the ruckus, Tige. Count up any damage inside and I'll settle up with you in a day or two. In the meantime, I had better go get cleaned up before I draw more attention for assault."

Puck grinned and gathered his animals. Mounting Gentry, he ambled north along the storefronts, still amazed at the growth of the once-simple skyline. Ironically, across the alley (it was more of a relief or cul-de-sac than an alley), from the saloon, stood Gray's Bible and Book Shop. Puck was humored by the thought that, true to tradition, good and evil were still facing one another down. The two businesses seemed to have different clientele, but there were some like himself who frequented both establishments without going to the extreme. Puck didn't like Bible-pounding patrons out of control any more than he liked drunks who couldn't manage themselves. Both types made one dizzy in their own way. Puck wondered what tired old Sandy would say about it, if an ass could speak. He thought he knew what the answer would be.

On down the street the threesome passed the apothecary and soda fountain shop, and Puck wondered why he had not come here for his drink rather than stopping at the saloon. Perchance, he might have averted the tangle with Buel Tankersley; then again, who knows, Tankersley being a drugstore cowboy and all, he might just as likely have found him here. Perish the thought! Puck laughed and pondered how really hard up for amusement he must be to have to conjure up his own.

The day was growing slim and Puck wanted to get by his aunt's dress shop to surprise her on his return. Bella's Dress Shop laid a good trot up the way, past the village jail, Junior Hayes' Gunsmith Shop, and next to the Village Bank on the adjoining corner, owned by Brandon Wise.

Bella Engstrom was Puckett's aunt on his mother's side of the family. His mother's name had been Clare Engstrom before she claimed the Puckett name in marriage to his father. Bella had been good in her care for him after his parent's death, though he was quite capable of fending for himself in life. The home life under her direction had been good for him, for which he had shown an appreciation over the past two years by sending money to help her extend her business and to care for his other two horses left behind in her charge.

The animals were now getting restless as Puck tied them in front of the dress shop. If they were as hungry as he was, he understood. He would just go in and greet his aunt, and then get on down the road to her house and barn at the edge of town. As he mounted the boardwalk, he noticed other structures across the street spread in both directions. There was the Westerly Hardware owned by Crip and Tellie Westerly, the Village Grocery run by Galin and Beth Marriott, Owen Sandafer's Barber Shop, the Pine Lodge Builder's office, and Doc Slaughter Judd's medical clinic. In the distance toward his aunt's small spread, Puck could see the livery stable and Dr. Timothy Breaker's veterinarian clinic and corrals. In between, cottages and cabins lined the street on both sides, giving the air of a quaint settlement at peace with itself.

The noise of the street was subsiding in the wake of people gathering their goods and children and repairing to their homes in time for the evening meal. Others had vacated the village somewhat earlier, owing to the fact that they lived on the outlying farms and ranches some distance from Jackson. The peaceful atmosphere, however, might soon give way to potential trouble, as drovers and cowboys were just now beginning to filter into the village for a weekend of drinking and carousing.

Puck lowered his head as he entered the dress shop, hoping to surprise his aunt, but not watching where he was going, he bumped into Jarrell Quincy, owner of the hotel, exiting with a package for his wife. Puck pardoned himself without much adieu, as Quincy was an acquaintance but, otherwise, not very familiar to him. He approached the dry goods counter where he found a young lass by the name of Faye Lincoln minding the store.

"The name's Puckett, Miss. I'm looking for my aunt, Bella Engstrom. Is she in the back?"

"No, Mr. Puckett. She went home early today not feeling too well. She left me to close up. I'm sure you will find her at home, but can I help you with anything else? Maybe a scarf for your girlfriend?"

"Well, thank you kindly, but I really don't have a girlfriend at the time, and as you can see, I'm not very presentable to be browsing in these clean confines. I'll just mosey along and check on my aunt.

But I must say, my aunt knows how to pick pretty ones for her clerks."

"Well, thank you, sir. I might add that she also knows how to pick handsome relatives. You'll have to come back and see me another day when I can show you something on the racks or in the boxes. But then, if you don't have a girlfriend, what would you buy?"

"Yeah, what would I buy?" Puck was struck with the female's beauty and wished now that he had not chanced coming in so bedraggled looking. He excused himself, backing toward the door, pirouetting around stacks in the aisles, looking back impulsively to get a last glimpse of the beauty, almost knocking items on the floor. He closed the door behind him, mounted his faithful steed, and rode north with dispatch. The little dun mule, reluctant to move out of his dozing stance, kicked up belligerently at the tug of the rope tied to the pommel of Gentry's saddle. Side winding up the road, churning up dust in their wake, the threesome challenged the slight grade leading to the Engstrom place on the outskirts of the village.

The gate was open to the front yard as Puck approached the cottage. He tethered the animals with a rope along the picket fence surrounding the house where they could munch on tufts of grass and wild flowers blooming shyly around each post. Maybe that would bide their time until he could get them fed for the night. Turning toward the house he walked briskly up the walk paved in flat stone. Before he could knock on the door, it opened and the lady of the house peered through the screen to see who the company might be. She lowered a wet cloth from her forehead to get a better look. Seeing the unmistakable Puckett frame, with jubilant outcry she mocked the town crier, lifting her head toward the ceiling and bursting forth. "Well, cancel my subscription, Postman, the boy's done wandered home!" The two grabbed each other like long lost weaverbirds returning to their clutch.

Aunt Bella kept patting Puck on the cheek and repeating, "I can't believe it! I can't believe it!" She sat down and ogled the sight before her and just as quickly rose to her feet for more patting and disbelief. The rag lay limply on the floor as she completely forgot about her headache. She had just gained new strength. Puck had come home. Puck smiled agreeably and insisted that it was true. He had come home for good!

CHAPTER 3
CATCHING UP

The past evening was a grand reunion on two fronts. The foremost front, of course, was that Aunt Bella was so elated over the appearance of Puck on her doorstep that she forgot about her illness. Either that, or she let it slide without much regard, in that while Puck took care of the animals for the night, she whipped up a country supper that a land urchin would kill for, consisting of braised steak tenders, juicy beyond imagination; mashed potatoes (or as Puck called them, *whipped spuds*); succulent wild asparagus sprouts sautéed in fresh garlic and country butter; early turnips and greens brought in by an Indian friend the day before, cooked with ham hock and extra morsels of ham, and hot cornbread that defied the touch without first moistening the fingertips. Cold fresh milk and cream, pulled from the side of an ice block, washed the country fare down, and when that was seated properly, it was chased with banana cream pie and piping hot coffee. Puck wakened in the night still thinking the meal was a stroke of fortune ordered from Paradise. He bet that even God was surprised that such a meal existed! But sweet old Aunt Bella knew. She was no belly robber like the ranch cooks he had known.

The other front of the grand reunion took place when Puck went to care for Gentry and Sandy. After unbridling them and removing the pack from Sandy, he fed them before being exultantly reunited with his other two horses. Sandy was beside himself, being freed of the encumbrance that had plagued his day since early light. He bounced and bobbed and bucked almost belly up at times. He rollicked and rolled in the dust of the corral, and scratched his rear against the gatepost. Then he, along with Gentry, settled down long enough to pig-out on a mixture of corn silage, oats, barley bran, and sweet molasses. Puck left them two giant pitchforks worth of prairie hay. Then he headed for the open bedding stalls inside the barn to greet his other horses.

As he opened the door and entered the straw-laden flat, something as black as midnight moved out of the shadows into the waning sunlight filtering in through a window above. Puck's horse, Carbon, had exited his bedding stall, flanked by Firebrand, a three-year old gelding. Carbon hesitated momentarily in the service lane of the barn to see who had entered. Almost instantly Carbon pricked his ears forward and bowed his tail in certain recognition of his owner. A low nicker and a few stamps of his right foot signaled Puck's welcome home by the big black. He cantered forward to the embrace of Puck's arms about his neck. The two swayed, almost as if putting their love for each other to motion, and the big horse's exuberance practically lifted Puck off the ground.

Carbon was an aging horse now, and Puck had never slighted him in any way. "Care" wasn't a big enough word to describe how he lionized that horse. His favor toward Carbon over the years was so ennobling that it had almost been a religious act. Even so, he had not laid in store better attention than Carbon had proffered him. The horse had gotten him out of a lot of tough places when the chips were down. He had once saved Puck's life by intervening during the charge of an angry bull, and had a scar along the flank to show for it. He seemed to naturally take charge of circumstances at times as though he were the leader of the two. Still, the big black knew who was master. For a year before Puck had left for Idaho, he had been gradually edging Carbon into retirement. Carbon seemed to sense as much every time Puck saddled Gentry and gathered up the mule for another ride.

Firebrand nosed his way along the withers of Carbon to make his presence known. He nipped gently at Puckett's wrist and nuzzled beneath his arm. Puck reached for his halter and pulled him slightly ahead of Carbon. He repeatedly creased his ears in his palm, stroking them through his fingers. He wiggled his hand on the foretop and brushed him along the neck. The horse responded with the gentle pitching of his head up and down.

"So this is what you have become," Puck intoned. Puck had not seen the horse since he was a young colt, owing to the fact that he left for Idaho shortly after acquiring him.

Firebrand was a quiet horse, more even-tempered than most, with a story behind his name. Puck knew that most cowboys on the range never took much stock in naming their horses. Reference to "the big gelding," "the gray mare," "the little sorrel," or the like, was good enough. They didn't think they should name something they might later have to eat, but that wasn't Puck. He named his horses to single them out from the masses. They had character of their own.

Puck had bought Firebrand from Jeremy Ames when the colt was only a strapping junior at his mother's side. On a stormy night, the colt had almost lost his life. Lightning had struck the Ames bedding stalls and set them afire. Awakened by commotion coming from the barn, the family dogs barking, and a general melee set in by squawking chickens and guineas, all four members of the Ames family broke for the barn to free trapped animals. Heavy rains were not slowing the flames, due to their being largely inside the structure. Mr. Ames flung open the double doors to the bedding barn and covered his nose with rain-soaked flour bags hanging to one side. He was able to free six animals without serious incident, except for their own wild cavorting in breaking through the maze of shuttle passes between stalls, in their search of the main exit. Firebrand's dam lumbered through the doors at the last moment.

The colt followed close behind, but his tail was on fire. The only thing that saved the colt, in its wild-eyed painful lunge, was the fact of the rain simultaneously pounding down in sheets. The colt was saved, but not without serious burns to the tail and the threat of infection in the days to come.

When Puck saw the colt a few days later, he feigned no grief, as his heart went out in sympathy for the young survivor. Jeremy Ames was more than pleased that Puck showed such affection for the marked animal and, therefore, was willing to sell him for less than an admirable price. Puck lost no time christening the colt "Firebrand." Sadly, he had to leave the colt with Aunt Bella to rear, so that Firebrand, in effect, had really become her horse. For three years she had cared for the colt and trained him not only to ride gentle as a lady's mount but also to pull the family buggy. Puck could sense he was a lady's man.

Time with Carbon and Firebrand at the barn was exceptionally pleasing to Puck, but he was hungry, needing a long-overdue bath, and fidgety for a good night's sleep. That is when he had returned to the house to be confronted, to his absolute delight, by Aunt Bella's sumptuous country fare.

The two had been too tired to talk that evening but vowed they would spend a good deal of time doing so come morning. His having completed a long-overdue bath in the old oval tub, Puck then had headed for bed.

Puck slept-in a few hours after dawn on that first Sunday home from the hills. The usual routine was to attend meeting at the church, but bones and brawn were too sore and aching to even consider it. Aunt Bella was putting on another country fare, this time a more modest assortment of bacon, eggs, biscuits, jam, and more piping hot coffee, and now ringing the come-and-get-it bell and hollering the old-time cowboy wake-up call:

> *"Bacon in the pan*
> *Coffee in the pot*
> *Get up an' get it*
> *Eat it while it's hot."*

Aunt Bella bowed her head to say grace and did a finer job than that once proffered by a cowboy who thought he ought to say grace but did not know how. He simply, if not genuinely, repeated, "Good spuds, good meat, good Lord, let's eat." By the manner in which he then took to the food, you just knew he was thankful.

The surroundings of the kitchen furnishings put Puck into his homiest mood. It was country in every way. The cupboards hung on one wall papered over canvas with a rendition of buttercups and trailing vines. The two were encompassed by beautiful hues of greens and golds. There was no running water, but a dish basin stood on a makeshift wooden platform overlooking the kitchen window, revealing a beautiful rose garden scintillating with early buds and blossoms. A regal sun spoke of the radiant day in store. To the left of the window was a rack for spices and condiments used in Aunt Bella's cooking. At the end of the counter to the right of the window, draped with tatted floral patterned flour sacks to hide the pots and pans on shelves below, stood the well bucket and ladle, the only water in the house. At the turn in the wall three feet from the bucket, stood the old black iron and white porcelain wood stove, and above it, hanging on the wall, an assortment of cast iron skillets and copper bottom pans.

Puck's eyes wandered past the stove to the door exiting to the outside, and just to the right of the door a fireplace arranged in the corner, still smoldering from use during the night chill. Against the adjoining wall stood a quaint china cabinet with framed doors, divided by wooden mullions and glass, a cabinet that had been built by his father not long after the family had moved to Togwatee Pass. Aunt Bella had rightly claimed it for her own use after the death of his parents. It sparkled with her best china. The heavy wooden table, where the two sat eating, stood slightly off-center of the room, and, behind it, a wall glutted with pictures and family heirlooms. The knotty pine wainscot and plank flooring glistened with a satin patina. Three kerosene lanterns hung shimmering from the ceiling. Everything in sight reminded Puck that he was home.

Rising chatter interrupted the penetrating silence. For once, Puck was actually more interested in talking than eating. So much had passed beneath the bridge since his departure into Idaho Territory that he needed to catch up. He now felt a bit lost among a fold of people that he ought to know well. He wasn't interested in the weather, the usual point of conversation, but as he thanked Aunt Bella not only for breakfast, but also for the delicious dinner the night before, he began with familiar things.

"Auntie, who brought in those delicious turnips and greens we had last night?"

"Those were brought to me by Noka Kona, the beautiful young Indian girl married to Reston Chandler. Her gift was special enough, but I really think she had some things on her mind that she wanted to talk about."

"What things?" Puck led her on, as he too knew the Indian girl.

"Well, she was depressed over talk in the village about her cross-racial marriage to Reston," Aunt Bella went on. "She said that she was making a special dress to wear to the annual celebration next month, but was afraid she would back out of going to the dance if talk persisted."

"Did Noka Kona indicate how Reston was taking the matter?"

"He understands her concern and is concerned himself about what is being said behind their backs, but he wants her to attend the celebration and let the chips fall where they may. He says that if she doesn't go, he'll stay home with her. It wouldn't be right, he felt, to leave her home alone, with his being out on the town celebrating."

Puck acknowledged the problem and registered concern. He knew something behind the thinking of both the women and the men in the village. The women were a little leery of the Indian beauty in the presence of their husbands, and the men were jealous that Reston had been so lucky to have won her hand. If the problem had racial roots at all, it was alluded to merely to save face. Many whites felt that if their kind married an Indian girl, he ought to live on the reservation, rather than bringing the Indian into the white domain. In the case of Reston and Noka Kona, their place in the village was partially tolerated because the Chandler family name had a place of honor in getting the village established. Apparently, such honor did not include total silence on the interracial question. Puck assured Aunt Bella that he would do what he could to befriend the couple. He remembered the couple being rather handsome, and he certainly agreed with the townspeople's assessment of Noka Kona's beauty.

Puck began to smile, and then questioned Aunt Bella with a bit of playfulness in his voice, "Auntie, speaking of pretty ladies, have you been hiding a special secret from me? You never wrote in any of your letters to me anything about your pretty store clerk."

"You mean Faye Lincoln, I presume?"

"Yes, I think that's the name she gave yesterday afternoon when I was in the dress shop. She's nice and quite a *looker*! Has she taken to anybody seriously in the Village?"

Aunt Bella mused a moment as if trying to recall a name.

"Well, I'm not sure how serious, but I think a *fella* by the name of Buel Tankersley has been sporting her around town recently." Puck's chin dropped two fathoms.

"Auntie, you could have gone all day without mentioning that name!"

"How's that?"

"I had no cause to mention it to you, but yesterday I had a run-in with him at the saloon as I came into the Village—I'm not sure to any lasting conflict—but he doesn't ingratiate himself to strangers by any means. He'd disgust St. Pius! You mean to tell me that Faye Lincoln—that lovely creature in your shop—actually would want to be seen with him?"

"Tankersley is somewhat new around these parts," Aunt Bella nodded, "and I suppose all the eligible girls at least want to check him out. He dresses nicely, seems to be clean, and has a little money that he doesn't mind spending on them. I guess it turns a girl's head. If you want to know anything more than that, I guess you can ask Faye."

Gazing out the front window into the distance, Puck toned down his answer as if taken by another soliloquy. "Maybe I will. Yeah, I'm sure of it. Maybe I will."

Aunt Bella, snapping her fingers as if to jolt Puck back into reality, questioned him. "Sure? Maybe? Which is it Puck?"

"Okay," Puck responded, "I will, but I'm not interested in finding out anything about Tankersley. I'd rather find out what makes Miss Lincoln tick."

"Well, don't go too far out on a limb too fast," Aunt Bella prodded, "and whatever you do, don't disrupt her flair for business. She's the best clerk I've ever had." In order to see if Puck were listening, Aunt Bella thought to humor him by adding, "She tried to sell me the shop one day, and I already own it!"

Puck, still somewhat in a trance, retorted, "How much was she asking for…" Then he caught himself, "Oh, Aunt Bella, what are you trying to pull? You know that I've been listening!"

With that, Puck changed the subject. "I've been thinking a lot lately, Auntie, about what I'm going to do since I've returned home? Of course, I've not had the chance to talk to anyone about matters, but you know me probably better than anyone else. I trust your acceptance of me, no matter what fool thing I come up with. But I don't even know where to begin."

Puck straightened up as if to take charge of matters, whatever that might be. He had always been in charge of his life, and there was no need to suspend the responsibility now. He was a man who wanted to make his impact felt. He just was not sure how he would go about it. As he had thought about his own early experiences, including the dangerous history with regard to Indian affairs and White dominance, in which he had often found himself vacillating, he began to construct a vision of his future. That he began to do so at the expense of bending Aunt Bella's ear was a new twist to his confidence.

"Aunt Bella," he began in earnest, "in the winning of the West, there has been enough killing and despair to last a lifetime. If the white man is not tired of it as a whole, I am! Whatever line of work I secure in the days ahead, I am going to live to correct some of the weak philosophies, the sordid worldviews, and moral inconsistencies taking shape in our reconstruction since the Civil War. I certainly will need a job, and I'm not trained for much of anything but highriding, but whatever I wind up doing, I want to be left free to pursue some healing advantage for the people of Wyoming—White and Indian alike! Your mentioning of Noka Kona's dilemma is merely a case in point. There is so much hurt and distrust since the Indian wars that someone is going to have to stand in the gap and help to right the wrongs. Oh, I recognize that the wheels of history cannot be turned back. We can never right all the wrongs. We can never heal all the wounds, but what matters is that there shall be no further wounds."

Aunt Bella interrupted. "Puck, you are a mighty man to pursue such dreams as you propose. I don't know of a better objective, and I know you will find a way to make a living and be of service to the peoples of this land. You've got it in ya, Puck! You'll not rest till you take this current age by storm and edge it upright, and God knows it can stand some uprighting!"

Aunt Bella paused and then continued. "You mentioned reconstruction a moment ago. If you are to help in the process, you must be up-to-date on what's been going on around these parts. You are aware, I suppose, of the talk of Wyoming Territory becoming a state of the Union?" The question was rhetorical. "There is some indication that Washington, D. C., will sanction the move by early July. Feelings about it are mixed around the village. Some are concerned that if we fall in with the Union, we will fall prey to its overbearing authority. We may find ourselves paying for it through the nose, much as the Indian territories fell victim to broken treaty after broken treaty. Those of this persuasion feel that we ought to remain a Territory so as to maintain some semblance of monetary independence. Others feel that continued self-government may leave us scrambling for subsistence and cut us off from any aid that a larger unitary body might avail in troubled times. We have already floundered on occasions and have had nowhere to turn. I guess I am leaning toward a place in the Union. Territories around us have already conceded, such as Colorado fourteen years ago. Statehood came to Montana and Washington almost simultaneously, Montana on November 8, and Washington on November 11, 1889. North and South Dakota also came in last year. Idaho is sure to concede next month and Wyoming could easily follow.

"We will not pride ourselves by our own sense of diversity if we hold back in arrogance. In recent days, many political arm-twisting barons have swept through our territory pumping up the people for welcoming the state billing. Many of our own townspeople, anticipating statehood, are already preparing to celebrate the transition in our annual extravaganza that will be taking place next month. These are things to give thought to, Puck, if you hope to get your foot in the door."

Aunt Bella settled back and waited for a response.

"Well, for one thing," Puck finally chimed in, "whether we become a state or not, I'm not looking to become some political figure in order to make a mark. I believe health comes to the grassroots by people of the grassroots. We will learn to serve one another and meet human need wherever possible, if wounds are to be healed. No position on a government board is required for us to help change the course of life around us. Better yet, in fact, that we not be hamstrung by some political office! Sometimes we wind up allowing people to die while we spend our time at the demanding job of keeping a political office alive. No thank you! I'm not interested even in the president's office. I'll stick to the low road where the thoughts and dreams and challenges of man in his shirt sleeves converge to produce life—not mere progress!"

"Don't miss my point, Puck. You must know what's happening with the people if you are going to help people."

"I know you're right, Auntie, and I'll do my best to come up to date with the real concerns in our day and time, and I'll proceed with as much adventure as I can muster. I'll try to make you proud."

"I know you will, Puck."

"Auntie, for starters, what else is going on around here?"

Aunt Bella thought for a moment. Then she informed Puck of the burgeoning railroad affairs, especially the Union Pacific Railroad that had established its way across southern Wyoming. Travel had already been made easier by its presence. Cattle movements had been greatly facilitated even though the business was now severely on a decline. Oil production, too, was getting established after the discovery of the Dallas Field in the state. Jackson Hole itself was apparently on the map to stay. The village was expanding, due to the encroachment of farmers into the area. Ranches were more than subsisting as family operations, but as far as being the big business centers they once had been was another matter. Newcomers must be well advised as to their current state of treading water.

Puck was enlightened about current history being made, but he also wanted to know about news more up-to-date. Aunt Bella knew he had more than local gossip in mind.

"Well, on one front," Aunt Bella began, "you may have heard about the recent rise of cattle rustling around the area and especially in Johnson County. Settlers have come in, bought up government land, and have begun to fence off their properties. Some of the newcomers have proceeded to stock their herds by stealing cattle from the established cattle operations. The cattlemen are certain to rise up in arms if the rustling does not stop, and some bloody wars are going to be the outcome. We've even had some rustling going on around here lately. If you take another highriding job, more than likely you will find the ferreting out of the culprits as part of your task."

This kind of talk interested Puck, so he urged his aunt on regarding current news.

"I'm reluctant to let you in on this latest bit of news," Aunt Bella went on, "but you will find it out soon enough, so I may as well go ahead and tell you myself. I would have told you yesterday but you looked so tired, and here you were just home—home for the first time in three years. It is ironic that you should show up right on the heels of the matter. I wish...." Puck, agitated at Aunt Bella's seeming avoidance, interrupted her with a slight stamp of his foot.

"Auntie, please, what are you driving at? Do you have something to tell me, or not?"

"I was getting to it, Puck. Don't be so impatient. Slow down a bit. You're not on your horse now. Okay, here it is! Yesterday a report came to the Village that an eight-year-old Shoshoni Indian girl had been kidnapped from her home on the Wind River Indian Reservation by two white men. The kidnapping happened right at dusk four days ago. Two older Indian boys pursued the two culprits but lost them in the night. The Indian nation has been up in arms ever since and is threatening to rally their own forces to hunt them down. Governor Warren has seen that as a potential hotbed between Indian and White and has stepped in with assurance to the Shoshonis that he will muster the necessary forces to search out all of Wyoming, if need be, until the girl is found. He promised immediate response and has offered $10,000 reward for any information leading to the arrest of the kidnappers."

Puck was puzzled. This was certainly an important concern and it raised his own sense of compassion and justice, but why was there such reluctance from Aunt Bella to tell him the news?

"Aunt Bella," Puck intruded, "at first you thought not to tell me about this matter. Why in the world would you not want me to know about such news?"

"Well, I haven't gotten around to the whole story yet. There is more. Apparently, some of your long-standing Indian friends at Crowheart and Wind River, Wyoming, met with the governor and convinced him that 'Puck Puckett' was the only person they knew who could revive a cold trail. They remembered your excursions throughout all of their territory, including the rugged area between Gannett Peak and Wind River Peak on the Continental Divide. They recalled how you also trailed Pawnee renegades throughout the uranium mining districts farther east, and put the Cavalry into their camps. The governor was impressed enough to send two soldiers from Fort Washakie to try to find you. They had no indication from your Indian friends that you would not be here when they arrived. The sheriff told them as much and then sent them here to consult with me. I gave them what information I had as to your whereabouts. Of course, I had no way of knowing that you would show up on my doorstep six hours later. The soldiers remarked that they would stay the day tomorrow and seek to contact you in Idaho by telegraph. If they had no success, they would then inform the governor and leave on Tuesday. Puck, you'll have to forgive me, but when I saw you on my front porch and later heard you state that you were home to stay, I just didn't have the heart to break the news to you. I guess I was selfish. I haven't seen you in three years!"

Puck placed his arm around Aunt Bella and assured her that she had done no wrong. He fully intended to go into the village on Monday anyway, and he would be sure to be informed by someone that the soldiers were looking for him. The news did not have to come from Aunt Bella.

"I suppose you know, Auntie," Puck averred, "that I have to pursue this request from the governor? At least I have to see if my going is feasible. When the soldiers show me the facts of the case, I may find my going hopeless. Then again, if circumstances are favorable, I'll have to find a way to comply. And, Auntie, I know it was hard for you, but thanks for telling me. You know where my heart is. This just may be some of that 'righting of the wrongs' I've been mentioning to you."

The two parted amiably with a vigorous hug and Puck spent the afternoon walking the grounds, drinking in the beauty of the Engstrom layout. Why would anyone, who had access to all this beauty, want to place himself in harms way anyway? Is a man not entitled to his privacy at some point in his life? Can't the Indian Agents handle the affairs of the reservations? Why should he entertain such an excruciating task just after a rugged ride across Idaho Territory? Are the Cavalrymen that inept at tracking offenders? A thousand such questions arose to convince Puck of his logic and to test his sanity. Quite suddenly, a sharp pang pierced his conscience and assured him all over again that none of us is an island when it comes to the suffering of another human being.

Puck fed the animals and then moved slowly, but more discreetly, along the fence line, across the freshly plowed garden acre, and eventually returned to the cottage. He spent a quiet evening with Aunt Bella reassuring her that whatever the outcome of his meeting with the soldiers, he fully intended one day soon to make home his headquarters for the duration. As darkness fell, he subsided with it, falling limply into bed, and thanking God for another glorious day.

CHAPTER 4
THE DECISION

Early Monday morning, Puck fed the stock and then saddled Carbon for the brief ride into the village. Usually, Carbon stayed back and watched Puck saddle Gentry, but this day belonged to Carbon. With Puck aloft, he pranced out of the barn like a show mount. A Tennessee walker would have had a supreme task to sidestep and swish like this big black. He danced amiably to Puck's gentle urging, neck and tail bowed, head alert, eyes gleaming in a distant gaze, high-stepping to the prompting of Puck's toes in the horse's barrel behind the legs. The gait was easy, as Puck floated in the saddle rather than anchoring himself tightly. Moving down the lane, two old friends picked up the pace toward the village.

The morning's itinerary was pre-set, with two major concerns forcing their way into Puck's mind. One was the dire importance of the soldier delegation and their charge by the governor of the Territory. The other was Puck's desire to speak with his banker, Brandon Wise, regarding a number of matters, not the least of which was his personal account at the bank.

The bank would not be open for a few hours, so before taking care of his own personal affairs, Puck dropped by the livery stable to see if Seldon Howard had been keeping the soldiers' mounts. The answer was "yes." Seldon Howard had been keeping the horses, and they had not yet been picked up for the day. Puck was relieved that the militia were still in the Village, possibly still at the hotel. In deference to their privacy he would first consult Sheriff Forgus Manley, who would know something of the soldiers' whereabouts and something of the nature of their orders.

Sheriff Manley was seated at his desk going over some papers, when Puck entered the door. Manley casually glanced up thinking to see his deputy coming in for work. When he recognized that it was Puck, instead, one would have thought he had seen a phantom. He jumped to his feet, inadvertently tipping his chair against the wall. He slapped his hands together and then lifted them toward heaven in a gesture of thanksgiving. His mind stumbled over his tongue as he began almost to shout.

"Puck? That can't be you, Puck! You're in Idaho! How'd you get here since yesterday? Does your aunt know you're here? Soldiers have been looking for you. The governor has..." The sheriff finally just stopped and plopped into a chair, amazed and out of breath.

"Well, for one thing," Puck volunteered, "I am here, and I'm not a ghost, so you can loosen your collar and let the blood flow back into your ashen face. Get hold of yourself and I'll explain everything." The sheriff wiped his brow, a pink hue began to irrigate his pallor like a rising temperature gauge, and a smile began to wash across his face.

"Puck, for a minute there I thought I was seeing things." He rose again and greeted Puck with a healthy slap on the shoulder.

Puckett himself questioned the ironic timing of his returning just when someone happened into the village looking for him. Stranger things have happened, but now he began to wonder if he had returned to the village for just such a time as this!

When everything about his return had been explained, Puck began to raise his questions.

"Sheriff Manley, you started to say something about the governor. I know about his sending soldiers here to look for me, and I have been told about the kidnapping on the reservation, but I have no details. Really, that is why I am here. I thought you would know."

"Yes, I could fill you in on a number of things, but I wish we could get the soldiers here. They have a portfolio with facts, which they did not relate to me, and full information regarding the request of Governor Francis E. Warren. I saw the orders and the charge, and they looked pretty official to me."

Just then the door opened and in walked Deputy Shane Newby, later than normal, but he excused himself by stating he had been stopped momentarily by the two soldiers. He had a message for the sheriff. After breakfast the soldiers were going to the telegraph office to try to contact a Mr. Puckett in Idaho and then come by the Sheriff's office.

"Newby," the sheriff broke in, "You don't know this man standing here, do you?"

"No, sir, I guess I don't."

"Well, this happens to be the man the soldiers are looking for. Newby, meet Puck Puckett." The two men shook hands.

"Well, sheriff, if this is Mr. Puckett, why are the soldiers looking for him in Idaho? Why don't they just come down here?"

"Good deduction, Newby. Now *howsabout* going back to the hotel for me and informing the soldiers that the man they have been looking for is sitting in my office."

When Newby was gone, Sheriff Manley informed Puck of Shane's simple approach to things. He had good common sense, but his education and social acumen were a little under normal. Most of the townspeople recognized his good intentions and the fact that he was as good as gold, but others chided him and thought he traveled with something short of a full deck. He was a good deputy and no one pushed him around when he was in charge of official matters.

Newby was not gone more than twenty minutes when he returned with the two soldiers and presented them to Sheriff Manley and Puck. The sheriff introduced the two men as Sergeant

Graves and Corporal Allen and arranged for the men to spread their papers on a round conference table in the center of the room. Sergeant Graves immediately took charge and got down to business, as they were taught to do in the Cavalry.

"Mr. Puckett," Graves began, "the governor has sent us here with a request for you to assume a commission, one which, if you choose to accept, will ultimately render a stipend based on officer's wages. The governor has also established a $10,000 reward fund to be shared by any who supply information toward the capture of two kidnappers of a Shoshoni Indian girl. He requests that you leave as soon as possible and rally any materials or alliances that you might require for the trip to Fort Washakie and for the ultimate pursuit of the kidnappers. We will try to answer any questions you might have that could expedite your decision. Do you have any questions, Sir?"

"Sergeant Graves, Corporal Allen, thank you both for coming. You are doing a fine service for your country and in this case for the people of the Wind River Indian Reservation. First of all, should I know the identity of the Shoshoni girl who was kidnapped?"

Corporal Allen responded, "Yes, the girl is the great grand niece of one of the retired chiefs on the Reservation. She is no small item of concern as a member of the tribe but more so because her father is one of the wealthiest leaders among his people. A sizable ransom of $150,000 has also been demanded for her safe return."

"For this reason, then, you think the girl has not been harmed?"

Sergeant Graves responded, "This is the fifth day since her kidnapping, so we feel there is a good chance that she has remained unharmed. At this point, any chase after the kidnappers has been low key, hopefully so they will not be driven into panic. The governor is concerned that any open attempt on the part of the Cavalry or segment from the Shoshoni people might cause undue alarm on the part of the offenders and drive them into some brash action toward the girl. This is why Governor Warren is commissioning a clandestine expert unit to handle the affairs. By what he has been informed about your skills, he feels that you are the man for the job."

"At what point on the Reservation was the girl kidnapped?"

Graves continued, "She was taken from outside her home just before dark in the southern portions of the preserve in Wind River Village, two miles below Fort Washakie."

"My aunt indicated to me, from news she had heard, that the men were pursued by two Indian boys. I'm sure you have questioned them, but are they still available for further questioning, if I were to assume the governor's request?"

"I'm sure of it," Corporal Allen replied. "Maybe you would have questions that we have not thought of."

"You said the perpetrators had demanded ransom money. How did they make contact?"

"Apparently," Graves answered, "someone among them has experience in tapping into telegraph lines, because the first communication came to the telegraph office in Riverton and could not be traced to its point of origin."

"Just how did they intimate that the ransom should be paid, and what was the point of pick up?"

Graves spoke up, "They wanted an approximation in gold or actual certificates placed in unmarked saddlebags and ultimately left at an undisclosed site, which they would later reveal. We have not been in contact with the Fort, so we do not know if further communication and instructions have come in."

"You used the word 'site,' Sir. Is that your word or is that the word they used?"

"That is the word they used, why?"

"Just curious," Puck concluded.

Puck felt that he had asked enough preliminary questions, except that he wanted to be clear on a matter before he gave them his answer. "Gentlemen, did I understand you correctly to say that the governor would leave me free to gather my own personnel and supplies?"

"You understood correctly, Sir," responded Corporal Allen. "And Sergeant Graves here," pointing to the officer, "is authorized to advance any initial funding you may require for the trip. Just say the word!"

"Mr. Puckett, Sir," intoned Graves, "if you need a little time to think over the governor's proposition, we could wait a few more hours before we telegraph our company head of your decision."

"Gentlemen, I know you have had a tough four days on the trail. You've carried out your orders responsibly and spent your time here efficiently, and I am not one to start wasting it for you now. You may telegraph the governor or your company command and inform them that I have accepted the request and will proceed immediately to gather my functionaries and ware and be on my way within the week. Whatever advance funding you feel appropriate will be welcomed, and any further expenses required when I arrive at Fort Washakie may be paid as needed. Beyond that, I will accept no further pay and will think about the reward being offered only if we have been successful, and only if those under my hire warrant that kind of remuneration. Have I made myself clear, gentlemen?"

"Sir," Sergeant Graves responded, reaching to clasp Puck's hand, "you have just added warmth to our morning sun!"

Sergeant Graves reached into his vest pocket, pulled out a wrinkled manila envelope with government markings, handed it to Puck, and remarked, "Mr. Puckett, you will find a cashier's check in this envelope made out in your name in the amount of $1,000. You may handle it any way you wish."

The two officers turned to the sheriff and thanked him for his services, bade the two adieu, exited the door, and crossed the boardwalk to their waiting horses. In a moment, they were hastening down the street and to the conclusion of their business.

Puck turned to Deputy Newby who had stationed himself over in a corner of the room and had overheard the full affair.

"Shane, did you notice that Corporal Allen was a crack shot with a rifle?"

"How could you tell that? His rifle was in his saddle holster, and how would you know anyway?"

Puck responded, "Did you notice the badge above Corporal Allen's left pocket? That was the insignia denoting him as an 'expert rifleman.' You will remember that the next time you see the crossing of two rifles on a badge like that. That is the Army's way of rewarding their men for exceptional attainment. Has the sheriff here ever offered you a badge other than your official deputy star?"

"Well, not that I recall," Shane responded humbly. "But he has always been awfully nice to me. Maybe I haven't earned another badge yet, and if I did, I don't know what it would be for. I'm not good at too many things, except making good coffee and keeping the office straight."

"That certainly speaks well of you, Shane. That's worth a lot more than you may realize. No one requires a badge for that, but one day the sheriff just may find some attainment for which you will deserve a badge of honor. If you ever get one, I want to see it, ya hear?"

"Yes, Sir, you'll be the first to hear. And thank you, sir, for your encouragement!"

Deputy Newby settled back in his chair with a smile on his face and looked longingly into the distance as if viewing the culmination of his own dreams. Sheriff Manley patted him on the shoulder and praised him, "You're a good man, Shane. I think I'll keep you."

With that, Puck excused himself and left to take care of personal matters with Brandon Wise.

Brandon Wise had just tossed his hat on the Shaker pegs on the wall, when Puck entered the office at the far end of the hall. He clomped and jingled his way furtively across the wooden floor, boots and spurs noisily announcing his presence.

The banker turned to see who had entered his chambers without knocking. His cleaning boy, Billy Yeager, had just left the quarters for the storage room, so he knew it must be someone else. Besides, Billy would never assert himself that stridently; he knew better than to do so in the banker's chamber. The banker was a bit stunned at first to see that it was Puck, and yet not overly surprised because he had just been informed that Puck was in town.

"Well, Puck, I swear! Can that really be you? I guess I should say that I am surprised to see you, but I got word just a moment ago that you were back in the village."

"It is certainly good to see you, Brandon, but now just how did the news get around to you so fast?"

"My cleaning boy, Billy, told me not more than five minutes ago. I guess you knew that your Aunt Bella had hired him to feed and look after your horses while you were gone. He told me that when he went to feed the stock this morning, Carbon did not come to meet him as usual. Then he saw Gentry and Sandy in the lot and hustled to the house to confirm with your aunt that you were home. He really was surprised and a little let down, too, I may add. Though he is going to be happy to see you, he feels that his job of caring for your horses will be in jeopardy. Do you know what Aunt Bella told him?"

"I haven't a clue, sir."

"She told him that, unless she missed her guess, he would be needed as usual, depending on what she heard of the outcome of your meeting with the soldiers today. My good man, Aunt Bella has you pegged all the way through the shell, the skin, and to the kernel of the peanut itself! She doesn't need a crystal ball, you know. She knows your moves merely by looking into your eyes. A dead giveaway, she claims! So what's the verdict?"

"You and Aunt Bella are two of a kind, you ol' cuss! I couldn't hide anything from either of you. Since I was a boy, you have known me as well as you know the back of your own hand. Okay, so Billy will be needed awhile yet. What do you make of that?"

"Uh huh, so you *have* accepted the Governor's request, haven't you? When Billy told me that he had seen you and the soldiers parting a few minutes ago, I knew they were not disappointed. And you're here to hit me up for a loan to finance your venture!"

"I now know why some of the townspeople have often called you 'Mr. Wisepockets,' but I've outsmarted you this time! You're only half right. *Yes*, I have accepted the offer, but *no*, I am not here to squeeze the till—unless, of course, there is no interest for as long as I need the money."

Puck pulled the envelope from his shirt pocket and handed it to Mr. Wise.

"This time, Sir," Puck added, "the Governor is funding the venture, but you can exchange this check for spendable cash if you're so's a mind to!"

"Have you taken a look closely at that check, son? That check is drawn on this bank, and you will see my name scribbled in the lower right hand corner. I made the check out actually thinking it would be a hopeless endeavor of finding you way over in Idaho. Yet, the Governor felt that if the transaction could not be completed as hoped, it would be easy for me to dispose of the check. But boy, am I gratefully surprised that you are going to utilize these funds. Welcome home, Puck!"

Brandon hugged Puck and slapped him on the back. Puck returned the gesture, and the two sat down to talk.

Puck was happy to be renewing old unions with Brandon Wise. He had once worked for him as a bank sentry, guarding special shipments of gold and currency. He had been in the bank the day the Quinn Bolton gang stormed the bank to rob it of its monthly Mountaineer shipment of gold nuggets. The Bolton brothers, Quinn and Seth, were both killed by Puck in the melee. Curt Bolton, their nephew, escaped with two other gang members. A customer died in the crossfire and Puck himself was winged above the left knee. The wound proved to be superficial, in that the bullet passed through the outer flesh missing the bone. The Bolton gang scattered and, from all reports, had broken up since the death of their ringleader.

If no one else documented the history as significant, Brandon Wise remembered not only the event itself but also Puck's blazing draw down. Realizing now that Puck would soon be in harm's way again as he began his search for the kidnappers, he wanted to know if Puck had maintained his prowess with the six-shooter. Puck acknowledged his concern and assured him that he was not out of practice.

What really concerned Puck now was his outlook for the future. When he returned from Fort Washakie, he would need a job, and as far as he was concerned, Brandon Wise would have an edge on the times better than anyone else he knew in the Territory. For years, Wise had followed historical events with an almost religious fervor and seemed to understand their meaning and movements. He understood their play upon the local economy. That was his job, and he did it well.

Puck was uneasy about what had happened and was happening with the cattle business, the burgeoning rise of pioneer farmers, the railroads, the planting of Indian reservations, due to their loss of a homeland, and the growing demise of the frontier life as a whole. His vocation as a highrider was now at stake. But surely the ranch was not a thing of the past! Puck could not bring himself to think such a thought. When he reminded himself of the rich history of the Plains, he wrestled with nostalgic wonder as to the role he would play, due to the changing times. How had it come to this? Where was it headed, and what would he do with it? Those were the main questions on his mind.

As the banker excused himself, momentarily, to retrieve some papers from the vault, a brief excursus of history brought Puck awake to the reality before him. History of the frontier had begun innocently enough. Emigrants, trappers, hunters, prospectors, and cattlemen were the forerunners of the homesteaders, who glutted the Plains following the Homestead Act of 1862. After the discovery of gold in California in 1848, innocence changed to insanity, debauchery, and opened doors to a fool's paradise.

The California Gold Rush began in 1849, taking in part of Nevada and later spreading back across the Plains, after gold was also discovered there. Fortunes were won and fortunes were lost. Grubstakes were planted and uprooted by failure to produce. Many prairie schooners (covered wagons) that had come bearing pioneers from the Mississippi Valley and as far as the Cumberland Pass in the East in search of fortunes in gold, went back the same route carrying their beaten investors. The hardships of life on the trail took many lives, but the experience of entering a new land with hopes of finding greater resources for the good life seemed to partly compensate for the struggles and losses.

Gold and silver had also been discovered in Colorado, especially in the areas of Cripple Creek and Leadville, when the Territory (later the state of Colorado) was first known as Jefferson. Then gold finds were established on the Great Plains along the major rivers of Idaho, the fields of Montana—especially at Alder Gulch (later Virginia City) and Last Chance Gulch (later Helena)—and in Wyoming Territory along the Sweetwater River. These mad rushes played out and parleyed to the new discoveries in the Black Hills of Dakota Territory in 1875—where, there again, the Indians were uprooted against broken U.S. treaties in favor of the gold-mongers.

Mining towns sprang up everywhere in the operation of small placer mines. With them grew up saloons, dance halls, bawdy houses, and gambling dens. These drew not only respectable adventurers but lawless outcasts as well. Violence constantly erupted in these places, including such characteristic acts as murder, robbery, sexual debauchery, and widespread drunkenness. Many mining towns died out as fast as they arose, but others developed into thriving cities of the West. The placer mine gave way to the great mining operations that resulted in such major multimillion dollar finds as the infamous Comstock Lode in Nevada.

During the late 1850's and early 1860's, the first pioneers began to populate the Plains. In the years before, they had crossed the plains along the Oregon Trail, beginning at Independence, Missouri, and stopping for supplies at such points as Fort Kearny and Fort Laramie. Then, moving through South Pass in Wyoming, they followed the Trail to Fort Hall and connected with the California Trail, eventually moving through Donner Pass and ending up at Sutter's Fort (Sacramento) along the Sacramento and San Joaquin Rivers. Others followed a more southern route, moving from Independence along the Santa Fe Trail to Cimarron Crossing and either going on to Bent's Fort along the Arkansas River, or taking the Cimarron Cutoff, either choice ending up in Santa Fe in

New Mexico Territory. From there they picked up the Old Spanish Trail, crossed the Colorado and Green Rivers and dropped down in a southwesterly direction weathering the Mojave Desert into Los Angeles.

Because these earliest of pioneers were merely passing through Indian Territory on their trek to California, rather than settling down permanently, they were often aided by the Indian tribes—being helped to ford the rivers, supplied with buffalo meat, and proffered opportunities for trade. Now that these frontiersmen were returning to the Plains, this time to establish settlements, the tribes were driven not merely to defend their hunting grounds but more so the land as a religious shrine, a gift to their people by the Great Spirit. Frontier life under these circumstances proved to be dangerous and taxing of every ounce of physical and moral fiber, as the Indian nation rose to meet the onslaught of frontier squatters and the rampant establishment of military outposts.

With the return of the banker to his chamber, Puck blinked away the moving picture of history rolling through his mind and got down to serious talk with the sheriff about the cattle business and his own need of a job. It seemed easy for the banker to put things into perspective for Puck. Puck listened as the man talked.

"Drovers who have heard of the once burgeoning cattle business in these parts have come seeking trail jobs moving cattle to market. As poor as the cattle business actually is here, there is an overabundance of seekers. So the *Butterfield Overland Express*, the *Wells, Fargo Line*, the regional *Sabreline Stage*, and the more local *Gray's Stage Express*, have not had any trouble hiring would-be drovers to ride shotgun on the various runs. Of course, experienced highriders like you are a premium. The ranches have locked your kind into service by high paying positions, so if you get established here, it is not likely you'll ever want to play wing man on the stage again."

Slapping himself gently on the forehead, the banker interrupted himself. "Puck, I just remembered something. A man by the name of Preston Taggart sent a letter stating that he would be in town next week on business. He will be coming by the bank. I know that he has been looking for a new hand for his ranch. He has two very good men already, but I think he is looking for a highrider to help manage the ranch operation and oversee its problems."

Puck began to raise a few questions.

"Where is the ranch from here?"

"It's the Twin Meadow Ranch south of here along the Hoback River. It *sorta* backs up into the hills east of the junction of the Hoback and Snake Rivers, this side of Snake River Canyon."

"Do you know anything about the job at all? I mean, what are the benefits as compared to other operations around?"

"Well, specifically speaking, Puck, I really don't know the nature of the work. We haven't talked about it yet, but there may be one benefit you might take a likin' to."

"And what might that be?" Puck prompted.

"Taggart has a daughter by the name of Marlowe. And if you ask me, Marlowe Taggart is the beauty of the territory."

Puck interrupted him. "Even prettier than Faye Lincoln across the street at Auntie's dress shop?"

"Well, let me put it this way," the banker continued. "She draws a crowd, and many a man has tried to court her, but Taggart is highly possessive of his daughter—especially around men whose character is held in question. That's a little unnecessary, though, because Marlowe is more finicky than her dad. She hasn't given many suitors the time of day. Oh, you'll be struck by her for sure, and if anyone could have a chance with her, you might."

"When do I meet this jewel?"

"She will be here for the Annual Celebration next month, if you get back from Fort Washakie in time to attend. I'll see if I can get a few things staged for you while you're gone. At least I'll inform Taggart of your availability for work. I'm certain he will want to meet you. I'll also introduce you to Marlowe at the dance."

Puck loved dreaming, but he had business with the governor awaiting him and knew that, if he didn't get busy, there would be no more homecoming or celebration for him. He thanked the banker for his time, folded the envelope containing the cash just exchanged for the cashier's check, and was excused to get things ready for the trip to Fort Washakie.

CHAPTER 5

PREPARATION

Leaving the bank, Puck walked across the street briskly, as often depicts a man of purpose, and entered his aunt's dress shop. Inside, only a few patrons browsed, marking time slowly, as often depicts people of no particular purpose. Of course, they would buy if they found something worth the taking and soon leave if they did not. Puck was happy to see that most of them were leaving. In the back corner of the store, the pretty Faye Lincoln was busy stacking items that had been left disarranged needlessly by the customers, as if they had been looking for a needle in a haystack. Puck saw his chance to get better acquainted with the pretty charmer.

"Say!" he called out, "Can't a fella get some service in this queen's den?" As soon as he said it, he was not sure of himself. In fact, he felt a little stupid, not knowing if the lady would take the gesture as a joke. Luckily, Miss Lincoln looked up from her work with a smile rather than a smirk. When she recognized Puck, the smile began to grow, and she immediately left her garments to their own stacking. Of course, that wasn't wise either, as they promptly fell to the floor. Puck hustled to aid the damsel in distress, stooping down at the stricken pile at the selfsame moment as she to retrieve the mess. Each picked up a few items and rose up together almost face to face—so close that Puck got a whiff of her cologne and a glimpse of an inviting glint in her eyes. He was so stupefied by her attractive form that he fumbled to stack the garments without taking his eyes off of her. The scramble of intermingled arms pushing the garments into some semblance of balance finally got the two laughing at one another. Each backed off, Puck whisking his hands together and wiping them across his vest, and she brushing her hair aside and flipping her head back in relief.

"Do you always affect your surroundings like this?" Faye chided. "I mean, the last time you were in here, you almost tipped the racks trying to walk out backwards, and now this!"

"Well, why don't you sell some of this stuff and make for some space. Do you always have an overstuffed room on your hands?"

"Maybe you'd like to get out your checkbook and take some of this *stuff* off my hands."

"Oh, I don't see too much here that I could use."

"Well, stop complaining then, and get off that shoe rack, its a display and not a chair." Miss Lincoln popped him on his biceps with the butt of her palm nudging him off his perch.

"Okay, Miss Faye Lincoln, I know when I'm not wanted," Puck retorted as he turned away as if to leave. The lady grabbed him by the forearm and coaxed him back.

"Oh, all right, you don't have to leave, but can't you talk standing up? Say," she interjected, "you're sporting some frightful muscles there. How'd you come by those?"

"I was about to ask you the sa—Oh, I, uh—I've been working on these muscles since birth playing cowboys and Indians—mainly cowboys here lately, but I'd rather talk about you."

"And what would you like to know? I'm five feet four inches, I weigh about one hundred and five pounds, and I'm *twishsha-foo* years old," as she "smooshed" her hand across her mouth, in order to leave that bit of information to the imagination. "Any other increments of size and distance, you'll have to guess. And don't go getting secret information from your aunt Bella. Leave her out of this."

Puck chided her this time. "Do you plan to always live in secret like this? I just wanted to get somewhat acquainted, seeing that I barely got my nose into your business the last time I came in here so grimy. You may be worth getting to know, don't you see?"

"Well, you're going to be around for awhile, aren't you? You can drop in any time. Maybe we can go down to the soda fountain and pass a little time over a malt or something."

"I'd like that fine," Puck responded, "except I'm afraid it will have to wait awhile. I've got a commission from the governor for a small task and will have to make preparations to leave right away. I'll take a rain check, if you don't mind."

"A commission from the governor, huh? Well, well! Since you have such important business, the malt will have to wait. Guess you'll miss the annual celebration next month, too?"

"That, I don't know," Puck replied, not knowing if she was being genuine or feigning sarcasm, "but if I make it back in time, will you save a dance for me?"

"I might do that if I thought I could count on it."

"And what, may I ask does that mean?" Puck was now certain that she was gibing and he fell into the same blithesome attitude.

"Well," she retorted, "you've been here only two days and you're already packing up to move out again. If you get back in time, do you think you might hang around long enough to get a dance in?" She lowered her head and then raised it slowly, batting her eyelids in a flirtatious manner.

Puck got her drift and wished he could hang around, but a commitment was a commitment, and time was getting away.

"I'll make a promise," Puck concluded. "If I get back for the Celebration, I'll expect that dance, even if I have to buck the cowboy who escorts you. How's that? Plain enough?"

With that remark, Puck clasped her hand in his, raised it and kissed it gently, and started to turn away.

"I'll wait," she said softly, as she cupped her hand about his neck and tiptoed to kiss him on the cheek. The two made their adieu at the front door of the shop, and Puck mounted Carbon for the ride home to inform Aunt Bella of his decision.

Lunch was on the table, as Aunt Bella knew Puck would be home if he had accepted the governor's commission. And he would be in a hurry. She met him at the door and noticed the haste with which he had approached it, just as she had expected.

"Well," she began, "I'm sure the governor found his man! You don't normally leave your horse tied up at the front gate! So what's the verdict, yea or nay?"

"Auntie," Puck intoned resignedly, "You know that unless the proposal was simply impossible, I couldn't refuse such a request. I now understand the governor's wisdom—with the reservation currently intact, he wants to keep the Indians from pursuit at all costs, and he's afraid soldiers might be too much of a threat for the culprits to linger very long with their intentions. They might spook, finding their undertaking too risky, and kill the girl. He wants a little more secretive approach to the case. Fewer detectives are less detective, no pun intended. So, I've placed my services in the governor's confidence."

"When will you leave? Or do you know? I mean—well, come on in here and eat and we can talk about this later."

"Sure, Auntie, but there won't be much 'later' left. That's why I left Carbon tied up out front. As soon as I eat, I need to go to the telegraph office to send a message and then get busy 'outrigging' for the trip to Fort Washakie. Then, as soon as I get the men together I'll need, I'll have to get underway. If all goes well, I'll be leaving early Thursday morning. This is still Monday, isn't it?"

"Yes, son, it's still Monday. You've only been here a day and a half and you've already done so much that it feels like a week. I had a feeling you would need to leave in somewhat of a hurry, so that's why I stayed home from the shop today. I've been washing your clothes. They're on the line sunning now, and I'll pack 'em up for you as soon as they're dry. I sure hate to see you leave so soon, but I understand."

"You are my favorite aunt," Puck warmly assured her, failing to mention also that she was his *only* aunt. "I hate to leave so soon, as well, but I promise to make time up to you when I return. It's certain at this point that I don't have any other woman to spend it with, so count on a little of it for yourself when I get back from the hills."

The ride back to the village seemed longer than usual, perhaps due to Puck's impatience to get matters accomplished for the trip. He went straight to the telegraph office and sent an urgent message to Chief Broken Bow at the Indian Worker's Lodge in Idaho where he had spent the night only a few days before. He sent it in care of the soldiers' outpost near the camp, under whose direction all the Indian braves were working daily on a government project—the building of a much needed water dam in that area. He outlined his commission with the governor and requested that the Chief send two of his best Indian scouts and trackers to help in the search for the kidnapped Indian girl. They were to ride without delay and intercept the route of the Sabreline Stage and pay their way on, trailing their horses behind, and arriving as soon as possible in Jackson Hole. The telegram could serve as a voucher for their trip, or they could get papers of leave from the outpost to guarantee their legitimacy for being absent from the bailiwick.

Within four hours, Chief Broken Bow, through the soldiers' outpost, had returned an answer with the names of the two scouts he would be sending. Humorously, Puck thought, the Chief had signed the telegram with the name the Spaniards had given him—*Arco Que Brao.*

The scout's names were Saragosa and Dellium. Saragosa normally went by the name "Trinket" because he liked to wear an extreme amount of beads and baubles that, earlier in his life, he had the habit of taking in his coups. He had heard how other Indians had saved such artifacts as buffalo beards, arrowheads from various enemy tribes, horseshoes picked up from farrier caches on the sites of burned out farm and ranch houses, and pieces of rope left behind by drovers on the great cattle drives. As for Saragosa, then, he liked beads as souvenirs.

Wearing the beads and finery, Trinket had wanted to be called "Pretty Boy," but his father convinced him that such a name didn't sound manly enough to describe a serious warrior. *Trinket* didn't sound much better, except that the appropriation of the finery came through the accumulation of booty taken in hostile forays, at least depicting courage in those carrying out the coups. Besides, beads had history to them. They were made from many things—copper, turquoise, quartz, and even seeds of various kinds, often in combination with porcupine quills. Some Indian tribes were known to make beads from clamshells, which they called *wampum*, a kind of money used in trading. Beads were often woven into fabrics with various designs, many of them being symbolic—a semicircle or triangle for rain, a zigzag for lightning, and a disk for the sun. Knowing all this, *Trinket* was descriptive enough for Saragosa.

Dellium was better known as "Three Toes," because he had once been bitten on the foot by a poisonous snake, and in order to spare his life, the medicine man had to chop off two toes where infection had set in. Dellium was a rendering of the mineral bdellium (pronounced *dellium*) or Indian myrrh, some forms being gum or resin, often formed like a pearl or stone, and in biblical times equated in value to gold. Dellium had gotten his proper name from the white man's Bible (Gen. 2:12; Num. 11:7), but "Three Toes" was the name he preferred.

Trinket and Three Toes, knowing the urgent nature of their assignment, arranged for their families' care and began their trip almost immediately. Not much time is required for an Indian to get ready for any undertaking—organizing sustaining contents of a *parfleche*, filling a gourd with water for times when water could not be found along the way, and out rigging his horse with simplicity. In most instances, he did not even claim the luxury of a night's sleep.

The sun was still up for several hours yet, and a rising moon would soon shed light on the encroaching darkness. There was not a cloud in the sky, so nothing threatened their journey. They moved along with dispatch hoping to intersect the stage line by midmorning the following day, by late afternoon at the latest.

Meanwhile, Puck was busy putting together the team of additional men he would need for the task ahead. He wanted two packers for handling the wagon and all the gear, a cook for the preparation of meals, and two riflemen who would serve with him and the Indian scouts on the various tracking engagements.

Before sunset, Puck had acquired his men and had advanced them a small stipend, sending them to the village outfitters for anything they might need by way of horses, firearms and munitions, clothing, boots, and rain gear. He had hired Jed Palmer and Johnny Lively as the packers and Pistol Bill Farley and Mel Engle as his riflemen. His old friend, Whiskers Benedict, was the best campfire cook around, and he was lucky to get him.

His riflemen and packers were not only experienced cattle drovers, they were also master shots with the Winchester model 1873 lever action repeating rifles. The riflemen could also shoot from the hip with uncanny accuracy, using the latest Peacemaker and Frontier models of the Colt .45 pistols. This was especially true of Pistol Bill, such marksmanship with the pistol being the source for his name. Puck was certainly not out of practice himself. He recently had shot the eye out of a snake at twenty paces on the Belmont Ranch.

As the sun came up on the Idaho panorama, Trinket and Three Toes had already passed through the rolling hills and were now entering the lower plains skirting the Snake River on the east. They had slept only two hours, seeming par for Indian scouts on the move. They flanked Liberty Hill, passing through Chalmer's Gap on its eastern edge.

As children, the two braves had run this country repeatedly and knew every niche of its spread. Now that they were to pass this way again, Chief Broken Bow had told them to take every shortcut possible, as "Big Man Puck," as the chief called him, must get on the move toward the Wind River Reservation. The ride would be tough, but "plenty of wampum" waited for them when the search was over. The two Indians especially liked the idea that they might also get to see Chief Washakie again. Saddle sores were no deterrent to their determined ride, though they feared their ponies would not hold up at such a pace.

Now, they were dropping down out of the plateaus and hugging the Snake River once more, crossing its shallows at one point to gain smoother footing along its western channel before fording it again at Peak's Crossing.

At Peak's Crossing, the horses were buckling under the strain of weariness as much as their riders' weight. A stop was necessary. On its eastern shore, the braves reined into a plush meadow to rest. They purposely stopped at its southern extremity where it jutted out onto Inks Point. Here they could view the meandering valley below and determine their next move. The remainder of the ride would not be as familiar to them.

The horses rolled and grunted, feigning to eat the grass beneath them as they frolicked on the ground, but they were really too tired to eat. Momentarily, one could hear the wheezing of nostrils amid snoring and low grunts trailing from the slumbering animals. Everything else settled down into a pleasant summer day's silence.

The Indians, too, had stretched out in the noonday heat, but soundless to avert attention should any stranger happen by as they slept. To accomplish this, they had sealed their mouths closed with camper's tape to squelch any possibility of snoring. They began to doze, welcoming the heat as a respite from the coolness of the morning ride. A warm breeze now replaced the early morning briskness.

The company had slept only an hour when Three Toes, who seemed to sleep with one eye open, heard a sound in the distance. He rolled over and placed his ear to the ground to be certain he had not been dreaming. In a moment, he heard another sound like the knock of an animal's hoof against a rock, followed by still another, and then the familiar sound of half-winded horses blowing the dust from their nostrils. He raised his head above the boulder that had partially hidden him from the open view and scoped the horizon.

Hardly two hundred yards away, coming in from the west, were two horsemen, trailed by a pack animal. They were descending a slope on a trail that would bring them within a stone's throw of the scout's position.

Trinket was roused from sleep by a handful of gravel sprayed across his bedroll by Three Toes. His companion's hand signals informed him of the presence of white riders, and he belly-crawled to where Three Toes was crouched surveying the situation. Although they had authority to be where they were, it was always unsettling when having to face white strangers on the trail. One could never be totally certain of their disposition.

As the riders came into plainer view, the scouts could now see the familiar blue and gold markings of the U.S. Cavalry. While such should give the scouts a fuller sense of security, it often did not, as they were never sure that some soldiers, bearing grudges for losses in the Indian Wars, might turn on them to avenge the death of some relative or friend.

Just then, the low nickering of one of the Indian ponies alerted the riders, as their own horses whinnied in response. A soldier instantly drew his rifle and reined up to meet the situation.

Now that the Indians' position had been given away, there was little use to remain secluded. Three Toes stood up and waved a red headband toward the soldiers, and Trinket stood wearing his around his forehead after the fashion of an army scout.

The readied rifle of the soldier was now gently cradled across his arm in a peaceful stance, until the situation could be ascertained. Straightway, the soldiers broke the trail and descended toward the scouts' position, while the scouts rose to meet the strangers.

"Yo, red man," shouted the lead soldier. "Are you alone?"

Three Toes placed his hand on Trinket's shoulder and returned it to his own breast, then indicated "no more" by a horizontal crossing motion of his hands back and forth in front of him. Both soldiers relaxed, dismounted, and raised their right hands in a peaceful greeting. The Indians returned the gesture.

The lead soldier spoke. "I'm Major Quentin Burns and this is Sergeant Jonce Dunham," pointing to his partner. "Are you boys strays, or do you have a reason to be away from the reservation?"

"Look see here," Trinket announced in broken English, pointing to the red headbands. "We here, on our way to Jackson, given good chance to help governor as scouts for 'Big Man Puck'."

"Big Man who?" the major retorted. "And any Indian can wear a headband, so how do we know you're telling the truth?"

"Oh, we are truth, sir," came the response from Three Toes. "Look see here these papers. One from brave's Chief Broken Bow. Other is tell it 'gram from Mr. Puck."

Major Burns shuffled through the papers until he was satisfied that the Indians were on the up-and-up.

"We to stop Sabreline when find it, and ride to Jackson in hurry," Trinket added.

"Well, even if you find it, you won't get anywhere in a hurry." Burns jabbered. "Our cayuses are faster than any stage wagon, and we know every shortcut from here to Kalamazoo. Besides, we're headed for Jackson ourselves to pick up an army deserter. You boys best ride along with us."

The foursome mounted their horses and trailed off to the northeast, moving with assurance toward Wyoming Territory.

Late evening found the riders approaching Fort Hall and the Fort Hall Indian Reservation. As they approached the colonnade, they reined in right at bugle call for the evening meal. Such welcome hospitality was a refreshing rest from the tiring ride. A few hours' sleep following the meal would prepare them for the last day's ride into the village of Jackson.

The moon was still high a few hours before dawn as the four riders mounted their horses to begin the day. With fresh food supplies and water secured, they headed almost due east, crossing the Blackfoot River early on, and then they struck a beeline toward Swan Valley. They would not likely see another face until they entered Jackson itself.

CHAPTER 6

ACCOMMODATIONS

The troop came dragging into the little village of Jackson approximately mid-afternoon on Wednesday. The horses were exhausted and the Indians were as good as lost. No one had told them where to find Puck. Still, they felt somewhat confident that the soldiers would hang with them long enough to get directions. They certainly had been a godsend on the last leg of the trip, being quite familiar with the territory and apparently every shortcut available. They had made good time, a highlight for which the Indians could be grateful.

Burns and Dunham pulled up to the hitching rail in front of the sheriff's office, knowing this was where they would find their prisoner. Three Toes and Trinket followed as a matter of course. The troop dismounted and entered the building to find Sheriff Forgus Manley sitting at his desk.

The sheriff rose and saluted the officers and introduced himself. "Manley's the name," he spoke up as he put forth his hand. "I've been lookin' for you. Been keepin' your prisoner fat and sassy, as well." He chuckled and retrieved his hand.

"I'm Major Burns, and this is my partner, Sergeant Dunham. Quentin and Jonce is good enough."

The Indians looked at one another, and, not to remain silent like some storefront wooden Indian, Three Toes stepped up and greeted the sheriff. "We are Saragosa and Dellium, army scouts. Trinket and Three Toes is good enough."

"These your men, are they, Major Burns?" Sheriff Manley questioned.

"No, sir. I was about to inform you that they traveled here with us with papers, to sign on with someone called 'Big Man Puck.'"

"Well, I've never heard him called that before, but I know exactly who you mean. In fact, he told me this morning to expect the Indians on the stage sometime today or tomorrow. Actually, I've been a little worried! Got word this morning by telegraph that the stage was held up by bandits yesterday on the other side of Coyote Canyon and had to stay over a spell at the Redwater Outpost. They pistol-whipped the driver, and one of the lady passengers had a nervous spell. They hoped to be getting underway again sometime this morning. Sure lucky for these Indians, though. Marauding gangs don't cotton much to Indians fraternizing too closely with the white population. Don't know what might have happened to them. Know one thing for sure, though—this fella' Trinket here, if he got away with his life he would have lost all those relics hanging around his neck there!"

Trinket hurriedly placed his hands over his chest in a gesture of hiding the necklaces hanging around his neck.

"No fear, now," Sheriff Manley assured the Indians. "You're safe and sound, now, and I'll help you find Puck in a little bit. Let me first get these soldiers accommodated.

Puck was busy binding some boxes for the trip on his aunt's front porch when the sheriff and the two Indians came riding up.

"Hey, Puck," Manley shouted, "I've got a couple of government scouts here lookin' for you!"

Puck stopped what he was doing and went to the front gate to meet the men.

"Howdy, my friends," Puck said, as he reached out to shake hands with the Indians. "You men look like you've been through the mill."

Trinket looked puzzled. He didn't recall going through anything like what Big Man Puck was calling the "mill." He looked down at himself to see what Puck had seen. Three Toes jabbed him, bringing him out of his stupor long enough to shake hands with Puck, then Trinket promptly fell back into his confusion over the mill.

"When you pullin' out of here, Puck?" the sheriff asked.

"Since my scouts are here," Puck answered, "there is no use hanging around here past morning. In fact, I told the other men to be ready at first light if the scouts arrived, but I need to get word to them."

"Well, let me round 'em up for you. I need to be headin' back into town anyway. I know where Jed Palmer and Johnny Lively are staying, and they can get hold of Pistol Bill, Engle, and Benedict."

Puck responded, "I'd be obliged, Forgus," calling the sheriff by his first name. "Just have them meet us here about an hour before sunup."

"Sure enough, Puck. And don't get yourself into trouble hunting down those kidnappin' culprits. I'd like to see you back here by the time the annual celebration rolls around."

"I intend to be back soon enough," Puck retorted, "but you never know."

"But you never know what?" the sheriff questioned with a hint of concern.

"Well, you never know how long matters like this will take. You ride the rogue wind and hope you come out on top—better sooner than later—but you never know for sure."

"Okay, I get you," the sheriff resigned. "But stay healthy, and I'll see you as soon as you return." With that, the sheriff pulled himself into the saddle and reined his animal in the direction of the village.

Trinket seemed to have come out of his fog over the "mill" thing, as Puck led the two Indians to the barn and bunkhouse. Puck showed them where to bed their horses and what to feed them. Then he took them into the bunkhouse next to the tack room and showed them two cots fitted with thin mattresses, cover, and pillows. The Indians had heard of beds like these, but they had never slept on one. They were not really sure, in fact, about spending a night suspended off the ground. They would have been content to spread their bedrolls on the floor.

Three Toes sat on one of the cots and was surprised to feel how soft it felt to his tired bones, and then he spied something in the corner of the room. There on the floor was an oval tub that looked as if it would hold twenty jugs of water, and to the right of the tub were two wooden kegs filled with cool water. Putting his hand into one of the kegs, it felt refreshing to his hot hand. The June evening was still warm, though not as hot as the scorching sun that beat down on them as they rode into town earlier in the day.

"What water for, Big Man Puck?" Three Toes asked.

"Before you can eat at Auntie's table," Puck announced, "You need to take a bath and put on some clean clothes."

"Where is the river?" asked Trinket. "We always clean in river."

"Well, there's no river around here, so it's the tub tonight," Puck spoke convincingly. "There's a keg of water for each of you and some soap to help get the grime off. You men have been through the mill!"

There was that word again. Whatever it was, Trinket hoped the water would take care of it.

"Also, men, Auntie rounded up some denim pants and wrangler shirts for each of you, guessing at your size, and it looks like she may have lucked out. And there are some new buckskins to go over the pants as you ride out in the morning. I'm going to leave you to taking care of your horses and getting your baths. When you're finished, come on back to the house where we will take our meal before bedtime."

The two Indians hurried to unload their ponies, led them into two large stalls in the barn, and gave them the grain mixture and prairie hay that Puck had showed them. They filled their drinking buckets with water and turned toward the door, looking back momentarily to see if the horses were taking to their confinement. The animals splashed the water and guzzled a lengthy drink, then turned to the grain like ravenous wolves over a fresh kill. Content that their horses were satisfied and safe for the night, the Indians headed for the bunk and their "river in a tub."

Two Indians never looked so clean, dressed in their finery, as they entered the front door of Aunt Bella's house. Trinket spoke up to Puck. "You say we to have another mill at your auntie's table, so we here."

"Not *mill*, Trinket. *Meal!* Ever since I mentioned it today, you've been concerned about the mill, so let me explain. There are people who work in places they call a sawmill where they saw trees into lumber, and there are places called grain mills where they grind wheat and corn into flour and corn meal. People who work in these places can get awfully dirty. And you know what a grinder will do to grain. I just thought you men looked as if that's where you'd been, but you sure look differently now. Come on in and let's eat."

Puck graciously introduced the two Indians to Aunt Bella as she carried foodstuff to the table. She politely indicated to each of them where they should be seated. Then she pulled Puck aside, momentarily. "Son, I overheard what you told Trinket. You shouldn't humor them that way. They may take it as your looking down on them."

"Well, Auntie, these men have had no education, and if I can't take a little time to explain a few things, how are they ever going to get informed? I may be doing them a service. They don't know the sayings and colloquialisms of the white man, and if they are going to spend any time around us, they need to learn a few of our mannerisms. I don't want to take anything for granted. I want to shoot straight with them—you know, just be on the up-and-up. In situations like this, I'm always reminded of something Ralph Waldo Emerson once said. He said, 'Nothing astonishes men so much as common-sense and plain dealing.' I guess that's my policy, Auntie."

"Since you put it that way, maybe you're right. Well, let's get back in there before they begin to think we are talking about them behind their backs."

The Indians hardly knew how to eat at a white man's table. Forks were new to them, so they watched Puck and Aunt Bella as they lifted food to their mouths. Their awkward use of the utensils was telling as the Indians attempted to bring food to their mouths from their plates, dropping much of it back onto the plate or onto Aunt Bella's tablecloth. Before long, though, they were getting the hang of it, shoveling in mashed potatoes, corn, green beans (which they had never tasted), and chunks of roast beef that would melt in the mouth. Fresh salad greens were not altogether new to them, only a different variety, as these men had grown up eating roots and leaves of many plants grown in the wild. Cold milk helped to wash it all down. When apple pie was set before them for dessert, the Indians tasted the sweet mixture before taking a serious bite. After the first bite, their hands never missed a movement, as they put away every piece in the dish.

When the table was cleared, Aunt Bella and Puck checked to see if the men needed anything. Then Puck walked to the bunkhouse with them, explaining along the way that the caravan would be leaving at dawn. The other men would arrive shortly before, and they would be on their way to Fort Washakie and the Wind River Reservation. When all was explained, Puck turned back and left the Indians to themselves.

In order to extinguish the light in the room for the night, the two Indians knew enough to turn the wick down on the lantern hanging from a rafter. They rolled into bed haggard and trail-worn. Everything fell into silence, except for one thing. Out of the night, and seemingly close by, came the sounds of *tic.. tic. . tic...tic!* Three Toes looked at a stand between the beds against the wall and saw the glint of a metal object as the moon reflected through the window on the opposite wall. He got out of bed and picked up the object as Trinket joined him.

"What's this with numbers and noise?" Three Toes questioned Trinket.

"I think that is white man's way of telling when moon goes down and sun comes up and when family come together for mills, I mean *meals*. They call it a *wash* or a *watch* or something like that—I guess because they watch it to see what it tells them. You better put it back where Big Man Puck left it, unless he is angry with us." Three Toes returned the object to the nightstand, and the two men returned to bed.

Tic.. tic.. tic...tic!

Three Toes tossed, covered his head with the cover, but to no avail. The sounds came through. He then got out of bed and looked around for something with which to cover the object on the table. In the corner was a metal bucket, which the Indian promptly turned upside down over the noisemaker and went back to bed.

Tink...tink...tink...tink! The noise had changed and had become much fainter, but the sound could still be heard. However, it was now faint enough that exhaustion of the two men won out, and the two soon fell asleep.

The night breeze blowing through the windows blew away the sultry air that had claimed the day. Two Indians, now without camper's tape on their mouths, snored through the otherwise silence, punctuated by the *tink, tink,* of the metal object. No one would be the wiser, as the two men rested motionless through the night, except for an occasional turn, and the hooting of a barn owl in the night. Hours later, while the men still sawed logs in their sleep, rest seemed to find its way into their weary bones. And then, suddenly, it happened. *Brrrringggggkkkkkkkk!!! Brrrringgggg kkkkkkkk!!!*

Trinket sat straight up in bed. Three Toes rolled out of bed, whooping as he hit the floor. Trinket knocked the bucket across the room. It was the metal object making a terrible noise. He picked it up and shook it without avail. The ringing continued uninterrupted, excruciating to an Indian's sensitive ear. Trinket pummeled it with the palm of his hand. The noise continued. He began to push buttons on the back of the clock and inadvertently must have worked some kind of magic. Suddenly, the noise stopped.

Three Toes rubbed his shoulder that had hit the floor and then looked at the wicked object with numbers. One of the sticks was pointing to five. What that meant, he did not know, but he knew it must be close to daylight, as some of the animals began to stir in the barnyard and a light came on in the house where Puck slept. Not knowing what else to do, the two men dressed, washed their faces in a pan of water on another stand in the corner and stepped outside to take care of other pressing business.

A door opened at the house and someone started beating a metal triangle hanging on the porch. And then they heard a voice call out in the distance, "Hey, boys! Get ready to eat!" That was the voice of Puck, and though the men did not know exactly what the triangle meant, they headed for the house.

CHAPTER 7

DEPARTURE

When breakfast was finished, the Indians stepped onto the front porch. Light was rising faintly in the east, but shadows were still tricky for walking around. Aunt Bella and Puck were busy bringing small items to the porch that would go on the wagon.

In the distance, the muffled sound of men talking could be barely heard. The sounds grew louder as they neared the house, until finally the dim figures of horsemen could be seen approaching. It was Palmer and Lively coming in with their packhorse trailing behind. Palmer was a brute of a man, appearing almost too large for his mount. Lively was tall and thin, whose horse looked as if it could carry two of him.

"Hey, Indian," Palmer called out, as he saw the two standing at the front gate. "Grab the lead of this pack horse and get it some water before we leave."

Puck, just coming onto the porch to see who was approaching, overheard the drover's orders. "Is that you, Palmer?" he asked.

"Yeah, its me, Puck."

"Well, get down and get your own water! These men will be doing their part but they aren't our servants, you know."

"That okay, Big Man Puck," Three Toes rejoined. "Me fetch water gladly. Need something to do!"

When Three Toes had left with the horse for the barn to get it water, Puck ambled over to Palmer, who had just dismounted. "Jed, take a little care how you ask one of the men to do something. We're all in this thing together and can and must help each other if we get through the ordeal out there before us, but we'll need to be a little less bossy if we make it. Savvy?"

"Yeah, I understand, boss! I'll tone it down. Sorry I came across so biting."

"Would you men help me get these things off the porch? I think I hear the wagon coming now. Trinket, give us a hand, please. The sun is about to pop over the horizon."

The morning air was brisk, with the smell of freshly mown hay coming from the meadow. Smoke from the neighboring cook stoves wafted on the air. A mockingbird started the wake-up call, followed by the barnyard roosters. Hens fluttered from their nests and the calves could be heard calling for their mamas, hungry after the long night.

Puck and Johnny Lively headed for the barn to saddle Gentry and bring Sandy to the gate for packing out a few things. Three Toes passed them on the way back to the house with Palmer's packhorse, where Trinket and Palmer were busy handling the portage.

Whiskers Benedict wheeled the incoming wagon around in a semi-circle to head the team in the direction of their exit, trailed by Bill Farley and Mel Engle. Benedict climbed out of the driver's seat and swung sprightly to the ground. He was quite nimble for a man in his sixties, short but hearty, with a patch of whiskers that covered the bulk of his face except for a set of robust cheeks and a bauble of a nose. Even in the dimness of the morning dawn, his black hat appeared dusty, creased upward in the front, and slightly tilted back on his head, so that his forehead tended to show.

"Hey, Bunter," Benedict called out to Bill Farley. "Give me a hand here, would you? Can't seem to get this drop gate open on the chuck wagon." "Bunter" is what he had always called Farley, ever since an Englishman traveling through had dubbed the young Billy with that name. "Bunter" was the name for "Billy" given to a typical English schoolboy. Farley didn't much care for the nickname, yet, coming from Whiskers Benedict, it seemed to be an honor. He stepped up to give the old man some aid with the wagon.

Mel Engle grabbed the lead rope of Sandy's halter and pulled him alongside to place some of the lighter packing onto its shoulders, as Puck tied Gentry to the front fence and headed for the house to say goodbye to Aunt Bella. Momentarily, everyone was rounded up and waiting. Puck mounted Gentry and rode to the front of the small brigade in advance of the two scouts. Then came the wagon with Farley and Engle on either side, and Palmer and Lively bringing up the rear.

"For'wrd Ho-o-o-o!" Puck shouted, pointing the way with an outstretched arm. Then he laughed at himself. These Indians didn't know "Forward Ho" from a mule's rear, but it got everyone started. The mules jerked at the traces to break the inertia, as chains and doubletrees clanked in the brisk morning air. The hollow pat of horses' hooves on the hardpan of the roadbed took up cadence with the creaking of the joints of the oak sideboards of the heavy-laden chuck wagon. In the distance, light was rising, with pink and orange breaking through the morning haze toward the east. The crew was on its way at last.

Whiskers Benedict was elated to be driving a recently reconditioned chuck wagon. He smiled when he thought of the good load he was carrying and all the previous runs he had made trying to make their meager rations serviceable and hold out the duration of the trips. This trip, barring any danger, would be the highlight of his profession.

Pistol Bill looked over his newly acquired rigging in the glow of the early morning light. His hand-tooled leather rifle scabbard swung securely to one side of his own refurbished saddle. Most cowboys of his genre had to settle for more modest trimmings, usually of their own making. Most of Farley's gear had come through trading, finagling, or winnings from card-sharking. Short of these means, he simply did without, as did many other cowboys like him.

Puck turned the men in a northeasterly direction along the Blackrock Creek and traveled below Union Pass on the west. Soon, the caravan had passed through Kelly and Elk and Moran Junction, and by early afternoon was now peeling over the first major rise approaching Togwatee Pass on the Continental Divide, twenty-five miles from Moran Junction. Mel Engle called it "Bullet Pass," because it was here that he had experienced his first harrowing shoot-out with the Tremont Gang. Those were moments to be forgotten, as he had come out of the foray with a shattered wrist. Luckily, it was not on his shooting hand. He could still level the business end of a firearm with precision.

Trinket and Three Toes skirted the regal party sewn firmly, in effect, to their own makeshift saddles. The best saddlers in town couldn't reproduce the comfort of these Indians' own time-formed "sillas," as they called them, like the ruts of a well-worn road. Their small frames fit the soft channels of their rigging like clinging vines. Owing to their smallness of size, the white man's saddle fit their butts like a lone plum in a two-gallon bucket. However, they were proud of their new saddlebags and rifles purchased for them by Puck. Their ammunition belts were slung stately across their chests from shoulder to side, and they rode against the breeze with their heads held high. They were proud to be on this mission to aid one of their own kin.

Lively rode with one foot in the stirrup and the other leg slung over the horn of the saddle. This seemed to be a reprieve for his lanky body, especially since the troop was moving at a brisk walk at this point.

Palmer was chattering under his breath about the smallness of his own saddle, not realizing that saddles for men his size did not come around often, unless one had the wherewithal to have one specially made. There wasn't time for that this trip, even if the stipend from Puck was enough to have allowed it. Time was of the essence, so Palmer, pulled his hat down over his brow and ceased his chatter for the moment.

"Hey, Palmer," Lively called out, "You know what your problem is?"

"No. What's that?"

"Your stirrups are not set right."

"Whadaya mean they're not set right?"

Lively spoke up authoritatively. "Haven't you heard of the age-old test for the proper length of stirrups?"

"No, but I have a feelin' you're about to tell me, aren't you?"

"Sure, if you want to solve your problem and get comfortable in that saddle."

"Okay, I'm game. What is it?"

"Just this: A cowboy's stirrups are the proper length if he can stand up in the stirrups and his rear end clears the saddle. Stand up and try it!"

Palmer retorted, "I am standing up."

Lively returned, "No wonder your butt's tired."

"Yeah, well maybe you should check your own saddle, Longbow. When you stand up your rear clears the saddle twice."

Like kids in a quarrel, Lively answered back. "Oh, yeah? Well, I could tell you somethin' else about your saddle, but you're already half mad, and I was only tryin' to help you."

"Okay, let's have it then, Mr. I. Q. Maybe it'll throw me over the edge and I'll get plumb mad!"

"Well, I've noticed you're ridin' a saddle with only a single cinch. If anybody in this troop needs a saddle with a double cinch, it's you. I bet your saddle keeps shiftin' on you. Not good on the horse either. That's a saddle for buckaroos!"

Palmer countered, "I'm sorry I'm not as rich as you, Money Bags, or maybe I could afford a better saddle."

"Okay, Palmer, I didn't mean to get your ire up. I really am just trying to help. Tell you what. I've had a little experience with saddle makeovers. If old Whiskers has any gimp cord or extra leather on the wagon, I think I can add a second cinch for you. I have a sewing awl in my gear. If you can make it to the Fort, I'll find the time to fix you up, or I'll make a deal with the soldiers for a better saddle for you. How's that?"

Palmer mumbled some faint agreement in lower cursive, and punched his pony ahead, probably ashamed for being so sensitive over nothing.

"Hey, Palmer, wait up. I have something else to tell you. As short as you are, never take a squat with your spurs on!"

Palmer could hardly keep from laughing, so he let it lie.

At Togwatee Pass, the caravan entered the Wind River Range. Traveling would be tougher now that they were entering that part of the forest known as Washakie Wilderness. They had rested only twice during the day, giving the animals time to relax, take water, and graze a bit. Now the men needed a longer rest and something refreshing to eat. Whiskers had already made arrangements for the mid-day feed. Leftover leg-o-lamb, cold biscuits, and fresh tomato juice, still cool from the overnight temperature, was the chosen fare. To his surprise, he heard no grumbling.

When the meal had been consumed, the platters cleaned, and everything returned to its niche in the chuck wagon, everyone, including the animals, stretched out for an hour's *siesta*. Even the mules were removed from their traces to give them a chance to frolic in the dust and chill out for a spell. Sandy, this trip, had the portage on his back removed so he too could join the other mules cavorting in the dust. After their horses were tethered to a long hitching rope, yet given plenty of room to bed down on the grassy slope, the cowboys picked out a tree and slung their saddles in the shade to serve as pillows.

It was late afternoon when the animals were harnessed again and the brigade was beating the trail ahead. Going was not easy, but Puck knew in advance what he would be up against before he accepted the governor's commission. There seemed to be no complaints.

The caravan moved at a snail's pace through the clay and sandstone rock ledges flanking Wind River on the east. At almost 10,000 feet above sea level, air was thinner, making their efforts more taxing on the human frame. The erosion of wind and rain had eaten out this range of canyons. By nightfall, still awhile before last light, the group entered the Valley of the Warm Winds at Dubois. This would be the end of the trail for one day. It had taken several hours to make the twenty-five or so miles from Togwatee Pass to Dubois, and yet the rovers were lucky to have gotten this far the first day.

The packers, Palmer and Lively, wasted no time taking control of the rigging and getting the camp laid out for the others, though not without help at their supervision. Whiskers decided they should have fresh meat for the evening meal, so he sent Three Toes and Trinket into the forest for game. Rabbits would have been nice, but deer were plentiful around Dubois, so it wasn't long before the two Indians returned carrying a small deer carcass between them on a Lodge Pole Pine, skinned of boughs to serve as a carrying device. No one could skin a deer faster than an Indian, so by the time Whiskers had the fire going and the pans ready, the Indians had dressed and filleted venison steaks for the evening meal. Cornbread was already on the fire cooking in the Dutch oven. Fresh onion was cut, and potatoes were being fried ranch-style in one of the irons, with a few onions thrown in for flavor, along with salt and black pepper for seasoning. Added to this was a pot of warmed over red beans sent along by Aunt Bella and doctored up a bit with chili powder thrown in by Benedict. The smell of coffee filled the air, and there would be plenty of it to wash down the grub. No one would go hungry, if Whiskers Benedict had anything to say about it.

Nightfall put the camp at ease. Bedrolls were lined out, and the weary men peeled away from otherwise interesting conversation to get a little shuteye. Palmer ambled over to Lively's pad, a little uneasy about the furor over nothing earlier in the day.

"Lively," he spoke up, "I want to apologize to you about the way I acted out there on the trail today, when we got into that bickering over my silly saddle. I really didn't have enough time to get it prepared for this trip, but I can't blame anyone but myself. And I really would like for you to fix the saddle if you think you can. I'll make it up to you somehow—maybe, if we get anything for finding that girl."

"Oh, shush, Palmer! Don't need no apologies for earlier today, and don't need no pay for fixin' your saddle. I haven't had a chance to do anything with the cinch, but when you get on your horse in the morning, check and see if the stirrups feel any better. I pulled 'em up two notches after we got the camp set tonight and you were busy laying out the campfires. Should be just about right. If not, we'll change 'em again. Better get some sleep now and rest those weary bones. See you at first light."

With that, Lively rolled over in his bedroll and exhaled a few last weary sighs. Palmer followed suit and began to shed his boots for the night.

A cool breeze blew across the encampment as men and animals slumbered in the silent forest; silent, that is, except for the sounds of rustling leaves and an occasional hooting of an owl and the lonesome wail of a coyote somewhere in the distance. The animals had long since cleared their nostrils for the night and were as still as statues spread among the grass. A deathlike tranquility enveloped the side of the mountain. The night air, itself, continued to move and spread its forest perfume over the brigade's temporary lodging. All lay unruffled in repose and peace in the hush of the night.

The camp was cleared away by daylight. Except for a few smoldering campfires, doused with leftover breakfast coffee, and matted grass left where the animals had bedded during the night, one would not know a camp was ever spread in this spot. Stomachs were full again, stuffed with scrambled eggs and salt-cured country ham. The landlopers were in the saddle and on the way again.

Soon the band had ventured out of the mountainous terrain and had crossed an expansive valley where there was easy riding. Though the area was rife with antelope, the timing was off for the need of fresh meat, but if they were still around when the trail ended for the night, some antelope might just wind up in the frying pan. Grasses of every kind and sage spread out as far as the eye could see.

Before long the caravan was crossing rolling foothills leading into the basin, flanked at a distance by an ascending mountain range to the east.

From Dubois, they followed the Wind River along its eastern shore, still heading in a southeasterly direction. They passed through Crowheart, thirty miles or so from where they had started early in the morning, and a little farther found fresh water at Bull Lake Creek. There they changed out their water barrels and gave the animals, as well as the men, time to drink and/or to bathe in the sparkling water. At this point, they could look back to the southwest and see Gannett Peak twenty-five miles away, rising 13,785 feet above sea level, the highest peak in Wyoming Territory. Togwatee Pass, at 9,650 feet, had been their highest point so far. They counted their lucky stars they did not have to enter Washakie Wilderness through Gannett Peak, or they might still be climbing. Because there was only about thirty miles to go, as the crow flies, the ramblers might make Fort Washakie by midnight.

The mules and horses had put in a tough day as the troop finally advanced to within ten miles of Morton Flats. Since the remainder of the journey would be headed due south, Puck determined that the brigade would spend the night and travel the remaining fifteen miles to Fort Washakie the next morning. There was no use going in late at night and then having to arrange for sleeping accommodations. That conclusion seemed to put a lilt into the drudgery the men had sometimes felt along the way. Even the animals sensed that the day was closing in on their workload as well. Tomorrow would be a new day!

The packers wasted no time preparing the camp. Earlier in the day, during *siesta* time, just after lunch, Pistol Bill had gone off and shot a small antelope, had field dressed it, and had wrapped it in cheese cloth to keep the flies from blowing it. For about an hour, he had hung the carcass among some willow branches where the breeze was blowing across a stream of water. This would partially hide it from the scavenging Magpies and cool it down enough for the remaining afternoon ride. But now, as camp was being established, Farley had turned the butchering over to the scouts who prepared it for Benedict's evening meal. Whatever was left over would be taken to the fort, along with the leftover venison from lunch.

The meal went quickly and quietly, fatigue having driven the men into silence. Stomachs full again, the men chilled out for another summer night's inviting rest. Moonlight filtering through the clouds cast a platinum glow over the gray-green meadow and enveloped the camp in a milky haze. Sleep seemed to gain a challenging edge as tonight seeped into tomorrow.

CHAPTER 8

FORT WASHAKIE

As the troop came over the last rise, the gray timbers of the garrison, bleached by years of scalding sun and inclement weather, could be seen glistening in the distance. The dust of a lone horseman also could be seen lifting in the distance, as he rushed toward the gate of the compound, apparently to alert the fortress personnel of the approaching wagon and riders. The gate opened and closed again. The faint noise of the sentry's bugle could be heard calling the militia to their various posts. Then quietness and a totally ghost-like front! Even the field mice stopped their scurrying to check out the situation.

Puck reined up and surveyed the morgue-like appearance of the fort lying still on a not-too-distant rise. Powdery dust boiled beneath the wagon wheels and then began to drift and finally to settle as Whiskers pulled the mules to a halt.

"Whadda ya think boss," Palmer questioned as he hustled his horse up beside Puck.

"Don't know, Jed. Somethin' strange, for sure! Hang loose a minute."

No one moved. Except for the sporadic blowing of the horses clearing the dust from their nostrils, there was nothing but silence. An eerie silence! The Indians looked at one another and then at Puck. Nothing. Puck never moved.

Buzzards circled between the troop and the compound. Two coyotes skulked warily from where the rider had bolted from the sage along the rocky eminence that had been his lookout. Puck was sure that, since the coyotes had moved in so quickly, there were no more men in the rocks.

No movement could be seen along the crest of the colonnades. No sentries could be seen in the crow's nest rising above the fortress. The emblematic flags that usually served as ensigns to the fort were nowhere in sight. It was as if the band had not seen a rider, as if they had not heard a bugle, but they weren't dreaming. Those facts were sure, but what about this nothingness now? Everything washed in silence?

Suddenly, out of seeming total absence—*Va-room!* Again, *Va-rooom!* And again, *Va-roooom!* Each canon volley burst forth louder than the one before it. Black smoke billowed above the compound walls. The gate swung wide. A vast horde of horseflesh and menacing riders broke into the open, forming an ever-widening funnel, and advancing like ravenous Army Ants upon the little brigade. Like the warbling tremolo of a thousand Indians, a horrendous, shrill cry went up. The drum corps pounded their drumheads as if to wake the dead. The buglers blew the "charge" with reveling staccato.

Horses were cavorting and snorting in the melee. Sabers rattled in their sheaths against their metal rings. Pistols cracked mercilessly, riveting the atmosphere with the acrid smell of gunpowder. A colony of Jack Rabbits darted wildly this way and another. Dust choked the air.

The little band of landrovers, taken by surprise, dared to retreat, but it was too late. The packhorse and Sandy, wild-eyed and nostrils flared, broke their tethers and bolted toward the east. The mules and the wagon went west, with Whiskers pulling wildly at the reins. Cowpokes and cayuses wheeled feverishly in circles trying to defy gravity and stay in the mount. Horses pulled one way and then the other, up and then down, breaking wind with every jump. Gentry went down sprattled loosely, like a puppet on a string, then up again. Puck reached for the sky, for handlebars, for anything to hold his own, but couldn't. Gentry went one way and Puck went another. He rolled across the ground, covering his head with forearms and handholds and pulling himself into a fetal position, praying, hoping that he wouldn't get trampled.

As quickly as the murderous cacophony had started, it ended. Everywhere riders dismounted and pulled their horses up, attempting to calm them and return them to sanity. Out of the settling dust and stabilizing herd of animal hooves and horseplay, a half-hearted strain of laughter went up. And then it stopped. Maybe it was too much. The foray had been intended as a welcoming committee; it turned out to be a grim and dangerous enactment. Even now there was no certainty that men and animals alike had escaped injury, perhaps even serious injury.

"Bring 'em 'round! Line 'em up!" shouted the colonel. "Nuchols, you and Blythe git after those pack animals. Talbert, Grayson, the two of you, help the driver with his wagon. Bertrand, see if the highrider and riflemen are okay. Tally, Branson, help those packers with their gear. Mocha, see if you can find out what happened to the Indians. Double time, men, double time! We created all of this, and I'm to blame!"

The colonel dismounted and hustled to where Puck was extricating himself from a pile of brush.

"Mr. Puckett, sir. My apologies! I'm red in the face over this, sir! Didn't mean for anything like this to happen. I'm Colonel Randall Meecham Stott—*Meech* for short. I'm at your service, sir!"

"So this is your idea of a welcoming committee is it Colonel?" Puck asked, trying to smile between grimaces at the pain in his shoulder.

"Well, let's say that's what it started out to be. Didn't expect anything like this sort of tomfoolery though."

"Excuse me, Colonel," Puck motioned. "Be back in a moment. Gotta find my scouts."

"Don't bother, Puckett. I sent a man to find them."

"You don't know Indians, do you Colonel? Those men might be in Apple Valley by now, or resting comfortably in your suite at the fort."

"Don't worry, Puckett. I sent my Indian, Mocha, to locate them. He'll find them for sure."

Puck hesitated and looked up to see Mocha bringing in the two Indians from the direction of the fort.

"How'd you find those men so quickly, Mocha?" the colonel called out.

"No problem, Colonel Meech. Men have only horses unshod, and Indians will almost always circle back on their attackers. Find them hiding in the rocks looking out the situation."

The entire cavalry, along with the government brigade, finally got the situation in hand and calm enough to proceed to the fort. As they streamed through the gate, Colonel Meech bellowed his orders. "Men, let's git these horses cooled down and bathed, and then git yourselves cleaned up. Chow time is comin' up fast."

The colonel took the new arrivals to their accommodations, giving the group sufficient rooms to maintain a little privacy. Mocha took the two Indians with him and showed them their quarters, as comfortable as any in the colonnade.

When the intended duties had been performed and the grime had been halfway washed out of the dust-ridden company, the lunch bell announced chow time. The men repaired to the main dining hall, each one in succession passing through the chow line to receive his tray.

Trinket, Three Toes, and Mocha conveniently came in right at the time the last man had received his tray and the company had been seated. The colonel had not yet arrived. When the Indians had secured their trays, Mocha led them into an anteroom next to the main chow hall where the company had been seated and were beginning to eat.

Puck looked up somewhat puzzled. There were plenty of seats and tables remaining open for several more men. Why were the Indians going off to themselves? Then, his face began to be flushed with embarrassment. A pink hue gradually formed about his neck and slowly rose to his forehead. He leaned over to one side and said something to Farley and Lively. Then, he leaned across the table and motioned similarly to the other three men. In a moment, each of them rose up, took his tray, and followed Puck into the anteroom where they sat down and began to eat with the Indians.

Colonel Meech entered the main dining room with his tray and surveyed the group, looking for Puck. He went to the head table, sat his tray down, and motioned to Private Rolly Nuchols. Nuchols sprang to his feet and presented himself. The colonel said something to him and he turned and headed in the direction of the anteroom. He entered the room and went to where Puck was seated.

"Mr. Puckett, sir," he addressed him, "the Colonel wishes that you dine with him at the head table. He wishes your riflemen, packers, and cook to join you as well."

"What about my scouts. Did he forget them?"

"Sir," Nuchols continued, "he indicated nothing about the Indians."

"Well, then, Private Nuchols, please inform the colonel that I prefer to eat in here with all my men, and if he would like to join me in here, he may do so."

"Yes sir, Mr. Puckett," Nuchols responded, as he turned abruptly and returned to the main dining room.

In a moment, Colonel Meech himself entered the anteroom. "Mr. Puckett," he announced, "I was hoping you would join me at the head table so we could confer a bit about your assignment here at the Wind River Reservation."

Puck answered, "I was hoping to eat with my men, sir, but if you wish, we could *all* join you in there." Puck spoke matter-of-factly with a bit more emphasis on the word "all."

"Sure thing, Mr. Puckett. Trinket and Three Toes can remain in here with Mocha."

"I can't do that, Colonel," Puck rejoined. "Is there any reason we can't all join you?"

"You mean the Indians, too?"

"Yes sir, I mean the Indians, too."

"Well sir, we just haven't done things around here like that yet."

"You mean Whites eating with Indians, don't you, sir?"

"Yes, is that anything so terrible? Kind eating with kind?"

"Look, Colonel, these men were created human beings just as you were. They had no play in being born Indian rather than White, just as you had no play in being born White rather than Indian. They were created with the same dignity and worth as you were. Therefore, they should be treated as such."

"But Puckett, I have to keep things at an even keel around here. My men wouldn't like it if I allowed the Indians into their chow room."

"*Even keel,* sir?" Puck retorted with more than a bit of firmness. "*Even keel* means *even—even for all.* If we can't eat in here with the Indians, or they with us in the main dining room, then we'll just pull our wagon outside the fort and set up camp there."

"No, don't do that, Puckett. You know," Colonel Meech bowed

his head toward the floor, "I've felt a little funny every time I've sent Mocha off to eat by himself, yet he is as loyal to me as any man I have. You may have something about this equal stuff." The colonel hesitated and then continued. "Okay, here goes! Mocha, take your Indian friends here and your food into the main chow hall. You're eatin' with us today, and from now on. I'll take care of any trouble. You can count on that."

All the riders of the wagon train, including the Indians, picked up their food trays and joined the men in the main dining hall. As they sat down, eyes from every table in the room lifted to survey the situation. The chatter toned down in response, and low mumbling could be heard, as the men questioned what they were seeing for the first time. Some looked away and continued eating, while others kept looking at the Indians, and then at their plates. They weren't sure of this at all.

Rucker and Solomon dropped their utensils on the table loud enough to be conspicuous, and then left the room. Colonel Meech laid his own plate aside and followed them out.

"Rucker, you and Solomon hold up," the colonel called out. "What's the problem with you men? You didn't finish your meals."

"Colonel," Rucker replied, "No offense, but I ain't eatin' with no Injuns."

"Look men, you like Mocha, don't you?"

"Yeah, we like him," Solomon responded, "but that don't mean we have to eat with him."

"Okay men, I realize its not customary to put the Indians and Whites together like this, but I've been thinking about this whole thing a lot lately, and Puckett in there just cleared up my mind on a lot of things. Think of it, men. Mocha works as hard as anyone around here. Never complains. More than I can say about some of the other men here. He's ready at any time to help any of you men.

I've seen him take it upon himself to see that some of you boys have a little extra comfort. He has never defied me in the least. He's totally respectful. Now the Good Book here lately has been tellin' me that we are all created equal. Guess that's why I've been feelin' guilty so much here lately. So from now on, we're gonna see if we can git things on even par around here. I hope you men won't buck me on this. So why don't you both go back in there and finish your meals?"

"Well, I don't know, Colonel. I'll need to give this a little thought," replied Rucker.

"What about you, Solomon?"

"Why uh, I uh," Solomon hesitated. "I *am* hungry, Colonel. Guess it wouldn't hurt me to try."

"Rucker," the Colonel entertained, "I'm gonna leave you with your thoughts, and for this time I'm gonna fetch your food for you. But from now on..."

The opening of the dining hall door and a clatter of tin plates interrupted the colonel suddenly! He turned to see Mocha standing there with the men's trays.

"Colonel Meech," Mocha spoke up, "I hope I no do wrong thing. Don't like see my friends, Rucker and Solomon, no eat their food. I no have problem that they no eat with me."

Mocha handed the trays to the men. Solomon stood motionless. Rucker was stunned. Mocha turned to go back into the hall.

"Hold it, Mocha," Rucker called out. "I, uh, I don't really know what to say. Guess I'm being a little childish. You're looking like the better man here. Maybe not looking—maybe you are. You're treatin' me better'n I've ever treated you. I guess this malarkey needs to stop right now."

Rucker handed his tray to the Colonel, approached Mocha, and put one hand on his shoulder and the other on the door. "Let's get back in here and eat, okay?" He turned and motioned, "You comin' Solomon?" he asked, retrieving his tray from the colonel.

The two men reentered the hall, followed by Mocha and the colonel, and sat among the other men, showing not a little embarrassment.

Mocha returned to his seat but he didn't sit down. He leaned over and said something to Trinket and Three Toes. Almost immediately they rose to their feet and the three Indians picked up their trays and returned to the anteroom where Mocha usually ate.

All eyes were on the three again. The room became almost silent. Then, seemingly for no reason, another soldier rose to his feet and shook his fist in the direction of the Indians and shouted, "All right! So *now* you think you're *too good* to eat with the rest of us!"

The colonel rose to his feet and trounced on the issue. "Settle down, McClary, or you'll eat your next meal in the brig. We'll have none of this!" The colonel could see that the tables had been turned, and that none of it made any sense. "Gentlemen," he added, "what we've seen here today ought to make us sit up and take notice of our attitudes. We've been pretty ugly, you know? 'Sides, ugly *is* as ugly *does*. So we better start gettin the ugly outa our systems. I'll have no more outbursts like this, so when this meal is finished, we better each go aside and think through this matter wisely. McClary, I've never called a man down in public, but you brought it on yourself. If you can find it in yourself to apologize to the Indian men, I'll certainly find it in myself to apologize to you. Now let's try to finish this meal before it gits thrown out, along with every man in here."

Fort Washakie had not always been called by that name. The fort originated as Camp Brown, but due to the extraordinary aid to white emigrants on the Northern Plains by Washakie and the Eastern Shoshonis, the camp had eventually been renamed in honor of Washakie.

Upon the death of the principal chief of the Shoshonis in 1842, Washakie had become the undisputed successor as head of the tribe. He not only had become a friend to such mountain men as Kit Carson and Jim Bridger, but from 1843 to 1860, he stood in support of the white man entering the territory along the Oregon Trail, and later along the Lander Road, in the development of the West. He formed a tireless bulwark of strength against the Arapahos, Cheyennes, Crows, and Sioux, who detested the intrusion of the white man. Hundreds of covered wagons felt safe to traverse the course if Washakie and his band were in the vicinity of travel. The riders of the Pony Express and the builders of the telegraph system felt safe if, when pursued by hostile Indians, they could make it to Washakie's camp.

In 1868, on behalf of the U. S. Government, Colonel Christopher C. Augur awarded the Wind River valley in Wyoming Territory to Washakie as a reservation to his people. This amounted to over a million and a half acres of land.

In 1876, for his support of the white man, both along the Oregon Trail and alongside General George Crook in the Battle of the Rosebud against the fierce Sioux, enemies of the emigrants, Washakie was honored ceremoniously at Camp Brown. President Ulysses S. Grant sent him a handsome saddle specially trimmed in silver. Indian Agent, James Irwin, who presented the saddle, gave a speech in Washakie's honor, ultimately bringing the old chief to tears. When asked what message he would like to send President Grant, the old man could not speak. Irwin continued to coax Washakie to make a reply even of a few words, whereupon Washakie finally began to speak—and in short. His speech consisted of only three brief sentences. He said, "When a favor is shown a white man, he feels it in his head and his tongue speaks. When a kindness is shown to an Indian, he feels it in his heart, and the heart has no tongue. I have spoken."[5]

Washakie ceased his active duty with the Army as a scout late in 1876, after the defeat of Chief Dull Knife of the Cheyennes. As a tribute for his services, he would remain on the Army payroll until his death, whether active or not, and in 1878 Camp Brown was renamed Fort Washakie in his honor.

Much of this history danced through Puck's memory as Colonel Meech led Puck and company to the headquarters of the Wind River Reservation. Other Army officers assigned to the kidnapping case were already assembled, awaiting them, ready to assist the search for the Indian girl any way they might.

As Puck entered, applause went up among the officers led by Sergeant Graves and Corporal Allen, who had first gone to Jackson to secure Puck's services for the Territory of Wyoming. Others in the room, the liaison of Indian leaders sent to help negotiate the work, sat sullen, gripped by the brutal confiscation of one from among their family—and a child at that. The applause was short-lived and dwindled into rapt attention of all in the room, as Puck rose to address the group.

"Gentlemen, I'll be brief, because what I may have to say will not be nearly so important as the questions I want to ask. My associates and I have come for one reason, and that is to locate the whereabouts of the little Indian girl and to bring her kidnappers to justice. I'll want any assistance you might bring to aid in that purpose, most of which I hope you will be able to give today, because after this session, I'll be instantly on the trail of the perpetrators of this crime, and you may not see me again until I am able to bring you good news. If you have any questions, you should ask them now before I start asking mine."

For a moment there was silence. Then from the back of the room an Indian figure rose to his feet and began to speak.

"Our people, sir, are grateful for your services. You can know how troubled we all are in the taking of this child, especially the girl's mother and father. Many days seem to have passed without much attention being given toward the hunt." The Indian spoke fluently and astutely, and continued, "Chief Washakie himself has shown much concern that the government is not being more actively in pursuit and has even spoken that if something more promising is not done soon, he will consider coming out of retirement as an Army scout and enter the case himself. Can you assure us, sir, that the effort to find this girl will be an all-out scouring of the Territory for our little sister of the Shoshoni family?"

"In response to your concern, Sir," Puck began, "when I have received all the information currently available from among the people in this room, my services will begin immediately, and I'll pursue the case both day and night, if that is what is required. You may assure your chief and the family of this girl that they can rest easy knowing that everything that possibly can be done will be done. You have my oath on that. If I may soften the pain of anyone else in this room by answering any further questions, please ask them quickly, because I am about to get busy with my own."

No other questions were forthcoming, so Puck rose to his feet and approached a table in the center of the room where a map of the general territory surrounding the Wind River village was being displayed. He motioned for the crowd to assemble around him. As they gathered, the two young boys, who had witnessed the kidnapping, squeezed in toward the edge of the table, so as to see the map.

Puck turned to them first and asked, "Boys, I understand that you witnessed the crime and followed the kidnappers on your own horses for awhile, until they finally outran you. Can you show me on the map the direction they headed and relate anything else that you observed that you think might be helpful?"

The older of the boys presented himself. "Sir," he addressed Puck, "let me first tell you what happened. When kidnapper pull Papu up on his *silla*, I jump up and git one hand on man's belt and one on his *silla*. I keep pulling and shouting, 'Let my friend go you *dammit* white man!' He hit my eye with his hand and kick my ribs with his spurs and shouted, 'Git away you little beaver brain.' I cannot hold tight any more. Then I fall to the dirt almost under his *cayuse*. My friend, Pokie, here come running fast with our ponies and we chase the white mans for two miles but our little ponies cannot catch the White mans' too fast *cayuses*. But we watch what way they ride."

Drawing an imaginary line with his finger on the map, the Indian boy moved it in a northeasterly direction. Puck could see that the kidnappers had passed about halfway between Fort Washakie and Ethete, each location being about two and a half miles from the riders' path.

"Boys, did the riders continue northeasterly, or did you see them turn at any time?"

"Mr. Puck," the older boy said, "we rode for about two miles before we lose them in the brush, but we never see them turn."

Puck mumbled something to himself, as though calculating matters under his breath. For all he knew, the riders could have ultimately gone in any direction after ditching their pursuers.

"Boys," Puck mused again, "do you recall seeing anything

peculiar or strange about these riders? I mean something that might distinguish them in some way?"

"Well, Mr. Puck," the younger of the boys spoke up, "one of the man's *cayuse* fall behind the one in front. He was throwing his back leg as if something be wrong with it. But he still fast enough that our little ponies can no keep up. My friend, Wilder, here see the face of one man who catch Papu, but we not git close enough to see other face. But the rider who ride in front, stand in the saddle once and have something black on the seat of his britches—like mud, or coal dust, really dirty looking. He was a tall, thin man. That's about all I see."

"Thank you boys," Puck responded. "You've been a big help. We'll consider everything you've told us."

Puck turned to the Indian men and started to question them, then stopped abruptly, as if something had just occurred to him. "By the way, men, how old is the little girl, and what is her name?"

One of the Indians closest to the family spoke up. "Her name is Papu Banta, and she is eight years old, maybe eight and a half."

"What was she wearing, and about how tall is she?"

Again, the Indian remarked, "She is about the same height as this young boy here—about three and a half or four feet tall. Her family told me what she was wearing but it is hard for me to describe."

"I know what she wear," the older Indian boy chimed in. "She wear a turquoise color skirt, long to her knees, a white shirt, and a buckskin vest over shirt. She wear high moccasins the color of buckskin with turquoise beads across toes and around ankles. I know this because we have all been playing together about an hour before these mans rode up and grabbed our friend."

Colonel Meech spoke up, "Puck, here is some paper and a pen. Don't you need to write some of this stuff down?"

"No need for it, sir. I keep everything in my head. Don't want any cumbersome bulk to carry around."

Trinket and Three Toes snickered at Puck's remark, finding it rather humorous. Three Toes whispered, "From now, maybe we just call him 'Paperhead Puck.' He writes everything on his brain."

Puck brought attention back to the map and began to assess matters in some detail. He began to calculate the possibilities. "Look," he said, pointing to the map, "the kidnappers may have continued northeast for awhile. That would take them somewhere close to Kinnear, but my feeling is that they probably skirted the village to avert detection and probably stopped at Ocean Lake just north of the village to refresh their horses. Or, they could have veered more toward Morton, passing it by to stop at Pilot Butte Reservoir. In either case, they would not likely proceed farther north, as the terrain is a combination of rolling hills and flatland with not much cover.

"If this is true, they would not have turned west, because there is no population in that direction and, therefore, no telegraph centers—and these men used the telegraph, according to Army facts, to submit their demands. Besides, except for the Wind River, they would not find fresh water lakes near enough to sustain themselves. My guess, then, is that they either turned due east toward Riverton, or dropped down in a southeasterly direction to Arapaho. The Beaver River is only about two miles east of Arapaho where fresh water can be found. Still again, from the lakes they may have continued around the southern tip of Boysen Reservoir and then turned due north to Shoshoni, to find hiding in the lower reaches of Wind River Canyon. They would then be just outside the borders of Wind River Reservation. From here they would always have water along the Boysen Reservoir and access to telegraph lines, both in Shoshoni or back south in Riverton. Unless the rider with the crippled horse changes mounts altogether, he is going to need a farrier to check out the problem, or at best a blacksmith, and there is one in Shoshoni."

Puck turned from the map to the group of men, thinking they might have observations of their own, and then turned back. "Oh, one other question. Sergeant Graves, you told me back in my village that the kidnappers demanded a ransom to be delivered to a particular site that they would name later. I asked you then if the word "site" was their word or yours. Do you have any more leads on this?"

"Yes, sir, I do have, sir. I secured a copy of the telegram sent by the kidnappers, and the word "site" is in their remarks. Don't see how that is of any value at this point though, since we have not heard from them again telling us just what specific site."

Puck twitched his fingers back and forth around his chin as if pondering, then concluded, "Don't know if it means anything Sergeant, just a hunch. Get word to me, though, as soon as you hear from them again. I'll let you know where you can find me."

Puck reached in his vest pocket and retrieved a clutch of paper. "I have one other item of interest. I want to test my own thoughts here between several of you men. Colonel Meech, Graves, Allen, and two or three of you other men, gather around closer to the table." As the men gathered, Puck gave them a slip of paper with nothing written on it.

"Now, gentlemen, here's my question, and you can jot down your answers on the slips of paper I just handed you. The question is, if you were a lone kidnapper, with no one else involved, and were demanding a ransom for the safe return of such a victim as this little girl, how much money would you ask for? I have already written my answer on this slip of paper here in my hand. Now, I want to know what you would say."

The men collected pencils from the table in front of them and began to jot down their answers, some thinking through the proposition longer than others. When the group had finished, Puck asked them to spread out their slips upright on the table. Every slip of paper, to a man, had as its amount, $50,000. Puck laid his slip on top of the rest. What he had written beforehand matched their answers identically—$50,000.

"Gentlemen," Puck concluded, "I could be wrong, but if the kidnappers were just the two who took the girl, they more than likely would have asked for $100,000 in ransom, so that the two-man split would be as we all suggested—$50,000 for each man. But they asked for $150,000. This occurs to me that there is a third party involved and perhaps the 'brains' of the operation. So, if my hunch is correct, I will be looking for three men—the kingpin and two rooks. This actually makes the search easier, because the two kidnappers will constantly have to answer to their boss with every successive bit of news they get. At least, it's a start. And speaking of starting, I'm ready to get with it!"

CHAPTER 9
THE SEARCH

As the chuck wagon pulled out of the gates at Fort Washakie, followed by Puck and his riders, soldiers lined their exit at full attention and in regal salute. Colonel Meech, himself an old southern gentlemen, had taught his men certain respectful hospitality and affirmation of wayfaring guests. Puck waved away the rigid salute by a quick hand to the brow in final tribute and hustled up his horse to the head of the caravan. The flag bearer dipped his colors in response. In a moment, the gates were closed again and the search for Papu Banta was on.

By mid-afternoon, the air smelled of rain. A cool breeze put a new spirit of enthusiasm in both men and animals. The Indians watched the honeybees gathering pollen, nervously, among the prairie blossoms. Sensing the approaching storm, many had begun to retreat to their hives. Birds flew into the cover of trees or fluttered into the brush. These and other signs, not the least of which was a bruised sky along the horizon, indicated that an approaching storm was imminent. Streaks of gray-blue curtains of rain could be seen in the distance through openings in the tree line. For better or worse, the men were headed directly into the storm's path.

Puck was startled suddenly by an uproar of some kind coming from the rear. He turned to see one of the Indian boys from Wind River Village riding wildly toward the caravan, flailing his arms in the air and yelling at the top of his lungs. Puck hurriedly made tracks toward the youth, wondering what could possibly be wrong.

Out of breath by the mad dash and constant hollering, the boy reined up and attempted to speak to Puck. Due to cotton mouth and a dry throat, his voice was but a strained whisper, an almost guttural rasp. He started and stopped, caught his breath, wheezed, and began again.

"Hold up!" Puck urged, taking his canteen from its saddle perch and handing it to the lad. "Here, drink some water, and get your breath," he prompted.

The boy gulped and coughed. In a moment, he began to speak with a sign of urgency.

"Mr. Puck, I just see the big man of the kidnappers, the one who rides a bad horse. I go on an errand for my father and I pass close to the old Indian arbor. It was beginning to rain, and this rider pull up under the cover to be dry. I hide in the trees when I recognize him. He stay until the rain stop and then ride away."

"Son, where is this arbor?"

"It's about five miles from village. It was built for tribal reunion gatherings a few years ago and they never take it down. Nobody use it much any more. I can take you to it!"

"Okay, son, let me think a moment." Puck became silent in thought, then turned to the men and shouted for Three Toes. Three Toes hustled to see what he wanted.

"Three Toes," Puck began, "our young friend here has just seen one of the kidnappers in an old abandoned arbor. I think it would be better that I not show myself there. Your being an Indian would not rouse too much concern. Go with the lad and check out the situation. Tie your horses some distance from the arbor so as not to add tracks on top of those left by the rider's horse. See if you can make out anything peculiar about the tracks. The rider was still on the lame horse. When you finish, meet us at the old Cripple Creek Mining Depot. Do you know where that is?"

"Yes sir, Mr. Puck. Some of my family used to bring silver and minerals to sell to the buyers. I was very young then, like this boy here, but I am sure I can still find the place. Just don't let old Whiskers put away the food too soon."

With that spoken, Three Toes and the lad were off toward the arbor. If they were to examine any of the tracks, then they would have to hurry; the storm was approaching fast. Any more rain would wash away the tracks.

Evening was coming on as the caravan approached the timeworn mining depot, dilapidated and dust-ridden with age. Some of the adjoining sheds had already fallen to the ground, but the main building was still secure. Though grizzled and bleached by sun and rain, it was still a sturdy old architectural wonder. Bedrolls would be dry in the inner chambers, and the men would be safer from the lightening that was already cracking in the humid air. A sturdy overhang on the outside perimeter would get the animals out of the storm that was already beginning to dance around their ears, whipping up the dust and tumble weeds and rattling the tin, flapping up at the corners of the roof line. Though Whiskers was not concerned about the chuck wagon, he backed it under a canopy that had once served as a grain chute for servicing the animals of the buyers and sellers.

Light was growing dim and a foggy haze was rolling in with the storm, whisking away what warm air was left of the afternoon. Through the haze, a rider could be seen approaching the old depot, and none too soon, as the first splatters of rain began to pelt the ground and blow across the venerable old porch stretching across the front of the main pavilion.

As the figure neared, the crew could make out a feather or two flitting in the wind, signaling at once that Three Toes was advancing. He pulled up, gracefully dismounted, and sprang to the porch, leaving his reins in the hands of Trinket, who was standing there to take his horse to shelter.

"Come on in, T.T.," Puck abbreviated, "Wha'd you find at the arbor?"

"How you say 'T.T.?' T.T., I mean Three Toes find something very interesting." He pulled the strings of his high-topped moccasins and slipped them off, placing them close to the fire that Whiskers had made in the age-worn fireplace. His feathers drooped, saturated with rain, signifying that he had already ridden through a line of storm. His raven hair glistened in the firelight. He shed his vest and hung it on a peg protruding from a support post near the fireplace.

"Okay, Mr. Puck, let me show you what Three Toes find. Now I wish you were not Paper Brains and bring paper Colonel Meech offer you. No paper. No ink. No quill. Here, let me draw in the sand."

Three Toes found a spot where the floorboards had rotted away and the sand had sifted in circular fashion on the adobe sub-floor. With the brush of his hand, he spread it to form a tablet, and with a twig he picked up from the floor, he proceeded to draw a picture. He first formed the outer perimeter of a horse's hoof and then drew that portion inside the perimeter known as the "frog." The "frog" is the elastic, horny substance that normally forms a "V" on the bottom of the hoof. If it gets punctured, stone-bruised, or damaged in some way, the horse will give in to its sensitivity. Three Toes had drawn a disfigured "frog" that he had detected in the tracks left by the kidnapper's horse—a "V" with a cavity along one edge.

"Mr. Puck," Three Toes concluded, "this horse is no fit to ride much longer. It is—how you say? 'Shoddy or with bad foot. We must find more tracks before this man gets other horse. But maybe he won't trade horse. He thinks same about horse as he does about Indian girl. He brings sorrow to both and does not care."

Puck affirmed the Indian's conclusion by saying, "Three Toes, you have done well. You're a good scout with a good head on your shoulders. And you are right. We need to find this man while he is still riding this horse, before he sends it to the glue factory and secures another one. I'll give this matter some thought, and by morning I'll know what our strategy will be."

The men ate their dinner in the safety of the mining compound, unable to converse much with one another, because of the blowing gale bearing down outside. Heavy rain was drenching the old pavilion and leaking into the sleeping chambers along the perimeter of the building where sheets of roofing tin had long since blown away. However, it was dry along the fireplace wall and some of the other inner partitions, so the men began to spread their bedrolls accordingly.

Bursts of thunder shook the rafters above them. The floor, what was left of it, creaked, as if bearing some ghostly presence. Cracks of lightning streaked across the night sky lighting up the horizon, looking for a place to strike, like bandits searching for the next best assault. Still, the horrendous night clamor, piteously distracting as it was, could not keep the exhausted crew awake. Only the fire in the fireplace kept vigilance with the menacing storm, and even it was beginning to dwindle at heart and smolder at the edges. Though fiendish of purpose, the din of the storm could not unsettle the camp that now lay undisturbed by it in the cradle of repose.

The night of belligerent skies soon gave way to a brilliant dawn, its morning air giving place to the shrill scolding of the Mockingbird and the low, bashful wail of the Mourning Dove. The aroma of bacon and coffee wafted throughout the sleeping quarters, as old Whiskers Benedict made as much noise with the pots and pans as he possibly could. If he were going to cook for a patchwork of grizzly cowhands and Indians, they were going to at least keep him company, one way or another.

Everyone helped square away the camp after breakfast and got his gear together for another day's venture. Puck had lay awake a good portion of the night giving thought to strategy for the impending search for the Indian girl. He was now ready to lay out the schedule for the day and get things moving. Time was really of the essence now.

Puck called the men together and presented the possibilities open to the kidnappers and their likely choice of hideout. He reasoned that they would get the girl out of the Reservation but not too far out to cause suspicion, just in case anyone saw the Indian girl in white man's territory. If they went to Wind River Canyon, they could drop down to Boysen Reservoir and to Shoshoni on the far eastern boundary of the Reservation. On the one hand, they might make headquarters in the Canyon, where they would have access to water along the river and reservoir and go into Shoshoni to make whatever transactions useful by way of ransom demands. Indians, for the most part, were living along the western front of Boysen Reservoir, but few on the eastern side except for those taking up residence on the western side of Shoshoni. The kidnappers' identities were virtually unknown, except for being white men, and whites lived in Shoshoni and came and went freely. The kidnappers, whether basing their operations there or merely using it for their basic needs, would be greatly unsuspected. A telegraph office was available in Shoshoni, as well. On the other hand, Riverton was only twenty miles southwest of Shoshoni where there would be access to governmental offices and banking facilities, in case of prevailing communication by the kidnappers. From Shoshoni to the southernmost tip of the Reservation, there was good hiding along the eastern stretch of the Indian boundary. Puck was familiar with this stretch of topography and was weighing heavily on this area where the girl might be hidden away.

The boss stopped his reasoning long enough to tell the men of his final plans. "We will all go to a place I know off the beaten trail near the southern tip of Boysen Reservoir. Until further notice, this will be our nightly camp and place of rendezvous. We'll return to camp each evening, except for you, Three Toes. If I play my hunches right, I'll have a job for you and a place for you to stay, which I'll explain later. If things seem a little hazy at this point, don't concern yourselves. It will all be clear later, but for now, let's head for Boysen Reservoir. We can make the trip by noon if we don't dawdle."

The ride was refreshing in the cool of the day in the aftermath of the rain the night before. Puck directed the course well west of Boysen Reservoir, hoping they would meet fewer travelers along the way. As soon as they could get to their destination and break up as a group, the sooner they could avert giving up any identity as a band connected to one another.

Just before noon, Puck veered off the beaten trail, leading the caravan through pockets of intervening brush and small timber. Half a mile later, he pulled up into a clearing, partially hidden by a series of small, abrupt cliffs. He then rounded a break of Cedars opening onto a small undulating stream of water, a freshwater stream fed by springs seeping from cracks in the cliff rocks. A small *cul-de-sac* came instantly into view, at the end of which was a dilapidated log structure that used to be a cabin. Only three walls remained standing. The roof and the front wall were no longer discernible. The shack had fallen in and the debris had long since rotted away.

Puck directed Whiskers to pull the chuck wagon alongside what used to be the front of the building. This would serve to partially enclose the log perimeter as shelter. They could span the walls with freshly cut tree limbs and cover them with canvas as a diversion in case of rain. They could then go in and out of the enclosure to one side of the front where Whiskers had intentionally left a three-foot opening.

Palmer and Lively lost no time directing the crew in preparing the shelter and unpacking the horses and mules. Whiskers prepared lunch. Puck and the Indians tethered the animals, so they could feed and drink at leisure, and then they began cutting tree limbs to span the cabin walls.

After lunch and a brief *siesta,* Puck called the men together again and mapped out his plan of operation. "Whiskers," he began, "you and Palmer stay with the wagon for now. You can look for small game to bide your time and look after the camp. Lively, return to the trail and go back down to Riverton. Hang around there and keep your ears open, especially around the saloon. Check in with the telegraph office, give the operator your name, and have him send any telegrams for me to Sheriff Bixley. Bixley knows what I am about here, so introduce yourself to him. Report back to camp each night. Engle, you and Three Toes head for Shoshoni, but break up before you enter town. Three Toes, go to the blacksmith shop and try to hire on as a cleaning boy. The shop is also a stable. Horses come and go. By chance, you may see the lame horse and his rider come in. Engle, go down to the telegraph office and present yourself. Then go meet Sheriff "Bullet" Larson. From that point, keep your ears open. Try to check with Three Toes once a day—but as secretly as possible—and be ready to relay any important information.

"Three Toes, if you get the job, ask the blacksmith, who also serves as the town farrier, if you can bunk in the loft. Engle, you will return to camp each evening. Trinket, I want you to ride the boundary of the Reservation between Riverton and Shoshoni. You will see Indians, of course, but you may see whites coming and going as well. Keep an eye open for the big man and the lame horse, or anyone you keep seeing on a regular basis that may appear suspicious to you. Come back into camp each evening. For a few days, I'm going to be all over, checking in with government and army officials, and trying to get some bearing on what's happening concerning the kidnappers' demands. Farley, you'll come with me, shadowing my moves in case I need you. So let's all make the best of the afternoon. We'll move out at first light. Anyone have any questions?"

No one had any questions, only a few pertinent comments. The afternoon went by uneventfully. Dinner came and went, and nightfall seemed to come early. Soon the camp was silent for another night.

Departure to the various posts came at early light the next morning. After breakfast, Trinket and Lively headed south toward Riverton. Three Toes and Engle headed northeast toward Shoshoni. Farley and Puck moved out together, heading first to Shoshoni to find out the latest reports regarding the kidnappers' demands.

Four miles out of Shoshoni, Three Toes and Engle parted, each taking separate trails into town. In town, Three Toes pulled up in front of the blacksmith and stable barn and presented himself to the man inside.

"I'm Three Toes, looking for a small job," he told the man. "Clean the stalls, feed and water the horses, keep the coal bucket full—anything you got. Indian good help for food and little pay.

Hope you can use me and give me and my *cayuse* a place to stay."

The man kept looking down at the Indian's moccasins, thinking he would learn the reason for the name, then introduced himself as Lambert Browning and kept rubbing his forehead, questioning whether or not he needed an Indian around the place.

"I've never hired an Indian before," he said, "and there are plenty of them around here, but I guess there is always a first time. The last white boy got lazy on me, so I let him go a few days ago. Guess I could try you, Toes. Won't be much pay, but I'll feed you and your cayuse and give you a cool place to stay. Just don't get in the way of my business. Since it is only nine o'clock and you just rode in, you may be hungry. I'll get you some food, and then you can get started."

"Oh, that's okay boss. I've..." He started to say he had already eaten at the camp. He hesitated and then went on, correcting himself. "I have some food in my parfletche." He then proceeded to eat some of the biscuits and ham left over from the camp breakfast.

Browning brought Three Toes something to drink and noticed what he was eating.

"Say, Injun, how is it you're eatin' white man's bread? How'd you come by that?"

"Oh, I not buy it, Mr. Blacksmith."

"I mean, how did you get it? You should be eatin' *pemmican* and deer jerky, not biscuits and pork."

"Oh, Mr. Boss, I traded some softened leather to some soldiers for it when I came down the trail. I ran out of food yesterday." His lie, if taken for face value, would be the first test for the clandestine role he needed to play. The work was a mere cover.

"Well, wherever you got it," Browning went on, "when you finish eatin', you can start by filling up the horses' troughs with water and pitching some hay out of the loft for the evening feeding."

Just then, the morning stage pulled up in front of the shop and the driver called Browning over to the traces. "Lambert," the driver spoke up, using the farrier's first name, "I've got a horse giving in to his right front hoof. Thought I'd better check it out before leaving town."

The smithy picked up the horse's leg and doubled it between his knees to check it out. He noticed immediately that a small flat stone had lodged beneath the inner edge of the horseshoe. He took out his pocketknife and pried the pebble free and flicked it to the ground. With the butt of the knife, he pounded at the shoe to help seat it again, and checked the foot for any other problem.

"Well, Johnson," the blacksmith reflected, "Your problem is solved for now. After your run today, bring the horse in and I'll reset that shoe. It's not bad enough to cause you trouble today."

The driver thanked Browning and flipped him a coin. He mounted the carriage once more and was off in the direction of Riverton.

Three Toes was finishing his snack as the boss returned to the building.

"Mr. Toes," the boss chided, "I'm glad you came by today. I'm need'n to go on a short errand. You can look after the place and bed any horses that come in. Tell anyone arriving that I'll return about mid-afternoon and settle up with them then." With that, he went to the first stall and mounted a horse already saddled to ride and rode off in the direction leading south of town.

Three Toes watered the horses, dropped the hay in the horse cradles below the loft, and swept out a few stalls. He then sat out front waiting to take in any new mounts that might arrive. He checked out any new rider coming in, hoping to find something interesting regarding the kidnapping case, although he had no idea what he might be looking for short of a lame horse and a big rider.

Until the boss returned, he would look around for any other work needing to be done.

Puck left Farley at the town saloon where Mel Engle had already arrived and sat over to one side having a drink. Though the two men noticed each other, they did not speak, or intimate in any way that they had connections.

Puck sauntered casually down the boardwalk, hoping to be inconspicuous as he entered the office of the Indian Agency. There he learned that a telegram from the kidnappers had come the day before, the second one in the past week. The messages were getting more serious, the culprits more impatient. They wanted some clear sign that the government was actively working on their ransom demands. The latest telegram demanded that a hundred dollars for food for the girl be placed in a red bandanna and left with the stage driver going to Riverton the next morning. The package was to be hung on a tree limb just after the driver crossed Hale's Ford. If anyone cared for the safety of the Indian girl, it was important that no one followed the stage or staked anyone near the crossing. This transaction would confirm the government's desire to comply in good faith toward the ransom demand. Another telegram would be forthcoming when the bandanna had been received.

This was actually the day for the hundred-dollar ransom delivery. Though it was timely with Puck's arrival, he knew his hands were tied. There would be no following the stage. Though he knew nothing about the stage's temporary stop at the blacksmith barn, he was sure it had already left with the ransom in the hands of the driver. The package certainly wouldn't hang on the tree long, so there was no use pursuing the matter for now.

Engle left the saloon and noticed Puck coming to pick up Farley. Without speaking, he mounted his horse and rode off in the direction of the blacksmith shop. As he passed the barn, he saw Three Toes, to one side of the building, busy at dusting horse blankets and saddle pads. He realized his Indian partner was set to begin his surveillance as directed by Puck. Rather than stopping, he went on to the telegraph office to introduce himself to the operator. He would then be ready to receive any pertinent messages relayed for Puck. On his return, he saw Three Toes sitting in front of the stable biding his time. As he approached, the Indian motioned to him to come over.

"Is it safe for me to be here right now, Three Toes," Engle asked?

"Very safe, Engle. The boss is gone on an errand. Be back in afternoon."

Three Toes told Engle about the stagecoach dropping by to check one of the horse's legs. Only one man had ridden in to stable his horse, nothing out of the ordinary. Engle assured Three Toes that he would touch base with him in some manner the next day.

A nice campfire and dinner welcomed the men as they filtered back into camp for the evening. As they ate, they exchanged events of the day from each one's vantage point. Engle told of Three Toe's good luck of landing a job at the stable and of getting a tolerable place to stay in the barn. He relayed information about the stage driver getting his horse checked before leaving on the Riverton morning run, and then the blacksmith's leaving Three Toes to mind the shop while he ran an errand. Puck told the group about the telegram and the ransom demand of a hundred dollars to be left at Hale's Ford by the stage driver. When Trinket heard about the stage and the ransom package, he interrupted the conversation to say something apparently important.

"Maybe this is important, Mr. Puck! I ride the border all morning and see nothing, but after lunch, I came to little creek and decided to water my pony. While he drink, I hear wagon coming and look up to see stagecoach coming pretty fast. I pulled my horse away and moved into brush to hide. When stage cross creek, it stop and the driver ran to a tree near road and put something in it. But then, he take it back and run to other bigger tree more off road and leave package hanging on a limb."

Puck interrupted, "I hope you stayed back from the tree."

"Yes, well..." Trinket hesitated. "When the stage go, I wait good time watching the tree and then think it important to have a looksee. But when I start to move, I look up and see a rider coming to the creek. So, I wait and get behind bigger pile of brush. Only have small peephole to look out the situation. The rider go straight to tree like he know about package. He take red, flat package and push it deep under saddle, not in bags on saddle. He turns horse and go back same way he come and then go off road into brush. I never see man again. What all this mean, Mr. Puck?"

"Apparently, you saw one of the kidnappers, or someone associated with them, picking up the ransom. Did you get a good look at the man, Trinket?"

"Hard to say what man look like, Mr. Puck He had big hat pulled down on ears and shadow over eyes. Maybe he weigh 180 pounds. Had gray shirt, blue denim pants like mine, boots, spurs, and riding bay horse. Look like every man on street. Maybe I would follow him if he stay on road, but when turn into brush, I not follow."

"Maybe it is best you didn't, my friend," Puck stressed. "If he sensed anyone following, the girl's safety might be in jeopardy. The fact that those culprits got money for the girl's food, will buy us a little more time. This tells us that she is probably still alive. It also tells us that our hunch was right; we're in the right territory."

"Oh, Mr. Puck, I forget to tell you one thing," Trinket broke in as he reached into his pocket. "After rider go into bushes, I wait and then ride to tree. I find these beads hanging on tree. Maybe he leave them. These are Shoshoni beads, but beads made small for children. Maybe these beads belong to Papu Banta. I hope you are not angry I bring them."

"Not angry, Trinket, but I need to take them to the office of Indian Affairs. They are staying closely in touch with the family at Wind River Village. The family will know if the beads belong to their daughter." Puck ended by saying, "You are a good scout, Trinket. You are doing exactly what I had in mind when I sent you to patrol the boundary. So, put some of this Indian pottery in your parfletche for tomorrow in case someone stops you and questions your presence along the boundary. And be sure to always stay within the Reservation. If anyone does question you, tell them you are on your way to the next town to sell your pottery."

Trinket smiled and retorted, "Mr. Puck, you are very wise man. Maybe next day I take arrows to sell to white men for souvenirs. I need reason to be on trail every day, so no one question why I ride the white man's path so often."

The next day Three Toes was cleaning stalls, while Browning was busy in his office. As he carried a bucket of trash past the office door, he heard a strange sound—strange to him anyway. It sounded like "Tic, tic, tic-tic-tic, tic-tic, tic, tic." He had no idea what he was hearing, and he had a feeling that he would not be finding out any time soon. Going into the office was totally restricted for him. Anyway, the boss kept the door locked when he was out of the office.

About mid-morning, Engle happened by, this time turning into the blacksmith shop under the guise of needing some assistance from Browning. He actually did need some help straightening out a decorative metal escutcheon applied to his saddle. He had been catching his clothing on it getting on and off of his horse. This would be as good an excuse as any to chat a moment with Three Toes.

Engle introduced himself to Browning and showed him the bent escutcheon. Browning called Three Toes over to where they were standing.

"Toes, remove this saddle from the good man's horse and take it back to my work bench. And show the gentleman a place to sit. I'll be back there in a moment to correct his problem."

Engle followed Three Toes back to the work area chatting with him to avert any suspicion. When they were well out of earshot of the blacksmith, Engle spoke up. "Any new developments this morning, Three Toes?"

"No one has been in today except a few people picking up their horses," Three Toes explained. "Nothing strange about any of them. They seemed to be going about their business. Only said 'hello' and 'see ya later' to the owner. But there is something strange—strange to me, since I never hear it before. When boss is in his office, sometimes I hear strange sound, sound like 'tic, tic, tic.' I thought it was a watch, or how you say, 'clock,' but it not keep even sound. It goes 'tic, tic-tic-tic, tic.' It's no tapping of hammer, but I can no see inside office. The boss keeps the door locked."

"Well," Engle began in answer, "No telling what it may be. Don't see where it would be important to us. The man has all kinds of business to take care of. It could be that he actually has one of those Remington machines they call a typewriter, a machine put on the market about sixteen years ago by a gunsmith in Ilion, New York. Or the noise may be related to something he is doing for a customer. Who knows?"

Three Toes did not raise any more questions and ambled off to take care of other matters as Browning approached the workbench to repair the saddle.

"Been doing repair work like this for long?" Engle questioned.

"Well, off and on, from since I was a child, but in this shop for only about three years. Got a little more acquainted with it in Laramie where I lived before coming up here to Shoshoni. Like it more here in this out-of-the-way place! People take you for granted and don't pry into your business too much. That's the way I like it. Friends and acquaintances are nice to have if they know when to keep their distance. Don't have much trouble around here. How 'bout you? You new around here? Can't say that I've seen you before."

"Guess you might say I'm sorta like you, checking out a new place to settle down. Spent the last winter in Teton country. That's all the cold I want for awhile. This is a good time of year to look for something new."

"Hope you like it here. We could use more whites around here." The man hesitated and put a few tools away. "Well, here's your saddle, good as new—no charge, being that you are new around here. Count it as a welcoming gift."

"Thanks so much, Browning. Maybe I can leave my horse at your stable when I'm going to be in town awhile. At least I can drop by and say 'howdy' occasionally, if I plan to stay. I'll push some business your way. And thanks for hiring that Indian. He takes care of your customers quite well. Nice boy!"

With that, Engle saddled his horse and led him out of the barn, thinking to himself that now he had a perfect excuse to come around anytime he wanted—even with the secure feeling that he could now be seen chatting with Three Toes without appearing suspicious. Strategy was coming together quite well.

Sheriff John "Bullet" Larson, the much-revered lawman of the town of Shoshoni and regions thereabouts, had sent word to Puck to meet him at the telegraph office. Puck and Farley arrived there about opening time and Puck went inside while Farley stood sentry along the boardwalk.

"Puck," Larson spoke up, pointing to the telegraph operator, "Mr. Morley, here, tells me that he has had all the telegraph offices consulted within a hundred miles radius of Shoshoni, and the kidnapping demands have been coming from somewhere other than these offices. They are at a loss as to just where the point of origin is, unless the lines are being tapped somewhere between Shoshoni and Riverton. I sent word to Sheriff Bixley in Riverton to put a man on the line this morning heading this way, and told him we would get a man on the job heading that way from here. The men could meet halfway and compare their findings. Do you have a man you could put on the line?"

"Yes, sir, I do," Puck answered, going to the door to summon Farley. Farley hustled down the boardwalk and entered the office.

"Farley, Sheriff Larson needs a man to follow the telegraph lines out of Shoshoni leading to Riverton, checking them out for possible wire tapping. You'll meet another man headed this way somewhere down the line. Compare your findings and bring your report back to 'Bullet,' and then be back at camp tonight."

Mr. Morley handed Farley a pair of pole spikes he could attach to his boots in case he found something suspicious and needed to reach the wires for inspection. With that, Farley turned to leave, but not without jesting a bit over the name of the sheriff being "Bullet."

"Sheriff, you and I would make a pair," Farley quipped. "They call me 'Pistol Bill,' and you've been dubbed 'Bullet.' I guess you realize that one is not worth much without the other. Get it?"

"Yeah, I gotcha, Farley. Why couldn't we just have a plain name like Buster, or George, or Puck, or something like that?" He laughed and glanced Puck's way, wondering what affect those remarks would bring. Not waiting for a reaction, he quickly shook hands with Mr. Morley and motioned Puck toward the door. Farley led the way across the boardwalk, mounted his horse, and headed south, out of town.

Back at the camp, Benedict and Palmer were busy getting firewood for the campfire, when a stranger came riding through the brush.

"Howdy, my friends," he called out, and chanced riding a little closer before speaking again.

"Looks like you boys have a good setup here. I was just passing through on my way to Shoshoni and heard some wood choppin' going on over this way and reined in to check it out. Hope you don't mind the intrusion."

"Can't say that we mind at all," Whiskers spoke up. "We were just fixin' to have some lunch. You're welcome to join us if you're hungry. Don't mind sharing a little grub now and then. 'Sides, we could use some company. We're a little tired of looking at the rocks."

"Maybe it's none of my business, but you fellas seem to be a ways off the beaten trail. You trappin' for varmint hides or something?"

"No, we're looking for those k—" Whiskers interrupted Palmer, breaking in excitedly. "What Palmer, here, was trying to say is that we're looking for those cattle that were stolen from the Billingsley spread a week ago. We settled down here for a spell to pan for a little gold in the creek and to rest our bones. You didn't see any cattle being driven this way did you?"

"No, haven't seen any cattle. And I sure wouldn't be any use to you panning for gold. Never found a nugget in my life. Sounds like work to me, and that's just what I don't like doin'."

"What do you do for a living?" Palmer spoke up.

"Well, I'd like to tell you that I rob trains, but the train doesn't come through these parts, so I just do a few odd jobs when I need a little money and mostly keep roamin' about the territory. I've helped out the blacksmith in Shoshoni a few times. In fact that's where I'm headin' now to see if I can pick up a little work."

The men finished the last few morsels of lunch and drank their coffee in leisure, not getting much out of their conversation. Soon enough the stranger gestured that he needed to be getting on down the trail and rose to mount his horse. As he turned to mount, Whiskers and Palmer noticed the grime on the seat of his britches—black, somewhat dusty, somewhat oily substance caked on his britches. They rose to see the same grimy look on his otherwise nice looking saddle.

"Say, mister," Whiskers engaged the man, "You ever work in a coal mine in your odd job practice?"

"The name's Wortham," the man bolted back, as if Whiskers had hit a sore spot. "And, no, I hain't never taken on a coal mining job. Why do you ask?"

"No reason, except it looks like you've been sitting in a coal bin or something."

"Yeah, well I hate standing, so I'll sit almost anywhere. No telling where I got this stain. Oh well, it'll clean up with a little kerosene and soap. Didn't know it was so noticeable."

"Okay, Wortham, no offense. Keep your chin up," Whiskers rejoined. "Maybe our paths will cross again sometime. Have a good ride into Shoshoni!"

The man gathered his composure, thanked the men for his lunch, mounted his horse, and rode off in the same direction as he had come into camp.

Along the eastern boundary of the Reservation, Trinket moved briskly along the trail, hoping to see something that might weigh on the kidnapping case. As he rounded a bend in the trail, he came upon a rider moving rather slowly. He reined up near enough to the rider to see that his horse was giving in to his left hind leg. The horse, a bay, matched the identity of the one the kidnapper was riding the day Papu Banta was taken. For a moment, Trinket was unsure about confronting the stranger, except this man was small in comparison to the one described by the Indian boys. He decided to chance a contact, but cautiously and unassumingly.

"Say, mister," Trinket called out, "I notice you movin' easy. Your horse walks on troubled foot." As he finished speaking, he noticed that the hoof print on the ground looked exactly like that described by Three Toes in his drawing on the mining depot floor.

"You got that right, scout," the man rejoined. "I bought the horse cheap, thinking I could correct the hoof. Bought the animal from a big man in Riverton this morning. I'm heading to Shoshoni to get a special shoe made, hoping it will solve the horse's problem. I traded my own horse and received a little cash to boot. I've been so long on this trail now, that I think I may have made a mistake. This horse may not make it to Shoshoni."

"What kind of horse did you have, mister?"

"I had a big black and white paint. A big man by the name of Trammel bought the horse from me. Said he was tired of doctoring this one's foot. I needed a little extra cash and thought I could mend this horse, so—stupid me—I proceeded to trade. Now I wish I had my horse back."

"I'm so sorry for your bad luck, mister, but if you like, I think I can fix your horse's foot good enough to get to Shoshoni."

"What can you do, scout?"

"I show you."

Trinket dismounted and reached into his *parfletche* for some items. He picked up a small carving knife he had made of flint and proceeded to cut away at a green tree limb about the circumference of the horse's hoof. When he was through carving, he had shaped an object almost like that of a horse shoe but with a shallow, flat pan at the heart of the object. When he placed it on the horse's hoof for measurement, he marked the spot where he wanted a concave cup that would align with the frog of the hoof. He removed the object and finished carving it and then took a sharp pointed trinket from his parfleche with which he drilled holes around the perimeter large enough to accept some leather lace for binding the piece over the horse's already existing shoe and around the hoof. He then took a very soft piece of leather to use as slight padding in the concave cup that he had specially designed and then strapped the "boot" onto the horse's hoof, tying the lace tightly enough around the upper part of the hoof so that it could not slip off the foot. He took the reins and walked the horse around, and surprisingly—or maybe from Trinket's view, not surprising at all—the horse walked on it without giving in to his lame foot. He then encouraged the stranger to mount the horse to see if the added weight would change matters. The man pulled himself into the saddle and urged the horse forward slowly. The horse walked almost sprightly and moved along without the slightest limp.

"My Indian friend," the man called back to Trinket, "You are a miracle worker. You deserve a medal." As he wheeled his horse about, he reached into his pocket and pulled out a crucifix with a gold chain on it and handed it to Trinket. "Take this," he urged, "for being so helpful. You have saved my day. Hope to see you again soon." With that, he urged his horse forward, moving at a faster pace, leaving the Indian standing in the trail.

The man now out of sight, Trinket whirled his horse about and headed for Riverton to get with Lively and to let him know about the lame horse having been sold by someone named Trammel.

Briley Wortham rode into the blacksmith shop late in the afternoon and caught Browning coming out of his office. The two men greeted, and Wortham sat down to chat awhile. Browning kept looking at the seated man and kept shaking his head disagreeably. It wasn't the man that concerned him but where he had chosen to sit.

"Wortham," he finally exclaimed, when he could take no more, "get off that coal box. Can't you find a better place to sit? You attach your rear to that box every time you come in here. Can't you see what you're doing to your clothes? I thought you were smarter than that."

"Okay boss. I don't mean anything by it. I like to sit, and I don't much mind where, but I'll get a chair." He reached around the corner of the stall and picked up a farrier's stool and perched himself on it, folding his gangly knees up practically under his chin.

"Say, when did you get your Indian help?" Three Toes was

cleaning out the next stall, being as inconspicuous as cleaning would permit, but hoping he might overhear something of importance.

"Oh, he wandered in here a few days ago needing a job, so I hired him. He stays at it too. So, tell me, Wortham, what's new?"

"Well, I was back down at the triangle again last night. Don't know how much longer I can keep traveling back and forth."

"Hang on a minute, Wortham," Browning interrupted. "A rider just entered the barn. Better check out his needs."

The blacksmith hustled over to what he hoped would be another customer.

"Howdy, mister. What can I do for you?"

The man dismounted, pointing to the horse's back hoof.

"Bought this horse from a man in Riverton this morning. Knew the horse had a bad hoof, but the man said you could probably devise a shoe to help correct the problem. I took a chance that you could. You are Browning, aren't you?"

"That's right," Browning rejoined, "and I know that horse. Came from a man by the name of Trammel, didn't it?"

"Yeah, how'd you know?"

"Well, I know Trammel, and he's been riding that horse in here for some time now. Never took the time to let me work on the foot though. Maybe I can give it some attention now. Put the horse in the stall over there and I'll see what I can do, but I'm not promising a whole lot."

"I'd be much obliged if you can get even a few months out of the hoof, until I've had time to get back on my feet financially and look around for another horse. I wouldn't be here now if it hadn't been for an Indian along the way who devised the plate that's strapped to the horse's hoof now. You might check it out as a pattern for something you might make for the foot. Well, have at it. I'll be back in late tomorrow to check with you."

Upon Browning's summon, Three Toes hustled over to where the two men stood with the horse and took the mount to a stall part way down the line. He untied the straps on the hoof and removed the wooden plate and soft leather pad. He looked curiously at the piece of work and knew instantly that the Indian that had placed it there was none other than Trinket himself. That information he needed to keep under wrap, but he was sure the horse was the one once owned by the kidnapper. The hoof print was the exact replica of the one he had seen at the Indian reunion shelter that day in the rain. This would be tremendous information for Farley and Puck.

Going about his business, Three Toes now became eager to see Engle come by to check on him. Unless he missed his guess, a lot of things were going to happen fast, now that the getaway horse had been found. And more than that, who was this fellow Wortham, who came in with blackened britches? One of the kidnappers had on blackened britches and was tall and lean like Wortham. Three Toes pondered what was to come of these latest findings seemingly connected to the missing Indian girl.

CHAPTER 10
THE SWITCH

In Riverton, Lively was having a drink in the local saloon, when a ruckus broke out in the back corner of the room. An unruly cowboy was tugging at the arm of one of the showgirls.

"Leave me alone," the barmaid wailed. "I said, no! Now get away from me! Ouch! You're hurting my arm! Turn me loose!"

The cowpoke did not stop, pulling more determined than ever, until the lady's blouse was slipping off her shoulder, the tousles in her hair becoming unburdened of their ribbons and falling loosely over one eye. Everyone in the bar watched the incident without moving.

Lively watched momentarily, too, then he moved. Like a bull crashing through a paper-thin fence, Lively broke through the maze of tables, knocking some of the chairs in his path to the floor, making his way quickly to the damsel in distress. He clutched the grappler around the shoulder and spun him around.

"Say, mister," he accentuated, "the lady asked you to leave her alone. Can't you hear?"

The lady fell back against the wall as the man handler loosed the hold on her arm. Turning to Lively, with the brush of his arm to ward off his assailant, he shouted, "Who are you, her guardian? I'd say mind your own business."

"Touch her again," retorted Lively, "and I'll make it my business!"

At that, the man reached behind him and gently touched the damsel who was brushing by the two to get out of the way.

"You ought not to have done that," countered Lively, as he placed a well-directed cluster of knuckles upwards and under the scoundrel's chin. The cowpoke buckled, momentarily, then retaliated with a blow to Lively's midsection. In the clutch, the two wrestled across the tables, spilling drinks and breaking glass in the melee. Bar patrons scurried to safety, out of the path of the contention. The two were on the floor, and then up again, stretched across a table in an eager death-hold, crashing more drinks and glasses to the floor, frolicking to the right and to the left, one blow following another. Lively, to his feet again, managed to plaster the man's cheekbone with a well-placed knuckle-buster. With one last surge, the cowpoke riveted Lively's left eye with a similar bruising hit, and then turned and headed for the door. Lively followed to show his manly fervor, but only daintily, happy that the fracas was over for now. He then plopped down into a nearby chair that just happened to still be standing. Already his eye was swelling to plum-sized proportion and taking on a bit of its purplish color, as well.

The saloon princess, having gotten herself intact, hurried to Lively's side with a damp cloth, along with a precious few ice chips, sacrificed by a grateful bartender.

Outside, the villain mounted his horse and was riding away just as Trinket rode up to the saloon to find Lively. The mad dash away from the hitching post by the rider especially caught Trinket's eye when he saw that the horse the man was riding was a big black and white paint. Just as Trinket got to the swinging doors to enter the saloon, Lively came barreling through them holding a cloth wrap on his eye.

"Man, Trinket," Lively spoke up, "It's good to see you, but where were you when I really needed you?"

"What's goin' on, Lively? What's that patch? Did man who just rode off like beaten coyote have sump'n to do with this?"

"Yeah, he had everything to do with it, and I don't even know the man."

"Well, Trinket think he know the man." His English was breaking up again. "That man is Trammel, the big man that ride the horse with bad foot, when Papu Banta was taken."

"And how do you know this?" Lively countered.

"Because I meet man on trail who bought bad horse in trade for a big paint horse like *cayuse* man just rode away on. He told me man's name was Trammel."

Just then, the bartender exited the saloon to check on Lively.

"Say Calvin," Lively questioned, "Do you know the scoundrel that started all this fuss in there?"

"Yeah, I know him. The whole town knows him. He's Pete Trammel, a sort of ne'er-do-well who has no business but that of someone else. He comes and goes. Doesn't stay around here much, just long enough to get everyone's dander up. Hope you didn't get too scraped about in there."

"Oh, I'll be okay. But I sure need to learn more about that Trammel fellow."

Trinket went to the hitching rail and picked up the reins of the horses, leading Lively's horse over to him. He looked back over his shoulder in an easterly direction to see if the rider was gone for sure.

"Well, Trinket, we've learned some things today. We better get on back to camp and relay our findings to Puck and the others." Lively spoke matter-of-factly as he eased up on his horse, grimacing with the slightest bend of his joints. Every muscle quivered. Every bone ached. His eye, by now the size of a small hen egg, was swollen shut completely and turning black with traces of blue. The sheen looked menacing.

The two detectives—rifleman and scout—headed north toward their rendezvous.

Late in the evening, the camp began receiving the returning trackers. Engle and Farley had met along the way, returning from Shoshoni. Puck arrived just shortly after Lively and Trinket. Whiskers and Palmer had dinner hot and ready to eat, and the men were famished after a long, but eventful, day.

As they ate, each man accounted for his daily movements, and Puck took in every detail with unusual interest. Farley and Engle really had nothing to report. Engle had not been able to talk with Three Toes during the day and nothing new had come his way. Farley had left Puck at the telegraph office to check out a lead on a lame horse west of Shoshoni, but nothing came of it, so he dropped down south and conveniently met up with Engle on his way to the camp.

Trinket and Lively had the surprise of the day for the group, laying out before them news of the discovery of the lame horse and subsequently its original owner in Pete Trammel. Of course, this brought up all kinds of snickering questions and jibes about Lively's now purple goose egg above his left cheek. They had to know all the details about his fisticuffs with the apparent kidnapping miscreant called Trammel.

When the laughter died down, Jed Palmer told of the stranger who happened into camp that day. They led Puck to believe that the man was a rambler, and worked only when needing a little change to buy food and the like. Yet, they felt that they might have struck gold after all, since that is what they had told the stranger they were looking for that morning. But this gold was more like black gold, coal dust or something similar blanketing the rear end of the stranger's pants.

Whiskers spoke up to add, "The man's name was Wortham. He told us he had connections with Browning in Shoshoni as a periodic hire-on to pick up a little change. When he left, Palmer and I began to think he might be one of the kidnappers, due to the dirty britches and the fact that he was long and lean, the precise description given to us by the Indian boys at Wind River Village. He was headed toward the stables when he left."

Puck registered all the details, and then spoke up, as he pulled a paper from his vest pocket. "I picked up this telegram at the telegraph office this afternoon after I left Farley. Looks as if we have some urgent detective work to be done, as the sound of this telegram has 'finality' written all over it. Let me read it to you." Puck read the following:

> *June 18*   *Stop Three weeks have passed and no ransom has been issued Stop The end of the week is our final deadline Stop Be ready to put money on the stage to Riverton when we inform you of the day, or else Stop We mean business this time Stop.*

Puck folded the paper and returned it to his vest pocket, hesitated in thought for a moment, and then addressed the group.

"Men, I think the culprits are dead serious this time. We are running out of time. We only have a few days to solve this mystery or the girl is in trouble. What I think we have to—"

Puck was interrupted by a noise coming from the edge of camp. He stopped abruptly and hushed the men into silence. Then he whispered, "Farley, take the left ravine coming in. Palmer, ease around to the right and overlook the trail opening into camp. Whiskers, make a little noise with the pots and pans. The rest of you mill around easy, but keep alert. I'll stir the campfire and keep my holster primed for action."

The noise did not stop but kept coming. Then a faint whistle sounded above the noise of a horse blowing his nostrils. One of the camp horses nickered lowly in response. Sandy hee-hawed to alert everyone. Whiskers made a little more noise to convey a busy camp.

Suddenly, a voice broke the night air, "Okay, drop off your mount," shouted Palmer. "Hurry, or you're a dead man!" he repeated. Before either Palmer or the rider broke into the opening, Palmer could be heard again. "Aw hell, Three Toes, don't you know better'n to sneak up on a night camp. What are you doing here anyway?" The next words were, "As you were men, I've caught our stalker!" Palmer and Three toes entered the camp leading the Indian pony, and Farley came in on their heels.

"Gentlemen, Puck," Three Toes spoke up guiltily. "I'm sorry if I startled the camp. I whistled so Trinket would catch the message."

Trinket had been busy quieting the horses and didn't hear the whistle.

"Anyway, men," he went on, "Three Toes have some very important things to tell you and not want it wait 'til tomorrow. Engle don't get by to see me today, so I ask Mr. Boss if I could go away for a night just to get away from the place of working. He think I was meaning to go get drunk, but he let me go anyway. Said I could have 'til noon tomorrow. I think he is not suspicious of me. No one followed me out. I make sure of that."

Puck handed Three Toes a plate of food and a cup of java and urged him to sit down and eat and share his findings. Between bites of food and sips of coffee, Three Toes told his story of the day. "Today, first thing that happen is tall man come ridin' in about mid-afternoon. He have dirty britches black in the seat and talk to my boss like they old friends. He have been sitting on the coal bin, not only this time but also every time he come to the stables, the boss say. Then, a rider come in ridin' the lame horse with wooden block shoe on hoof. I look at it good and know it have been placed there by Trinket. No too many Indians know this trick to help sore foot—

at least for a while. This man buy horse from man in Riverton and say Browning will make horse good. He tell Browning man in Riverton recommend him to the stables. Browning tell man that he knew this horse, and that he had try to get owner to take time for get horse some attention. Then, two hours before dark, guess who come ridin' into stables but big man from Riverton, ridin' black and white paint. The boss call him Trammel a few times and Pete a few times Maybe he is Trammel Pete or Pete Trammel. The big man also know the tall man and call him Briley. The boss call him Wortham. Now, my boss seems good man, so I no understand why he pow-wows so much with two men like these two."

Three Toes caught his breath momentarily as he finished his meal and took the last sip of coffee.

"Another thing happen earlier in morning. When the boss opened his office to go in, I was carrying a load of pickets to the back fence. As I pass by the open door, I see a suit of Cavalry clothes and boots hanging on peg. Don't know if that means anything, but he must have been in army at one time in his life. When I come back by the office, door was closed and I hear that strange noise coming from inside again—that *tic, tic-tic, tic-tic-tic, tic*. Nothing else happened until the Wortham fellow come into stables. I guess that's about all I know. What do you think, Puck? This stuff any good to help us?"

"You can count on it, Three Toes," Puck responded. "I think we have found at least some of our men, but how we're going to keep tabs on them is the question. Then we have to prove they are involved with the kidnapping, and somehow corner them without jeopardizing the safety of the girl—and finding her, as well. We may have most of our puzzle in place, but the picture is not clear yet. I'm going to think through all this overnight and come up with our next move for tomorrow. Except for you, Three Toes, the others will have a different plan than usual for tomorrow and the rest of the week. You need to get back to the stables before noon tomorrow, and just as a cover for your night's absence, take one of the empty whisky bottles out of the chuck wagon, and act a little tipsy tomorrow when you enter the stables, but not drunk at all, or the boss might fire you. Let the bottle fall out of your pocket, which will leave no uncertainty in his mind as to where you spent the night. Tell him you are ready to go to work, and work as hard as you usually do. That will show him that you were at least responsible after your supposed night out on the town. Okay, men, let's get some shuteye. We have some important business tomorrow."

The moon was high, lighting the surrounding cedars and sparkling against the spring seeps trickling from the ledge-rock above. The little brook, meandering at the foot of the cliffs, a stone's throw from the camp's clearing, made its pleasant music as it gurgled over the rocky stream bed. Crickets fiddled to one another looking for love in the night, while the cool breeze wafted through the brush and across the slumbering encampment.

That is, everyone slept except one. Puck lay awake musing over the glut of evidence uncovered during the day, seemingly implicating the two men who had ridden into the Shoshoni stable. A new telegram had arrived also, but from where? Other telegraph offices had received the same message according to Mr. Morley, yet he still had been unable to trace its origin. Nothing had been found on the telegraph lines themselves, according to Farley who rode the length of them. Had they been tapped, he would not have missed it—well, more than likely he would not have missed it. Browning also seemed too good a man to have any connection with men like

Trammel and Wortham. Both the sheriff and the stage driver know Browning quite well. They hold him in high honor. Once, when they thought they wanted a mayor in Shoshoni, the two backed Browning for the seat, before the idea fizzled with the town folk.

He could be an honorable man, and yet, according to Three Toes, Browning seems a little secretive, especially around his office. Army clothes hanging inside. What could that mean, if anything? The busy sounds of the typewriter heard by Three Toes earlier in the morning don't mount up to much. A man has to stay on top of his business and his bill deliveries. Still again, with the telegram coming in today, one would almost entertain the thought that Browning might be playing on a telegraph sender rather than a typewriter, but no, Browning has been a blacksmith and farrier most of his life. Where would he learn the intricacies of telegraphy? Then irked at his own befuddled state, Puck rolled over to pass it off in sleep. Suddenly, startled by his own line of questioning, his eyes opened, gleaming in the light filtering through the cracks of the log cabin. "Puck," he said aloud to himself, "you are a fool! Where does *anybody* learn telegraphy? In the Army, of course! Do those Army duds hanging in Browning's office tell you anything now? Well, sure enough they do, don't ya see?" Puck continued to berate his own intelligence, or lack thereof, then he concluded, "It's worth checking into, by all means!"

In an instant, Puck pulled himself out of the sack and slipped into his trousers and boots, then pulled his shirt around his shoulders and donned his hat. He eased through the sleeping cabin of men until he came to Farley. Gently he nudged Farley, not enough to startle him. Then again, he pushed gently at Farley's foot, putting pressure on it enough to rouse him. "Hey, Farley," he whispered! "Farley, wake up!"

Farley turned in his sleep and started to settle down again when

Puck tapped him on his forehead. He jerked and opened his eyes at the intrusion, and Puck quickly settled him down.

"It's Puck, Farley. Wake up! I need your help."

Farley eased up, looking around at the other sleeping trail grinders. "What's up, Puck?" he questioned.

"Farley, I've got to go back into Shoshoni tonight."

"Tonight!" Farley bolted.

"Shhh," Puck cautioned with a finger across his lips. "Not so loud. You'll wake the camp. Yeah, I need to go tonight, but I need to ask you something. When you rode out the telegraph lines the other day, where did you start your inspection?"

"Right at the edge of town, Puck. I saw no reason to trace them back to the telegraph office the distance is so short. Why?"

"I'm not sure, Farley, just a hunch. Go back to sleep. I'll return by breakfast in the morning. Let Whiskers and the others know where I've gone when you get up."

Puck eased his gear off the chuck wagon tongue and went for his horse. He led the horse quietly to the edge of camp, half-carrying and half-dragging his gear. Taking very little time to saddle his horse, he was soon mounted and easing off toward Shoshoni. Winding down the moonlit trail, he urged his animal along with somewhat of a dispatch, as he had some urgent business to take care of before first light.

Entering Shoshoni some two hours later, Puck headed straight for Mr. Morley's house. He hated to wake the telegraph operator, but time was of the essence. Morley, with tasseled hair, barefooted, scratching his head, and yawning, came to the door to see who was banging on it in the middle of the night. When he opened the door, he was surprised to see Puck.

"What's up Puck," he questioned curiously.

"Need to talk with you, Morley. I know it's late, but it can't wait until morning. I may need your help tonight."

"Come on in and sit down," Morley motioned. The two men seated themselves in the vestibule, and Puck began his questioning.

"Morley, you know Browning pretty well. Do you know anything about him ever being in the Cavalry?"

"No, can't say that I've ever heard."

"Where would the army keep records where we might get some information on Browning?"

"We could probably contact Colonel Meech at Fort Washakie. I'm sure they keep some records there."

"Can we get a telegram to Meech tonight?"

"Sure. We can try anyway. Let me get my boots on. I'm curious though. What difference does it make whether or not Browning has been in the Army?"

"I'll tell you," Puck responded. "Where did you first learn telegraphy? In the Army, right?"

"Yeah, and then I took up a course in it."

"Well, I may be wrong, but I think Browning may have telegraph equipment in his office at the stables. If so, he may be mixed up with our kidnapping situation. That may be the source of our ransom demands. When we finish with sending a telegram tonight, I'm going to check out the alleyway behind his place. The lines pass right by the blacksmith facility on its way out of town."

"You're right, Puck. In fact, when the lines were being erected, Browning let the linesmen place a pole at the corner of his shop. If he knows anything about telegraphy, he could easily tap into the system at that point."

The two men left immediately for the telegraph office and entered but did not turn on the lights. Back in the equipment room, Morley lit a lantern and pulled down the shades. Then he went to his work desk, got out his codebook and began tapping out a message to Colonel Meech. Morley had already informed his wife that he might spend the night in his office. This way he could wait for any answer that might be returned.

"Morley," Puck spoke up, "I'm going to leave it with you for awhile and go down the alley to check out my suspicion. I'll be back later."

Puck went out the back door into the alleyway and began to ease down the conglomeration of wagon wheels, implements, and otherwise profusion of junk that lined the rear walls of the buildings. He had to almost hug the walls in order to escape being detected in the moonlight, if anyone should happen to be up milling about at such an hour.

By the time he had reached the blacksmith shop and stables, he had alerted only one dog and kicked over a bucket that wakened a town drunk sleeping in the shadows of one of the buildings. The drunk mumbled something and then went back to sleep. Puck proceeded cautiously, looking to the telegraph lines overhead, hoping to detect some unusual structure. He finally came to the post at the corner of the shop mentioned by Morley. At first, nothing appeared amiss. Then, upon second inspection, Puck saw a small makeshift canister of some type protruding under the cross-member of the post, with a very small entanglement of wires leading to the telegraph lines. Were it not for the moonlight reflecting off the metal, nothing would have been detected. Even with that, the canister and wire were not that conspicuous. Anyone not looking for them would have missed them altogether. Then, below the canister, a series of wires were stretched tightly against the pole between it and the shop. Puck followed the length of them with his eyes until he saw that they ended right at the base of the pole and attached to another makeshift cartridge of some design—small and indiscriminate, except for two tiny metal posts capped with two brass nuts.

What seemed strange was that no wires were entering the building itself. However, upon further close inspection, Puck found two small holes in the wall of the building cased with porcelain grommets. Now he knew that anyone could easily push two strands of wire through the openings, attach them to the screws on the adapter, and be fully tapped into the telegraph system. Gratefully finding what he anticipated finding, this time moving along in the moonlight away from the buildings, he turned and eased his way back down the alley toward the telegraph office. Luckily, he had left the alley undisturbed as he entered the back door of the telegraph office.

"I've been waiting for you, Puck." Morley motioned. Here's what I found out from Colonel Meech. He didn't need to search the files for Browning's records. He knew him well. Said he was a well-liked officer by all his subordinates. Knew horses inside out, and always shoed his own mount. Even so, I hate to tell you, this Browning is not our man."

"How's that?" Puck questioned.

"Puck, Colonel Meech went to Browning's funeral about two years ago!"

"Well, that's out then," Puck resigned.

"Not so fast, Puck," Morley added. "Meech said he knew of a man who was sent to the penitentiary in Laramie for impersonating an officer, stopping a stage on its way to Rock Springs, robbing it of its payroll for the coal miners there, and taking all the passenger's valuables as well. It turned out that the officer that he was impersonating was Lambert Browning."

"Well, how does that help us? I had placed Browning in the Army in my mind only because he could have learned telegraphy there."

"Puck," Morley broke in, "Guess where else one can learn telegraphy?"

"I give up. Where?"

"The penitentiary teaches telegraphy, among other trades, to any inmate who wants to learn a vocation while serving his time."

"Then, we need to find out about our friend, Browning," Puck concluded. "If we only had a likeness of the man, we could go to Laramie with it. No. Guess not. Where would we get a picture of the man? And besides, Laramie is a four to five day journey round trip. Can't chance the loss of time."

"Wait a minute, Puck," Morley interrupted. "When Browning was urged to run for mayor, along with some of the other potential board members, we had tins made of everyone to make posters for the occasion. I have the tin in a drawer somewhere around here."

"We would still have to get the tin to Laramie," Puck interjected.

"Well, guess what again Puck? It just so happens that a special stage is leaving at daybreak to take a prisoner to be incarcerated in the prison at Laramie. Two soldiers are riding shotgun. Traveling hard, the stage will make it there in two days. We can get a message to the Warden through the soldiers and make the tin available to him. He can telegraph his reply to us. So, if the officials there can hustle up with their search in the records, we would only lose two days at most, or possibly two and a half if the stage is slower than expected."

"Its worth a try, Morley. But can you find the likeness tonight?"

"It may take us awhile, but we can start looking."

Three hours before daylight, the men found the package of tins and hurriedly separated the slates to find the one depicting Browning. They polished it to enhance the image and then wrapped it in a clean piece of flannel material. Morley sent Puck on his way back to camp, assuring him that the tin would be in the hands of the soldiers at daybreak, when the stage struck a beeline for Laramie.

Puck rode into camp as light began to break in the east. The moon had waned somewhat earlier and travel had become a little difficult in the dark. The tired rider had depended on his horse to detect the now well-traveled trail, so daylight was a welcomed reverie to the end of a hard night.

The smell of breakfast cooking on the open fire perked up both horse and rider as the two rode into camp. The camp hands, eager to know what Puck had learned in Shoshoni, greeted them.

Whiskers handed Puck a cup of coffee and Trinket led Puck's mount over to where the other animals were having their morning feeding of oats and barley. As the men ate, Puck explained what he had discovered about the telegraph lines leading to the base of the pole at the corner of Browning's stable. Addressing Three Toes, he said, "My friend, you are working for one of the kidnappers, I'm quite sure. Time will tell. If so, our next task will be to set a trap for flushing out the villains. As careful as we will have to be to keep matters from turning sour, I fear a wrong play that could jeopardize the safety of the little Indian girl. Time is now short, and we don't want to make any mistakes, if we can help it."

Puck told the men about the Army officer known as Lambert Browning, the fact of his death a few years ago, and that the blacksmith may be using the name to conceal his real identity. He further informed the men about the impending inquiry with the prison in Laramie, thinking that Browning may have served time there. Then, he addressed the group as to plans for the week.

"Trinket," Puck spoke up, "Go back along the trail as you have been doing. One of the kidnappers will have to be returning to take care of the girl's needs. More than likely, it will be the man riding the paint horse. See if you can trail him at a distance. It may lead you to the place where they are holding the girl. Take some food and a bedroll with you. You'll have to camp somewhere off the trail at night."

Turning to Three Toes, Puck continued, "Three Toes, get back to the shop, and without Browning seeing you, work your way quietly through the hay loft on the upper floor. Go to the corner of the barn where the telegraph pole is stationed and see how you might get to the wires going down the pole from their connections on the lines above. Put these cutters in your parfletche. You'll need them to cut the wires when you get the proper signal from Engle.

"Engle, I'll inform the sheriff that you will be bunking in his extra bed at night. You'll be receiving word from the telegraph operator when the last message has come in from the kidnappers as to where and when the ransom package is expected. You'll then take your horse to the stable and leave it there to be bedded and fed. This will be the signal for Three Toes to get to the wires on the pole and cut them. Three Toes, the wires need to be cut high on the pole in such a way that they can't be detected. We are doing all this so that when the message comes over the wires from the prison at Laramie regarding Browning's past, he won't be able to receive it. But we do need to get the final word from Browning before the wires are cut. I won't go into it here, but I have a plan that I think will cause Browning to place his telegram early. Leave that part to me.

"Palmer, because you have seen Briley Wortham and can recognize him, I'm sending you into town, for the time being, and letting Lively remain here with Whiskers. Get a room in the hotel across the street from the stables and keep a surveillance of people coming and going. Farley will relieve you for the night watch and you can come to the telegraph office to bunk in the back room. If you see Wortham leave the stables during your watch, get to your horse and follow him, but at a distance, so he doesn't suspect anything.

"Farley, you will shadow my moves as usual, but for now you will be staying at the telegraph office awaiting word from Laramie. I'll be there, too, but I plan to get some sleep in Morley's back room.

"Whiskers, you and Lively should pack up everything and move the wagon into Shoshoni. You can camp near the holding pens at the edge of town and pay the attendant for a place in the bunkhouse to stay the night. Lively, since you might be recognized by Trammel, stay by the wagon. You need to nurse your swollen eye, anyway. Whiskers, you can go into town occasionally and frequent the saloon in case Farley or I need to find you. If anyone—"

Puck hesitated momentarily and viewed the beautiful surroundings that had served as home base for the past two weeks. The little creek sparkled in the early light, rippling over polished stone and washed sand. The stock nibbled contentedly at tufts of plush grass growing in the openings around the verdant cedars rocking gently in the cool morning breeze. Light on the horizon symbolized the continuation of life after the sedentary but refreshing effects of night. Birds flitted among the low-lying brush, some stopping long enough to greet the morning light with familiar song. With this kind of beauty and potential available, it seemed incorrigible to Puck that kidnappings and crimes of any sort could prevail, and that upstanding citizens had to put up with such scourge or dare to put it down. Interrupted by the silence around him and the men awaiting his next word, Puck could hear duty calling once again.

The mesmerizing spell now broken, Puck continued, "As I was saying, if anyone has a significant message to get to me, and you can't find me, take it to Sheriff Larson. We'll leave at intervals after breakfast so as not to be noticed as a group. Trinket, you can go at any time. Three Toes, you should be the first heading back to Shoshoni. The rest of us can pick a time about twenty minutes apart. Any questions?"

Shoshoni was bustling when the men arrived in town. Puck headed for the back room of the telegraph office to get some shuteye. He met Morley coming out of the room from having caught a few winks after getting the tins to the stage office. The soldier escorts knew exactly how to handle the requested secrecy of the mission, and the stage was already on its way to Laramie.

For at least a day, Puck could do nothing about establishing contact with Browning. Although he knew exactly how he intended to weasel another telegram out of Browning regarding the time and place of the ransom pickup, it was too early to do so. On the second day, when the stage was nearer Laramie, he would slip a joker in the deck that would force Browning's hand.

For all intents and purposes, the day went uneventful. The men had all established their lookouts and, as far as Puck knew, were carrying out his instructions. Morley left his assistant handling the telegraph office, while he went to check on things at home. Puck faded off into dreamland, knowing that the next several days would demand all the strength he could muster. Palmer, stationed at the hotel, was bored to tears watching the street below, seeing nothing but buggies come and go and barristers ducking in and out of the little shops along the boardwalk. Whiskers had put away too many drinks already in his attempt to case the saloon, hoping to hear some tidbit of information that might unintentionally slip off the tongue of some mischief-maker associated with the kidnappers. Nothing! The place was dead. No one was talking. Lively, sequestered back at the holding pens at the edge of town, cursed his uninspiring lot of having to nurse a swollen eye.

Three Toes kept busy, duty-bound to stay on good terms with the mystifying man who had hired him and had so kindly kept him on, in spite of the fact that he was an Indian. And who knows, maybe his boss was in fact caught up in the sinister act of kidnapping one of his own Shoshoni people. His distrust was growing but not his impatience. Patience was part of being full-blood Indian unless pushed to the limits, when no Indian could remain unruffled. Farley was off with the sheriff somewhere hoping that any moment something would break in the case and he could get on with the showdown. For everyone under the governor's special mandate, time seemed to press on to no real purpose.

When the sun came up the next morning, trouble was brewing halfway between Fort Washakie and Riverton. A delegation of Shoshonis, having become impatient with the progress being made toward finding Papu Banta, had left Wind River Village before dawn and was bent on entering the case.

A military courier, who was returning from Riverton, came across the delegation and noted that rather than their proceeding single file, the usual formation for travel, they were advancing in groups of six or seven. He counted twenty-one in all. In his mind, this meant trouble. Being away from the village in such numbers required military escorts, but none were present.

Pulling alongside the delegation, the rider warily addressed one of the braves, "My good man, why are your people on the move?"

The brave did not answer.

"I am a friend of the Shoshonis, my good man. Why won't you answer me?"

The brave turned abruptly and spoke. "I am not your good man, and you are not my good man. My people are busy. You must not disturb our concentration. Go!"

The brave tweaked his horse away from the rider and rode swiftly to the front of the commission never looking back.

The courier reined up his horse and let the caravan parade by him. When the group had passed, he spurred his horse and hightailed it toward Fort Washakie as fast as his horse would permit. Colonel Meech would need to know about this irregular state of affairs.

The caravan picked up its pace, now moving by twos along the trail, with not a little fearfulness flushing the faces of occasional white passersby. Other Indians linked up momentarily with the delegation to find out its intent but were soon waved away by braves flanking the deputation.

Just before noon, the delegation entered Riverton and stopped in front of the sheriff's office. Sheriff Bixley came out to greet them but was surprised to see such a band unattended by a military man.

"Are you Sheriff Mr. Bixley?" the apparent leader spoke up.

"Yes, I'm Sheriff Bixley. What can I do for you?"

"I am Broken Heel of the Shoshonis, uncle to Papu Banta. Many suns have come and gone since she was kidnapped. We are unsettled in spirit that nothing has been done to bring her back to her family. We have been patient, yet no good word has been returned to us. Mr. Puckett has not kept us informed about our Papu. We have come to find her and the men who took her from our village."

"Broken Heel, listen to me," Bixley spoke up. "You are right that many days have passed since the little Indian girl was taken from you, but you are wrong that nothing has been done to find her. I have been in touch with the sheriff at Shoshoni, who has direct contact with Mr. Puckett. They are on the verge of a break-through in the case, and they think they know who the kidnappers are, but if you come out here hoping to force their hand, you will only muddy the waters. You may even put the safety of your niece in jeopardy. Don't you see?"

"What I see is that I don't see. I don't see the little girl who is loved by our tribe. I don't see Mr. Puckett telling us what we want to hear. I don't see two white renegades brought to justice. What I don't see is all that I see."

"Look, Broken Heel, I can understand your great concern for the life of your little niece, but you must turn back and wait for things to develop, or you will be sure to lose her. At all costs, you must be sensible and give Puck and his men the benefit of the doubt. I know for a fact that he is almost ready to spring the trap on those 'wolves' that took your child. Please give it a little more time. Don't put me on the spot to have to detain you. Can't you and her parents be patient for a little while longer?"

"Broken Heel is the one who is impatient," the Indian reacted, "not her parents. They do not even know that we have formed this party to find their little girl."

"Oh, my!" the sheriff countered with amazement. "Are you telling me that her parents know nothing of your intentions?" Bixley did not wait for the Indian's reply. "If Papu's mother and father knew that you were here, despite your good intentions, they would be horrified. They have trusted the authorities to find their daughter without jeopardizing her safety. So far, this has been the case, and the kidnappers are still contacting the authorities about reward money and, at one point, even retrieving money to buy food for the girl. We know that she is alive. Unless you want her dead, and never to be found, you must turn back and wait for a proper outcome. Mr. Puckett knows what he is doing."

"Where is Mr. Puckett? We want to find him and listen to the words from his own mouth."

"Broken Heel, I could tell you where Mr. Puckett can be found, but if you were to advance on his territory, you could easily bring down everything that has been accomplished up until now. If the kidnappers in Shoshoni were to see you and your braves descend on their domain, they would likely shut down all contact with the authorities, and any hope of seeing the little girl alive again might be lost for good,"

"Mr. Sheriff, I thank you for your time. You have told me what I want to know. I can now find Mr. Puckett. I must hear what he knows." With these words spoken, the Indian delegation turned and headed straightway for Shoshoni.

The constant racket along the boardwalk in Shoshoni gave Puck the feeling that life was going on totally oblivious of the fact that a little Indian girl was still being held against her will somewhere in the territorial vicinity. But Puck was not unmindful of the sinister act still being carried out by two, maybe three, heartless scoundrels, names of whom he felt certain had now risen to the surface. Evening would be coming on soon, and he wanted to see how things were progressing before sundown. Today looked to be an eventful day, with the hope of getting some word from the prison in Laramie before nightfall.

Nightfall was a ways away, and Puck was just impatient enough not to twiddle his thumbs. The time was urgent, so he had already informed the telegraph operator, Stan Morley, that he had activated his plan for weaseling out of Browning one final telegram that would clarify just when the ransom money was to be placed on the stage for pick up. The sheriff had sent the stage driver, Vern Johnson, on the errand, and Puck had told Morley that he should expect a telegram at any time, as the driver was at the livery stable as he spoke.

The stable was not as busy as it often was at this time of day when Johnson pulled the stage into the repair bay to consult with Browning.

"Look, Browning," Johnson began, "I guess I can confide in you. You've always kept my word in confidence. I've brought the stage in to get a couple of axles checked and greased. Sometime this week I'm supposed to deliver some ransom money to the kidnappers of that little Indian girl. The sheriff is just waiting for word from them as to when they expect the delivery to be made. They're hoping to hear, and the sooner the better. They want to get this whole ordeal over and the child back home. Anyway, Browning, I want this rig in mint condition. None of us can afford for anything to go wrong now. Do you have the time to check it out?"

"Yeah, sure, Johnson. Why don't you leave the rig here for an hour or so. You can take my horse. He's still saddled from an errand I ran a few minutes ago. And if you see Sheriff Larson tell him the rig will be ready, and there'll be no charge."

"Well, better not do that Browning. I'm not sure I'm supposed to be confiding this information to anyone. I just felt I could trust you. You've always been up front with me."

"Okay, Johnson, whatever you say. In any case, the stage will be ready when you return to pick it up."

Browning watched Johnson as he rode off down the street, then turned up the stable breezeway and hurried to his office. When he came out, he had a wry smile on his face, as if he knew something no one else knew. He quickly went to work on the stagecoach.

At the telegraph office, Morley's assistant called Morley in and informed him that a telegram had just come in that was certain to interest him. Morley looked at the paper and smiled a wry smile, too, as if he knew something that Browning didn't know. Puck's weaseling had paid off. The telegram stated that the ransom money was to be placed on the stage to Riverton on Friday morning and that anyone attempting to follow it would be shot on sight.

Morley tucked the note inside his vest and headed for Sheriff Larson's office. As he arrived, the sheriff and Engle were just coming out the door.

"Hold up, Sheriff," Morley called out. "Got something of interest here for you!" Morley handed the sheriff the telegram and stood back to see Larson's expression as he read it. The sheriff chuckled like a child does when handed a new toy. Then he spoke.

"Okay, Engle, its time for you to take your horse to the stables and leave it. Don't dawdle. We need to get those telegraph wires cut. We should be getting word from Laramie any minute regarding our man Browning, and we don't want him being privy to the information. Morley, you might want to get back to your office in case the word comes in, and I'll go find Puck and let him in on our ransom schedule. Good job men!"

Browning was still busy with the stage axles when Engle rode into the stables. "Morning, Browning," he called out. "I'm leaving my horse here a spell, if you don't mind. I'll pay you to have your Indian bathe and curry him. Should be back by noon. Can I bring you some lunch?"

"Looks like I'm going to be too busy for lunch today. I'll just chew on a little jerky, but thanks for the offer. See ya later!"

When Engle walked out of the livery, Browning hailed Three Toes and told him, "Take Engle's horse out back to wash and curry. There's some new soap in my office. I normally ask you to keep out, but it's okay this time. And just leave the door open. I may be back in there shortly."

Three Toes led the horse out the back of the breezeway to a wash trough in the rear and returned to the office for the soap. As he entered the office, he could see some machinery to the right in the corner. As secretly as possible, he checked it out, and found two wires going through the wall. He knew that the telegraph post was just outside the wall. Somehow he had to get into the loft and over to the corner of the building where he could get at the wires. He had already placed the cutters under some hay on that level.

Straightway, he went back to the horse and began to wash it down. He couldn't afford to do anything else until he had followed Browning's orders. Then he got an idea. He went to the front where the blacksmith was working on the rig and spoke up. "Boss, I've finished washing the horse, but he needs to dry before I can curry him. I've tied him to a post out back, but he keeps trying to roll in the dust. Maybe if I go up in the loft and get him an armful of hay, he will settle down. Then I can curry him."

"Good idea, Three Toes. Do what you have to do, but be sure he is clean when you're finished."

Three Toes headed for the loft and climbed the ladder quickly. He eased over to the corner of the building where he could get at the post bearing the wires. He had already spent some time working loose a bit of the siding from the inside so as to have a large enough hole to reach the wires, but he had been careful to replace it temporarily so as not to raise suspicion if his boss came meddling. He looked back toward the ladder making sure Browning had not followed, then he retrieved the cutters from beneath the hay in the corner and reached for the wires. Two quick snips and the job was done. He covered the opening and hustled back to the ladder carrying an armload of hay for Engle's horse. In a moment, he was feeding the hay to the horse and working over him with the currycomb.

As Three Toes walked the horse in the mid-day sun to complete the drying of the animal, stopping intermittently to curry his coat, he heard a commotion coming from inside the building. Leading the horse to the back entrance, he looked in to see Browning coming out of his office, kicking items one way then another as he exited the door, and mumbling sharply to himself, "Where's that confounded Indian?"

"Hey, Indian," Browning called out with an ear-piercing shout. "Git in here, Indian!" Three Toes tied the horse to an entrance post and hurried inside.

"What's wrong, boss. I do something wrong?"

"That's what I want to know, Indian. You been messin' with my machines here in the office? I told you not to touch anything in here."

"Mr. Boss," Three Toes cowered, "I do not touch any machines in your office. I just take the soap you tell me to use."

At that moment, Engle entered the stables, heard the hollering going on and saw Browning stamping around like an enraged mental case.

"What's the trouble, Browning," Engle coaxed.

"What's not the trouble," Browning railed. "I'm about to kill me an Indian, that's what's the trouble. I told him not to mess with my office, and—"

He was interrupted by Engle again, "What's Three Toes doing in your office?"

"Aw, it's a long story. Not your concern. He went in to git some soap. Well, never mind. I ain't got the time or patience right now to git into it. It's not your problem."

Engle knew the wrangling was more than likely over the now nonfunctioning telegraph equipment, but that was not for Browning to know. Engle was satisfied that Three Toes had done his job, but not from inside the office, for which he was now being maligned.

"Well, I don't want to meddle in your business, Browning, but don't be too hard on your Indian help. He's been a good boy for you. He couldn't have done too much wrong while I've been gone; he has my horse in beautiful shape, and that undoubtedly took some time. How much do I owe you? I'll get out of here and let you get things back in order."

Browning continued to mumble as he handed Engle a bill for the horse's care, and, looking up, he saw Johnson riding into the stables, back to pick up the stagecoach. By luck, everything was ready. Engle turned and made a low-key exit, not to raise any more dander, as Johnson ambled over to settle up with Browning.

After Sheriff Larson had gotten word to Puck regarding the ransom schedule, Puck was so relieved that he let go of everything for the moment. He had been taking a bit of restful meandering around the village of Shoshoni, just hanging loose, and biding time, which was becoming more and more precious. The afternoon breeze, cool for a summer day in June, felt good blowing through his hair. The din of the village was fading, and Puck began to relish the near silence as he ambled over to the boardwalk and parked his weary carcass on a padded bench just outside Herman's Dress Shop.

The smell of perfume wafting from inside, left over from damsels coming and going, reminded him of home and Aunt Bella's dress shop, not to mention his recollection of the pretty Faye Lincoln who usually adorned the premise. He looked to the horizon longingly, basking in jaded dreams that once spoke more lively of something other than work, responsibility, and constraint. Momentarily, he nodded off in a half-doze, his chin slumping to his chest then bobbing up guiltily again as if it were a crime to slumber in the broad of day. All was quiet for the moment.

A hand pushed his booted foot from its resting place on his knee and startled him awake as it hit the floor. The hush was over.

"Glad to catch up with you, Puck," the overbearing voice of Sheriff Larson announced with more decibels than anyone ever needed to use. "Sorry if I startled you, but Morley has some information you've been expecting."

Puck came alive as the two hurried their pace toward the telegraph office and quickly entered once they arrived.

"There you are, Puck," Morley spoke up. "The prison at Laramie came through on our inquiry. You're gonna like what you read," he added, as he handed Puck the telegram.

Puck began to read:

Greetings Stop Our records show that your man in question was released from our facility three years ago Stop He served time for robbery of the coal mine payroll at Rock Springs and for impersonating an army officer Stop He worked in our stables as a farrier and graduated with honors in our telegraphy program Stop His name is Perk Anson Stop As your inquiry represents official government business, we are sending photographs of his prison records with the couriers Stop Let us know if we may be of further service Stop

Puck returned the telegram to Morley and slapped his hands together briskly. "Gentlemen," he announced, "we have our man without question. Likenesses don't lie! What a switch—from Browning to Anson! And yet he seems so honorable. His whole life has been lived as a con artist, right under respectable people's noses. Being given the benefit of the doubt from good citizens of Shoshoni, he goes on choosing to be dishonorable. He's lost all conscience, and we have to take him in as the only cure."

CHAPTER 11

THE SURVEILLANCE

Puck and Sheriff Larson sat in his office making plans for the ransom delivery on Friday and determining the strategy for catching Perk Anson red-handed. Though they realized that the longtime alias Browning had now betrayed himself as the ringleader of the kidnapping gang, they had to catch him in the act of procuring the ransom money. Also, on Friday, one or both of the other instigators in the crime would be in on the retrieval of the ransom from the stage.

"Sheriff," Puck addressed Larson, thinking aloud, "I have some ideas as to how to go about the trapping of our prey, but we really have to be cautious. First, we can't risk surveillance of the stage's movement to Riverton—that is, with anyone who might even appear to be official in any way. The man who'll be ridin' shotgun is okay, because that's normal, but even he'll be limited in what he can do. Confronting any fracas on the road, their shootin' any of the pickup men is out of the question. We simply have to keep them alive if we want to find the location of the little Indian girl.

"There's one way we can get away with flanking the stage, even if it has to be at some distance. I've sent Farley to find Trinket and to bring him back here. When the stage leaves on Friday, he'll be stationed on its route south of town. He's one of Chief Broken Bow's best trackers, and he knows how to weave in and out of the brush along the trail, keepin' his distance. Any of the culprits who notice him in the vicinity of the stage will more than likely regard him as just another Indian traveler on the reservation. There'll probably be other Indians moving in the area as well. Once the ransom is picked up, Trinket can shadow the rider or riders' trail, in case they go in a direction other than Shoshoni.

"Then, Larson, we should wait to call Browning's hand—I mean Anson's hand. Unless I miss my guess, whoever picks up the money, even if it is Anson himself, will more than likely return to the livery stable. I have a feelin' that Anson will let Trammel and Wortham do the dirty work. In any case, we'll somehow stake out the stable and be waitin' when the riders return with the goods.

"We can then—" Suddenly, Puck was interrupted by a commotion coming from outside the office. The barking of dogs and the pounding of hoofs dancing around outside sounded a bit strange. Puck and Larson rushed to the door.

There standing abruptly in front of the office were twenty-one half-naked Indians on horseback, some of them swatting at the barking dogs, others beginning to dismount and move in closer to the boardwalk.

Addressing Puck, the leader spoke up. "You are Mr. Puckett, are you not?"

"That's right," Puck responded. "What can I do for you?"

"I am Broken Heel of the Shoshonis. We have come from Wind River Village to talk with you. We have come to find the kidnappers who took our Papu Banta. We believe their capture has been too slow. We want to hear words from your own mouth. What have you done to find our little Indian girl?"

"Wait a minute, Broken Heel," Puck enjoined. "You have come at a very bad time. Who sent—"

Broken Heel interrupted, "We have come at a very good time. Papu must be found now!" The Indian sounded firm and authoritative.

"Who sent you on this mission?" Puck asked, with even more expressed authority.

"We have come without consent from our chief or any of our leaders. Papu is of our blood. I am her uncle. That is enough!"

"That may be enough for you, my friend, but that is not enough for us. You have not only brought twenty braves unsupervised by army personnel, but, if you remain, you have brought trouble as well. You are putting Papu's life in jeopardy."

"What's this 'jeopardy' you speak of?" the Indian retorted.

"I mean that you are risking her life by being here. For your information, we now know who the kidnappers are, and if they find out why you have come, the life of your little girl will be in danger. You'll destroy everything we've accomplished so far. You must return to Wind River now."

"Mr. Puckett, you do not understand the Indian ways. We will not return. And we have not come to destroy. Tell us who the kidnappers are and we will find them. We have our ways of getting words out of them. When we are finished, they will want to talk like flowing water. They will tell us where they have hidden our Papu."

"I am sorry, Broken Heel, but we cannot possibly let you enter this case. If you will not return to Wind River in good conscience, Colonel Meecham of Fort Washakie will be called in to remove you and your braves from Shoshoni."

"Your tongue moves without understanding, Mr. Puckett. Broken Heel does not fear the white man's army."

"Broken Heel," Puck countered, "I am fully confident of the army's ability to detain you from your plans, but I know one thing for certain—if I consult Chief Washakie of your presence and intentions here, your very life will be in danger. He himself will raise your scalp on a pole, without hesitation."

The Indian looked around at the braves attending him to see how they reacted to Puck's sharp words. He knew that in order to save face, he had to respond in some way, and without showing weakness.

"If I find Papu, Mr. Puckett, my chief will praise me. He will not only praise me, but he may honor me by giving me a place next in line to be chief after him."

"Broken Heel, you are not thinking clearly. Not to be disrespectful, but your heel may not be the only thing that is broken."

Two of the younger braves snickered at the comment, not weighing the dismayed effect it made on their company leader. They straightened themselves in the saddle as Broken Heel turned in their direction.

"Look, Broken Heel," Puck continued, "maybe you and your braves can be of help later. Once we have cornered our prey, I may have use for you. When we learn where they have hidden Papu, we may need help in locating her. If you can be patient and remain down at the holding pens at the edge of town, I can find you when I need you. This is the only way you will be of help to us. I'm going to give you one hour to make up your mind what you want to do. I hope you will choose the right thing."

Puck turned and held the door open for Sheriff Larson, as they went back inside to continue making plans, locking the door behind them. The ultimatum having been given, they didn't even bother to see if the Indians had turned away. Plans continued for a while, when there came another rattle at the door.

"Those Indians are going to be the death of us," Puck remarked with a sigh of exasperation, as he went to the door!

When he opened the door, there stood Colonel Meech on the steps of the boardwalk, flanked by a small group of his right hand soldiers.

"Well, come in Colonel," Puck motioned. "Knowing what I know, I guess I should have expected you, but this is a bit of a surprise. Take a seat and I'll get you some coffee."

"No, don't bother, Puck. We ate a late lunch along the trail. I guess you know that we are here to alert you about a contingent of Indians, who have come off up here to concern themselves with your job? We came through Riverton and got the word from Sheriff Bixley. My courier saw them earlier this morning heading in his direction. I'm sure you don't need them interfering in your business, but then, they should not be away from their quarters in such numbers without proper supervision. Bixley said that before he could rally enough forces to detain them, they headed this way."

"They've been here all right, Colonel. We've already laid down the law to them, but we don't know yet what's going to come of the matter."

"You mean they're still here after your counseling them?"

"I'm sure they're still here, but I don't know what they may plan to do. Rather than making them furious, by totally shutting them out, I conciliated them by telling them they might be of help later. I sent them to the holding pens at the edge of town and gave them an hour to think over what I suggested."

"Well, in our relationship with the Indians of the reservation, we don't do much 'suggesting,' as you put it, Puck. We need to stay up front with these people or we'll be chasing bands everywhere. We want them to have their freedom but with some limitations, otherwise, their being on a reservation has no meaning. We'll get down to the pens and see if we can talk some sense into them. If they're willing to comply with your offer, I'll leave a detachment of men with them for supervision, and we'll let them remain until further notice. The rest of us will camp further out of town at the old Ryrie Place, in case you need us for anything."

"Do as you think best, Colonel," Puck conceded. "We're just too close to solving this case for them to start meddling, even though I can understand their concern and impatience."

With that, Colonel Meech bade adieu, left the office, mounted his horse, and waved his men toward the north end of town.

By the next morning, nothing disturbing had happened regarding the delegation of Indians at the north end of town. Puck assumed that Colonel Meech had at least temporarily won the battle of authority. That was something to be grateful for, since this was the day before the ransom was to be placed on the stage to Riverton. Any disruption now could be critical.

Farley and Trinket had arrived late in the night and had slept in the sheriff's spare room where Engle was staying. Engle did not think to take Farley's usual place relieving Palmer, so Palmer would have to stay awake on the night watch, as well. Trinket had to lay low until Friday morning, so as not to be seen in the company of any official people, especially the sheriff, the telegraph operator, or even the stage driver. So far, he was neutral with respect to any recognition on the part of the kidnappers. Even Trammel had not been aware of his riding up to the hitching post the morning Trammel and Lively had their scrap in the Riverton saloon. Puck would be lining him out later in the day. His having slept on the trail for over a week now, made the sheriff's cot a welcomed accommodation. Until Puck came by, he would make good use of it while he could.

Palmer was getting a little tired of his watch at the hotel. On many days, as he came in for his watch, he had to go right back out. Wortham had come and gone from the stables more than once, never staying long, and each time on his way out, Palmer had followed him at a distance, hoping that his trail would lead to Papu Banta. The man never left town and never wound up at any place that would be conducive to hiding an Indian girl. These false alarms were getting downright wearisome.

Timing could not have been worse. Farley had sent Engle in to take Palmer's watch, but just as he came in to relieve him, Palmer saw Wortham leading his horse out of the stables. *Here we go on another false alarm,* he thought to himself. Luckily, the hotel manager had brought him a good breakfast earlier, but because no one had come to relieve him in the night, he had to remain awake. The night had been a grind trying to stay awake, but in the wee hours he had inadvertently fallen asleep. Five hours later he was awakened by the manager's knock on the door. For all the wear and tear, he actually felt refreshed, a blessing he could now cherish, knowing he had to trail Wortham again. He grabbed his saddlebags packed with food and water and headed for the door.

Wortham headed south, this time actually leaving town, but Palmer could see that the trail he was taking did not lead to Riverton. The trail was heading farther east and not as much used as the one directly to Riverton. This seemed odd to Palmer, and yet he recalled that Lively had told the group that when Trammell left the saloon that morning after their scrap, he had headed due east from Riverton. This could mean that Wortham was now taking a shortcut southeasterly from Shoshoni, which might end up east of Riverton. Palmer delighted in the idea that Wortham could be heading straight for the hideout housing the little Indian girl.

As time passed, Palmer found it more and more difficult to keep himself hidden from his advanced rider, passing as it were through a lot of clearings without many trees or brush. During these times, he would lay farther back, and when the trail led into cover again, he would hustle his mount down the trail, reining up periodically, so as not to overrun Wortham, or alert him in any way. The pursuit had now ground into two tedious hours. His lack of sleep was now taking its toll. A few times he had to catch himself from dozing off on his mount. The situation was too important now to muffle its hope of finding the Indian girl. This man, Wortham, had to be headed directly for the lass. Maybe he had to see to her food and water supply, and make sure of any other welfare concerns. With the ransom pick-up scheduled for tomorrow, nothing should go wrong now. If the ransom were received without threat to the kidnappers' own welfare, they had assured the authorities the girl would be set free.

As the two riders rounded a bend, still maintaining substantial distance, Palmer could see a pool of water ahead. As Wortham neared the watering hole, another rider pulled away from its edge and stopped to chat with him. Palmer dismounted and led his horse into some brush and then resumed his surveillance of the two riders. Then something extremely strange happened. When the horses had finished drinking, the two riders pulled them away, mounted, and began returning together down the same trail Wortham had just covered. Palmer took his horse farther into the brush and tethered the reins to a limb. He then slipped back closer to the trail so he could see the approaching riders more clearly. As they passed, Palmer could see the big black and white paint and knew that it must be Trammel riding it, though he had never actually seen Trammel. The horse and rider fit the descriptions he had been told by the others of his company.

Palmer was puzzled. Surely, Wortham would not ride for several hours to meet someone along the trail just to turn around and retrace his steps. The only thing that made sense to him was that when Wortham met Trammel, Trammel must have assured him that the girl's needs had been taken care of, and there was no use of his going on to the hideout. If this were true, Palmer was now left in the lurch. The girl could be sequestered anywhere. The hiding place could be nearby. Then again, it could be several miles away, and on or off the beaten trail at that.

There was one thing Palmer knew for sure—he would not need to follow the riders, because they were apparently headed directly back to Shoshoni, and probably for the purpose of finalizing plans for tomorrow's ransom pick-up. He hurried back to his horse and headed toward the watering hole. As he approached, he dismounted so as to survey the hoof tracks, thinking he might be able to backtrack Trammel's ride from the hideout. The trail leading away from the pool was a hardpan of clay and rock, with intermittent patches of sandy loam. Palmer followed the trail slowly until it finally appeared useless to pick up the tracks any longer. Looking around, he could see nothing that seemed a likely place for a hideout. At least the hideout might be somewhere in the vicinity, if something went wrong on Friday and Puck had to order an extensive search of the area. For now, he would head back to Shoshoni and inform Puck of what he had experienced today.

Whiskers Benedict and Lively had spent the previous night at the holding pens, agitated and restless over the chanting of the Indian unit bedded down nearby. Every now and then, a sharp yelp out of an unruly brave would bring them out of their bedrolls. Then silence pursued for a while, but even the silence was not restful, with the two always on edge, waiting for the other shoe to drop. The soldiers were just as miserable, with two sitting watch while eight others tried to get some much-needed shuteye. The shuffling of moccasins around the campfire in a moderation of frenzy, or spirit dance as the Indians called it, may have enlivened them and prepared them for any contention they might face when the sun came up, but it had not done anything for Whiskers and Lively. Having gotten no sleep, they had rolled out early, hoping they would be able to find Puck.

Puck had just left the sheriff's office, having made final plans for the ransom package, when Whiskers and Lively found him.

"Boy, are we glad to find you," Whiskers assured Puck.

"Yeah, what's up men?" Puck responded.

"We've both had it with the holding pens, Puck," Lively intoned. "Wasn't so bad until the Indians showed up, but their heaping up noise in the night air has taken its toll on our comfort, not to mention our patience. A few nights sleeping in a jail cell would beat what we've been experiencing. We need something to do before we go batty."

"Well, you're in luck, men. Timing couldn't have been better," Puck replied. "Gentry and I were just gettin' ready to come look for you. Hope you haven't lost all your patience. You may need a little of it for what I want you to do."

"Anything will be better than biding our time at the holding pens," Whiskers assured him again.

Puck continued, "I need two men for surveillance tonight and in the morning at the stables. We have to keep Anson in our sights from this point on. No telling what he may have Three Toes doing. At least, he doesn't suspect anything about Three Toes yet. That leaves him free to help, if needed. For now, go down to Flaggerty's Café and have a good breakfast, and I'll get with you later.

Palmer, returning to Shoshoni, found Puck's horse tied up in front of the hotel. As he entered the front door, he met Puck and Farley coming down the stairs. Palmer greeted the men and told them of his experience of the morning, explaining the odd meeting of Wortham and Trammel along the trail. He presumed the two had already returned to Shoshoni.

Puck spoke up, "Yes, Farley and I saw the two men riding up to the stables about twenty minutes ago. I was about to send Farley over there to consult with Three Toes under the guise of getting his horse bathed and curried. Maybe Three Toes has overheard something that might be of significance for the big day tomorrow. By nightfall, I need to get Whiskers and Lively in the stable hayloft, and Farley here is going to see just how."

Puck, thinking aloud to himself as to the next step, remarked, "Palmer, since you've had a tough ride this morning and not much sleep last night, you might just as well go up to the room and get a few more winks. Someone will come for you if you're needed."

Puck headed for the local bank where he would meet Sheriff Larson to secure the ransom package and get it to the stage office for the next day's run to Riverton. Farley headed for the stables to leave his horse and to check out potential strategy for getting Whiskers and Lively into the loft late in the evening. When he arrived, he chatted cordially with Anson and told him what he wanted with respect to his horse.

"Browning," he addressed the blacksmith, remembering to maintain his alias, "don't bother yourself, I'll just get with your Indian and tell him what I want done."

Three Toes was in the rear of the building moving boxes when Farley approached him with his horse.

"Hey, Three Toes, lucky that I found you to yourself. How're things going? Have you overheard anything of importance?"

Three Toes responded, "Not much of anything, Pistol Bill," calling Farley by his nickname. "The two other men came in earlier and were talking with the boss, but they made sure I could not hear their words. All I know is that when they left, they told the boss they were heading for the café to eat. That's all I heard."

"Oh boy!" Farley injected.

"Oh boy, what, Mr. Bill?"

"Oh boy, tongue-tied lizards, that's what! Whiskers and Lively are there now, unless they've had time to eat and get away. Wortham knows Whiskers from the rendezvous site, and Trammel is the fellow who had the run-in with Lively at the Saloon in Riverton. Hope they can explain themselves. We can't have any suspicion cropping up now. Well, I'll know soon enough. I have to get with them later in the day for Puck's next move. By the way, Three Toes, part of Puck's move is to get whiskers and Lively into the loft here tonight to keep an eye on Anson. Do you have any ideas how we might do that?"

"Sure, I know. I mean I know if the boss does what he normally does each evening. He goes to the café to eat just before sundown and leaves me to handle the stables. He always brings me some food. Maybe he'll go again today."

"Okay, Three Toes, I'll bring Whiskers and Lively around back just before dark. If you will, try to find a secure place in the loft where they can hang out for the night. And, by the way, your English is getting better. Keep it up."

With that, Farley headed through the front passage of the stables thanking Anson on his way out for caring for his horse.

When Wortham and Trammel stepped onto the boardwalk to enter Flaggerty's Café, Whiskers and Lively were just coming out. Wortham made a double take when he recognized Whiskers.

"Say," he called out, "you're the gent I met on the trail. Did you ever find your stolen cattle?"

Whiskers replied, "No, and we've stopped looking." In a ploy to divert attention, he went on to add, "We've decided to look for real jobs. We didn't find any gold back at camp either. I see you have a friend with you."

"Yeah, this is Trammel, boys. He's lookin' for a job too. And who's this fellow with you? Can't say that I've met him."

Trammel, who had been eyeing Lively, spoke up. "I know who he is! He's the wisecrack who interrupted my play for a girl in the Riverton saloon. I've a mind to settle our differences right here and now!"

Lively stepped toward him, as Whiskers put out his arm and blocked him from proceeding. "Okay, gents, I don't know what this is all about, but there's no need to get something started all over again. Lively here hooked up with us to help us look for a job. He knows something of the territory. Palmer is out looking now. I hope we can be civil to one another. Looks like we're all in the same boat—jobless and edgy! If we're going to square off, let's square off to some purpose. It's not going to do us any good breathing down one another's collar."

"Trammel don't mean no harm," Wortham spoke up in poor country grammar. "He just don't like nobody jumpin' into his affairs. Maybe we ought to let bygones be bygones. You fellas look like you're tryin' to git ahead the same as us. In a day or so, we're gonna be on our way anyway. Right now, we're hungry, so maybe we'll see you around." Wortham paused momentarily then continued, "By the way, what did you do with your rig? Haven't seen it around."

"Oh, we're keeping it at the holding pens at the north end of town. We needed some place out of the way, and that's about as good as any. Drop by for some vittles sometime. Maybe we can get to know each other a little better."

"Yeah, maybe," Wortham went on, as he and Trammel turned and entered the café with a wave of goodbye to Whiskers and Lively. When the two were gone, Whiskers wiped his brow. "Whew! Glad that's over," he said. "I'll be glad when we can stop putting up this front. I've never had to lie so much in my life!"

Inside the café, Wortham and Trammel exchanged mental notes about their separate encounters with Whiskers and Lively. They thought it a bit coincidental that Lively was now linked up with the old man when Lively had been in Riverton and Whiskers had been riding the range looking for cattle. Strange that they should meet up in Shoshoni and strike up a friendship so quickly. When lunch was finished, the two decided to pay a visit to the holding pens just to check out the situation themselves.

As the two riders approached the area housing the holding pens, they reined up abruptly. Trammel piped up, "Look at all them Indians. What're they havin', an Indian convention? And look over there to one side. Those are soldiers. What are they doing here? And look over there. There's the old man's chuck wagon. I don't know about you Wortham, but something looks fishy to me. We better get back to the boss and see what he thinks about all this. A lot of strange things are happening all of a sudden, and I'm not sure what to make of it."

The two took no extra time getting back to the stables to present their findings to Anson. The boss was a little concerned about so many new figures staying in town, but then, he had seen soldiers having to corral dissenting Indians more than once since his stay in Shoshoni. And as for the old man, he was an old man! There couldn't be too much worry with an old codger like him. Then he assured his men, "We'll keep an eye open, but I don't think we have anything to worry about. Tomorrow it will be all over anyway, and we'll leave our tracks behind when the girl is returned to her kin and everything cools down. Just concentrate on your job tomorrow. We're almost there."

As evening approached, Farley located Whiskers and Lively and informed them of the plan he had devised to get them into the hayloft at the stables. They were to tie their horses in a shed behind Rafferty's Dry Goods store for the night, which was only two doors down from the stables. They were then to sit on the bench in front of the store and wait for his signal. Farley would be going for his horse, and when he saw Anson leave for the café, he would secure his horse and ride out of the stables. This would be their signal to move behind the store and down the alley where they would meet Three Toes at the back of the stables and find their niche for the night in the hayloft.

Puck had informed Trinket of his task of moving onto the stage road at the south of town come first light. He would stake out the run about a mile out of town and be ready to shadow the stage's movement in the brushy trails alongside the road to Riverton.

Puck and Palmer would take turns watching the entrance to the stables, and Farley would join them after he had gotten Whiskers and Lively sequestered in the hayloft.

The night watch was now about set. The busy traffic along the village street was grinding to a halt. A few lights were now coming on ahead of time in the nightspots, and the town custodian was proceeding to light the street lamps for another evening. The sun was fading on the horizon. A few old drunks staggered along the boardwalk seeking shelter for the night, stopping long enough only to entreat a few passersby for a bottle or for a bit of change to buy one. Subdued horses, tied to the hitching posts, relaxed on their haunches and nodded their heads in half-slumber. All the earmarks of a completed day were evident down every side street. Night was coming on.

Into the evening glow, Farley emerged from the stables, thus signaling to Whiskers and Lively that the coast was clear. He then headed for his night rendezvous at the quaint village hotel. In a moment, the darkness would signal that his day was over, and the town would sleep unwittingly of the high drama that would transpire come first light.

CHAPTER 12

THE SHOWDOWN

Just before the break of day, lights came on in the livery stable. The night had seemed long, and while Palmer and Farley were dead away in slumber, Puck had taken the last watch. He had seen the lights come on in the stable and was now watching figures coming in and out of the building. He reached over and jarred the foot of the iron bedstead to awaken Farley, and then moved over and nudged Palmer, who was sleeping in a bedroll on the floor. The two men moved slowly but began to come alive to meet the day when Puck told them the showdown was about to begin.

In a moment, two men emerged, one a big man leading the big black and white Paint—Trammel for sure—and the other a tall slender man, too thin to be mistaken for Anson. It had to be Wortham. They mounted and rode toward the south end of town, apparently to connect the road to Riverton and to get a head start on the stage that would not be leaving Shoshoni until about eight o'clock.

As sunlight began to flare in the east, Puck could more readily see any activity entering or leaving the stables. Shortly, two more figures emerged from the building leading two black horses and tethering them, momentarily, to a railing outside the door. Something about these figures looked baffling, as well as a bit familiar to Puck. The familiar sight was that one of the figures, unmistakably, was Three Toes, and the baffling drama was that the other figure was wearing a U.S. Cavalry outfit, one that depicts an officer. But why the black horses? Puck watched as the two mounted their rides and became more puzzled as the officer rode over to Three Toes, placed a lasso around the Indian, gave it about ten feet of slack and tied the rope around his own saddle horn. As the two shadowy figures rode south, with Three Toes in the lead, the scenario gave the appearance of an officer escorting an Indian as prisoner.

Instantly, Puck recalled Three Toes' telling him about the suit of Army clothing hanging in Anson's office, and Colonel Meech of the incident of Anson's impersonating an officer under the alias of Browning, for which he had drawn prison time. Something was seriously wrong. Now Three Toes was caught in the mix. This changed the whole demeanor of things.

As the two rode out of sight and Puck racked his brain as to what to do next, he looked up and saw Lively riding onto the town's main street from behind Rafferty's Dry Goods Store, then heading south as well. Something was up, and Puck sensed that something radical had happened that would cause Lively to leave his post in the hayloft.

"All right, men," Puck spoke up, "I've got to get over to the stables and contact Whiskers to see what has happened. We've got a pickle of a fine mess here with Three Toes apparently being held as a hostage, but why? That's the question. You men grab a bite to eat and be ready to ride. Put some vittles in a saddlebag for me and meet me in front of Rafferty's in fifteen minutes."

Puck donned his hat, left the hotel, quickly crossed the street, and slipped between Rafferty's and the building next to it. In a moment, he entered the broad door opening back of the stables, looking for Whiskers.

Whiskers started climbing down from the hayloft when he saw Puck below.

"You'll never guess," Benedict responded excitedly. "After Trammel and Wortham left, Anson came out of his office dressed in an officer's uniform. He stepped out back, went across the alley and came back with two black horses ready to ride. He then began to rough-talk Three Toes. He told him that he now knew that he was the one who had cut the wires on the telegraph pole outside. 'I don't know who put you up to it,' he went on, 'but you'll pay for your blunder before it's all over. I've got your horse saddled. You're going with me, and don't try to make a run for it, or I'll plug you before you reach the doorway. Git with it! We're about to leave.' With that, Anson watched every move Three Toes made until they left the building and headed south. With things changing as they were, Lively thought it best to follow them at a distance, risking as little as possible Anson's detecting his presence. Hope that was all right, boss."

"Yeah, I guess that was the right thing to do," Puck responded. "Whiskers, you had better stay here in case any of the culprits return. You can keep tabs on them from the hayloft. If they do return, we'll be close behind, so don't concern yourself about being alone. Farley and Palmer will be with me, but they'll return with me unless we have to split up for some reason."

Puck left the stables, picked up Farley and Palmer at Rafferty's, and headed south out of town.

By the time the stage was ready to leave Shoshoni, Trammel and Wortham were stationed along the stage route approximately halfway between Hale's Ford and Riverton. Anson had convinced them that by the time the stage reached them, any trackers would have been detected, and they would have clear access to the ransom without any interference. He had assured them that he would be in surveillance of the stage as it reached the point of Hale's Ford. If everything were in order, with no one following, he would then return to the stables to wait for them to bring in the money.

Earlier in the morning, Trinket had seen Trammel and Wortham pass along the trail, moving quite rapidly. It was too early for the stage to have left Shoshoni, so he knew the two were not running with the ransom. He let them go, as his job was to shadow the stage when it came into view.

Momentarily, though, Trinket became confused when he saw an army officer and Three Toes moving along the trail. By this time, Anson had removed the rope from Three Toes, so Trinket had no sense of foul play, except that he could not understand why Three Toes would be on the trail. Surely, Puck had not sent him. Then he remembered about the army clothes hanging in Anson's office and realized that the officer with Three Toes must be Anson. Still, Three Toes had no dealings in the ransom pick up, so what was up? He thought for a moment and realized that if this was Anson, as it had to be, and Trammel and Wortham had passed earlier, then he would not jeopardize anything if he shadowed Anson and Three Toes rather than waiting for the stage.

As Anson and Three Toes proceeded, Trinket moved along the brush, keeping them in sight. At one point, however, his trail split to the right and he had to make a quick semi-circle around the brush in order to get back into view of the stage road. When he finally got back into view, he noticed that he had gotten ahead of Anson and Three Toes. If he could only alert Three Toes of his presence without alerting Anson as well, that would be the ideal move. As the two riders passed a line of heavy brush, Trinket saw his chance. He cupped his hands over his mouth and let out a loud wail of a dying rabbit, followed by a shrill screech of a hawk attacking its prey. At that moment, the two came back into view along the road. Anson looked quickly toward the brush, startled enough to grab for his pistol.

When he saw nothing amiss, he eased off the holster and settled back, satisfied that the noise was actual prey in the brush. Trinket quickly made only the cry of the hawk again. This time, Three Toes perked up, alert to the sound. He knew that an actual hawk would never cry out a second time after having clutched its prey. As they rode along, he watched the line of brush along the route until he saw, in a brief flash, the movement of Trinket along the trail.

"Say, boss," Three Toes spoke up, "you hear that rabbit and hawk back there?"

"Yeah, I heard it. What about it?"

"Well, can you make sound of hawk?"

"Can't say that I can, Indian. What of it?"

"Well, I can make sound easily," Three Toes rejoined. "Listen!"

The Indian cupped his hands over his mouth and intentionally let out a shrill, but faulty, screech of the hawk.

"Ha!" Anson jolted, "that sound wouldn't scare a flea, much less git the attention of a rabbit." Three Toes knew that, but he didn't let on. He knew Trinket had gotten the message.

"Guess I'll have to practice up, boss. But right now I feel like rabbit back there. I no understand why you bring me out here with a trigger-happy finger at your side. I do everything you tell me at the stables."

"Yeah, well I'm telling you some other things to do now, so keep on ridin'."

With that said, the two were approaching Hale's Ford, where Anson directed them across the shallow water and to a good stone's throw down the road on the other side. He then urged them into the brush and behind a small bulwark of rock, where they would wait for the stage.

The stage billowed dust as it lumbered along the bumpy road to Riverton. It moved along intentionally empty of passengers, so as not to subject anyone to danger unnecessarily. Only Johnson, the stage driver, and a rifleman, riding shotgun, were aboard, pushing the four horses into a slight gallop, then breaking their stride intermittently to cool them down. With no riders aboard, once the ransom was delivered, the stage still had to push on to Riverton, because passengers there had been scheduled for the return trip to Shoshoni.

The stage was precisely on time, as it rounded the turn, approaching Hale's crossing. When Anson heard the oncoming rush and saw the billowing dust, he reached into his saddle pack and pulled out an Indian headdress formed into a mask. He handed it to Three Toes, ordered him to put it on, and cautioned him against removing it for any reason.

"We are going to stop the stage, and if you give our identity away you'll git the first bullet." Anson then reached into the other side of his saddle pack and took out a wig of hair longer than his own, which he placed on his head, combing it neatly beneath his officer's hat. Then he placed a fake moustache tightly above his upper lip and pressed it fastidiously into place until he was certain it was secure. So far as he knew, no one suspected him as one of the kidnappers, and though Johnson knew him, the army regalia and newly applied facial features were certain to hide his identity. The two black horses that he and the Indian were now riding would enhance the cover, because no one in Shoshoni had seen these mounts.

The coach and half-jaded horses slowed moderately as they entered the shallow water of the crossing, and then picked up their pace again as they came out on the other side. Just as the dust began to billow again, Anson motioned to Three Toes to move out. The two horsemen exited the small rocky eminence and skirted the brush that had been their hideaway, barreling onto the roadway at a gallop. Perk Anson drew his pistol and fired one shot into the air, shouting as he rode.

"Pull up there, driver! Keep your weapons plainly in sight. Move a muscle, and you're both dead! I mean business, so don't try me."

Johnson pulled strenuously at the reins, seesawing one rein and then the other, pumping repeatedly at the coach's mechanical brakes. "Whoa, Blackjack! Whoa, Stormy," he called out to the two lead horses. The horses flipped their heads in the air and bounced to a graded halt. Dust followed the coach, overtaking its riders briefly in a powdery haze.

"Okay, gents," Anson called out in a muffled tone to disguise his voice. "I think you have some cargo for me. Where's it stashed?"

"Two saddlebags just inside the coach, Officer," Johnson called out nervously. "Keep your firearm cool. We don't need any trouble. Take what you came for and we'll be on our way, no questions asked."

Motioning with the barrel of his gun, Anson gestured toward the door of the coach. "Git the goods, Indian, and decorate my saddle horn with them. Don't anybody move!"

Three Toes hurriedly dismounted, swung himself into the coach and just as quickly dropped again to the ground carrying the saddlebags. He raised them high, swaddling them across the horn in front of Anson and then retrieved his own mount, swinging himself, Indian-style, into the saddle.

"Your job is accomplished, gentlemen, harmless and efficient," Anson shouted, still muffling his voice. "Now, unfetter your brakes and proceed as planned. Keep her rollin', 'til you pull into Riverton. That's an order!"

Without hesitation or a second glance, Johnson flipped the reins and shouted, "Up in there, Blackjack! Ho! Roll 'em, Stormy!" The four-horse team jerked the traces in unison and bolted forward with dispatch, the road rising up plenty fast beneath them. The coach was on its way again.

Trinket observed the entire production without moving a muscle. He was only glad, after the fact, that Three Toes had not drawn a shotgun blast. So far, his friend was safe. He now made ready to trail them realizing that he and Three Toes were now in the majority.

As the two riders moved out toward the crossing, Anson registered a sly smirk. He had played his cards well. Unknowing to Trammel and Wortham, there was a joker in the deck! Anson had the ransom money, which his partners were waiting to retrieve when the stage approached them along the road. Wouldn't they be surprised? Once he got to the stables, Anson would grab a few personal items and head for high country. His ultimate plans for Three Toes had not yet been determined, but he kept his trigger finger limber just in case his move had to come prematurely.

Meanwhile, the stage lumbered along empty of cargo, heading pell-mell for Riverton. There the sheriff would be informed of the ransom drop and alerted by the drivers of any unusual riders that might be following them into Riverton. Waiting passengers could then board the stage for the return trip.

Halfway between Hale's Ford and Riverton, Johnson saw a rope, draped with red flags, stretched across the road ahead. He began slowing the horses and readied his gun for whatever might be awaiting them. Suddenly, and seemingly from out of nowhere, two masked riders appeared running beside them, having approached from the rear. Waving their pistols in the air, they hollered out at the stagehands, "Hold up there, driver, and keep your hands in the open. We're not lookin' for trouble, but you have something we've been waitin' for."

Johnson spoke up, "The reins are tied, partners, but I think you're too late. What can we do for you?"

Trammel reacted boisterously, "Whadaya mean, what can you do for us? You're carrying some ransom money and we're here to fetch it, so throw it down *pronto* and we'll be on our way."

"Like I say, mister, you're too late. The ransom package was picked up back at Hale's Ford half an hour ago."

"Picked up by who?" Trammel retorted, without the use of good grammar again.

"By a man in a Cavalry officer's uniform and a masked Indian, and they didn't leave us any instructions, except to get on into Riverton. That's where we're headed."

"Okay, sidekick, search the coach," Trammel motioned to Wortham. "See if they're telling the truth. If not, they're in trouble. I ain't playin' no games at this point."

Wortham went through the coach and came out empty-handed. He then climbed on top of the stage and looked beneath its rails and along its side panels. Then he ordered the two coachmen to their feet so he could examine the floorboard of the rig. In a moment, motioning to Trammel, he swung to the ground.

"They're tellin' the truth. There's nothing in the coach."

Trammel spoke up, "Tell me, mister, what did the officer and the Indian look like?"

Johnson countered, "The officer had long hair under his hat and sported a moustache, but frankly the moustache looked a bit crooked. Can't say if it was real or not. The Indian wore a headdress formed into a mask. They rode black horses. When they got the ransom from the coach, the officer slung 'em over his saddle horn and the two headed back across the ford in the direction of Shoshoni. That's all I know."

"Okay, gents," Trammel blurted out, "we're letting you go for now, but we've had a good look at you, and if we find you've been lying, we'll find you. You can count on that."

Wortham began pulling in the rope that had been stretched across the road, and the stage eased on down the way.

When the stage was fully on its way, Trammel spoke up again, "Wortham, unless I miss my guess, I think we've been boondoggled. There's no real army officer stupid enough to show himself unless in some disguise. Remember those army duds hangin' in Anson's office? Well, I think Anson was in 'em today. And that Indian he's had working for him must be in on the take. I don't know where they got the black horses. Whadaya make of it?"

"I think you're right, Trammel," Wortham responded. "Anson has the cookies and we're left here standin' with milk on our chins. That's what I think."

Halfway speaking to himself, Trammel rejoined, "Well, he won't git away with it. Git your mask off and lets ride, Wortham. We may be too late to overtake him, but he is sure to head back to the livery stable for cover. Ain't nobody going to suspect him—being the trusted town blacksmith and all. According to our plans, there's no reason for Anson to have stopped the stage. And he never told us he was takin' the Indian with him to Hale's Ford either. He's done pulled a fast one on us, but he'll be sorry. It's either him or us! Limber up your trigger finger and let's ride."

Lively had followed Anson and Three Toes in the early shadows, but as morning light came on, out of fear of being detected, he veered off and followed a major rise west of the route leading out of town. He was quite certain that Anson was heading for Hale's Ford or beyond to intercept the stage. He felt he could make good time on the rise that eventually would parallel the stage route near the crossing.

As predicted, in the panoramic view below, Lively's position had placed him in the whole theater of events that transpired when the stage came barreling down on Hale's Ford. He had seen Anson and Three Toes leave their sequestered place among the rocks and hold up the stage. He had seen Trinket moving in and out of the brush surveying the same action at close range.

Now that the stage had moved on, and Anson and Three Toes were heading back north from whence they had come, he entertained what his next move might be. There was no time to go down the rise, and even if there were time he had to use caution not to put Three Toes in jeopardy or to startle Trinket, who was shadowing their movement along the road. His only option was to backtrack along the rise and gradually decline toward the intervening trails below. This would eventually get him back to terrain on a level with the road. His only hope was that he wouldn't get lost in the brush when he had to leave the upper trails.

He retraced his tracks until he began to wind downward at a slight angle into the brush. Being off the trail, his pace was slower, sidetracking the bushes one at a time, weaving his way toward the valley below. Presently, he found himself on an open bench viewing more brush down the hillside. While resting his horse a moment, something caught his eye in the brush about two hundred yards below and to his left. Dismounting, he eased downward to get a better look, leading his horse delicately around the obstructions. Approaching the mystery spot, now about seventy-five yards in front of him, he saw two horses tethered under a large tree surrounded by a rocky, crescent-shaped *cul-de-sac*. A trail came up through a clearing below the rocks. How strange to see two horses sequestered, as in a hiding place, with no riders to be seen anywhere. The longer he looked, the more certain he became that one horse was Three Toes' horse and the other, a bay, like the one he had seen Anson ride in town.

Questions troubled him. How did these horses get out here? Why was one of them Three Toes' horse? Clearly, Anson had Three Toes constrained against his will. Did Three Toes even know his horse was here? The black horses they rode out of the stables early this morning had to be a screen to veil identity. Lively knew this for sure, or why would Anson have doffed the Army officer's uniform and have left Shoshoni in the dark? All he could conjure up about the scene before him was that Anson would be coming for these horses. The best thing he could do at this point was to wait and see. In any case, Trinket was along the trail stealthily keeping Anson in sight. Lively could afford to wait out the drama. Accordingly, he hid his horse back up the hill in some scrub oak and, with rifle in hand, returned to wait out the eventuality overlooking the tethered horses below.

Puck, Farley, and Palmer, had arrived late at Hale's Ford. Three horsemen simply could not safely follow Anson and Three Toes, who had moved with haste out of Shoshoni. The pursuit of pounding hooves would be a dead giveaway. Thereby, as they had chosen other meandering trails leading to the crossing, even the stage had gotten ahead of them. Now that Anson and Three Toes, with Trinket hot on their trail, had already begun to retrace their tracks back across Hale's Ford and into the brush, the threesome, unknowingly, had missed out altogether. They had seen nothing.

Seeing the stage tracks in the roadway, and not knowing at what point the stage would be held up, the three had pressed on warily in the direction of Riverton hoping to come upon some activity regarding the ransom pick up.

Presently, they were making their way along the road, split up on either side and hugging the brush for seclusion. As they moved along, they were suddenly startled to see two horsemen coming down the road from the direction of Riverton. They quickly veered into the brush and watched the riders approach. It was Trammel and Wortham moving at a hurried pace, apparently on their way back to Shoshoni. The saddlebags that Puck had personally picked to contain the ransom were not with them, the stage was nowhere in sight, and Anson and Three Toes had not been seen. These were the strangest turn of events that Puck had ever seen.

Meanwhile, Lively kept vigilance over the rock quarry below and the uneasy horses tethered in the shade of the tree. They began to move about even more restlessly now than before. Shortly, one of the horses nickered and pricked his ears in the direction of the clearing below the rock. As Lively squinted to shade the morning rays from his eyes, he saw two riders move into the opening. It was Anson in his soldier's uniform and Three Toes, riding the two blacks up the trail. He could not make out what was being said, but he could hear a muffled conversation going on between the two men.

The two rode to the tree and dismounted. Anson pulled back some brush, banked against the rock, and pulled a valise from behind it. Leaning his rifle against the rock wall, he proceeded to open the case and then to shed his officer's attire. Three Toes stood by helplessly, holding the two blacks, possessing the good sense not to make a break for it. Anson's position was only an arms-length from the rifle.

When Anson had made the change into street clothes, he placed the others in the cavity behind the brush along with the valise. Recovering his rifle, he moved toward Three Toes and the horses. The mumbling began again and Three Toes went to the bay and retrieved the saddlebags. Apparently, Anson directed him to transfer the money from the stage bags to his own and to secure them again to the saddle on the bay. When that was accomplished, Anson quickly unbridled the blacks and, with the dangling reins, slapped one of them on the rump. Both horses lumbered down the hill and across the clearing, wasting no time with their newly found freedom. Trinket had been slowly edging his way upward along the trail. The two blacks, passing through the brush below, almost knocked Trinket from his horse. Trinket quickly dismounted, momentarily confused about the rider-less blacks barreling past him. He tied his horse to a protruding limb and reached for his rifle. He then eased up the hill in the direction from which the horses had come. When the dust had settled, and only a faint knocking of hooves could be heard coming from the blacks' escape below, he heard voices rather clearly. He belly-crawled to a slight bench above him and stationed himself where he could see what was taking place. Then a voice began again.

"Okay, Toes, you're in luck! I had meant to do you in, but you've done me no harm and have actually been a lot of help. So, I'm letting you go. Where I'm headed from here, you'll never know, and when I'm gone, you'll never see me again. Of that I can be sure."

While Three Toes did not know what to make of the man's turn of heart, the man himself knew exactly what he had planned. He was headed for high country several days' ride across the border into Canada.

Anson motioned Three Toes toward the clearing below. Without looking back, Three Toes rode slowly into the flat, knowing fully well that when he reached the other side, he would bolt into the brush and break into the roughest terrain he could find. His horse was especially surefooted and Anson would not be able to follow where he would go.

As Three Toes reached the center of the clearing, Anson, having plainly lied about setting him free, raised his rifle and leveled down on the Indian to put him away. Trinket, sequestered below, saw the rifle go up and instantly raised his own, but before he could fire, two shots rang out. Anson's rifle had fired but his aim went awry as he slumped in the saddle and then to the ground. The other shot had come from about fifty yards up the hill where Lively had eventually settled to hear more readily the conversation going on below.

When the shots rang out, Three Toes had slithered like a snake down the side of his horse to the ground and had started crawling for the brush. He didn't look around until he had reached cover. The shot had whizzed past his ear and the other had hit the dirt ten feet to his left. As he looked up the hill, he saw Lively running toward the fallen Anson. To his left, Trinket was bolting toward him from his perch below the clearing, shouting some Shoshoni words, seeking a response and hoping Three Toes was still alive to answer. Thankfully, an answer in Shoshoni met the wind. Three Toes was okay.

The melee now over, the three convened around Anson to check his condition. Was he dead, still alive, wounded slightly or severely, or what? Rolling him over, Lively detected the rise and fall of Anson's chest. He was still breathing. The bullet had hit above his right ear, and somewhat more than a graze, had passed through his scull and out the side of his right lobe. He was totally unconscious, showing no movement except for his breathing, which seemed fairly normal. The blood had stopped except for a slight trickle.

Three Toes retrieved Anson's horse and removed the water bag strapped to the saddle. Lively saturated his own bandana and began to bathe Anson's wounds with the kerchief.

"What we do now, Mr. Johnny?" Trinket asked Lively.

"The only thing we can do is to get him on his horse and down the hill toward the road. Maybe a wagon, the returning stage, or help of some kind will come along so we can get him to the doctor in Shoshoni. Whether or not he'll make it, who knows? But if he dies, we may be in trouble about finding the girl, unless we capture Trammel or Wortham." Lively spoke with no little worry showing on his face.

With that said, Lively and Trinket hoisted Anson over the saddle. Three Toes had retrieved Lively's horse from the scrub oak on the hill and whistled for his own horse that waited in the brush below the clearing. Horses all recovered, the three men, with their wounded victim, gravitated slowly down the hill toward the main road.

When the shots rang out, not only did Puck and his men wheel about to survey the noise coming from behind, but Trammel and Wortham reined up in the middle of the road. Upon seeing Puck, Farley, and Palmer enter the road, they instinctively made a break for the brush.

"Farley, Palmer!" Puck shouted, "Get after Trammel and Wortham. I'm heading in the direction of the shots. Our men may be in trouble. And don't you get into trouble. Keep your heads down and watch your step. Hustle! I'm gone!"

Puck was breathless when he made his move, heading back down the road at breakneck speed. The fact that no more shots sounded, concerned him. Either the intended target had moved out of range or someone was hit, and unless he heard another shot, his finding the source was going to be extremely difficult. There was nothing he could do but keep on riding. He crossed Hale's Ford in a haze of splashing water, then slowed to give his horse a breather. He looked and listened, but nothing! Getting his second wind, Gentry leveled out again in an unrestrained gallop, moving sprightly along the roadway for a quarter of a mile or so.

Up the hill to his left, Puck spotted a faint puff of dust and reined up along a trail meandering upward toward the western rise. By the time he had stopped, the dust was gone, but the noise of sliding rock and the knock of horses' hooves could be heard above Gentry's blowing nostrils. Puck retrieved his rifle from its leather and waited. His wait was short-lived. The two blacks that had come off the western rise broke into a clearing and down the meandering grade and dashed in front of him—saddles still intact, but bridles missing.

Puck thought to himself, *Two shots, two rider-less horses, no bridles! What could this mean? Where were Anson and Three Toes?* He swallowed tensely and scoured the hillside for a solution to his nervous questioning.

In a moment, evidence toward an answer came tearing down the hill in the form of Trinket. He had hurried ahead of Lively and Three Toes in their slow descent, hoping to find help for them when he reached the bottom. He was surprised, but relieved, to find Puck and Gentry shuffling excitedly in the roadbed.

Puck was just as surprised and relieved, as he interrogated Trinket about what had happened. Hearing the facts, he was visibly alarmed that Anson was unconscious, yet relieved that Three Toes was safe. Anson may have deserved everything he got, but his death would greatly jeopardize the search for Papu Banta. Every effort should be made to keep him alive. To that end, Puck would direct his attention. That mindfulness was about to begin, as Lively and Three Toes were now easing down the footpath with their wounded felon.

CHAPTER 13

THE VIGIL

Farley and Palmer hustled, as Puck had directed, but with every precaution that any sane gunmen would take, riding blindly into the brush after dangerous men. Hazard could lurk around any bush, and these two seasoned gunslingers were not about to run into an ambush.

Farley hollered for Palmer to pull up.

"Look, Palmer," Farley pondered, "if we follow them in, then we're goin' to be in trouble. It's only about a mile across this patch of brush in front of us. On the other side is a long, open park that stretches out two hundred yards, before the brush begins again. Unless I miss my guess, they'll be crossing that flat to get into heavier cover. Which way they'll turn after that is anyone's guess. Apparently, they were headed back to Shoshoni, so they may turn north, but havin' been detected, they may go south and wait things out awhile.

"Here's what we need to do. You head south down the road about a half of a mile and find a trail leadin' to the clearing. When you arrive at the clearing, station yourself at the edge, so you can view the flat. I'm heading north and cutting back to do the same. Once you cut back, never mind the noise getting' down the trail. We have to be in place when they ride into the clearing. They should come out somewhere between us. If they cut back on us, we're out of luck, but then they'll have to get past Puck."

The two split up and moved out in a race against time. Farley had a feeling that though Trammel and Wortham were doing the same, they were probably skittish enough to stop, intermittently, to see if anyone were following. This would slow them enough to allow him and Palmer to gain on them and hopefully to pass them.

Time seemed to have crawled as Farley and Palmer finally reached their stations overlooking the flat. Farley was concerned that they might be too late. By the time he got his breath and his horse settled down from the brisk run, time seemed to have mounted beyond any possibility that Trammel and Wortham would still be in the brush. He had no real option but to wait, and he hoped Palmer was doing the same. The vigil was on, sink or swim.

Directly, hearing a crackling noise down a ways to his right, Farley stretched out to survey the edge of the brush line. The noise had stopped but there was a curious movement of some branches on a willow bush. Something was there. Farley kept his eyes trained on the spot, and surely enough, two doe broke into the open in a fast trot. He was quite certain they had been disturbed from their bedding ground, because they would have been laying up in the shade this time of the morning. They lost little time getting across the clearing. Trammel and Wortham, Farley surmised, would be coming out any moment.

As suspected, a horse and rider eased out of the brush and stopped long enough to survey the clearing, and then returned to the brush. Moments passed. Suddenly, as if a bell had rung signaling the start, a horse and rider lurched into the opening at breakneck speed and bolted toward the brush on the other side. It was Wortham.

Farley resigned within himself that Trammel and Wortham were not as ignorant as he had thought. There was no way he could pursue Wortham, and unless he missed his guess, Trammel would likewise break out of the brush and proceed across the flat, under the cover of Wortham's gun. If such were the case, Farley was in a dither. He had to stop Trammel before he could get to the other side, or the two would be gone, and yet he needed to take these men alive, if the

Indian girl were ever to be found. No sooner had he entertained such thought, than Trammel broke into the clearing with pistol drawn and headed for the other side.

With two guns against him, Farley could not pursue Trammel into the open. He had no idea where Palmer was at this point, but he knew he had to take some kind of action. Resting his rifle barrel on a protruding limb for support, he leveled down on the rider, now some seventy yards away. When the rifle's peep was finely tuned on Trammel's shoulder, Farley eased the trigger gently, knowing he had only one chance. The burst of the rifle added to the rumble of the horse's hooves, and the bullet hit its mark. Trammel fell from his mount writhing on the ground. Wortham instantly bolted into the clearing, firing indiscriminately in Farley's direction. Farley entered the clearing, riding low along his steed, firing only discerningly, hoping Wortham would turn chicken and retreat. No such luck! Wortham rushed alongside Trammel and pulled him up behind the saddle, turning in the same motion and heading pell-mell for the cover of the brush.

When the firing began, Palmer had possessed the presence of mind to cross the clearing south of the foray and move along the brush on the other side. He now waited in the precise spot where Wortham had exited the brush to aid Trammel. At the risk of killing one or the other, Farley could no longer fire, but continued the pursuit to keep the pressure on and to draw Wortham's attention. What would happen when they reached the other side and entered the brush was open to speculation.

As Wortham and Trammel neared the point of entry, Palmer fired a shot into the air. Wortham's horse startled to a halt. Now, with rifle leveled on the rogues, Palmer shouted, "Rein up, Buster, or you'll meet your Maker with holes in your vest!"

Wortham dropped his reins and pitched his pistol on the ground, while Trammel slid off the horse half-conscious. Farley bounced to a halt behind them and dismounted, placing his rifle back into its leather. While Palmer held Wortham at bay, Farley went to his saddlebags and extracted a small vial of Laudanum and handed it to Trammel.

"Here," he said. "This medicine will help deaden the pain. You were getting away and I couldn't let that happen. You are both accessories to kidnapping, with the intention of receiving ransom for the victim."

Trammel reacted, "What's this kidnapping and ransom jargon? You don't have evidence for any of this. We don't have any ransom on us. And what proof do you have that we are part of any kidnapping?"

"Well, we have evidence of both, and we'll try to make it stick, but for now, we're taking you into Shoshoni."

"You're wastin' your time, Slick," Trammel contended, grimacing in churning pain. "You boys'll look like silly asses when you cain't prove anything."

Luckily, Trammel's shoulder wound was not too serious, the bullet having passed through flesh below the collarbone and the arm pit. This made for easier travel back to Shoshoni as the foursome headed north.

Arriving in Shoshoni, Farley and Palmer went to find Dr. Orland Metcalf, while Sheriff Larson placed Trammel and Wortham under lock and key. They then went to the stables to inform Whiskers about the events of the morning, including their capture of Trammel and Wortham.

"Well, where's Puck and the others?" Whiskers inflected. "Lively went out on his own, you know. And what's happened to Anson and Three Toes?"

"We don't know yet," Farley responded. "We heard shots earlier, just before Palmer and I took after Trammel and Wortham. Puck headed to check out the shots and that's the last we saw of him. We're banking on the ingenuity of Trinket and Lively to take care of themselves. Three Toes doesn't have a gun, but he's smart. Of course, *smart* isn't equal to an ex con with a gun, so we're more worried about him than anyone. Puck can take care of himself. But this doesn't tell us much about what's taken place and whether or not any of them need our help."

About that time, Palmer interjected, "Looka comin' here!" Trotting toward them were the two rider-less and bridle-less black horses. Whiskers and Farley eased out to stop them. Palmer reached for two short lead ropes draped over a tethering rail and met them in the middle of the road to help secure the horses and to lead them into the stables.

"Whadaya make of this?" Whiskers queried. "Saddles, but no bridles! Someone has turned these horses loose and they were conscientious enough to remove their reins so they didn't get hung up on the brush. But this means that Anson and Three Toes are afoot." Whiskers rubbed his beard and appeared to be thinking. Then he darted into the stable barn and went to the cubical where Three Toes kept his horse and then to where Anson kept his. Both horses, of course, were gone.

"This doesn't make any sense at all," Whiskers began again, half talking to himself. "No one took the horses out of the barn this morning. I haven't been sleeping. Yet, I didn't even notice that they were missing. None of this makes sense."

"We don't have any answers either," Palmer spoke up. "We never even ran across Anson and Three Toes this morning. Unless Puck has done some good, or Lively, or Trinket, we're going to remain in the dark."

"Yeah, well dark hasn't got here yet," came a voice from behind the three men. The men wheeled to identify the intruder. It was

Sheriff Larson. "We've got some time men, and we'll have to make the best of it. I just got a telegram from Sheriff Bixley in Riverton. The stage was held up by a man in an officer's uniform and an Indian, and the ransom was picked up."

"Well, what can we do?" Farley spoke up. "We don't know where any of our own men are at this point, not to mention Anson and Three Toes. There's no certain trail to follow except the main road. We brought Trammel and Wortham in on a trail east of the main road, so we don't know who might be on it."

"Well, gentlemen, it's my guess," Larson pondered, "that—"

Sheriff Larson's words were cut short by the noise and shouting of an incoming rider, who reined up in a fog of dust at the entrance of the stable barn.

Above the snort of his horse's breathing and his own excitement, the rider spoke, half gasping for air. "Saw you standin' here, Sheriff. Uh, they're bringin' him in! They asked me to hurry ahead to inform you and Doc Metcalf."

"Settle down, man," Larson countered. "They're bringing who in? I mean who's bringing who in?"

"Don't rightly know all the details, Sheriff, but a Mr. Puckett, another man, and two Indians commandeered a buckboard driven by an elderly couple. They have a wounded man on board, shot through the head. Mr. Puckett told me to tell you he is a man named Anson—whoever that is—and that he will need the attention of Doc Metcalf. That's all I know. They're about eight miles out."

The sheriff asked Benedict to go to the jail and alert Doc Metcalf about the injured man coming in, and to have him meet at his clinic, as soon as he is finished with doctoring Trammel's wound.

When Whiskers entered the jail, Doc Metcalf was just closing his doctor's case.

"Doc Metcalf," Whiskers spoke urgently, "Sheriff Larson sent me. When you complete your work here, he wanted you to meet him at your clinic. They are bringing Anson in with a gunshot to the head."

Hearing the name *Anson,* Trammel and Wortham looked at one another with a look of surprise.

"Anson?" Doc questioned. "Who's Anson?"

"You know, Doc, the blacksmith and farrier at the stables."

"You mean Browning?"

"Yeah, Browning to you, I guess. In any case, he is going to need your attention."

"Well, we can be on our way. I'm through here for now."

"Say, old man," Trammel gestured as Whiskers turned to leave. "What's the state of this Anson you speak about? I mean, is he going to make it? And what was he doing to come by a shot in the head?"

"Can't say that any of this is your concern, young buck. Anyway, I'm not at liberty to get into it, and I don't know much about it myself. But if he does make it, he may wind up in the cell next to you."

As they left the jailbirds in the hands of Larson's deputy, Whiskers asked the doctor if he would need any assistance getting things ready at the clinic.

"You can come along, if you like. Things are about as ready as you can get for a man with a shot to the head. Don't know if an operation will be in order or not, but he'll need to be kept quiet. You may want to stay by the bed and alert me if anything crucial develops. We'll find some others to sit shifts with you. As far as I know, Browning doesn't have any family here."

Two hours had passed when the buckboard carrying the gunshot victim rolled up to Doc Metcalf's clinic. Puck and Lively helped Whiskers and the doc carry Anson into the building. As Puck started up the boardwalk, he called back to his scouts, "Three Toes, you and Trinket can go get your things out of the livery stable. You won't be staying there any longer, and hang around close. Sheriff Larson may need to talk with you. I see Farley and Palmer coming with the sheriff, now."

Whiskers stayed with the doc as he examined Anson, while the sheriff and other men waited outside, eager to know the doc's prognosis. Shortly, Doc Metcalf emerged the examining room and walked slowly to where the men were standing. There was an unmistakable look of concern on his face as he stroked his chin in concentration.

"Orland," Sheriff Larson addressed the doc familiarly, "what'd you find? Anything promising?"

"Well, I'll tell you Sheriff, it certainly doesn't look good. He may make it, but then again he may not. He didn't lose too much blood, but enough to weaken matters. He's still unconscious and with that kind of blow, he may stay that way for several days, if he comes around at all. The bullet passed through cleanly, so there's no operation to be performed. About all I can do for him until he rallies is to bathe his wounds with antiseptic and give him a little Belladonna for pain, along with a few vitamin injections. If he doesn't come around to where we can get some water down him, he'll get dehydrated and we'll lose him for sure. If we can get that far with him, we can even get some broth down him for foodstuff, which he will certainly eventually need, or everything will become hopeless anyway. Weakness will shut down his organ functions. Right now, all we can do is stand by and hope for him to wake up enough to respond to our treatments."

Puck thanked Doc Metcalf for his analysis and assured him that he would be well paid for his services. He left Whiskers to sit out the first shift in what might be a long vigil, waiting for Anson to recover from his comatose condition. He and the other men would relieve Whiskers and each other in turn, in the watch. The doc seemed appreciative of their helpfulness and noted that he would be available to respond to any unexpected change in the patient's condition.

Sheriff Larson took the saddlebags containing the ransom to the bank for safekeeping and settled in for the evening at the jail.

The men made their adieu to Doc Metcalf and headed for the hotel, making connections with Three Toes and Trinket for a well-deserved dinner and late afternoon *siesta*. The day would soon wear away, and night would bring a welcomed reprieve from the day's rigors of danger and duress. Hopefully, tomorrow would bring a change in Anson's condition and Trammel and Wortham would come clean on their role in the kidnapping. Though the ransom pickup had been foiled for them, expectation reigned supreme that the two would concede and reveal the whereabouts of the Indian girl. Puck would invariably be on the job come first light.

Come morning, there was no change in Anson's condition, as Puck went by the clinic to inquire, so he proceeded to the jail to help the sheriff interrogate the inmates.

Sheriff Larson was already beside himself, frustrated that Trammel and Wortham were playing the innocence game. They admitted nothing regarding the kidnapping and dared the sheriff to prove anything otherwise.

"Puck," Sheriff Larson invited, "see what you can do. I've done nothing but waste my breath."

Puck ambled over to the cell where Trammel and Wortham were secluded. "Gentlemen," he spoke up somewhat congenially, "we've got a problem here. Maybe you can help me with it for everyone's sake. We've got a little Indian girl out there somewhere being held against her will, and unless she is released soon, her survival is questionable. We have good evidence that you both know where she has been placed. For your own good, as well as the girl's, you might want to tell us where we can find her."

"Well, Mr. Detective," Trammel reacted, "Yeah, we've heard about a little girl being kidnapped. Who hasn't? It's been spread around everywhere you go. But we can't help you any more than anyone else in town."

"Can't or won't?" Puck countered.

"Well, we would if we could," Wortham piped up.

"Look, my good man," Puck enjoined, looking squarely in Wortham's pitiable eyes, "we have had the two of you under surveillance for a good week. We've watched you pay visits to Anson, the blacksmith, on many occasions. Our Indian scout has been our cover as a hired hand in the stables, and he has seen you fraternize with Anson many times, overhearing some of your conversations. Not only that, Briley Wortham—does the name sound familiar?—you told two of our men at our camp outside of Shoshoni that you personally had worked for Anson. Anson picked up the ransom yesterday morning, a task originally meant for you, but he double-crossed you and beat you to the draw. Our stage driver will verify later today that the two of you attempted to pick up the ransom that you thought was on the stage.

"If that is not enough, we'll be bringing in the two Indian boys, who saw you kidnap their little friend, and they will identify you before the courts. It appears to me that it would be to your advantage to come clean and help us locate the girl. Maybe the courts will be lenient in some way. So, what do you say?"

"We don't know about any Indian boys, mister," Trammel responded, "and we'll be glad for you to bring in the stage driver. We don't know him, and he don't know us."

"What were you running from yesterday, then, when we startled you coming toward Shoshoni on the main road?"

"We heard shots about the time we saw you in the brush along the road and we thought we were in line for an ambush of some kind," Trammel countered. "We got out of there quick! What would you have done?"

Puck saw that he was getting nowhere, so he made one final attempt to be convincing. "Okay, men, let me confide in you something that might be of interest to your own safety. Down the road here, is a band of Indian braves from Wind River Village where the girl was kidnapped. They are sure to be down here this morning, and if they even think you are not complying with us to help find their little Indian girl, they won't like it! They have ways of making people talk. We'll turn you over to them, and when they finish with you, either they will know where to find the girl, or you will regret that you still have breath.

"Now, gentlemen—and I use that word loosely—you know, as well as I do, with what seriousness they dredge the truth out of persons. Did you ever hear of them staking out their victims in the broiling desert sun, tethered with green deer hides? When those hides dry, they begin to shrink and will almost cut the wrists and ankles in half, not to mention what damage is done by the strip that has been stretched across the forehead. I've seen where others have staked out their victims over a red anthill and then have put the whole den into a frenzy by stomping around their entry hole. You might just as well be burned with fire. Knowing this, you might want to reconsider your decision about the girl."

Puck didn't wait for a response but walked slowly away from the cell and ambled over to where Sheriff Larson was standing. Larson turned to him and placed his hand to the side of his mouth and spoke in low tones, so the prisoners could not hear. "Puck, you know we can't turn these men over to that band of Indians."

"I know that, Sheriff, but maybe they don't."

Wortham, noticeably shaken, turned to Trammel and asked feverishly. "They can't do that, can they?"

Putting his hand on Wortham's shoulder, Trammel called out, "Hey, Sheriff, surely you ain't going to turn us over to them savages, are you? I ain't no lawyer, but you know, as well as I do, that your job is to keep us safe until we get our day in court. If you let them Indians get at us, we'll have your job, and you'll have a cell of your own. So, you better inform your assistant there of the facts."

Puck walked back to the cell and spoke with finality. "Look, gents, I have a promise to make. If you fail to help us find where you have placed the girl, and she dies as a result of your insolence, I'll do everything in my power to see you hang by the neck until dead, and I'll personally request the role of executioner!"

With that, Puck turned and left the jail, followed by Sheriff Larson. When they stepped onto the boardwalk, they were pleasantly delighted by the presence of Colonel Meech and his troops.

"Well, Sheriff, Puck," the Colonel addressed the men, "we've learned of yesterday's developments and have come to see what help we might be. We've played out our welcome at the Old Ryrie place, and the men corralling the Indian band are tired of their watch at the holding pens. I told them to give us thirty minutes to check out the situation and then to bring Broken Heel and his braves to meet us. The Indians are about played out, too. So, what's up, gentlemen? How may we be of service?"

Puck spoke up. "Colonel, We're glad you're here. And I think you can be of help. In fact, what takes place at this point may turn out to be our only hope—at least under present circumstances."

"What circumstances do you refer to, Puck?"

"What I mean is that, on the one hand, Anson is in a coma and is currently of no help on getting information on the whereabouts of the girl. His regaining consciousness appears doubtful at this point. On the other hand, Trammel and Wortham have shut us out, denying any part in the kidnapping, and we're at a loss as to how to make them talk—legally, that is. Unless those men stocked the girl's confines with adequate food and water, time is running out. So right now, our only option is to get all the interested bodies we can find, to begin a hill-to-hill, canyon-to-canyon, cave-to-cave search for the girl. We have only some faint indications of where the search might begin. Piecing together a few bits of information, if we blanket the area with enough people, we just may luck out and locate the hiding place. I'm personally going to keep vigil with Doc Metcalf on Anson's condition and keep trying to persuade Trammel and Wortham to pony up with directions to the girl. When Broken Heel gets here, we'll get him and his men involved, as well."

As he spoke, a shading of horsemen, breaking through the morning haze, appeared to be heading their way. The closer they came, the more apparent it became that it was Meech's men and the Indian band. The soldiers reined up in virtual silence, but the Indians were chattering outlandishly, indicating thereby that they had not lost their vim, vigor and vitality.

Broken Heel bounced to the ground and addressed Puck and the sheriff. "All is *okee-dokee* with you, is the hope of Broken Heel!"

"Thank you, Broken Heel. Yes, all is okay with us this morning," Puck averred.

"And have you caught the evil ones who have taken our Papu?"

"Well, yes, and no," was Puck's response.

"What do you mean *yes* and *no*. If it is *yes*, it cannot be *no*, and if it is *no*, it cannot be *yes*. Yes?"

"Yes, you are right, my friend." Puck had been equivocating, hoping that he would not have to tell Broken Heel of the culprits in jail, though he halfway might like to see these Shoshonis get their hands on them long enough to shake the dust off their tongues.

"We have to tell you the truth, Broken Heel, and then tell you how you may help us. I promised you a place in this deal earlier in the week, and I'll keep my promise. One of the men involved in the kidnapping of Papu has been shot in the head and is unconscious at Doc Metcalf's clinic. Unless he wakes up soon, he will be of no help to us. The other two men have been captured and are locked behind bars over there in Sheriff Larson's jail. Though we do not believe them, they tell us that they know nothing about the kidnapping. So—"

Puck was interrupted by Broken Heel's brushing him to one side as he headed for the jail.

"Wait," Puck shouted, as he and Sheriff Larson took after him.

The door of the jail was flung open as Broken Heel barreled through the entry, crossing the room and grasping hold of the cell bars. The big Indian, swarthy and turning red with anger, jolted the entire building with his booming voice.

"So, you are the tight tongues who won't tell us where you have taken our Papu Banta?"

Sheriff Larson lunged to pull the Indian away, but Puck grabbed his shoulder and pulled him back. "Wait, Sheriff," he coaxed, "Let him have his say. He just might put the fear of the Etruscans in those goofballs, and do some good."

The sheriff held back and gave place to the fuming brave.

"Look-see here, you weak-faced child keepers!" the Indian's blast continued. "You will soon tell us where you have taken our little girl, or we will feed your flesh to the vultures, and your bones will be spread among the whitened animal skulls of the prairie! If my people have to break these doors to catch you by the throat, we will bend these bars like iron men and nail you to the wall! Only one question to you, that empty heads can understand—where is our little Indian girl? Be with haste to tell us your answer!"

Trammel and Wortham turned pale and cowered in the corner of the cell, coughing and almost choking at the Indian's words, perspiring and blinking away the salty brine bathing their eyelids. Then silence. Outside, Indian drums began a mournful timpani beat. Broken Heel, with arms akimbo, walked slowly toward the cell again, still angry but more subdued.

"White eyes," he began again, "you have one last chance to choose your fortune. Do you hear those drums? They are beating for you. When they stop beating, you die!" In mock portrayal of instant death, the Indian punctuated his promise with a quick slash across his own throat with his stiffened hand and the click of his tongue. He then turned and walked away.

Outside again, the sheriff and Puck, with some difficulty, gathered the men around them. The drums continued to beat. To hold forth his promise, Broken Heel sent two drummers to station themselves on the bench outside the front door of the jail. They would continue day and night until they were directed to cease, one always beating the same mournful dirge, the other caring for their needs—eating, drinking, resting, and sleeping in turn—but the drum was never silent. It looked as if Sheriff Larson and his deputy would have to find another place to sleep, if they intended to get any.

Puck addressed the group of servicemen and Indian braves.

"Look, men, we have the difficult, and almost blind task of searching for the little Indian girl. Our area of concern, so far as we know at this point, is along the eastern border of the reservation, somewhere between Shoshoni and Riverton. That is a large area, so in a little while I will be sending a telegram to Sheriff Bixley in Riverton asking him to bring together as many professional and otherwise willing townspeople to scout out as much of that area as possible. Colonel Meech, would you take your men – and call on any others back at Fort Washakie that can be spared—and scout out the area two miles in breadth outside the reservation on the eastern front?"

"We'll do it, Puck."

"Broken Heel," Puck continued, "first, I would like for you to send a runner to the Wind River Village and have him bring back to Shoshoni the two young boys who witnessed the kidnapping. Then, if you would, please, take the rest of your men to scout out the eastern border inside the reservation. Don't cross the border. If you would like, your runner may bring ten more men to your aid when he returns with the boys. For the sake of abiding by reservation rules and keeping down confusion, please limit the number to ten. I am sending Trinket with you, as he knows every nook and cranny of the territory into which you'll be moving."

One of the Indians shuffled and mumbled something to Puck. Puck responded, repeating his question. "What's nook and cranny? Well, that means every important trail, watering hole, cave, and that sort of thing."

The Indian seemed satisfied with Puck's explanation, so Puck continued addressing the group.

"Gentlemen, I hope you'll not feel that I am shirking duty by my remaining behind. There's enough here to keep me plenty busy, not the least of which is to keep up the vigil on Anson's medical condition, and to try to think through the known details of this case. I'm asking my wagon man, Whiskers Benedict, to stay behind and help Doc at the clinic. Doc's wife has consented to help with the bedside sitting, as well. I also need Three Toes to stay with me as my right hand man. He served as our cover at the stables and often overheard the conversations of Anson and the other two suspects. The rest of my men, Jed Palmer, Johnny Lively, Bill Farley—*ahem*, excuse me—Pistol Bill Farley, and Mel Engle will be pursuing a southeasterly route to a destination where Palmer once saw Trammel and Wortham meeting along the trail. They could likely heat up a cold trail in that vicinity.

"Okay, today is Saturday. If everyone can get into position by early afternoon, we'll have the rest of today and Sunday to cover our assigned territory. Somewhere along the way, Sheriff Bixley's group will merge with our parties.

"Now, gentlemen, two other items. The governor of this territory has given me a blank check, so to speak, to purchase anything that may be needed for the assignment I accepted a few weeks ago. Go to the café before you leave and get a substantial meal for the ride. Then go to the local mercantile and purchase enough food supplies to carry you through two days. These places will know to charge everything to my account. And finally, men, if the girl is not found by Sunday evening, everyone should gather at Hale's Ford by noon Monday. I'll meet you there at that time. This is the best strategy that I have at the moment, so good luck, and may God, the Great Spirit, be your guide."

Everyone, now resolved to take matters into his own hands, following his specific assignment, mounted and turned to prepare for the ride. Puck headed for the clinic to check on Anson's condition, and Sheriff Larson headed for the telegraph office to send a telegram to Sheriff Bixley in Riverton. The day was still early, and the air seemed cooler than usual, a welcomed condition for waging what hopefully would be the final search for Papu Banta.

CHAPTER 14

THE HIDING PLACE

A low, sad whimper pierced the blackened walls of the hiding place. Nothing but a candle or two lighted the grim surroundings, and even they were almost melted away. Little Papu Banta wiped away her tears and hoped for the light of day. Today no one had come. No one had heard her sobs. No one had discovered her misery. Mournfully she began to speak above her sadness, to drown out her throbbing heartache. A soliloquy of sorrow, grief's slow stain, filled the vacuous hall, as she mimed to herself.

"There's no one to listen," she said. "No one to talk to! Little girls like me should not have to be lonesome. Maybe if I talk to myself, I will feel better."

And so she began. "Little Indian girl, can you hear what I say? Listen to me closely, because I won't be able to say it again. It hurts too much. Do you remember when you were free, when you played together with your little friends with so much happiness? Oh, but to see my little friends again—little Joachim and Willamette; Pokie and Dardanelle; Madra and Helena; Wilder, Rampart, and Kelly Jo. I would never be angry with them again. There is no reason ever to be unkind.

"Do you remember, too, little Indian girl, the loveliness of summertime in the open air, how the sun warmed your spirit by day and the moon lighted your path by night? How every little bird seemed to whisper a song of joy in your ears? How the raindrops gently pelted your lashes making it hard to see, and yet, how you loved their silent trickle down your dusty face?

"Do you remember the call to suppertime of *pemmican*, stew, and choke cherry pudding? How bedtime from a tiring day meant sweet dreams of romping through meadows and catching lovely butterflies to caress with care, and then to let them fly away to freedom once again? How I miss that happy playground made of earth, stone, and fresh green grass, flowers dancing in the golden sunshine, given to us by the Great Spirit. But my sorrow is not golden, my heart cannot shine, and I'm lonely as a cloud that has lost its way in the sky. My mother's words have taught me well, to know by heart her Wordsworth poem.

> *I wandered lonely as a cloud*
> *That floats on high o'er vales and hills,*
> *When all at once I saw a crowd,*
> *A host, of golden daffodils;*
> *Beside the lake, beneath the trees,*
> *Fluttering and dancing in the breeze.*

"Do you remember, little Indian girl, how the sweet touch at your mother's breast seemed so warm and safe? How she cried when you cried and laughed when you laughed? And now, you are not safe, little Indian girl. You cry, and no one cries with you. You laugh no more, but then, what does it matter? There's no one here to join the laughter. You sob alone tonight and hope for joy tomorrow.

"Evil men have hidden you in a dark place, little Papu. Even your name sounds sad in the darkness. No one comes to get you. Has everyone forgotten? How I wish they would remember me. I remember them. If I could, I would love them again. I do love them, even if they don't remember. Oh, Great Spirit, are you there? Please send someone to my lonely side."

With that somber quest for hope quivering on her lips, the little girl cried herself to sleep.

With the morning light came the rain. After two weeks of sweltering heat and powder dry days, Papu was so happy to see moisture that she shouted for joy. And while she was shouting, she turned it into a plea for help, calling out to anyone who might happen nearby and hear her baleful cry. But no one was likely to hear. The hiding place no longer had trails leading to it that might draw human traffic of any kind, even that of adventurers, trappers, or hunters. This shaft of a cave hidden in the bush was a long-forgotten place. Weeds and brambles had long since covered over the entrance except for a small opening beneath a rocky eminence above, just large enough for crawling into its darkened confines. A few surface holes in the rock ceiling brought intermittent streaks of light into the chambers, with somewhat brighter light at high noon. An old gate of metal wickerwork closed off the opening from the inner berth, twenty feet within the cloister. Papu could not proceed beyond this point. The gate had been padlocked and its surround chinked with mortar.

One of the greater openings had fresh rainwater trickling down its stony walls and beginning to puddle on the cavern floor. Papu rushed for the water buckets left for her by the kidnappers, three empty and one with only a quart of water left in it. She had been rationing the last bit of water, not knowing when, or if, the evil men would return with more. The food had been rationed away almost completely now, and Papu was getting hungry, so hungry that she had even wished at one point that the men would return with food to restock her supply, though she detested seeing their dreadful faces again.

A frightening thought momentarily recurred reminding her of the nightmare she was experiencing. She recalled a day when the two good-for-nothings came to the mine together. She remembered something she said to them that made them so angry that Wortham slapped her across the face. She had gone into a tirade when they would not let her leave the cave. She shuddered again as she recalled her remarks. "You two white peoples look bad at Indian peoples. You are not like other white peoples I know. When I want to be free, you spit in my face and tell me shut up. You push me down in the dark corner and take away my food. You say nasty things to me and take away my clothes. Only when I begin to cough and shiver, you give them back, or maybe by now I would be sick to death with fever. One fat man and one tall, skinny man think they are strong to keep little, weak Indian girl from going home. But you are weaker, and your mothers and fathers were weaker than you, to let you become the evil men you are. My great Chief Washakie would say you are not real men, but bastard men. He would tell to you that you are not good men but little boy sons-of-bitches, who have not grown up."

It was at that point of her tirade, Papu recalled, that Wortham slapped her hard with the back of his hand, knocking her to the floor. When she recovered and got back to her feet, she had added one more remark. "Your mean action is the sign that I tell the truth. It is the truth that makes you angry."

Those grisly faces now coming to mind, Papu's thoughts wandered back to that awful night when those evil men first took her away from her village. She didn't even get to say goodbye to her mother or father or to her three-year-old brother, Timeron. She recalled yelling to her two little friends, Wilder and Pokie, to help her, and they tried, but their little ponies couldn't catch the bigger horses of the wicked men. She had tried to get away, biting, kicking and screaming, but the stout arm of her captor held her like a vice to his chest. They rode into the dark night, and she remembered being weak with fear. Even now, she realizes, she has been in the dark practically ever since that terrifying night.

Papu almost screamed out again, recalling her misery and fearing that she might end up in total darkness in this vile, prison-like den.

With the rain getting heavier, the usual noonday sun could not be seen, and the light in the chambers was limited almost entirely to the two small candles. If those candles either went out, or burned away, she would be left to the mercy of the least amount of light during the day and total blackness at night. How she would dread darkness so dark that she would not even be able to see her hand before her face.

What should she do about the candles? Somehow she had to conserve her source of light. She looked around for something to burn, though she knew she would have to build the fire in front of the metal gate as close to the entrance as possible. The draft from inside would draw the smoke out the entrance and keep from threatening her with carbon monoxide. In her village she had been taught the importance of a flu or open flap in the peak of their teepees to keep fresh air ventilating and pushing the dangerous air out of the tent. She remembered that, just outside the gate, a pile of old dried brambles had been bunched against the wall. Could she reach any of them through the opening in the wickerwork gate? That was the question. Arriving at the gate she reached through the opening closest to the brambles, but even they were too far out of reach. What was that she faintly recalled, that the big man once left behind? He had used it as walking support to help hold up his seemingly giant frame—giant to her anyway—because she was just a little girl. She hurried back to the central quarters where she spent most of her time and searched around and under everything in the surrounding area.

She found nothing on the floor, but when she looked up toward the ceiling, she saw what she thought she remembered—a four-foot, dead tree limb hanging against the wall on a small ledge-rock above. It was caught by a shorter limb protruding downward like a wishbone away from the butt end of the stick. She reached for it, lifting it from its lodging, and headed for the gate with it.

Papu guided the stick through the gate opening and latched the wishbone hook around a substantial stem and began to pull. The brambles were matted together and a good portion of the pile tended her way as she pulled at the mass. With concerted effort and a bit of luck, the little Indian finally drew the heap against the gate. With precision, she pulled stem after stem through the openings until she had a considerable bulk inside the chamber. She moved it to a remote place away from the gate for dry storage, and then took sufficient fragments of it back to the gate to start a small campfire. Removing one of the candles, she ignited the dry faggots until they were blazing. She then blew out the candle to conserve it for later when the other candle would be depleted. She would also feed the fire slowly, so as not to use up the brambles unwisely, always keeping enough back to restart the fire, if necessary.

Now that she had solved her lighting problem, at least for the moment, she began to concentrate on food. She went back to change the buckets as each one filled with rainwater, knowing that all of them would soon be filled if the rain continued much longer. As she moved one of the buckets to replace it, she saw a large grasshopper on the chamber floor that apparently had been washed through the hole above by the incoming rain. As she reached for it, another one washed across her hand from above. She grabbed them up quickly and stashed them in an old rusty canister the men had left for food storage. To her amazement, more of them were washing down the funnel-like opening above, the good thing being that most of them had not drowned but were still quite alive. As grotesque as it sounds to most people, the eating of certain insects was a means of survival. It was a foregone fact that many Indians in lean years had kept from starving by eating roasted grasshoppers. Even in good times, the practice was still maintained, and Papu herself had eaten them, although she might certainly have wished for almost anything else, given a choice. But now, push had come to shove, and Papu was hungry enough to eat almost anything.

The little Indian girl broke a long, slender twig from the pile of brambles. Without giving it another thought, she skewered three grasshoppers onto the slender spear-like extremity and turned them slowly over the fire long enough to roast them thoroughly. One by one, she ate them as they cooled, even relishing the taste, she was so hungry. She prepared two more and saved back six for morning. She knew, however, that if she left them in the canister, they would all be dead by morning. That would not be good, as bacteria would set in and spoil them for purposes of eating. Accordingly, she gathered handfuls of small stones that she stacked in a small corral-like circle, forming a small, dome-like enclosure, in which to secure them. She placed the remaining grasshoppers in the stone igloo through a small opening in the top and then placed a small stone over the opening. The insects would be able to get sufficient air to remain alive and yet be unable to escape.

Satisfied with her ingenuity, Papu turned to the pails that were now all filled with rainwater. The increasing trickle of water instantly gave Papu another thought. She would bathe as best she could and wash her hair that, by this time, had become matted with dirt and left powdery dry. The kidnappers had shown the presence of mind enough to leave a small cake of lye soap with her, if for no other reason than to help her keep down dangerous bacteria. Sickness now would greatly inhibit their purpose. They needed her alive and well.

The rain lasted just long enough for her to rinse the soap from her body and out of her long black hair. The sun had actually already begun to shine through the opening, but the water was still meandering through the rocks to the chamber below, giving Papu time enough to complete her bath. She dried her body sparingly and ruffled her hair with an old piece of blanket, other than the one she used for cover at night. Combing through her hair with her fingers, she finally formed it into a flowing, silky flock. In the stream of light, filtering down from above, it glistened like the back of a raven.

Papu was pleased with all she had done to survive her ordeal, but she was not able to displace her loneliness and fear of what might happen if no one found her soon. Night was on its way again, a time when all searching had to cease, if in fact it was being carried on by anyone. Yet she hoped she was loved enough, and important enough, for her people not to give up looking for her. She held her head high and attempted to smile, but in the dank confines, she found very little to smile about, and sadness swept over her once again.

Darkness came on, and Papu spent a fitful night, rising often to add bramble twigs to the fire. Given a choice, she had rather have the light and a bit of warmth in the cool night, than the sleep. With very little else to do, she could sleep any time. She faced the morning still hungry, unsatisfied from the frugal meal of grasshoppers last evening. She immediately placed more faggots on the fire and headed for the rock dome she had devised to hold the remaining grasshoppers. What she found startled her. When she opened the dome, the grasshoppers were gone. Inspecting the structure, Papu discerned that a lower rock in the quarry frame had been pushed aside. How? That was the mysterious question. The grasshoppers would never have been able to move the stone. She sat against the wall, looking forlornly at the pile of rocks, stunned that her only remaining meal was gone.

As she watched, something moved in the shadows along the

cavern floor. As it moved into the light, Papu could see that it was a lizard edging its way back to the rock pile. She now knew where her grasshoppers had gone during the night.

"Well, so much for the grasshoppers," she groaned, realizing to her disadvantage that lizards are not edible. For that, the plump little slithering reptile could count its blessings, because Papu was angry enough to skewer its slender frame onto her roasting lance. Papu sat motionless for a moment thinking frantically about what she would do next. She had already searched through the area where food had been stored, and there was not as much as a crust of bread to be found. All she could find now, as she rose to search one more time, was a teaspoon of sugar, some salt and pepper, and a thimbleful of peanut butter left in a metal tin. She ate the sugar and devoured the peanut butter, wiping the tin clean with her fingers, and licking them furiously for life. She drank a cup of water and sat down along the wall.

In her desperation, Papu's mind began to churn again. When the grasshoppers had been washed into the opening the day before, had she actually found all of them? Could there be others that she missed, or some trapped among the rock formations that were possibly still crawling around somewhere in the cracks? She rose again to make another search. Regrettably, every place she looked came up empty. As she diligently continued to search, something caught her eye that she had not seen before. In the damp, musty soils caught in the cracks and rotting, like compost, along the base of the walls, small toadstools or mushrooms had appeared. Apparently, the spores had germinated in the rain-laden formations. There they stood at attention like little umbrellas saluting the morning light.

Papu knew toadstools as well as mushrooms, and these were not toadstools. She raised her arms in applause to the Great Spirit. He had not let her down. She would eat again and began immediately to do so, salting and peppering one mushroom at a time, eating some of them raw and others toasted over the fire. Only the seasoning made the mushrooms more palatable. There were more to be had lined in decorative rows along the walls and in the cracks. She could farm even more of them by keeping the soils moist with limited portions of her water.

Patting her stomach gracefully, Papu could not believe her good fortune. For once in three days, she was no longer hungry. Her mind off her stomach, momentarily, she now automatically turned her attention back to getting free from her grievous confinement. She had already settled the fact that there was no way digging through the rock. There was also no climbing through openings in the ceiling. The walls were too steep and slick, and the holes were too small even for her tiny body.

If she couldn't get out, maybe someone on the outside could get in, if they had any way of locating her. A thought instantly came to mind. She had more bramble limbs, which, if tied together firmly, might be conducive to raising a flag through one of the openings in the ceiling. With that ingenuity established, she set to work industriously laying out limbs stripped from the brambles. She overlaid them lengthwise slightly and tied them firmly with strips of cloth torn from her makeshift towel. Periodically, she raised the thin pole to check for stiffness. When it began to bow, she stopped adding limbs and tied a white handkerchief to its tip. Luckily, her mother had always coached her to keep a handkerchief inside her buckskin vest. How grateful Papu was now that she had been obedient to her mother!

The little Indian then raised the pole carefully along the wall toward the largest of the openings in the ceiling, resting it temporarily to add more lengths of bramble, one limb at a time, until the white flag pierced the opening above her. She continued to add more limbs to raise the flag as far above the opening as possible, until it began to bend with the added weight. When that happened, she stopped, sat the butt of the pole on the cavern floor against the wall, and blocked it with rocks to keep it from slipping.

Papu's greatest hope was that someone, who might possibly wander into the area, in their search for her, would notice the flag and come to her aid. She had literally done everything she knew to do, and all the activity of the morning had at least taken her mind off her loneliness, momentarily. With a tweak of her thumbs beneath her armpits, she smiled and affirmed her accomplishment, "I'm proud of you, Papu Banta, you little Indian marvel!" Sitting back against the wall, she pulled her blanket around her. All she knew to do now was to wait and to try to stay alive. With that resignation settled, she lay back against the wall in the restricted chamber and was soon fast asleep.

CHAPTER 15

THE CAMARADERIE

Ever since early afternoon, as the Cavalry, the Indian braves, and Puck's men, departed Shoshoni for their assigned territories, the town had been abuzz with the news. It was mid-afternoon, and church bells rang out calling the townspeople to prayer. Not all, but many of the shops closed in deference to the urgent invitation, their owners gladly giving up a few sales to join the effort.

After sleeping off his binge from the night before, Buford Townsend, known as the town drunk, had just been released from his cell by Sheriff Larson. Now that the bells were ringing in the distance, the sheriff felt that it was time to turn him loose, at least for another day. People were rushing from everywhere, all seeming to be headed in the same direction. That seemed strange to the sobering old man, so he stopped a passerby on the boardwalk and asked, "Whar's everybody goin' in such a hurry, Mister?"

The man drew back to shield himself from the man's still stringent breath and answered, "We're all headed for the church to pray for the little kidnapped Indian girl. They haven't found her yet."

"Wal, I can pray, too," the half-inebriated man averred. "That little girl deserves to be found. I know I don't count for much anymore. I've practly rooned my life, but maybe my prayer for that little girl might count for sump'n. And maybe while I'm thar, the church can do sump'n for me, too. You know, I've been hearin' a lotta talk about that little Indian, lately. Fact is, I heard those two men in the cell beside me talkin' 'bout her 'while ago. They acted like they knew where she is. Couldn't gather everythin' they was sayin', for those confounded drums abeatin' outside the door, but they kept talkin' 'bout her. Why don't the sheriff pounce on them 'bout what they know? Maybe when I finish prayin' for that little girl, I'll come back here and talk to 'em myself."

The man turned briskly to look back at the door of the jail and called out, "Hey, Indian man, cain't you go play that drum somewhar' else? We're tryin' to get a prayer meetin' goin' down at the church. I think they might 'preciate a little quiet. You kept me 'wake half the night with that confounded noise. Don't you pay no respect to your neighbors?"

The beat went on. Neither Indian brave said a word. The old man shook his head and ambled off toward the church. Sporting a few apparent jitters, he finally reached the church and could still be seen shaking his head. Townspeople continued to gather into the little frame Overland Presbyterian Church, led by the Reverend Gorman Settler. He was a southerner, who had come from Georgia about ten years earlier. Everybody liked his down-home style—a little formal at times, genteel for sure, but simple and down-to-earth, for the most part. When everyone that was apparently coming was seated, the pastor rose and addressed the crowd in his southern drawl. "Now, I want ya'll to give eah a bit heah. As ya'll know, we have a great amunt of camaraderie heah in this little village. In this church, in particular, you have learned that God's people are called to *koinonia*—translated "fellowship" in the Authorized King James Version of the Bible. But the word means more than ouwah English word conveys. It actually means "the mutual sharing of life."

What concerns one, it seems, concerns all. What affects one, affects all. I'm lookin' ovah a good bunch of people in this place. If you weren't quality people, I would have been gone long ago, because we have those in ouwah community who are needin' the likes of people like you to help get them on the straight and narrow.

You are learning well how to minister to people's needs. And before this ordeal is ovah, we will all be needin' to be supportive in one way or 'tuther to those connected with that little Indian girl. And we need the great Gawd on ouah side moah than evah. So that's why we've come today. We're gonna pray as genuinely as we know how, put the mattah before the Lawd, and accept whatevah verdict He gives us.

"Now, Mr. Puckett, the man on this case, is not able to be with us today, but he plans to be heah for chutch in the mornin' For any of you who can be back with us in the mornin', Mr. Puckett wants to address the group briefly and hold anothah prayer meetin' at that time. If anyone has anything to say today before we start our petitions to the Lawd, please rise where you are and address the group."

Only one among the faithful rose to speak, Selma Getting, one of the elderly pillars of the church. She added to the pastor's words that their prayers should also include the condition of Perk Anson, who, if he ever regained consciousness, might be willing and able to supply the information necessary for locating the little girl. And, as bitter as she was at Pete Trammel and Briley Wortham, she averred that maybe God could get a word in edgewise to them, since no one else had been able to do so. She avowed that, while the group would not be praying around the world, its prayers should at least cover all fronts pertaining to this regrettable predicament. When she was seated again, Rev. Settler called the group to prayer.

The prayer meeting lasted about an hour before the people filtered away a few at a time, most of them holding out hope for the little girl, due to their faith, but openly disgruntled that more had not been done to get the kidnappers to talk. Though they believed firmly in love, they believed also in tough love. While they gave credence to unconditional love and acceptance, even forgiveness, they also affirmed the accountability of love. There is a great difference between unconditional love and indulgence. People must be held accountable for their actions, when those actions involve bringing down others. For the sake of justice, offenders must not be mollycoddled. Clearly, there is no justice without mercy and no mercy without justice. Even God is a God of love and a God of wrath at the same time, and the two characteristics are not contradictory. God's anger or wrath is the justice side of His love without which His love becomes purely indulgent. He is a God who also must bring justice to bear or He is not moral, and a God who must express love or He is not merciful. People here in the Overland church certainly want mercy for all, but they also want justice for all. Though they prayed caringly for the kidnappers, they look at the consequences of their actions and know that for the sake of Papu Banta, they must also be held accountable.

Buford Townsend was not very steeped in theology, or even of thinking logically. His addiction clouded the issue most of the time. But he had a softness of heart when it came to anyone's being humiliated or harmed in some way. Clearly, the little Indian girl had been harmed by indignity and trauma, defacement and suffering. The old man intended to get some word out of the kidnappers by hook or crook, and he had been good at both in his day.

Accordingly, the old man left the church on his way to jail by way of the saloon. He came out of the saloon with a bulging package under his coat and a stiff scent on his breath that would assault the nostrils. Mixed with that odor was the ripe stench of unwashed feet and unkempt clothing, a smell that would almost stink a buzzard off a gut-wagon. He had sat alone in the church meeting, and had wondered why. But, unbeknownst to him, good old Sheriff Larson had already planned for a major cleanup when he returned to the cell. And he would return to the cell, no question about that!

When Buford entered the jail, Sheriff Larson was busy fumbling with papers on his desk, fuming over his workload in the absence of his deputy, and sipping half-guardedly on a cup of strong leftover coffee. He winced and whistled through pursed lips with every sip, and yet it never occurred to him that he really didn't have to drink it. So he kept on sipping to the point of shuddering with every swallow.

The old man, noting the Sheriff's state of mind, spoke up. "Say, Sheriff, why 'on't you jist take a little breather and check out things in town? I'll watch care over your shop here. These men ain't goin' nowhere. Won't be no trouble fer me to sit a spell. I owe you sump'n anyway for givin' me a place to sleep so often. Don't ya see what I mean?"

"Okay, Buford, maybe I can take a break. I need to go check on Doc Metcalf's patient anyway, and the deputy, being out of town on the search, is taking care of honorable business. I certainly don't begrudge him that, even if it does put a bit of a load on things around here. You think you can handle things for an hour or two?"

"Why, shore, Sheriff. Take all the time you need. I don't have anything else to do."

The sheriff rose to leave, then as an afterthought went to the cell wall and retrieved the cell keys from their hook. If he trusted Buford at all, it certainly was not over his having access to the keys, except when the cells were empty. Looking back over his shoulder, he spoke back to Buford. "Say, Townsend, I have a surprise for you when I return. See you later."

When the sheriff closed the door behind him, Buford was stammering to himself, "Yeah, Sheriff, I may have a surprise for you too." With that he went to work. Slowly ambling toward the cell, twisting a little to the right and to the left as he walked, and fidgeting with the package under his coat, he finally stopped abruptly in front of Trammel and Wortham.

"Say, gents," he addressed the miscreants, "bet you haven't had any of this stuff fer a spell," tottering a bottle of whisky by the neck before them.

"Hey, old man," Trammel gestured, "where'd you come by a whole bottle of booze like that? It sure looks smooth."

"I'll have you know, I jist 'bout used my whole life's savins gettin' this amber wash."

"Well, how about givin' us a swig from that beautiful piece of art you brought in here? As you say, we haven't had a touch of that in quite a spell."

"Oh, no you don't! You ain't gettin' this bottle in that cell. I'd be a plain fool. You'd never give it back, and with the sheriff gone, I'd have no way to git it back. But now, if you two had some shiny coins on you, we might jist make a deal."

"Yeah, friend, I guess you're right, but the sheriff took all our goods when he put us in here. He put it over in that cabinet yonder against the wall with our shootin' irons. Say, that's it, if you could get into that cabinet and fetch our money belts, we might just be able to make a deal you can't turn down. But, hey, don't try to double cross us. You know, you could just take our money and run, beings the sheriff is not around. But if you do, we're certain to clue him in on your swindle, and you'll have a cell uninterrupted for a long time. So do we make a deal or not?"

"Well, I could consider," Buford whined, twitching his whiskers with his thumb and index finger. "I kinda know what you two are goin' through. I've been there before without a squeeze. Maybe I can make a deal."

The old man went to the door to be sure the sheriff was not returning. He turned toward the cabinet so the men couldn't see his face, snickered a bit beneath his breath, and thought merrily to himself: *They bit, hook, line, and sinker. Now let's see where it all leads.*

Buford had no intention of taking the money from the money

belts, but he would let them think that he was. He took the belts to the men and told them to fork over whatever they thought was a fair price for all the trouble he had gone through to bring the bottle in, and he urged them to be generous, or else. He would then put the remainder back in the belts and return them to the cabinet.

The two hustled to get coins out of the belts and were overly generous in the transaction. What good was money to them, chinked away in the cell as they were? They handed him his due and the belts and reached for the bottle.

"Now, don't be too hasty. You're gonna git your bottle. Don't you have any manners?" The old man slowly reached out with the bottle of whisky until Trammel, in a flash, snatched the bottle from his hand. Fumbling with the container, the two snickered with pride. The old man had sold them a fifth of whisky!

While they were busy opening the bottle for a too-long-awaited chug, Buford slyly put the money back into the belts and returned them to the cabinet. He then returned to the cell to watch the two drink themselves sick. It wouldn't take long now before he would have two lightheaded drunks spilling the beans about everything in the history books—including some choice pieces of information regarding the whereabouts of the little Indian girl. He put his hands into his pockets, crossed his fingers, sat down, and waited.

The two men drank feverishly, passing the bottle with intervening haste, first the one and then the other. They began to slow up only after half the bottle had been guzzled. Within thirty minutes they were both tipsy, then sottish in another ten. When the bottle was nearly empty, the two were rolling with laughter, slapping each other on the shoulders and recalling memorable events in their recent past. They were now pie-eyed and happy, experiencing a kind of jolly hooch heaven. They began to talk, to reminisce, confess past guiltiness, and lay everything bare that came to mind.

Buford saw his chance. He began to play along with their stories, adding a few of his own, and laughing just as heartily as they were. He ultimately began to affirm them, which they relished with gratitude. Then the affirmation turned to the subject of Papu Banta.

"Hey, you guys really did yourselves proud," he attested "You hid that little Indian girl where nobody around could find her. You fellas have a head on you. And you've kept her safe, keepin' food and water for her and all. If you think you might want me to pick up from here and take care of her while you're in here, I'd be proud to oblige—if you think I could find the place."

Trammel piped up, "Hey, Worthless, where'd we stash that kid? You remember?"

Wortham countered, "What're ya callin' me Worthless for? My name ain't Worthless. Its Worthman, uh, Worthal…well, something like that anyway. But to give you an answer, Trafford, I think we went south a long way. Which way is south, Triffer?"

"Shore, you don't even know your own name, much less mine. My mother named me Peter Tramdon. I think it was Tramdon. Or was it Tramble? Eh, who cares?"

The old man thought, "I've overdone it. They can't even remember their names." Just the same, Buford continued to coax. "Which old shack did you put her in?"

"Aw, old man," Wortham chided, "You don't know. We didn't put her in a shack. They ain't no shacks where we took her. We had to crawl into this shelter, don't you see? It don't have no door or nothin', except one a ways inside, an' it has a few holes in the roof, dirt and all, an' its sorta damp inside most of the time. We know how to get back there, too, if we ever git out of here. We got it marked in our heads. We call it the Triangle. She can't get out though, so why do we need you to check on her for us?"

"Well, I mean, you being here, how ya gonna see to her needs—

food and water, and that kind of stuff?"

"Oh, Injuns don't have needs, old man. Anyway, we can't let on to the sheriff about any of this. He and the judge will throw the book at us. Now, old man, you like us, don't ya? You ain't gonna snip on us, are ya?"

"What's snippin' got to do with it? If the sheriff don't believe you, why would he believe me? Most people in town take me with a grain of salt. Don't ever really believe anything I try to tell 'em. I'm just concerned 'bout the little girl. Ain't no use that she should die, don't ya see?"

"Old man, we sshee—see all right. If we could git outa this here tank, we could make sure the Indian wouldn't die, but if we own up to kidnappin' her, we'll not only never get out, but we might fairly well be hanged. Now you wouldn't want to see good friends hang, would you?"

Buford tried everything he knew to coax more information out of the now drunken prisoners, but the more he talked, the more they nodded off, until both were passed out in sleep.

The timing could not have been more appropriate. As Trammel and Wortham fell across their cots, Sheriff Larson entered the jail carrying several large packages.

"What did you do, Buford, talk the jailbirds to death?" the sheriff quipped. Not waiting an answer to his rhetorical question, he walked over to the cell door and looked in on the two passed out prisoners. Then he sniffed, sniffed again, and then looked back at Buford in disbelief. "Buford, is that smell what I think it is?"

Buford responded with nonchalance. "Don't know, Sheriff, what do ya think it is?"

"Well, from the looks of that bare bottle over there in the corner of the cell, I guess I really don't have to think. Have any idea how they may have gotten that bottle, Buford?"

"Okay, Sheriff, I'll tell you, but you gotta listen to me. I mean really listen to me! I got the wild idea that if I could get them prisoners drunk as coots, they would spill the beans 'bout the little Indian girl. I got some information 'bout the hideout where they put her, but, try as I might, I couldn't ever git them to tell me exactly where it is. Here's what I got from them. Maybe you and Puck can decipher it. I can't make heads or tails of it. They said it was a long way south of here and sump'n about havin' to crawl into the shelter, whatever the shelter is. And they said it didn't have a door, except for one further inside. They seemed to think the roof had holes in it—as they put it, 'dirt and all.' Sounds like a dirt roof to me. Then they described it as being damp inside. And that's all they said, except that they named the place the Triangle. I've thought of triangle dinner bells, draftsman drawing instruments, and cattle brands of the Triangle S Ranch. None of that makes sense. But somehow the description sounds like a cave of some sort to me. Now, I hope you won't be angry with me, Sheriff. I was only tryin' to help."

The sheriff went over to Buford and put his hand on his shoulder. "Normally, doing what you did, Buford, would not be jail-worthy, but under the circumstances you might have done the right thing. We'll think it over, and then we'll get with Puck tomorrow after church, and put the details to him. Maybe he'll understand more than we seem to at this point. But now listen, Buford, if you stay around here you're gonna have to start being more careful how you handle yourself. I keep an honorable jail. Okay?"

"What'd you mean about after church tomorrow, Sheriff? I'm a guessin' I won't be goin' to church tomorrow. I didn't git much of a welcome over there today. Ain't nobody in the house would sit by me."

"Now, Buford, what would you think kept them from being more hospitable? You think the fact that you haven't had a bath in over a week might have had something to do with it? Put yourself in their shoes. Well, no pun intended, my friend, but actually my drift is the surprise I told you I had for you. Come over here with me."

The sheriff led Buford over to his usual cell and pointed to a curtain hanging across the corner. "Buford, go back there and look behind that curtain."

The old man curiously pulled aside the tail of the curtain, which revealed a large oval tub sitting on the floor and fresh towels hanging on the wall above it.

"Now, Buford, I've got plenty of hot water in the back that we can fill your tub with, and you can enjoy a cleanin' like you haven't had in a spell. Then, you can shave looking in that mirror over there. When you're done with that, you're gonna be surprised at what I brought with me in here this evening. In fact, I may as well tell you. I have some new underwear, a new suit of clothes, and a pair of boots. And they're yours, without charge.

"Look, you're better than you look, and better than you act—I mean with respect to your drinking and all. You don't have to be this way any more, and I'm taking it upon myself to see that you get all the help you need to stay sober and make a decent place for yourself in this town. And I'm going to start by hiring you to be my jail hand, with pay, of course. I'll have things for you to do that will be different than what my deputy does. But the place I want you to start is by going to the church in the morning. Puck is going to be sharing some things with the congregation. And then they're going to have another prayer meeting. You'll look fine in those new clothes I brought you. And even if we did take those boots off a dead man, they'll fit you fine and help to make the man. You know, Buford, a man can be dressed to the hilt, but if his shoes are dirty or tattered, the whole outfit is ruined. So, keep a spit shine on those boots. You can use my shoeshine kit over there in the corner."

Buford was dumbfounded and kept saying things like, "But Sheriff..." and "Lordy me," and questioning, "Why would you do this for me, Sheriff?"

"Because I've taken a liking to you, my man. So, get in there and get ready for your bath, and I'll start carrying water."

A few miles east of Riverton, just over the border marking the perimeter of the reservation, a great parcel of townspeople had been searching since noon for any sign of the little Indian girl's place of concealment. They were still going at sundown. They had come from all sections of the town and intervening countryside to do everything they could to be successful. They were a congenial group of people, people who had suffered in many ways together in the past. They shared their lives with a sense of unity and brotherliness. Like the people in the Overland church in Shoshoni, the people of the Wind River Baptist Church in Riverton knew the meaning of real *koinonia*. What hurt the one, hurt the other, and what thrilled the one, thrilled the other. They had laughed and cried together on many occasions, and now, to go about their business as if the little girl and her family were not of importance to them was unconscionable. They would stay with it until it appeared absolutely hopeless. Night came on for them, but Sunday offered a full day in which to resume the search.

Along the eastern front of the reservation, the Indian braves, led by Broken Heel, had split into groups of four and were checking out every familiar and unfamiliar spot where an eight year old girl might be hidden. They went into caves, checked out dilapidated shacks of every imaginable kind, and climbed down into old abandoned mines. Their efforts showed their respect and love for tribal kinship, their recollection of the great pow-wows that brought them, in unity, through the great Indian wars, and their keen vision for the potential of one lonely little Indian girl. If she were found, this would be a ride and a search like no other coup they ever experienced. There would be no quitting until she was found.

Southeast of Shoshoni, Farley, Palmer, Lively, and Engle, along with Sheriff Larson's deputy, Roland Blue, had gone to the watering hole where Palmer once saw Trammel and Wortham meeting, apparently after Trammel had been to check on the girl. Palmer had never been able to make anything of their meeting, except that the girl might be hidden nearby. There had been no way of knowing, since Palmer had no idea how far Trammel had traveled before ending up at the watering hole.

In any case, the five men had split up and had searched every cave and rock quarry, every deserted shack and bush camp. When they met back at the watering hole at sunset, several of them had covered nigh on five miles of territory, to no avail. They ran coyotes out of dens, and one mountain lion out of a rock-hewn cave, but found no Papu Banta. They set up camp and prepared themselves for a ride farther into the territory, come Sunday morning.

Colonel Meech and his right hand men had taken territory farther south and east of Shoshoni, almost to the Riverton area where the townspeople had set their boundary for the search. This area was not well traveled by anyone, as it was greatly overgrown with brush and, where there was no brush, it was plagued with medium to heavy rocky under pavement. The men's work had been cut out for them from the beginning. The half-day they spent getting into the heart of the area would mean another half-day getting out The area seemed a hopeless place for any likely hideout – too rough, too difficult to traverse, and too far from sources of sustenance. Sunday, the men would choose a more congenial region, one they would think lazy men like Trammel and Wortham might find more compatible with their taste.

The church doors opened early Sunday morning for anyone who wanted to pray, or for those who may or may not be able to attend morning services. In the pastor's study, Rev. Settler was putting the final touches to his message for the morning. He jotted down a scant outline of his thoughts to be used as a guide. He was not like Puck who kept everything in his head. He still felt that paper was cheaper than brains. He seldom made use of the notes, but they were there just in case he got off track in his thoughts.

Buford and Sheriff Larson were busy admiring Buford's new look and waited until they heard the church bells before leaving the jail. A cousin of Larson's had offered to sit the jail while the sheriff went to the church services. Outside, the Indians were still taking turns at the incessant drumbeat. Trammel and Wortham were pacing the floor, waiting impatiently for lunch, and cursing the day the Indians had ever crafted a drum. Everyone else was just as tired of the drumbeat, but if the meaning behind its nerve-racking noise would break down the prisoners to a more docile submission to the truth, they would tolerate it.

A while before the ringing of the bells, calling the worshippers to the meeting place, Puck had gone to the church to meet briefly with the pastor. People began to gather, until every seat available in the house was filled, with many other celebrants standing in the vestibule. A small choir began to sing a few old time hymns as Reverend Settler and Puck entered the auditorium from the rear and ascended the podium. An elder closed the front door and Reverend Settler rose to address the crowd.

"My good friends," he began, "before ah bring a brief message on 'Suffering the Insufferable,' Mr. Puckett has come today for the purpose of addressing the congregation with respect to the case of kidnapping that has so concerned people everywhe'ah in the Wyoming Territory. You will find him to be a man of faith, but one who knows that both man and man's faith are limited. He is well awa'ah that humanism, as a philosophy, is dead, that man cannot pull himself up by his own bootstraps. Therefore he relies on what Gawd can do in partnership with His people, how He can heighten man's native abilities, and bring insight, wisdom, and energy to all his efforts. He comes heah today looking for Gawd's leadership in his life in these gruelin' days of searchin' for the little Indian girl. Ah hope you will heah him gladly. And so, ah present to you, Mr. Puck Puckett."

Puck rose to his feet and stood to one side of the large wooden pulpit, with its stained patina glistening in the sunrays entering the side windows. A cool breeze lilted across the assembly as he addressed the congregation.

"Ladies and gentlemen, let me set your minds at ease. I do not know exactly how our little Indian girl is going to be found, but I have absolute faith in God that He is not going to let her die.

"We have one human potential left, and that is that if Perk Anson ever comes around from his coma, he may be willing to tell us where the child has been confined. But if he is as despicably hardhearted as those two in the jail, he may not help us either. Right now, I am banking on no one but God and all the noble people who have volunteered to look for her. I've been piecing together every possible clue I can think of, and so far what I've been able to come up with has been quite slim. I may just as well be honest and up front with you on that. What I am looking for now is wisdom that I don't have, and the only place I know to go for it is to God Almighty. That's why I'm here today.

"Rev. Settler, my pastor, back in the Village of Jackson, the Rev. Taylor Shadwell, has shared with me some particularly meaningful passages of Scripture that have helped to equip me in the faith. I want to share the reading of those passages with the congregation this morning. Then, among prayers from others in the gathering, I would especially like for you to voice a prayer for us that God will supply the wisdom, strategy, and whatever else we need that will lead us to the little girl. Now, let me share the passages of Scripture.

"First, we must recognize our own spiritual bankruptcy. From the Prophet Jeremiah, chapter nine, verse twenty-three, I read:

'Thus saith the Lord, Let not the wise man glory in his wisdom, neither let the mighty man glory in his might, let not the rich man glory in his riches: But let him that glorieth glory in this, that he understandeth and knoweth me, that I am the Lord which exercise lovingkindness, judgment, and righteousness, in the earth: for in these things I delight, saith the Lord.'

"The other passages are from The Epistle of James in the New Testament. In chapter three and verse seventeen, James describes the wisdom of God. He says:

'But the wisdom that is from above is first pure, then peaceable, gentle, and easy to be intreated, full of mercy and good fruits, without partiality and without hypocrisy.'

"In chapter one and verse five, James entreats us to do what we are about to do this morning. He says, 'If any of you lack wisdom, let him ask of God, that giveth to all men liberally and upbraideth not; and it shall be given to him.' In verse six he qualifies how we are to make the petition, by saying, 'But let him ask in faith, nothing wavering.'

"I ask the pastor now to voice for us the desires that he must know are heavy on all our hearts, and then some of you, in turn, may voice similar concerns in your prayers. Pastor, please pray." Puck left the podium and went back to the rear of the church and sat down beside Three Toes, Sheriff Larson, and Buford.

Rev. Settler rose to his feet, then knelt beside the pulpit and began his prayer: "Lawd, we come before you as your humble servants. We stand next to you as your creatures and know that we are not Gawd. But you, Lawd, are the triune Gawd, the Holy Trinity. And within that triangle rests our wholeness and our hope. Now, Lawd, that little girl, who has been kidnapped, is in danger of dying if she is not found soon. We appeal to you for wisdom. Direct someone to the place of her confinement. Keep her safe from harm until she is found. Please honor this pray'ah in the name of the Father, the Son, and the Holy Spirit. Amen."

Others began to follow in prayer, but none of them were registering with Puck. Something the pastor remarked in his prayer had drawn his attention away, which was still rolling around in his mind. "The *triune* God," Puck repeated to himself, followed by "the Holy *Trinity*," and then those words that struck thunder in his memory—"within that *triangle*." Closely behind that revelation came the recollection of another word that had aroused his curiosity from the very beginning. "Site, site, site," he repeated, as well, a word that Sergeant Graves used as coming from the kidnappers early on regarding the ransom money. Puck then poked Three Toes on the knee and motioned for him and the Sheriff to follow. They rose and quietly left the church, followed by Buford, as well.

When they were outside, Puck quizzed the men. "Did you hear the words in there, spoken by the pastor?"

"Why of course we heard the words, same as you," the sheriff responded.

"I mean, did you *hear* the *words*, and one in particular—***triangle***! Three Toes, you—listen closely now—you told us at the camp one day that one of the men came into the livery stable and called Anson 'Boss,' and then said that he had just come from the 'triangle.'"

"That's right, Mr. Puck. But he never did say what or where that was. And the boss seemed to know, but he didn't say anything about it either."

"Hey Mr. Puck. I mean, Puck," Buford chimed in. "That's exactly what the Sheriff and I have been savin' to tell you. You see, I got the wise idea to get some whiskey to those men in the cell—"

The Sheriff abruptly interrupted him, "Aw, Buford, don't go into the whole scenario, just tell Puck what you learned from them."

"Well, anyway, Puck, I got the men drunk so they would spill the beans about the little girl. They did, to an extent. They admitted they had kidnapped the girl and had hidden her in a place they named the Triangle." Buford went on to describe the place with its small entrance without a door, except for one further inside, with its holes in the roof—probably a dirt roof—and the dampness inside, and its being quite a ways south of Shoshoni.

Puck said, "That's it, Townsend! They're talking about a mine, or a mine **site**! That's the word they used in their telegram to you, Sheriff, when they talked about where you would leave the ransom money. Apparently, from the beginning, they were going to direct you to the mine site as the pick up place for the ransom. They must have thought it through and realized that it would be too dangerous an exchange. They would have no security, so they changed it to the route of the stage line, knowing they could get the money, and release the girl later almost anywhere they pleased so that she would be found by authorities. And they would be absolutely free of danger, knowing that if they were harmed, the girl's life would be in jeopardy. That's just what we've guarded against from the beginning. It just hasn't played out the way we had it planned."

"But which mine site, Puck?" the sheriff questioned. "Throughout the whole area between here and Riverton, inside and outside the reservation, there's a good number of old abandoned mine sites."

"Yeah, Sheriff," Puck agreed, "and I just got a shot of wisdom that I've been looking for, don't you see? Look, Sheriff, I know its Sunday, and all the shops are closed, but go see if you can find Ralph Lingerman and Willy Flanagan and have them meet us down at their offices. This is really important. We'll pay them extra if we have to, but get them down there, okay?"

"Yeah, Puck, anything you say. I'll get right on it."

The men departed, Puck and Three Toes going their way, and Sheriff Larson and Buford going theirs. Something was in the air, and it was just about to get exciting!

CHAPTER 16

THE INTERROGATION

Church now having let out, Selma Getting, with her sack lunch, had just reported to Doc Metcalf's clinic to relieve Whiskers Benedict of his shift at sitting with Perk Anson. Whiskers had left immediately to meet Puck and Three Toes at the village café.

After the three had eaten, Puck told Whiskers and Three Toes to hang loose for a while, until he had time to check out some matters down at the Shoshoni Assay Office. By evening, he would check with them at the hotel and would probably have an errand for them to carry out for him.

Willy Flanagan ran the Assay Office, and Ralph Lingerman made use of a room at the back of the office for the Lingerman Print Shop. By the time Puck arrived at the office, Sheriff Larson had located both men and had them waiting.

Willy Flanagan was a redheaded, barrel-chested Irishman. His only day to have a toddy was on Sunday afternoon, and he tried to keep it small enough not to be atoned for. On his way over there, Puck was hoping that this was one of Willy's smaller nip days. He needed his services urgently.

Puck entered the office elated to find both Flanagan and Lingerman in good shape for questions he had for them.

"Willy," Puck addressed the man, after amenities had been made, "Don't you have topographical maps of all the old mine sites in the general area surrounding Shoshoni and Riverton?"

"Well, yes, I do, and all the new sites as well. Lingerman, here, does all of the map work for us, after we take care of the surveying and platting of the various mines. Do you have something in mind?"

"Yes, I do. Of course, you will have a general map of the towns, villages, rivers, lakes, and such. Would you, by any chance, have a map of the old mine sites printed on the same scale?"

Lingerman spoke up, "I think we do, but if we don't, I can print one on the same scale."

"Do you have any maps printed on clear sheeting of any kind? Or if you don't, can a map be printed on something clear that you can see through?"

Lingerman said, "No, we don't have anything like that," and then he thought a moment. "I've not tried to print anything like that for two reasons, I guess. First, no one has ever asked for anything like that, and secondly, we don't have much in the way of clear sheeting. Some of the places in Montana are making vermiculite from flakes taken out of the mines there, but most of it is not really clear enough. I was just thinking though, I have a few pieces of Muscovite on hand, which is a form of Mica. This is sheeting that is common in Russia today. They use it as a substitute for panes in their windows. I think it may be stiff enough to use for printing purposes, but I have no idea whether or not the ink will transfer properly onto its surface. We can try."

As Lingerman started off to check on what he had on hand, Puck detained him a moment to ask another question. "Can you use indelible India ink in your printing, so if it doesn't work on the clear sheeting, you can print it on paper of a low rag content?"

Lingerman and Flanagan looked at each other amused that Puck was asking so many strange questions, without indicating what use he would make of the printed items—clear or paper.

Finally, Lingerman said, "Yes, I do have India ink, and one that has a high durability content, and if it doesn't work on clear sheeting, I have a paper that lacks the density that rag content possesses."

"See what you two men can do, and I will gladly pay for any cost you incur doing it for me. My problem is that I need it this afternoon. That's why I asked the sheriff to locate you for me. This whole printing matter is a hunch I have regarding the whereabouts of the little Indian girl. I'm leaving for Hale's Ford in the morning, and I hope I have the information I need for those volunteers who will be meeting me there. Can you do it?"

"We'll give it everything we've got," Flanagan replied. "Come back in two hours, and maybe we will have what you want."

Selma Getting had completed her lunch and was sitting by Perk Anson's bedside, when suddenly she noticed an unusual stir of the man. He raised his left arm and placed it behind his head on the pillow. Then he took it down again. He then reached over with his right hand and scratched his nose. He kicked at the covers with his feet. He tossed his head gently from side to side and with an almost muffled sound coughed and winced at the pain in his head as he did so. Then, to Miss Getting's surprise, the man opened his eyes. He closed them, only to open them again. He looked around the ceiling looking confused. In a moment his eyes turned toward her and he appeared more confused.

"Where am I, lady," he asked. "And who are you?"

Miss Getting rose and came alongside the bed. "Mr. Anson—oh, it sounds strange calling you that. I mean, you've always been Mr. Browning to me. I'm Selma Getting. Don't you remember? You've cared for my horse and buggy many times, and I've been sitting with you. You're in Doc Metcalf's clinic. You've had a gunshot to the head, and you've been in a coma for days. Take it easy now, and I'll send someone for Doc Metcalf. He'll be happy to hear that you've come around. Now you be still a moment while I fetch the maid to go get him."

Miss Getting went for the maid and then returned. She pulled the chair up to the bedside to talk with Anson.

"My dear boy," Selma spoke up, "you remember how you got shot, don't you?"

"Well, yeah, I remember something about it, but for the life of me, I can't place who shot me. I know where I was when I got shot, but I don't recall getting into a shootout with anyone. I think I know why I got shot. I'm sure it had something to do with a bag of money I was carrying."

"Mr. Anson, do you know what that bag of money was."

"Yeah, of course, I know, and I guess I'm a damned fool for ever pickin' it up. Look where I am now. And there's no tellin' where I'll wind up from here, if I live. I wish that whoever shot me woulda just finished me off."

"No need to talk like that, Mr. Anson. You know all about the little Indian girl then, don't you?"

"Sadly to say, I remember all too much."

"Well, if you would just inform the sheriff where that little girl can be found, you just might get off with a much lighter sentence. Then, maybe all won't be lost."

"Miss Getting, you've always been one of the nicest ladies in the village, and I hate to present myself as such a culprit that the beautiful relationship will now be ruined. I've been a damned fool, and if I don't hang for it, I'll be shut up the rest of my life. Well, I deserve it! If I could retrace my steps though, I'd do things a lot differently. I had everything going for me in this village. Everybody liked me. Even wanted to make me mayor! And, like a fool, I blew it! Thought I needed more in the form of money, rather than the good friends I enjoyed. What a nightmare!

"And you mentioned my telling the sheriff the whereabouts of the Indian girl. If I could help anyone find that girl, I would, but I don't even know where Trammel and Wortham placed her. They never told me exactly, and I never asked. I'm telling you, I've been a pure fool on this thing. And now that I double-crossed Trammel and Wortham, they're probably laying to put me out of my misery if they get half the chance."

"Well, you won't have to worry too much about those two. The sheriff has them locked up down at the jail. But they have refused to tell anyone where they confined the little girl. I mean, they even renounce any tie with her kidnapping. It's as if they think they can beat the rap by pleading innocent, thinking there's not sufficient evidence to convict them."

"Well, the way I've treated them on this thing, I wouldn't have a thimble of clout getting them to tell me where they hid the girl. I couldn't even pay them to tell me, or I would. Where they are now, and where they are likely to wind up, what would money mean now? I've burned my bridges on all fronts. What a mess I'm in now!"

"Mr. Anson," Miss Getting mused pensively, "did you ever know anything about the Nazarene of the Book?"

"You mean, Jesus, the guy from Nazareth, talked about in the Bible, what you call the Book?"

"Yes, we're talking about the same man—Jesus of Nazareth."

"Well, my mother—God bless her soul—used to talk about Him a lot. She used to tell me that if I ever got into trouble, to look to Him. I never thought too much about that then, and I've been in trouble before, but probably not even close to the trouble I'm in now. If I knew how to look to Him, I guess I would, but He'd have a tough job getting me outa the mess I've put myself in. There's probably no one who could help me now."

Miss Getting felt she needed to respond in some way. "Mr. Anson, you've a right to be despondent about your present situation. Except for the good name you have presented to this town in a professional way, you have messed up quite royally. I mean, you have been in prison once already, you've ended up here with a gunshot wound that almost took your life, and now, unless you can do some quick work in helping to find and free that little Indian girl, you will be going back to prison, or worse. As to your looking to Jesus when you face trouble, your motive is altogether wrong. I'm sure your mother was a godly woman and meant well in her admonishing you about the Lord, but looking to Him only when trouble arises is using Him for your own self-seeking, rather than loving Him for what He can make of your life. I could hope that your interest in Him would be such that you would let Him change your life, whether or not you ever get out of trouble.

"If He were to get you out of trouble in these circumstances without changing your inner nature, your staying out of trouble would only be short-lived. Even if you find total forgiveness, you must still face the consequences of your actions. Whatever the Lord does for you now, I hope you will be willing to take your medicine. And please don't get me wrong; I don't wish you a continuing nightmare in your life, rather a chance to do something royal with it from this point onward. You can make that change, you know! I hope you will."

"Yeah, Miss Getting. I know you're right, and you're kind to take an interest in me. No matter where I wind up from here, I'm going to think seriously about what you've just told me. I hope other church people are as caring as you. You've been a real comfort, even in my misery. Right now, I really have no way to go but up."

When Puck returned to the Assay Office, Flanagan and Lingerman had good news for him. They not only had printed a new territorial map with brighter markings, but a map of the old, abandoned mine sites had also been printed on the Muscovite sheeting on the same scale as the territorial map.

Puck took the maps and laid them on a table. He then placed the clear map of the mine sites over the territorial map and began a prodigious survey of every site on the map, especially those in the general area of Shoshoni and Riverton.

"What are you looking for?" Lingerman asked.

"I'm looking for a triangle," was Puck's reply.

"A triangle?"

"Yes, a triangle of any kind. You see, Trammel and Wortham went to check on the little Indian girl periodically. Sometimes one or the other left Shoshoni to get to the place, and at other times they left from Riverton to get to the same place."

Puck's finger moved resolutely across the clear sheet, and then it stopped abruptly.

"Here, Flanagan. What's this marking here?"

Flanagan took his spectacles from his nose and moved them closer to the map. "Puck," he remarked, "that would be the old Chamberlain Coal Mine site."

Puck took a ruler and drew a line from Shoshoni to Riverton on the map, then proceeded to draw a similar line from Riverton to the Chamberlain site and another line from the site to Shoshoni. It made an almost perfect triangle. The site was only about two and a half miles outside the reservation. It was some fifteen miles southeast of Shoshoni and about the same distance northeast from Riverton.

That meant the site was about forty-five miles from Wind River Village, from where Papu Banta had been kidnapped.

"Sheriff," Puck addressed Larson, "would you telegraph Sheriff Bixley in Riverton and tell him the girl might be found in the old Chamberlain Coal Mine."

Puck stayed on, still looking for any other possible triangle that would also reveal an old, abandoned mine. Before long, Sheriff Larson returned with a telegram from Sheriff Bixley stating that no one in Riverton knew anything about a Chamberlain mine site.

Puck was getting frustrated, trying to think in two places at once, being in Shoshoni, yet needing to be with those searching the vicinity where the girl might be found, if only someone could get there. He sat down to think, not knowing what might be the next move until tomorrow.

In the meantime, Whiskers had gone to Doc Metcalf's clinic to check on Anson and Miss Getting. He was greatly surprised to see Anson awake and talking with the doc. Miss Getting took him aside and told him everything Anson had said about not knowing where Trammel and Wortham had confined the girl. This was not good news to relay to Puck, but when he left the clinic looking for Puck, he walked into the Assay Office just about the time Puck sat down to take a breather.

When Whiskers conveyed the message to Puck, Puck immediately got up and excused himself, letting everyone know that he was going to get with Doc Metcalf and Anson. Maybe something could be said that would refresh Anson's memory. Puck spent no little time conferring with Anson about the confinement of Papu Banta, but for all his cajoling, prompting, even threatening Anson, he was not able to get a smidgeon of help that he so dearly needed. The man had left her whereabouts totally up to Trammel and Wortham, and he was grieved, if not for the little girl, at least for himself, that he had not been more interested in their handling of the matter. Now that his own safety hinged on finding the girl, how could he have been so stupid?

Puck took what he learned, which was very little, back to the jail with him. He would make Trammel and Wortham believe that Anson had spilled the beans, and that they would be in dire trouble if they failed to come across with the pertinent information needed, with which to find the girl.

Forthwith, Puck stood at the cell and addressed the miscreants one more time. "Gentlemen—and again, I use that term loosely—I now know about the Triangle. Want to tell me about it?"

"You've been talking to old man Townsend, haven't you," Trammel questioned?

"Maybe, but I've also been talking to Anson."

"So, the old boy didn't die," Trammel submitted?

"Yeah, he's alive and well, boys—not completely, actually—but he's on the mend enough to transfer him into a cell in a few days. He told me about your frequent runs to the Triangle."

Wortham spoke up. "He don't know where the Triangle is; we never told him."

"Well, well, Wortham, you've finally slipped up. Sheriff, did you hear what the man just said? Okay, Wortham, to save your own skin, you might want to just come clean. The longer you refuse to help us, the deeper the hole you're digging for yourself."

"Mr. Detective, I don't know nothing about no hole, and you can't prove nothing on us anyway!"

Puck reached through the bars, caught Wortham by the lapel, and pulled him up tightly against the bars, pressing his face against the irons. "Look, Paleface without a cause," he prompted, "I ought to come in there and shorten your damned skinny frame a notch or two, but I'll just warn you one last time. When we find the girl, and we will, if she is alive, we'll put you on the shelf for good, but if she is dead, we'll hang you at the end of a rope." With one last jolt against the bars, Puck thrust his apathetic prey back into the cell and walked away, turning back abruptly for one more remark. "By the way, do you hear those drums? You can rely on Broken Heel's word. When the drums stop beating, it will be curtains for you. Count on it!"

As Puck left the jail, the light of day had waned, and night was fast coming on. He had done everything he knew to do, and he realized that everything was now on his shoulders. When the sun came up in the morning, barring any telegram or message in the night that the little Indian girl had been found, he would be on his way to Hale's Ford to meet all the volunteers. From there, they would hunt for the old Chamberlain Coal Mine.

During the night, a knock at Puck's door brought him into the hotel hallway. Sheriff Larson had awakened him to inform him that one of the braves sent to Wind River Village to get the two young boys, who witnessed the kidnapping, had come bringing the boys. Not only had he brought the boys but the parents of Papu Banta, as well. The sheriff had put them in one of the hotel rooms for the night.

Puck had lost all hope that anything would turn the sentiment of the two kidnappers, even the two young boys, if in fact they were able to identify the men. In any case, the boys would be on hand for the trial later, and their testimony would be crucial to the conviction of the villains. The sheriff would see to the boys' well being until then. What Puck would do with the parents of the girl was something that concerned him, but he was too tired to give it much thought in the middle of the night. Maybe his answer would be forthcoming after his mind had a chance to rest. With that lingering thought, he thanked the Sheriff for his message and then went back to bed.

Monday morning came all too early for Puck. His being disturbed during the night, while it was necessary, left him tossing in his sleep, his mind still looking for answers in spite of every effort to tell himself that he needed sleep.

Regardless of his need for rest, he brushed aside all self-pity and went through the hotel looking for the parents of Papu Banta. When he found them, he spent time informing them about everything that had been done to date to find their little girl. If all went well today, he seemed to think, there was a good chance that their little girl might be found. They would be the first to hear of any good news.

Puck consoled the parents as best he could and then left the hotel to meet Whiskers and Three Toes at the café for breakfast. As they ate, Puck seemed preoccupied, such that Whiskers and Three Toes noticed his absorbed mood.

"What's wrong, Boss," Whiskers broke the silence?

"Well, I've been pondering what to do with the parents of the little girl."

Three Toes broke in, "What's this pondery you speak of, Boss?"

"*Pondering*," Puck repeated. "That means that I've been thinking."

"Then, why you not say *thinking*, Boss?"

"Probably because I was pondering more than thinking, I guess, Three Toes."

Whiskers broke in, "When you two get through with your

English lesson, we'll get back to the concerns you have about the girl's parents. Now what's up, Boss?"

"Okay, for the benefit of all, here's what I've been thinking. Whiskers, after breakfast you and Three Toes go find a nice hack somewhere—a hack, or a carriage, but something that is covered in case of rain—and get the use of it for a few days, even if you have to rent it. I'll give you the money. Pick up a small supply of food and water while you're at it. Then, pick up Papu's mother and father at the hotel and meet the searchers and me at the cut-through on the main road that leads to Powder River Station. You know the one I mean, don't you? It's the same road that leads to Casper. The cut-through, if you recall, is about halfway between Shoshoni and Riverton. Bring the carriage there. I want the parents to be on hand when we locate their little girl."

Whiskers dropped his head solemnly and then raised an important question. "Puckett," he intoned, "Uh, don't mean to counter your decision, but do you think it wise to bring her parents with us. I mean, what if we find the little girl dead?"

Three Toes chimed in, "Yeah, Boss, what if what we discover is not good?"

"I've considered that, gentlemen. I know it would be a grueling sorrow for them to find their little girl dead, but it would be grueling wherever they got the news. And, on the other hand, what if we find the little girl alive? I want her parents to be the first to see her and take her into their arms. In either event, we honor them by allowing them to be present. If I'm wrong, I'll take the responsibility."

"We're on our way then, Boss," whiskers acknowledged with a casual, but obliging, salute, and the two headed for the hotel.

CHAPTER 17

PAY DIRT

Sheriff Larson left his cousin in charge of the jail again while he went to see the progress of Perk Anson. He would have to incarcerate him as soon as the doc indicated he was able to function on his own. The sheriff also left Buford cleaning shop and especially straightening up the cabinet in which prisoner paraphernalia was being stored.

Puck filled his saddlebags with essentials, picked up his horse at the stables, and headed for Hale's Ford where he was to meet all the volunteer searchers at noon.

The morning was especially radiant and cool for the ride south, and though Puck was tired, he was pleased that he had in mind the most probable place where Papu Banta could be found. He rode along grateful to be part of the force but plainly preoccupied with thoughts of home, perhaps as a slight escape from the duress that goes with such a job. Now at the end of June, it wouldn't be long before the Annual Celebration would take place in the Village of Jackson. Puck hoped he would have reason to celebrate, realizing that if the little girl could not be found, there would be no revelry for him.

Visions of home intrigued him, momentarily, a diversion he could afford, only because he had time before reaching his morning destination. He wondered how his aunt Bella was doing, what her charming sales lady, Faye Lincoln, might be thinking at the moment, and whether or not his chance to meet Marlowe Taggart would come of anything interesting. What kind of job would he find when he returned? Would Taggart have interest in him as a highrider? He wondered, too, if Tankersley was still fuming over his soiled duds, and whether or not he was taking advantage of Faye Lincoln's eligibility. Was Carbon and Firebrand enjoying their summer, eating the scrap greens from Aunt Bella's summer garden? How were the grounds coming along that would house the celebration, with its bandstand and dance floor decking? Had Noka Kona changed her mind about attending the dance? Finally, he questioned, would he even make it to the dance himself?

All too soon, his mental bubble burst before his mind's eye, as strategy for the final search loomed before him. How would he divide up the volunteers? Or did they need only to form a linear brigade and march due east from the cut-through leading to Powder River Station? He knew that he and his men, along with the parents of the girl, would be directly seeking Chamberlain's mine, according to his calculations devised from the map.

The tired rider and his horse reached Hale's ford before noon. A few volunteers had already arrived and were cooling their horses' feet and legs in the stream and refreshing their own faces with splashes of cool water. Others were preparing their lunches, hoping to be ready to move out again once they conferred with Puck. After cooling down Gentry and letting him drink, Puck staked him along a grassy knoll to graze and then delved into his own saddlebags for lunch. He then sat down among the group to eat and to learn of any developments they had encountered, and to wait for the others to arrive. Little by little, the searchers filtered in, Broken Heel and his braves down the main road from the south, his own men and the deputy from their points in the east, and Colonel Meech and the troops riding in from the southeast. Those from Riverton had returned to Riverton, which suited Puck well, since he hardly knew where to send everyone anyway.

Sheriff Larson had chosen to remain behind, because the judge was to be coming through to consult with him about scheduling a hearing for his prisoners. Doc Metcalf had released Anson to him, assuring him that he was now out of danger. What treatment he would require could be handled from his jail cell. Having placed Anson in a cell next to Trammel and Wortham, he looked around for Buford. When he could not be found, he asked his cousin where he had gone.

"Well, I don't know Bullet," he addressed the sheriff by his nickname. "He cleaned and straightened the cabinets over there, swept a section of the floor and then went out the door without saying where he was going."

The sheriff was a bit ruffled, mumbling halfway to himself and otherwise to his cousin, "Guess he couldn't take it any longer. Can't seem to stay away from the bottle. I've done all I know to do to help him. He'll probably return drunk later in the evening, hoping to find a cell to sleep it off again. I've a mind to send him away."

Back at Hale's Ford, Puck knew that if he needed the sheriff for anything, he could send a courier with a message, so he wasn't too concerned that the sheriff had opted to remain behind. When everyone appeared to be present, Puck rose to address the group.

"Gentlemen, I am really appalled to see that no one has been able to report any sign of Papu Banta. You men—and look at the numbers—have covered acres and acres of territory, not to mention the townspeople from Riverton, and still no sightings of anything hopeful. Of course, we have today and days following, if need be, but after today, the little girl is going to be in real trouble. Unless she has really conserved by rationing, her food has probably already played out. What she has been doing for water is unknown, as well. Some of you told me that it rained over the majority of the area where you searched yesterday. Depending on where she is confined, maybe she has been able to utilize some of the rainwater. Whatever the present circumstances, they can't really be good, so we are in a race against time for sure.

"At least for today, my men are going to go with me to the cut-through to meet Whiskers, Three Toes, and the parents of the girl. I have had the good omen, wisdom from God, or whatever you may want to call it, to have located on territorial and topographical maps what I think may be the place where the kidnappers have confined the girl. For your information, it is the old Chamberlain Coal Mine. According to the Assay Office, the mine has been out of use for years, but, due to its location, it could be a good place to hide anything or anyone. Because it forms a triangle with Shoshoni and Riverton on the map, it coincides with the name the kidnappers gave to their hiding place—the Triangle. If I miss my guess, and we don't find the girl, you boys are going to see the most despondent being you have ever laid eyes on, because I'm at my wits end on this deal. So, men, I'm going to line you out, and when we break up here, give it your best shot, because this may be our last chance.

"Colonel Meech, if you will, take your men along the border of the reservation, beginning from about four miles before the cut-through, and line them out along that four miles. Then proceed due east outside the reservation and check out every potential place of confinement, especially any old abandoned mine shafts. Move east for at least two and a half miles. At that point, stop and everyone proceed due south toward Powder River Station.

"Broken Heel, please follow us to the cut-through and to the border of the reservation. We will part at the border. You and your braves string out for two miles south along the border and then, as with Colonel Meech, move due east searching everywhere for the same two and a half miles. At that point turn and head back north to meet us near Powder River Station.

"I hope each of you will travel with optimism and a prayer. If we fail, our only hope will be the direct providence of God, the Great Spirit, to put someone at the right place at the right time. I don't need to tell you to be eager and expectant. Keep your eyes open to any movement, to any noise, and help me present that young Indian girl to her parents by nightfall. Even if I'm being overly anxious, we haven't much time to be anything else, so good luck men. I'll see you again before dark."

Not much time elapsed until Puck's strategy was put into place and all volunteers were moving into terrain beyond the reservation's border. Puck and his men had converged with Whiskers and Three Toes, who were riding alongside the carriage, being driven by Papu's father, with her mother sitting beside him, expecting a miracle. Puck drew out his maps and took one last look at calculations he had penned on their surfaces. The hunt was on, as everyone proceeded east.

Puck had never remembered a time in his life when he was more concerned and fearful at the same time. In earlier years, before most of the Indian wars had come to a close, he had been in situations in which he was certain his life hung in the balance, but God had been faithful and had made a way out for him. He recalled the exhausting period surrounding the deaths of his mother and father, and the sadness associated with their passing. God had sent him Aunt Bella to pick up the slack and move him securely into life. There had been other times when he had been alone in the hills, hungry, and half-sick with the fever, not knowing if he would die or not. Now, here he was, as alive as ever, not much worse for the wear. Still, someone else was in jeopardy, not merely his own circumstances, and everything inside him was churning with a mixture of hope and fear. He looked at the sallow faces of the two Indian parents and noted the signs of grief, and yet sensed their sternness of heart, as well. Though stricken, they seemed quiet inside. Maybe he could calm his own soul, as they seemed to be looking to him for strength and guidance. As always, he would do his best.

Puck's group rolled along, periodically spreading out to search out potential places of concealment. Then they would filter back together, negotiating the heavy brush, finding a way for the carriage to proceed.

Two hours had passed before Puck neared the area where he calculated the mine to be situated. The brush was now becoming almost impenetrable for the carriage, so Whiskers found a clearing with a shade tree under which to park it. Three Toes stayed with the parents, as he spoke their language and was family at heart. Puck and the others continued on into the thick brush finding very little pathway to negotiate, even on horseback. Winding his way around the barriers, he came to a brief rise, and the terrain opened up more congenially for horse and rider. Trinket was right behind Puck, the other men bunching up behind. Movement was slow, but Puck sensed that he was still on course, according to his own calculations.

Suddenly, Trinket hustled up his horse and came alongside Puck, startled, and attempting to speak. "H—Hey, Mr. Puck, looka… looka through the light in the brush," pointing through the thickness.

Puck looked in the direction toward which Trinket was pointing. There, tied to the brush, was a large black and white paint horse. Trinket whispered, still startled over the sight, "Boss, that is the horse of Trammel. How can his horse be here? Mr. Bill and Mr. Jed took him to jail on that horse."

Puck nodded a gesture of surprise, as well, and moved toward the horse. He dismounted and eased up behind the Paint, moving his hand gently along the rump, across the saddle to the neck, patting the horse gently and looking around at the same time. And then he stopped abruptly!

There it was—the flag! Waving like a royal ensign against an Imperial sky, it protruded from a small hole in the earth. Located here in a desolate place, as it was, had to mean something to Puck.

But there was more! Coming out of the brush at the mouth of the mine, walking hand-in-hand were Buford Townsend and the little Indian girl, Buford smiling from ear to ear and Papu Banta chewing wolfishly on a fried chicken drumstick, Buford's canteen dangling over her shoulder.

Puck fell flat on his rear on the ground mumbling to himself, "Well, I'll be . . ." – and the words stopped. He had never been more dumbfounded.

Buford began to laugh, and then to weep. He loosened his hold on the little girl and she ran to Trinket and grabbed him around his neck, though she knew him only as one of her kind. He took all the beads from around his neck and looped them over the girl's head and kissed her on the cheek. The others, along with Puck, gathered around and patted her on the head, speaking words of endearment, and shaking hands with Buford. And now, all were crying, including Papu Banta.

Quickly, Trinket whispered something in Papu's ear and headed toward the waiting carriage, carrying the little girl as rapidly as he could negotiate the brush. The others grabbed the horses and moved as sprightly as possible behind him. Ahead lay the clearing. Suddenly, the two broke into the opening and began to shout, waving arms in air, the others mounting horses and running on ahead. The girl's parents spotted their little girl and leaped from the carriage, running like old Indians only can run when love is the question. Papu slipped to the ground and ran like a fawn to their waiting arms. They hugged, kissed, rocked back and forth, shouted, and then sat down on the ground and wept together.

After Whiskers had done his shouting, laughing, and weeping, he cleared his eyes and quickly began to spread a feast from knapsacks, saddlebags, and whatever else into which he had placed the food and drink. The parents led their little girl to the carriage. They had something to show her. Her father reached under the carriage seat and pulled out a box, one with more than a dozen holes in it. The little girl opened the box, and there on a cloth, stretched out shyly was a little pale yellow kitten. She picked it up and hugged it adoringly against her cheeks, looked up, and smiled gratefully at her parents.

Light was receding in the west as the others funneled in from north and south, finding the group by the light of a campfire already generated by Whiskers and the bunch. To a person, they could not believe their eyes when they saw the little Indian girl nestled in her parents' arms. The Indian braves, friends of the family, surrounded her, offering every form of adulation they could think of. This would be a night of all nights, as the happy throng gathered around the campfire.

When all had eaten, Puck drew Buford before the mass of volunteers and coaxed him to relate how he had come to know how to find the little girl.

"Well, it was like this," Buford began. "This past Saturday, I took a chance to sell the kidnappers some hooch, thinkin' I would get 'em drunk enough to tell me whar they had hidden Papu. They gave me only a few clues, one bein' that they had named the place the Triangle. When I made the trade of the whiskey for some of their money that the sheriff had placed in the cab'net next to their shootin' irons, I noticed a strange bill among the gold certificates. I didn't pay much attention to it as I placed all the money back into the cab'net.

"This mornin', however, the sheriff lined me out to clean the shop and to straighten the cab'net where he kept all the prisoner paraphernalia. He went to check on Anson and left his cousin in charge. As I shuffled through the items in the cab'net, I came 'cross that strange bill agin. Lookin' closely at it this time, I realized that it was a Continental certificate once distributed during the Revolutionary War, no longer of any value, of course. That's whar the current saying about anything worthless came to be described as bein' 'not worth a Continental.' I supposed that either Trammel or Wortham had been keepin' it as a souvenir. When I turned it o'er on the backside, I noticed some markings. The markings turned out to be a roughly drawn map of the location they were calling the Triangle.

"The cab'net got straightened up in a hurry, and I started to sweep the floors, when it occurred to me that time was awastin'. I hung up my apron on a peg and headed for the stables by way of the café. Puck had been gone for a while, so I figured finding him would be outa the question. I knew of a shortcut to this area, so I saddled Trammel's Paint, threw my saddlebags, with the food in them, o'er the horn, and headed out as fast as that animal's spotted carcass would hustle. When I got in the right vicinity, I looked at the map agin and finally got 'nough bearin' to eventually stumble o'er the old mine site up thar whar you found me.

"When I was fumblin' through the items in the paraphernalia cab'net, I came 'cross some keys that apparently belonged to one of the prisoners. On one of the keys was scratched the letters 'Tri,' which I presumed stood for Triangle. That key actually unlocked the padlock on the metal gate inside the mine. My little Indian friend here was so hungry and thirsty that she almost ripped open the saddlebags gettin' to the fried chicken I had brought. I had a time slowin' her down to keep her from chokin'. I guess you saw that she came out still eatin'.

"Now, ain't that the wildest story you've ever heard? In an old, abandoned mine, whar thar probably ain't an ounce of coal, we hit pay dirt!"

Every head began to shake back and forth with amazement, unbelieving what had just been revealed. Talk went on into the night. Cowboys and Indians made Spartan arrangements for sleeping in the open air, making the carriage the most comfortable spot for the parents, Papu Banta, and the little kitten, which Papu named "Mushroom." Morning would bring with it the most glorious celebration in Wyoming Territory, as everyone would head back to Shoshoni to bring this sequence of events to a close, and break the news to a waiting population.

CHAPTER 18

THE REVELRY

By noon Tuesday, everyone associated with the final search had returned to Shoshoni. The news had already broken; in fact, had been heralded across all of Wyoming Territory. A town crier raced through the streets of Shoshoni shouting, "Indian girl found! Papu Banta safe! The governor is on his way! Meeting this evening in the Town Hall! Come one, come all!" Over and over again he shouted, racing to and fro, just short of frenzy. People rushed to the doors of the shops to hear the clamor. Children clapped their hands, not knowing altogether what all the noise was about, but understanding enough to know that some little girl had been safely found. What a feeling of security and excitement it all exhibited.

The voice of the crier faded at last into the distance—"Come one, come all"—and melded with the Indian drumbeat as it passed the jail. Not a beat had been missed during the last three days and nights. The monotonous cacophony of the tom-tom had just about unnerved the town, and those for whom it was beating were doubly unsettled, almost stupefied by its undaunted message. Now hearing the crier announcing the finding of the little Indian girl, Trammel and Wortham were stunned. Time of reckoning was creeping up on them. In the other cell, totally resigned that the fiasco was over, Anson turned a wistful eye toward his one-time cohorts and remarked, "We should have known it would come to this. We've all been stooges, and now we pay! You might have helped our case by telling them how to find the girl, but you refused. Now, they've found her, and I, for one, am glad she is still alive. Maybe they won't hang us!"

"Aw, stop your bellyaching, Anson," Trammel countered. "If it weren't for your setting us up as stool pigeons, we'd all have money in our pockets and be on our way to no-man's land. But, no, you had to be greedy. You cut us out of the deal. If they don't hang us, you'd better hope that they send us to separate prisons, because for your sake it won't pay for us to get our hands on you."

As the kidnappers wrangled with each other, the sheriff entered the jail flanked by eight townspeople. He proceeded to the cell containing Trammel and Wortham, opened the door, and allowed four men to enter, then locked the door behind them. He then took the remaining four men to Anson's cell and placed them in it.

"Hey, what's the idea, Sheriff," Trammel protested. "There's enough of us in here already!"

The sheriff did not respond but went to his desk and sat down, folded his arms, plunked his feet on the desk, leaned back, and waited.

Shortly, the jail door opened again. In walked the judge, who would try the kidnapping case, wearing a long black frock coat and a wide brim, black hat. He was leading Papu Banta into the jail by the hand. The two Indian boys, who had witnessed the kidnapping near Wind River Village, were linked together holding Papu's other hand. The foursome approached the cells and stopped, first in front of the cell holding Trammel and Wortham.

"Now, my dear," the judge spoke up to Papu, "can you point out the person or persons who kidnapped you?"

The little Indian girl did not hesitate. Looking through the maze of men, she pointed to Trammel first, then moved to one side to locate Wortham and pointed him out, as well.

"Thank you, my dear," the judge said as he led Papu to Anson's cell. "Now, my little friend, do you recognize any of these men?"

Papu's eyes moved from man to man before she finally spoke up.

"No sir, I have never seen any of these people."

The judge turned to the boys and asked if they recognized any of the men. One of the boys was not certain about their identity, but the other boy pointed to Wortham as the thin man, who wrestled Papu onto his horse, and Trammel, the big man, who rode out of Wind River on a lame horse. He was now sure of Trammel's identity, as he had seen him again later at the Indian arbor the day Puck and his men left Fort Washakie. He then stated that he had seen the taller man with black of some kind on the seat of his pants the day of the kidnapping. As an afterthought, the lad pointed again at Wortham and said, "He is the *dammit* white man who kick my stomach and call me 'beaver brain'."

The judge asked Wortham to turn around. As suspected, his britches were mottled with patches of black.

The sheriff then went to each cell in turn and released the eight townspeople and informed them that they had just witnessed what the little girl and the boys had pointed out to the judge. Some of them, more than likely, would be on the jury at trial.

Outside, the drums became louder. As the judge turned to leave the jail with the children, he stopped to address the kidnappers. "Men, enjoy today. You may never enjoy the light of day again. See you in court tomorrow."

The judge walked out of the jail and closed the door behind him. The drumbeat that had accosted the ears of the entire township for so long stopped abruptly. One of the braves walked into the jail and mimicked Broken Heel's original gesture by slicing across his throat with his hand in mock symbol of execution, then turned and walked away. Trammel and Wortham turned ashen. They began to curse Anson, the judge, and the Indian race in general. Nothing in their attitude had changed. Anson slumped on his bed and whispered to himself. "Like a man, I'll receive whatever justice is coming to me.

I've made my bed. Now, I'll lie in it. Maybe Miss Getting's Nazarene of the Book will forgive me!"

The Town Hall was packed as the sun began to wane in the west. People had come not only from within Shoshoni but from Riverton, Casper, and other outlying places, as well. The governor had called for revelry on behalf of Puck, his men, Buford Townsend, all the volunteer searchers, and in honor of the little Indian girl, whose life had been spared.

Puck and his men had already loaded their chuck wagon and bedded their horses early in preparation for the trip back to Jackson, come first light. While they were grateful for consideration by the townspeople, as well as the governor of the territory, they were equally happy that their mission was complete. They were tired and longing for home. Three Toes and Trinket had wives and children of their own, which they had not seen in several weeks. The other men, including Puck, had attachments back home that beckoned, as well. They were sure that Colonel Meech and his soldiers, having been away from Fort Washakie for almost a week, needed to return to important duties there. The parents of Papu, and her uncle, Broken Heel, wanted their little girl back with family and friends, who waited so anxiously for their return.

Sheriffs Larson and Bixley had put in tireless hours on the case, having been on call at almost any hour of the day or night. There were so many people, who were instrumental in the recovery of the little Indian girl, that Puck hardly knew where to begin in commendations that he would make later in the evening, following Governor Warren's speech. For now, he sat back in his seat and breathed a sigh of relief that everything had turned out to the good and that justice was already being served. But he was saddened that men like Anson, Trammel, and Wortham had chosen to play out the scenarios of their lives against the potential of their God-given nature. What a waste, he thought, that they would succumb to a darker side in a land obviously flowing with milk and honey. He wanted to weep, and then, again, he wanted to shout, as the governor, now being introduced to the crowd, rose and walked to the lectern.

"Ladies and gentlemen," he began, "let me be simple tonight, because I am simple. We have much to be thankful for with respect to the wonderful outcome of the kidnapping case that has been so disheartening for the people of Wyoming Territory in recent weeks. I refer to our great area of livelihood as a territory guardedly, because in a few days—I may gratefully announce to you—the Territory of Wyoming will become the State of Wyoming. As I speak, Congress has already passed on its incumbency to enter the Union as the forty-fourth state, and on July 10th, it will become official. Although it is not of importance to you tonight, in light of the occasion for which you have gathered, I, Francis E. Warren, will become the first governor of the State of Wyoming on July 11, 1890."

The crowd rose to its feet in applause and cheers, appreciating not only the man, but also their prospect of statehood. When the house quieted and everyone was seated again, the governor continued. "Truth to be told, there is no way to commend all those who were instrumental in the recovery of our precious little Indian girl, Papu Banta, from her terrifying, loathsome nightmare. There are a few who were on the job day and night giving themselves, unstintingly, to the breaking of the case, putting together the dovetail joints that would turn the puzzle into a glorious picture. We know now, that if Mr. Buford Townsend, through a quirk of luck or providence, had not found Papu Banta first, her freedom would have been almost as immediate, as Mr. Puck Puckett had correctly calculated her whereabouts, and, timely enough, had located the cave almost simultaneously.

"Because he has a knack for reviving cold trails, Mr. Puckett was commissioned by the Territory and promised a stipend of $10,000, for him and any personnel required to aid his mission. In conference with our banker here in Shoshoni, Puck opted to divide the stipend eight ways, so checks have been drawn up, each in the amount of $1,250.00, and made to the order of Puck and each man of his crew. On behalf of the Territory of Wyoming, the Wind River Village of the Shoshoni Reservation, and the village of Shoshoni itself, I am happy to honor Puck and his company by submitting this reward. Along with this stipend, there is one other commendation of merit that has been arranged by the territory, as well. A ninth check, in the same amount as the others, has been made to the order of Mr. Buford Townsend for his insightful and caring action when it counted the most. It would be my pleasure that checks could also be written to many others who played a significant role in the case, but I cannot legislate such a prospect. Sheriffs Larson and Bixley, for example, worked closely with Puck and fulfilled a rather thankless job, but this territory thanks them, and when annual salaries are renegotiated at the end of the fiscal year, I have a feeling that these two will find a measurable stipend added to their pay. Others of note who were invaluable to the task were Mr. Morley at the telegraph office, Mr. Johnson, our stage driver, Colonel Meech and his men, Broken Heel and his braves, Ralph Lingerman, the printer, and Willy Flanagan at the Assay Office. I suppose I could go on all night naming others who played a role. Hopefully, they will recognize how appreciative we are of their efforts. They will be paid in their own coin of having been part of a beautiful service. May I add, in closing, that we are going to see to it, as well, that three others receive the pay coming to them, namely Perk Anson, Pete Trammel, and Briley Wortham. And now, before the night gets away, may I present to you Mr. Puck Puckett, who wanted to share a few comments with you."

Puck went to the lectern and looked over the crowd a moment before beginning. He could see Papu Banta seated with her parents at the rear of the packed room, warmly cradling Mushroom in her arms. Not far from them sat Buford Townsend, still smiling from ear to ear. The audience was a mixture of whites and Indians bunched together in the crowded hall, like sardines in a tin. Puck would not impinge on their time, beyond what was essential. He intended to be brief and to the point. And so he began to speak.

"Governor Warren, ladies and gentlemen, thank you for coming. What a proud day we face in light of the turn of events that brought our little Indian girl back to us safely. On the one hand, I find honor and satisfaction in just knowing that we were able to locate her before she was seriously harmed or suffered a shameless death. There needs to be no pay for that! On the other hand, those who perpetrated such a crime must be brought to justice, if for no other reason than to point up the preciousness of life, which no man has the right to disgrace or destroy at will. I have never been more pleased at the industry and energy shown by so many people at one time than those of you associated with this case. You formed a chain of concern and effort, links of which no man could break. As with the governor, I share his gratitude for all those he has already named, among them being my own men, who traveled with me here, and, who worked their wonders in such an intricate fashion, each contributing to the efforts of the others, no action ever getting in the way of progress. My role among such men seemed to be little more than as a coordinating coach, looking for evidence, and lining out tasks to be performed in the interest of recovery. Shoshoni has been accommodating in every way, it's officials, it's people, along with the same from adjoining villages, not the least of which was the town of Riverton. This kind of *unity* seems to me the greatest symbol depicting our readiness for joining in *union* as a state. If this kind of camaraderie and care continue to be initiated, then our future is safe.

"Governor Warren, as to the reward, or maybe I should say 'stipend,' since we already have our reward, if you don't mind, I would like for my check to be cashed out and divided between Three Toes and Trinket. In a few days, though they will resume their work as laborers on the Army reservoir project in Idaho, they do not make in excess of a meager living wage. They both have children. The money can be used to send their children to school.

"Also, Governor, you honor this city by providing an additional stipend for Buford Townsend. He has shown, by his courage and care in this great recovery, that there is more to this man than meets the eye. He has vowed a major turn around of his life, of which Sheriff Larson has been an uplifting initiative. His contribution to this village in the future will be measurable. Perhaps his stipend may aid him in the reconstruction of his home, helping to establish his place in the community, and getting him ready for a life of sobriety and service. Our prayers will be with him. Thank you, ladies and gentlemen, for your attentiveness."

With that, the crowd rose to its feet, applauding, whistling, and shouting until the rafters seemed to tremble. And then, suddenly, the applause dwindled abruptly and heads turned toward the back of the room. Coming down the aisle was little Papu Banta carrying Mushroom in her arms. The room became deathly silent. The little girl had tears trickling down her cheeks. She stopped momentarily at the front row of seats and handed the kitten to Selma Getting, who was seated in the first chair, and then she proceeded to the lectern. But it was too tall, so she moved it aside. She wiped her eyes with a little white handkerchief, apparently supplied by her mother before they came to the Hall. Haltingly, she began to address the crowd, as if she were the keynote speaker.

"Friendly people, I am just a tiny little girl. I do not fear you because you are kind, but I am shaking inside me because I cannot speak like Mr. Governor and Mr. Puck." She wiped her eyes again with the cloth, her hands shaking visibly. "I say a great big thank you for being good to me. When I was locked in the old damp mine, I thought I was going to die. I thought everyone had forgotten me. No one came. But I was wrong. You were remembering me and you were coming, but I could not know. I could not see, and I could not hear. Before Mr. Buford and Mr. Puck came, I was hungry and thirsty. But the Great Spirit sent rain, grasshoppers, and mushrooms to feed me. That means that He likes me, too. If you like me, and He likes me, I am a very rich little girl. And I forgot! Mushroom likes me, too." The crowd laughed amid the wiping of tearful eyes, as the child continued.

"I will always have love in my heart for you, and one day when you need someone to remember you, I will remember. I have sorrow in my heart for the men who took me away from my mother and father. They were evil to me, frightening me, and hurting me in my body, but I will not be evil to them. I hope the Great Spirit can be good to them like the Great Spirit and you have been good to me. If they could know what I know, they could never be evil again. They cannot go to their homes, and I feel sad for them. Tomorrow, I will go to my home with my father and mother, see my little brother, Timeron, and play with my little Mushroom. I will leave you now and hope that you will always remember that little Papu Banta loves you very much."

With that, the little Indian girl descended the platform, hugged

Selma Getting for keeping Mushroom, picked up the kitten, and headed for her seat. The crowd was still silent as the people began to exit the Hall, followed by Puck, his men, the governor, Colonel Meech and his men, and Papu and her parents, everyone moving with gestures of gratitude to one another, until the Hall was empty at last.

Tomorrow, Puck and his men would head back to the Village of Jackson, and Puck would pick up where he left off.

FOOTNOTES

[1] Benjamin Capps, *The Old West: The Great Chiefs* (New York: Time Inc., 1975), p. 146. Hereinafter referred to as *The Great Chiefs*.

[2] *The Great Chiefs*, p. 130.

[3] *The Great Chiefs*, p. 146.

[4] *The Great Chiefs*, p. 154.

[5] *The Great Chiefs*, p. 137.

CPSIA information can be obtained at www.ICGtesting.com
Printed in the USA
244533LV00001B/3/P